WHYCHOOSE HALLOWEEN WITCHES

AMELIA SHAW

ALPHA MAGIC

PROLOGUE

Halloween night. One year ago.

Our mothers said that three of us were Fated—blessed. What they meant was, I would be stuck with these two pain-in-the-ass best friends until my dying day.

"So, are we going to do this, or not?" I asked my friends, staring at each of them in turn. "Because there's no going back after this." My heart was pounding like a runaway train. If we didn't cast the spell now, I was afraid we'd never have the guts to do it.

The wind moved through the trees around us, rustling the leaves and signaling a fall storm was well on its way. We were gathered outside beneath the full moon, and the dark, starless sky, on a large, countryside property in the middle of nowhere. From here we couldn't be seen, so as long as we never said a word, no one would ever know about our little adventure or what we were up to on this sacred Halloween night; and our joint twenty-first birthday.

Tiffany, the blonde bombshell of our little group, nodded fiercely.

I could see the determination in her bright blue eyes.

She wanted this as much as I did.

I turned to Bella.

She had her teeth buried firmly in her lower lip.

I rolled my eyes. "Come on, Bella. You know we can't do this without you." And I meant that literally. Bella was a powerful witch and without her magic, I wasn't sure Tiff and I could pull off a spell of such magnitude.

She frowned and I could see the hesitation in the set of her shoulders and in the uncertain flicker of her dark brown gaze.

I narrowed my eyes at the girl who'd been practically a sister to me since the day we were born. "Come on, Bella. *Please.*"

We'd been talking about this spell for years, now, planning every part of the complex incantation. Waiting until the night we were old enough, powerful enough, and gutsy enough to pull it off.

Suddenly Bella's gaze hardened.

Relief poured through me. I knew that look. She was on my side now.

"Okay, Ruby. I'm in. Let's do this."

I grabbed my two best friends' hands, and they grabbed each other, forming a perfect triangle of strength. Our mothers were best friends, united in the abandonment by the fathers of their children. They'd made sure we grew up together, strong, bonded, and most of all, loyal to one another.

We clasped our hands and glanced down at the old book between us. I'd found it ten years ago, hidden in a stash of my mother's things.

It was a powerful spell book that had once belonged to my late grandmother.

Without delay we began our chant, reciting the incantation in an ancient language lost to time and memory.

I closed my eyes and tried to relax, having memorized the spell years ago. I spoke my part and my friends spoke theirs. Each verse was a call to the magic that rippled in our veins—to Fate—and most of all, to the unconditional love that we all so desperately desired and craved.

Over and over, we chanted our words, our rhythm growing, while the magic in our blood, in our very ancestry, simmered, ready to burst at the seams.

I could feel the enchantment's mystical heat swell within me, building until sweat rolled down my face. I didn't stop. *I wouldn't.* And neither would Bella or Tiffany. The power of our combined magic swirled around us, alive and violent like a hurricane. I clung to the spell with all my might, focusing everything I had on this one moment. This spell would change our destinies. If we succeeded we'd never end up like our mothers—abandoned and alone.

I opened my eyes. The ancient book floated in the space between us.

Bella was watching the phenomenon with trepidation.

Tiff grinned when she caught my eye.

Buoyed, we chanted louder, the words in our hearts building naturally as the spell came to a great crescendo.

I stared in awe at our joined hands, filled with excitement as a bright white light shone between our clenched fingers.

A sudden surge of power rippled between us, and the urge to finish the spell gripped me with a sense of urgency. I nodded at my honorary sisters and together we forged on with the spell. There was no going back now. As we uttered the final words, the white magic we'd conjured shot into the air above our heads with a cosmic *boom*, exploding in a spectacular eruption of color, like fireworks sparkling against the dark night sky.

The impact of the explosion blew us back with surprising force, each of us landing awkwardly with a *thump* on the dewy grass.

I groaned as I rolled onto my side to relieve the pressure on the bruised flesh of my backside, quickly looking back to the sky as the magic sprayed outward like a wave, then seemed to disappear. A small measure of disappointment hit me square in the chest. I'd expected more than some magical fireworks, followed by an unsatisfying dissipation. Though what I'd actually thought might happen, I couldn't really say.

Silence enveloped the night once more in the wake of our All-Hallows' Eve casting. The stars shimmered, the trees swayed in the breeze, and the moonlight shone down on a gorgeous country house a long way off in the distance.

"Is that it?" I asked.

As though in answer, the spell book that had been hovering in the air, dropped and landed in the dirt between us. The front cover closed by itself, all signs of magic, gone.

Tiffany stood first, brushing the dirt from her tight pants and groaning as though annoyed by the mess.

Bella and I got to our feet too, the anticipation and build-up finally beginning to leach the strength from me.

It was over. It was done. Now, all we had to do was wait for the spell to come to fruition. For the men—our men—to seek us out.

And patience, although a virtue, was definitely not one of my strengths. "So... back to the house for a celebratory drink?" I suggested, forcing some upbeat excitement into my tone.

We'd brought some alcohol with us, so why wouldn't we? Especially as we could finally *legally* drink in the human world.

"Sounds like a plan," Tiffany said with a flick of her long, blonde hair.

Then together we turned and trekked back to the house that Bella's family owned.

I glanced down at my hands, expecting something to have changed

—anything. But as I glanced at each of my friends, it seemed that nothing was different for any of us. At least not physically, anyway.

I wondered if our loves, wherever they were, had been struck by our magic. Could they feel it, even now? Were they maybe already searching for us?

Once inside the little house in the woods, we flicked on the lights and used our magic to mix up cocktails with the colors of the sunset— red, orange, yellow, and a splash of dusky purple.

"Perfect." I raised my glass from the counter.

Tiffany and Bella plucked up their drinks as well, lifting their glasses to clink with mine.

"Happy birthday, ladies," I said, and they chorused the cheerful sentiment back to me. Sharing a birthday with my two best friends had been trying at times, especially growing up. I'd never had a party of my own, or a single day where I felt special just for being me. But now that we were grown and my more selfish childhood tendencies had dissolved into a real sense of sisterhood, I loved it.

We all took a sip of our first legal drink and mutually grimaced at the sheer amount of liquor I'd poured in the mix.

"Wow, that's strong," Tiff said, blinking rapidly as the vapors burned her eyes.

I nodded ruefully, swallowing hard as the vodka and gin cocktail blazed down my throat.

Bella gulped awkwardly, coughing and shuddering before she set the drink back down firmly on the counter. She waved her hand over the table in front of us and conjured us up a whole feast of savory and sweet snacks to celebrate. Chips, chocolate cake, cookies, and crackers with cheese littered the surface in front of us.

She was the best at making food. Actually, truth be told, she was the best at everything when it came to magic. But luckily for us, as the most introverted of our little trio, she never big noted herself or threw it in our faces.

"Oh, perfect. Thanks, Belle!" I grabbed some chips and stuffed them in my mouth without shame. I hadn't eaten dinner. I couldn't, not with all the nerves surrounding tonight's activities.

Bella sighed.

I glanced up at her, raising my eyebrows in question. It was obvious she wanted to say something.

"What's up Bell-Bell?"

"Do you think it worked?" she asked, giving voice to the question we were all thinking about, and we all wanted answered.

I shrugged, forcing myself to appear nonchalant, though I was anything but. This spell would hopefully change the course of all our lives for the better. I gave her the only answer I could. "I don't know. I hope so. I mean, I guess we'll find out."

"I hope so, too!" Tiffany said, her tone exasperated. "We've only been planning this since forever."

I conjured up some stools for us and we all sat down around our tasty birthday spread.

We chatted and ate, drank and laughed, celebrating our whole lives ahead of us.

All through the night I hoped that our magic was working its way to the men for whom we were destined, because the spell we had woven together tonight was a spell that called out to Fate, itself for our one, true love.

Our mothers had been abandoned before we were even born. We'd grown up surrounded by sorrow, loneliness, and heartache. None of us wanted that for ourselves or any future children we might have. Finding the perfect match was clearly a game of Russian Roulette, and we weren't taking any chances!

That's why tonight, we'd sent out a call for the men who would love us for all eternity. Our perfect matches. The men who would stand by us, love us, and never leave us. We wanted them to manifest in our lives quickly of course, but they would answer the call of Fate when they were good and ready. Or at least, that's what I assumed.

Whether that would be tomorrow, next month, or next year—I would wait. And I knew Bella and Tiffany would, too. Because only

Fate could be trusted with such an important a decision as the person we were meant to spend the rest of our lives with.

Born to three single mothers, not a father between us, we certainly had trust issues aplenty. I, for one, wasn't going to date just anyone. And I wasn't going to fall in love with the first guy who happened to look my way and smile. I'd rather be alone forever than live with the pain my mother wore upon her shoulders like a heavy coat of sorrow.

So, with any luck, Fate would conspire with our magic and wouldn't let us down. We'd risked everything, tonight, to ensure that our futures would unfold in a drastically different way to our mothers'.

CHAPTER 1
RUBY

One year later.

My day job at the local florist certainly wasn't glamorous, but it passed the time all the same. "Have a nice day," I said to the human woman who'd just bought a bunch of beautiful roses for her sick mother. I waved her out the door. What I really should have done was tuck in a spell for her mother's flu, but we were forbidden to do magic around the humans in town.

I let out a huge sigh and looked around the large shop filled with neat buckets of brightly colored flowers and lush potted plants. What was I doing here again?

"Making yourself useful until you work out what you want to do with your life", my mother's voice sounded in my head.

The witches in my family were healers, fortune tellers, and teachers. But unlike all the women who had come before me, I had no idea what I wanted to do with my life. I'd graduated high school with good grades, gone to community college, then... nothing. I was adrift, but that wasn't my personality generally speaking. I wasn't a flake. But unlike so many of those within the witching community who were addicted to the coven lifestyle, I just... wasn't.

I wasn't even sure if I wanted to hang around this town forever. Travel sounded more interesting to me; the chance to really see the world. If only I could convince Bella and Tiffany to come along.

"Ruby, I'm just heading out to the bank. Do you want me to grab anything for lunch?" Andrea, my boss, smiled at me as she picked up her handbag from behind the counter and headed to the front door.

"No. I'm all good today. Thanks, Andrea." I smiled at her as she left. Such a lovely woman, especially for a human.

When my mother had realized I couldn't make up my mind about what I wanted to do with my life, she'd forced me to get a job with a non-magical person. To learn, to expand my horizons, and to be of use to the community. Which, at the time, I'd thought was a horrible idea. But as it turned out, there were a lot of nice humans here. It really wasn't so bad.

The school I'd attended had been mostly for witches, and I'd kept my head down at college and mostly associated with those I knew. Again, mostly witches. Now, it was kind of nice to be able to weave between the different communities; not that the humans knew what I was, of course.

I turned back to the flowers I'd been artfully arranging when my last customer had come in. A phone order had come through for a large bunch of white lilies and sweet violets. Simple, but lovely. I was so tempted to use my magic to make them brighter, bigger, and even more spectacular. But the consequences for revealing magic to the non-magicals was far too severe to risk.

So, instead, I focused on my more artistic skills. I arranged them in a nice bunch, wrapping paper and plastic around the stems, before tying it off with a large orange ribbon to contrast with the vivid purple of the violets.

The bell above the door tinkled, alerting me to a new customer.

"With you in a moment," I called over my shoulder toward the front door. An unexpected tingle of awareness shot up my spine like sizzling electricity. I shivered, not with cold but with the feeling of impending change. My breath caught in my throat as I twisted around to see who had set off such a drastic shift in the world around me.

A huge man stood in the shop, staring at me with quiet intensity.

His rugged beauty struck me like a slap to the face. Soulful, dark blue eyes regarded me, while brown locks fell to his shoulders. His features were so stunning it made me want to crawl over the counter and jump right into his arms. The only thing that stopped me in my tracks was the fact that the striking man standing before me who was staring at me like he'd never even seen a woman before, wasn't *just* a man. I took a deep breath through my nose and shivered at the gruff, animalistic notes.

He was a shifter, but not just any shifter. He was a wolf, and not just any damn wolf, but an Alpha.

I'd come across one once by accident when I was a child in the forest. The scent of an Alpha was like barely leashed power, earthy sweat, and a strong animal musk. I'd never forgotten the way I'd felt that day, and now I was standing before another one—this time in human form.

I placed my hands on the counter in front of me, digging my nails into the wood, grounding myself. I didn't want to embarrass myself by squealing or screaming. But it was incredibly hard to remain calm in the face of laying eyes upon who I felt was surely my one true love... the one the spell had summoned. I cleared my throat with a cough and forced myself to smile up at him. "Hi, can I help you?"

His beauty was intoxicating, and if he wasn't something like six feet six, well, I'd bite my own bum!

"You're a witch," he said. It was a statement. Not a question.

"Shh..." I said, hushing him as my brow furrowed. "You're lucky my boss has ducked out to the bank."

He frowned. "She doesn't know?"

"We don't tell humans what we are. You know that." I crossed my arms over my chest and quirked my brow at him. "Do you go around shouting to them that you're an Alpha wolf shifter?"

His eyes went wide, and he stared at me with his mouth open, an expression of shock written all over his face. He looked as if I'd just hit him over the head with a frying pan.

"What's wrong? Cat got your tongue?" I asked, grinning at him for several long moments. *Damn, he's beautiful. So beautiful.* Though that was probably the wrong word to describe his appearance. His jawline was darkened with the beginnings of a new beard, and the muscles bulging under the gray hoodie he wore hinted at an incredibly lethal body. Hot... that's what he was. *Damn HOT.*

"But what are you, exactly?" he asked. It sounded almost like an accusation.

"What do you mean, what am I?" I repeated and frowned at him. He knew I was a witch. What more did he want? "I'm Ruby. Why are you here? What's wrong?"

"How did you know *that* about me?" he asked, his tone growly. "I'm not the Alpha... not yet, anyway."

"But it's in your blood, isn't it?" I asked, second-guessing myself now. I couldn't be wrong about that, could I? The other Alpha I'd met was in wolf form.

He took a few steps forward, his intense blue gaze focused on me. "Yes, it is. So, answer my question. How'd you know that?"

My breath caught in my throat the closer he moved, the scent of him seemed so familiar, like a long-forgotten memory. But how was that possible? I'd never met him before in my life. I was sure of it.

"I..." I swallowed and dropped my arms, grabbing for the counter again as my knees threatened to buckle beneath me. "I met an Alpha wolf when I was child. He smelled the same as you," I explained.

The Alpha crept closer, until he stood right in front of the counter I was leaning on for support.

I had to tilt my head up to look into his eyes, and when I did, a noise slipped from my mouth. One that I couldn't decipher. Was it a moan? A prayer? A curse? *What is going on?* I gripped the counter more desperately as my trembling legs finally gave way. This was going to hurt if I didn't save myself—and fast.

I muttered a spell and conjured a chair beneath me. I fell into it, feeling as intoxicated as I assumed being drunk felt like. Witches had a great natural resistance to alcohol, like most paranormals, so I'd never felt what being tipsy was actually like, let alone been fully intoxicated. But I had to assume it felt something like this strange, hot, tingly feeling that pulsed through my veins, making me weak at the knees, weepy, and ridiculously and inexplicably aroused.

Damn, that's what this is! Arousal. Heat pulsated from my core, radiating through my belly and down my still trembling legs. I forced myself to look up at him, and he was staring at me as though he were waiting for something. "Um…" My brain had gone frustratingly blank. "Um, sorry, did you ask me another question?"

He shook his head and growled a little, swallowing and coughing as though he suddenly couldn't speak.

What was going on? The bell tinkled again over the front door and Andrea strolled back in. I jumped to my feet and made my chair vanish before she saw it.

"Welcome back," I greeted her, putting on my cheeriest smile and happiest voice, though inside my head, my world was positively spinning.

This guy… this wolf shifter… he had to be my soul mate. The one I'd called for on Halloween last year. *Didn't he?* Nothing else made sense. He was so much hotter, bigger, and older than I'd imagined. But I'd never expected a wolf shifter. *Damn.* How was my mom going to take this news?

Andrea placed her black handbag on the counter and frowned at the Alpha wolf in front of me. "Can I help you?" she asked rather brusquely.

I was surprised by her non-welcoming response, especially coming from one of the friendliest women I'd ever met. Didn't she feel his strength, his power? How wasn't she affected by his otherworldly beauty? Then something my mother had once told me swam up into my subconscious. *"Humans don't like shifters."* Wolves, especially. They could feel the danger in them, which to us, was an aphrodisiac. However, for a human, it just smelled like trouble.

And boy, am I in trouble...

The guy nodded at Andrea and pushed a piece of paper across the desk at us.

I glanced down at it. It was an order for a bouquet of lilies and violets.

"Oh, these are for you, sir!" I squeaked in my nervousness to diffuse the situation. I didn't want Andrea showing any aggression at him. He wasn't doing anything wrong—not yet anyway.

I twisted around, grabbed the flowers I'd just finished arranging, and turned back to him in a hurry. I leaned over the counter and offered the bouquet to the huge man, even though I felt pretty certain they were meant to be mine.

"Thank you," he managed to say, though he sounded garbled, and his teeth were unusually pointed as he forced the words out. Almost... wolf-like. His teeth didn't look like that when he'd first come into the shop. He pulled out a credit card from his wallet.

I glanced down at the name before sliding it through the sensor on the side of the register monitor. I couldn't help myself.

Jackson Davis.

Oh, I liked the sound of that. But where did he live? Where was he from? Was he just passing through town or did he belong to a local pack? *I have to find out!* I processed his payment and handed back his plastic.

He plucked the card from my hand with his fingertips, careful not to touch me as he took it.

A flush of disappointment washed over me. I ached to touch him, to see if I could feel something tangible and physical between us. It was still early days in my training as a witch, but all my teachers had always said that I had a natural affinity for scrying and future predictions; that my instincts were always right on target. And every instinct, every vibe, and every ounce of my witchy genes was telling me that Jackson and I would be seeing *a lot* more of each other in the future.

"Thank you," he mumbled again as he backed away, though he barely opened his mouth to speak this time.

I cocked my head at him and watched as he turned on his heels to leave. What was with the weird talking thing? Or more precisely, the lack of talking?

Was he fighting the urge to shift? Did he feel the attraction between us that radiated as bright and brilliant as the noonday sun? I wanted to know so badly what was going on inside that beautiful head of his.

"Oh, ah..." I tried to call out to him as he left, but he strode for the door as if in a hurry. The bells clanged unceremoniously as he all but launched himself outside.

I stared at him through the window as he climbed up into his truck and high-tailed it out of his parking spot in front of the shop before I even had the time to walk around the counter.

Andrea shook her head and *tsked* loudly as she opened the cash register and began unloading the change she'd gotten from the bank. "He sounded like such a nice man over the phone. I'm sorry you had to wait on him while I was out. I'm sure he scared you."

"Scared me?" I repeated, moving away from Andrea to arrange some nearby roses. Idle hands... devil's work, and all that.

"Oh, yes," Andrea said, shuddering. "Didn't he bother you? The size of him... the feel of him. Ugh." She shuddered again.

I clenched my jaw, feeling surprisingly defensive. Why couldn't she see that there was nothing wrong with him? That instead, something wrong with her? I swallowed down my sudden anger. It was for the good of all humanity that they were afraid of the shifters. It was natural. And I shouldn't allow myself to be offended—even though my face was flushed with heat, and latent rage simmered away inside me.

It's a good thing. It's a good thing. Don't get mad. I repeated it over and over. I faced the roses I was toying with so she couldn't see my reddening face and forced myself to continue with a completely normal and casual turn of conversation. "Who were the flowers for, do you know? His wife, maybe? Did he say?" There hadn't been a card ordered, so I was left hoping someone hadn't snagged him before I could.

"His grandmother, I think," Andrea said absently as she went into the back to check stock.

I was left staring out the window. Was this the man I was meant to love? The one that our Halloween spell had called upon? Everything in me said *yes*.

But none of us had so much as even had a single date since that fateful night on All Hallows' Eve exactly twelve months ago. But from the feel of Jackson Davis and the prickling hairs at the nape of my neck, I was pretty sure I'd just met my *one*. My only. My soulmate.

And he was a wolf shifter. *Damn. I hope the coven doesn't mind!*

CHAPTER 2

JACKSON

"What the fuck was that?!" I growled at myself from the inside my truck cabin, slamming the palm of my hand over and over on the steering wheel.

Thump. Thump. Thump.

My skin was on fire, my wolf shifter leaping within my gut to break free. He wanted to rip through me and roar to the sky that he'd found his mate. *No!* No, it couldn't be. She's not a shifter! She wasn't even a human! And I wasn't ready to find my mate yet. I was barely twenty-eight! I wanted more time to travel, to explore, to be free.

If she'd been a shifter, *maybe* I'd be able to wrap my head around the fact I'd just found my mate. It would have been fine, and ideal long-term, actually. But she wasn't even human, which would have been inferior, but at least accepted within my pack. A witch, though? *Hell, no.* Our children would be some strange, terrible half-breeds. *Don't overreact*, I chastised myself.

Exhaling sharply, all the fight went out of me as I slumped in my seat. "Just focus on the road, you idiot."

A large part of me—namely the sane, non-wolf part—was screaming that it couldn't be true. Just couldn't be. That part—my more human part—said that this was some weird mix-up and that my shifter was just horny or something. *Though she had the scent of an innocent...*

"Damn it!" I slammed my clenched fist into the steering wheel, hard this time.

A witch and a virgin as well? She'd probably blow my damn head off the first time we had sex. What was Fate up to now? Because she was seriously screwing with me. With a sigh I turned right off Main Street and followed the road around to my grandmother's house; the only human relative I had.

My brothers never visited her, but she'd been a good and stable influence in my life since I was a child, and I wasn't interested in shunning her. And no one else had, until Grandpa had died. Weird how that had changed everything. I parked my truck in her driveway and turned off the engine. "Wonder what she'll think about this twist?"

The front door opened, and Grandma stepped out onto the porch, waving at me with a huge, welcoming smile on her face.

I sighed heavily and grabbed the flowers, which still smelled vaguely of my mate's touch. I grimaced as I hopped out of the truck. Her scent had me hardening like a pond in winter. I needed to think cool thoughts, and fast.

"Jackson! What brings you here?" Grandma called out as I rounded the truck and headed toward her. Her long, gray hair was piled on top of her head in a large, round bun, and she was looking paler than normal.

I frowned as I approached. "Hey Grandma, Mom said you weren't feeling so good."

"Pah," Grandma said, swatting at the air as though there was a fly nearby "I'm fine."

I lifted the flowers and offered them to her.

She sighed and made a huffing noise at the same time. "You shouldn't have," she said, but she smiled as she took them and leaned down to smell them. "Thank you."

I waited patiently.

Finally, she waved me inside. "Oh, come in, come in."

We strolled inside, away from the sounds of the humans next door, and I could relax a little. There was something about town that always set me on edge, and now I had an extra reason for it.

"Let me get us some lemonade. I even made an orange cake this morning," Grandma said as she gestured toward the large couch in her sitting room. "Sit, sit."

I grinned as I collapsed onto the couch.

She toddled off to grab whatever treats she had created.

There was nothing like homemade baked goods. They soothed the soul.

When she came back into the room, she put the flowers that were now in a vase on the table. But the best part was that she also returned with a plate of desserts the size of my broad chest.

"Ah, expecting guests?" I asked, quirking my brow at the mound of cake and chocolate chip cookies.

She poured me a glass of homemade lemonade. "Well, it's Halloween tomorrow," she said, as though that answered the question.

"And...?" I asked, before shoving a chocolate chip cookie into my mouth, groaning as the chocolate melted on my tongue. *Just out of the oven. Perfect.*

"And I like to give the little trick-or-treaters a homemade treat. None of that town-bought candy rubbish," she said, shaking her head as though the tradition of hoarding candy in a bag for months after Halloween was a bad thing.

I chuckled. "Well, you do go all out. These cookies are amazing." I grabbed another one then picked up the glass of lemonade she'd poured. "Thank you, this is great."

Grandma leaned back on her sofa and narrowed her eyes at me. "What's going on, Jackson? You don't seem quite like yourself."

I tried to smile, but it came out as more of a grimace. "Just came to see you." Which was true, I had initially.

"Mmhmm..." she hummed, giving me the eye that meant she didn't believe me.

I sighed. "I *did*. I had the day off work and Mom said you hadn't been well, and I realized that I've been slack in seeing you."

"Then what happened?" she asked, raising one eyebrow.

"I... ordered flowers from a florist in town. Just to, you know, apologize for not coming to visit more often."

She nodded sagely. "Yes. Then what happened to make you so antsy?"

I grabbed another cookie. This was another reason I loved my grandmother. She read me better than anyone else in the family. It was confrontational sometimes, but it was reassuring to know that someone loved me enough to check in on me and see how I was really doing.

I swallowed hard, my tongue thick and my throat tight. God, this was more difficult to say than I'd expected. "The girl who works at the florist..."

"The new girl? With gorgeous red hair? I'm not sure of her name," my grandmother mused, her eyes lighting up with interest.

I shook my head. "I don't know it, either." I hadn't looked, hadn't wanted to know. If she'd been wearing a name tag, I hadn't seen it.

"So? What about her?" my grandmother probed.

"I think..." I clenched my jaw, forcing myself to say it. *Come on, Jackson! You're from a fucking Alpha bloodline. Pull your shit together.* I cleared my throat roughly and tried again. "No... I mean, *I know,* she's my mate."

My grandmother clapped her hands together, bouncing softly on the couch in her excitement. "Oh, Jackson, darling. That's wonderful!"

I scowled at her unintentionally. "It is not. She's a witch, Grandma. Did you know that?"

"Pah," my grandmother said, waving her hand to dismiss my agitation. "So what? In this town, everyone's *something*."

That wasn't true. Most of the town's people were human.

"But she's not a shifter! Don't you understand what that means?"

My grandmother nodded. "Yes. Instead of turning into a wolf whenever she wants, she'll be able to work magic every day of her life and probably make me some absolutely kickass great grandbabies."

I put my empty glass down and collapsed against the sofa back. "You don't get it, not my long shot, Grandma."

She sighed. "Of course, I get it. Why do you think I live in town rather than being closer to my kids, and grandkids?"

I shrugged. "No idea." I hadn't really ever thought about it. I mean, I'd wondered about it a few times. Like, why had she moved away from us after our grandfather died? I'd assumed at the time that it was to be close to her human friends. For support or... something. I ran a hand through my disheveled hair in annoyance.

She picked up a cookie and inspected it. "It's because your pack is full of species-ist *assholes*. Despite all the years I'd lived with the pack, they made me feel wholly unwelcome after your grandfather passed. All because I'm human—even though I was family."

"Species-ist?" I repeated. Was she serious?

She laughed at me. "Why do you look so shocked? You're a prime example of it, yourself."

"Me?" I repeated. I'd never been called such a thing in my life.

"Yes, you." She narrowed her gaze at me, though there was very little heat in the look. "Just look at you, all horrified that Fate dared to send you a beautiful young girl as your mate! You're all twisted up simply because she's not a wolf shifter. Well, I'll be the first one to say it. I'm glad she's not! That pack has become far too inbred. Look at the lack of females being born, if at all. Look at the infertility of your generation." Grandma shook her head in dismay.

"The..." *What?*

I hadn't even thought about it. We were lacking in females. *Yes... I suppose we were.* Not that I had any issues finding a nightly bed warmer if I needed or wanted one. There were a dozen packs within an hour's drive, and there were willing women in all of them.

But Grandma was right. There weren't many females that were available to mate with. I'd heard my father say it once. That in the past twenty years there hadn't been a single pack female born. But it didn't concern me. After all, there were other packs. Other shifters. Why should I care? And now that I thought about it, there were very few babies being born in general. I hadn't even seen a pregnant woman in... I don't know how many years.

She nodded slowly. "You need to talk to some of your friends, and your parents, too, Jackson. That pack is in trouble, and if you ignore this call from Fate, you may end up like half the other men in your pack —alone and childless."

"That won't happen," I said, sitting up straight. I was Alpha born. No female shifter in her right mind would deny me. "Not that I'm ready for that kind of commitment, anyway."

Grandma rolled her eyes at me. "Oh, cut out the Peter Pan shit. You're twenty-eight years old. Your father was twenty-five when he married your mother, and your grandfather was barely twenty-one when we were married. I'm surprised it's taken you this long to find her."

I rolled my eyes. "Come on, Grandma. That's not fair."

"What's not fair is that you've gotten away with being rootless this long. It's time, obviously, or Fate wouldn't have sent you this girl. Now, forget all the crap you've been taught—that you *must* mate with a shifter." She rolled her eyes for emphasis. "You wouldn't exist if your grandfather had ignored the pull of Fate and decided not to marry me."

I nodded slowly, dumbstruck. "That's true."

Even as a pure human, my grandmother had produced five strong sons for my grandfather. All excellent fighters. There was obviously nothing wrong with mating outside of our pack, I'd just never expected the need.

My heart suddenly swelled, and happiness pulsed along my veins. "Thanks, Grandma."

She nodded. "You're welcome. Now, have some cake." She shoved the plate at me, and we went back to less heated subjects.

On the way home I was left with a strange feeling in my gut, which was odd as my grandmother's words had me rethinking all of my preconceived notions about with whom I'd mate and when. She was right. Fate always knew best. But still, something was wrong. There was something missing. I just wasn't sure what it was.

CHAPTER 3
DARREN

My grandmother had been a full blood witch, one of the few accepted by pack men in the past. She'd died a few years ago but throughout my life it had become obvious that I'd inherited a few of her traits. An uncomfortable ability to know when something was wrong was one of those things.

I spotted the guy I was looking for as he walked out the front door of his parents' house. I called out, "Hey, Billy. I need to speak to Jackson. Do you know where he went?"

Billy, who was Jackson's cousin, stopped in his tracks to answer me. "Yeah, I heard he went to the florist in town to pick up some stuff for Grandma, then was going to see her."

I nodded, tension eating at my gut.

"I need to go find him," I said, knowing full well what Billy would say next.

He stared at me for a minute, then shrugged. "Sure. I'll come with you. Haven't seen Grandma in ages, anyway. Wanna take my truck?"

"Yeah. Thanks."

Billy had the better vehicle between us, a black truck with a bull bar and massive wheels. Not my style, but it was comfortable.

Once we jumped into the truck, he turned to me. "You sure you don't wanna wait until he gets home? He probably won't be long."

I opened the door and shook my head. "Nah. I've got to find him now."

Billy shrugged but didn't argue, settling into his seat in the cab alongside me. "Okay."

Most of the pack ignored my heritage, but they also did what I asked when I asked for it, irrespective of how weird it sounded at the time. They knew I had some strange insights and just went with it. We drove fifteen minutes into town, looking out for Jackson's truck along the way. As we slowed down for the traffic on Main Street, the florist caught my eye.

A tingle unlike anything I'd ever felt passed over my neck. It felt like a warning, yet there was something positive and good behind the feeling as well. Something I shouldn't ignore, perhaps. "Hey. Stop there." I pointed.

"Where?" Billy asked, slowing down regardless of the fact he didn't know which way I meant.

I pointed toward the front window. "The flower shop! There. The store with the pink sign."

Billy pulled hard on the wheel, and we turned straight across the road and parked outside the florist.

Billy glanced at me, a puzzled look on his face. "Yeah, I don't think Jackson will still be here."

"Probably not, but I.... want to go in. Just for a minute." I stepped out of the truck, surprised to see Billy getting out too. "You don't have to come," I told him, another strange sensory premonition passing over my skin. Something was about to happen.

He shrugged. "May as well buy something too. Can't have Jackson showing me up."

I had a retort for that but bit my tongue. Jackson and Billy, and most of their siblings, had practically abandoned their grandmother when she'd moved into town. I'd always wondered why. Other than the fact she was human, of course. But that shouldn't have been a reason to ignore the woman who had cared for them practically their whole lives. However, the pack was weird like that.

I pushed on the glass door as we entered the shop, the tinkle of a bell sounding above our heads.

An older woman with dark hair and a cheery smile greeted us as we walked inside. "Hello. Can I help you?"

I smiled back at her, but soon recognized that this person wasn't the reason that I'd been called to come into the shop, but I responded to her just the same. "Yes, you can hopefully. I was just looking for a friend that came this way today. Jackson—"

Billy sidled up next to me and said in a low voice, "Hey, can you smell that?"

Being part witch rather than full shifter meant that my wolf senses weren't as attuned as his. Especially my sense of smell. "No. What do you..." Then I smelled it. A sexy, sweet, all-consuming scent that made me want to go down on my knees and thank the heavens for the person it belonged to. "Who?"

We both looked around the room. It couldn't be the old lady. There had to be someone else.

"Did you say Jackson?" came a voice from the right.

We both turned to stare at the angel who was walking through a staff-only door, toward us.

She had long, red hair and the most beautiful face. I'd never seen anyone so perfect, not even in my dreams.

My heart thumped in my chest as my mouth ran dry. Who was this magnificent creature and why was Billy growling beside me?

I forced myself to swallow and answer her question. "Ah, yes. He was headed this way and we stopped by to see if he was still here." Then it hit me with the force of a tornado. The knowledge. A fact. An irrefutable truth... She was a witch. And she was *my* Fated Mate. My knees trembled and I willed them to lock. If there'd been something nearby to grab, I would have hauled myself over to it.

"And you are?" I managed to say, glancing to my left.

Billy was shivering like he was freezing cold.

What is his problem?

She swallowed visibly, her eyes growing as round as the full moon.

I could see her magic pulsing like a silver halo radiating all around her.

"I... ah... Ruby. I'm Ruby."

"Ruby." I couldn't stop myself from repeating her name. It suited her, from her glowing red hair to the precious, beautiful jewel she obviously was.

"I'm Darren," I said. "And this is Billy."

Billy growled a little then snapped his jaw shut.

She stepped closer, biting her lip in a way that made me ache to kiss her. "Did you say you were looking for Jackson?"

"Yeah, why?"

Her cheeks warmed in a strange way, as though blushing at the mere mention of his name. "He came in to pick up some flowers, then left. He didn't say much."

I glanced over at Billy. It seemed like he was having the same trouble. I looked back to her, smiling broadly. "Do you always have that effect on men?"

She shook her head. "No! Oh my God. Not at all." She glanced away as though embarrassed.

Billy tugged on my jacket, pulling me toward the front door once again.

I didn't want to leave, but I could feel Billy's anxiety and the need to get away. I chuckled and indicated to Billy with my thumb. "Ah... looks like I need to go, but I hope I'll see you again."

She nodded. "It's Halloween tomorrow night. I'll be around." She smiled brightly and there was a hint of understanding in her eyes.

Could she sense the witch in me also?

"Will you come back for All Hallows' Eve?"

Normally I wouldn't venture into town on Halloween, not even if someone paid me.

Billy continued to tug on my jacket.

"Definitely. See you then," I called back, following Billy outside, a laugh escaping me.

Billy ran straight for the truck like his life depended on it.

"Hey. What's going on with you?" I asked him. Then out of the corner of my eye, I saw Jackson in his black truck fly by. I nodded toward the retreating vehicle. "There's Jackson. Looks like we missed your grandmother's meeting. You still want to see her or go back to the pack?"

Billy paced the pavement by the truck like a man possessed, his hands clenching and unclenching. "The pack. Now," Billy managed to get out, before twisting around to jump in the truck.

I shrugged and followed his lead, then we took off after Jackson.

Billy was shaking like a dog trying to get water out of his coat, and he kept clenching his hands around the steering wheel as though he was attempting to wring the very life out of the poor truck.

"What's going on, Billy?" I asked casually, glancing hesitantly at the speedometer and hoping there weren't any cops nearby.

He was way over the limit, and we were catching Jackson fast.

I glanced ahead and pointed out the obvious. "Look. There's Jackson. You can slow down now," I said, injecting my tone with light-hearted laughter, hoping it would relax the wolf shifter beside me.

Billy didn't say anything, but he took his foot off the gas so that we were following Jackson at a safer and much more legal pace. He didn't even try and speak to me for the rest of the trip.

So, I just sat back and enjoyed the strange new feelings flowing through me. Now that I wasn't so focused on Billy and his weirdness, I could daydream about the glorious fact that I'd just found my mate. She wasn't a wolf, and she wasn't a human. She was a witch! How perfect was that? For me, anyway.

I'd always secretly wished I had more power than the small amount of intuition and fortune-telling I was gifted with. Of course, having Ruby as my wife wouldn't increase my own power, but our children would be *incredible*. Also, it would be a joy to see Ruby come into more of her power as she got older. She only looked to be about twenty-one, twenty-two, maybe. Most witches had only just started to develop their skills by that age. But this way, I would be there to see it all.

My dad wouldn't be thrilled about my news, but Mom wouldn't mind. After all, it was her mother who was the full blood witch in the family.

The truck slowed down as we headed into our borough. Our pack had built the houses and roads a century ago, beginning with a large farm that had just a few houses on it, it had increased to a substantial settlement now. Though we relied on the town for most of our needs, we did grow some food and had our own local tradesmen. I, myself, was a sparky—one of about five electricians in the pack.

Billy pulled his truck up behind Jackson's, who had parked in the driveway in front of his house.

Most of us single guys still lived with our parents, or in bachelor housing set up for the extra males our pack seemed to be having.

Jackson was one of the few single men in the pack who'd already built his own house, but then again, he was a proverbial jack of all trades. He did construction, plastering, some plumbing, as well as brick laying. And to top it all off, he was an Alpha wolf, one of the few we had in our current generation. They were born and bred to lead by example and step up in times of stress and uncertainty. Luckily, we hadn't fought a battle or a decent enemy in decades, so Jackson could relax and just be another member of the pack.

Billy turned off the engine and jumped out.

I followed suit, a strong sense of contentment making my limbs feel warm and relaxed. I casually strode after Billy as he went straight for his cousin.

Jackson was just opening the front door to his house and called over his shoulder, "Hey, Billy. Come on in. Boy, do I have news for you."

"Hey," I said, lifting my hand and waving at him.

Jackson smiled at me in return, though he tilted his head curiously, as though confused as to why I was there.

I jumped in to explain, "I, ah, had a... premonition that I needed to find you. So Billy and I went into town to look for you."

"Oh." Jackson frowned, then like most people in the pack, just shrugged and went with it. "Okay. Come in, then." He waved us inside.

We stepped into the large living area, and I couldn't stop myself from having a look around. I hadn't seen inside the house since it was finished. It was impressive, with natural exposed beams and a large, open plan kitchen.

"Jackson, you won't fucking believe it!" Billy said, running his hand agitatedly through his hair.

"What?"

"I met my mate," Billy spat, as though it were the worst thing he'd ever admitted to.

Then it kicked me square in the balls. I spun back to face him. "What are you talking about?" He couldn't possibly be talking about *my* mate, could he? Because I was pretty sure that wasn't how all this worked.

Jackson chuckled, heading to the fridge. He opened the door and pulled out a six-pack of beer. "You guys want one?"

"Hell, yes," Billy said.

I didn't usually drink, but my instincts were telling me that today was going to be one of those rare times I did. "Yeah. Thanks."

Jackson cracked three of the cans and handed them over. "Well, it looks like it's the day for finding mates," he announced, puffing up his chest as though he was about to say something important. "Because I found mine, too."

I shuddered, an overwhelming sense of destiny shivering down my nerves and through my gut. "Fuck," I swore, as I shivered again. I gripped my beer tightly as I grabbed a nearby kitchen stool and pulled it abruptly towards me. I fell onto it, my legs giving way. This was *bad*. So very, very bad.

"You okay?" Billy asked from beside me.

I managed to focus my eyes long enough to look toward him. "It's her."

"Who, her?" Jackson asked.

I swallowed hard. I didn't want to say it. Not in a room with an Alpha and his cousin. Their wolves and their tempers were legendary. But there was no way around it. I had to tell them. I licked my lips. "I met my mate today, too. All the signs were there. Instant attraction, incredible smell. Visible shock and awe. Everything."

"But you and I only went to the..." Billy stopped talking and stared at me, his eyes wide. "You don't mean..." Billy's eyebrows lowered suddenly as he glared at me with surprising intensity.

I nodded. "It's Ruby, isn't it?" I glanced from one glowering wolf to the other.

"Ruby?" Jackson repeated.

I exhaled sharply then lifted my tone, making my words seem far more casual than they felt. "Yes, *Ruby*. My mate is a red-haired, gorgeous young witch who works at the florist in town. How about you guys?"

"No!" Billy practically yelled, slamming his beer down on the counter and causing it to fizz and froth over. "That's impossible."

I shifted my gaze to Jackson.

He was shaking his head. "You have to be mistaken," he said. "She's *my* mate. I met her earlier when I picked up Grandma's flowers. She's got long, red hair and..."

I huffed out an uncomfortable laugh and pinched the bridge of my nose. "Yeah, and blue eyes, pink lips, and an unmistakable silver aura of magic all around her."

Jackson looked at his cousin.

Billy slammed his fist into the frothy mess on the marble counter-top. "Fuck!"

Yeah. You can say that again.

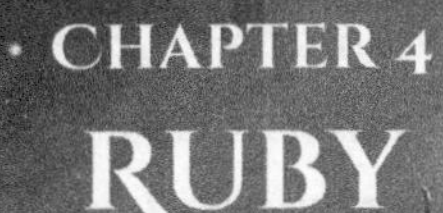

CHAPTER 4
RUBY

I ran home practically screaming after work. I'd met three men —*three*—all of whom I had an incredible attraction to. Were they all my men? Or was I supposed to choose between them? How did this work, exactly? It's not like magic was a precise science...

Could one of them be for Bella and one for Tiffany? Had I somehow called all three of them to me by accident? No, I didn't think so. There were no accidents or mistakes where Fate was concerned.

When I got home, I found a note Mom had left on the table.

Going to be late. Dinners in the fridge. Love you.

I pulled out my cell phone and messaged Bella and Tiffany, barely able to contain my excitement.

Got AMAZING news! Come over as soon as you can.

Both responded immediately, saying they'd be over in about an hour.

Perfect. I put Mom's homemade chicken casserole in the oven and jumped in the shower. I smelled like a heady combination of roses and lilies. It was strange how much I loved the many fragrances of the shop but also found it extremely overwhelming at the same time.

Stepping out of the shower, I dried myself, and dressed in comfy sweatpants and my favorite hoodie. I was psyched for a night of hot chocolate and movies with my two best friends. That was, if they wanted to stay after what I told them! Hopefully they wouldn't feel jealous, since they hadn't found their Fated men yet.

I devoured the delicious and flavorful casserole Mom had made. She loved to cook from scratch, rather than choosing to use magic. She found it therapeutic and enjoyed the time in the kitchen. And I had to admit, her homecooked meals tasted better than the meals I could conjure up.

I was just putting my plate in the sink when the doorbell rang. "Come in!" I called out and a cacophony of sound burst through my front door. I couldn't stop the grin that spread across my face as I called out to them, "In the kitchen!"

Tiffany strode through the door holding bottles of soda.

Bella had blocks of chocolate in hand.

"So, what's the occasion?" Bella asked, straight off the bat, her eyes sparkling.

"I met him today!" I said with a squeal and a ridiculous little dance.

"Him?" Tiffany repeated, brow quirked.

I nodded, an insane smile stretching my lips. "Well, *them* actually. But that's the next part of the story. You know... him. My man? The one we cast the spell for on All Hallows' Eve last year?"

Bella clapped her hands together and grinned at me. "Oh my God.

That's awesome! So, it really worked? Who is it? Do we know them? Is it one of the guys in town? Or—"

Tiffany put her hands up silencing the conversation. "Hang on just one second. Did you seriously just say, *them*? As in plural, Ruby?"

She never misses a beat, this one. I bit my lip, unable to contain the nervous energy bubbling within me. I still hadn't worked out that part. "Yeah, well, I'm not quite sure exactly what's going on in that regard."

Bella leaned over the counter conspiratorially and rested her chin on her hand.

Tiffany sat on the kitchen stool beside her. "Tell us everything."

I laughed at the happiness fizzing through me and explained it all, from the moment Jackson had exploded into my life. How I'd felt and how he'd reacted. Then, what had happened when the other two guys had walked into the flourish just an hour later.

"And they were all wolf shifters. You're sure?" Bella asked. She was standing to attention, her eyes wide and shocked.

We didn't have much to do with the shifters in the witching community to be honest. They didn't seem to like us for some reason. "Yeah, pretty sure. Well, two out of three of them were, anyway. Jackson, definitely. And the other big one. Both went all growly and basically couldn't speak when they met me."

Tiffany shivered and sighed. "Oh, that sounds so sexy."

I laughed. "Yeah, it kind of was. I've never experienced anything like it!"

"And the third guy?" Bella asked, hungry for more details.

I tilted my head to the side, thinking about what made him different. "Um... he was something else, I think. He had some wolf in him, but he was smaller than the other two, and... you know what? If I didn't know better, I'd say he had some warlock about him."

"Really?" Bella asked, her eyebrows climbing higher up her forehead.

Combinations of witch and shifter blood were uncommon, which would mean that if I was correct, tracking down his lineage would probably be relatively easy. I thought about it for a minute. "Yeah. I'm pretty sure that's what it was, because he had no problems talking to me, even though I had the same reaction to all of them."

"More toward one than the others?" Tiffany asked, opening one of the chocolate wrappers with her long fingernails. When she got frustrated with the fiddly packaging, she flippantly waved her hand over the counter and magicked us up some platters of snacks and arranged everything to her liking.

I grinned. "Um, do you mean, if I had to choose?"

Tiffany shrugged. "I suppose so."

I pressed my lips together. How would I even start to evaluate something like that? They were all so unique, each with their own particular quirks and beauty.

"Well, I don't really know them yet, obviously, but Jackson—the first guy I met—he is just gorgeous with a capital G!" I grinned at them, heat flushing my cheeks at the mere thought of him.

"And the other two?" Tiff prompted.

"Billy didn't speak at all, but he was hot, too. He seems more of the bad boy type, which could mean trouble."

Tiffany laughed. "Sounds like my kind of guy. And how about the third one?"

"Hmm... he was the one that I think has some witch or warlock in him. He spotted me right away and had no issues chatting. He's smaller than the other two, but super sweet. The kind of persona you could easily be best friends with."

Bella put both hands out in front of her like she was stopping traffic. "Hang on a second. Are you saying you hit the trifecta? The boy next door, the bad boy, *and* the protective Alpha?"

I hadn't really thought about it like that, and it made me giggle. "Well, when you put it that way..."

"Then how are you going to choose between them?" Bella asked again.

I shrugged and picked up a chip, munching on it. "Who says I have to?"

"Ruby!" Bella exclaimed; horror written all over her face.

"What?" I asked dramatically, rolling my eyes. "If they're all meant to be with me—and that was how it felt—why would I choose?"

"You may not get a choice in keeping them all. Wolf shifters don't share. When they mate, they mate for life. You know that." Bella said, shaking her head as if it were obvious.

I groaned. "How would you know? We pretty much have nothing to do with them."

Bella crossed her arms over her chest defensively. "I've heard about them, okay! They're very possessive, especially the Alphas. They'll never share you. Not well, anyway. None of you will be happy in a relationship like that."

I shrugged and continued to chomp on the salty chips and chocolate sweets before me. I didn't necessarily like the idea of dating all three of them at once, of course. Like, how would that even work? But at this point I was just enjoying the feeling of success. Our spell had worked! I looked at my friends and grimaced, a little crestfallen by their reactions. "Why are you being so negative about all this? I thought you would be happy for me."

Tiffany waved her hands as if raising a white flag of surrender. "I'm not. I think it's totally cool. If it's Fated, it'll all work out, I'm sure."

I looked pointedly at Bella.

She sighed and rolled her eyes. "Because it's totally unfair! That's why. How could you meet three guys in one day when we haven't met even one? And how are you going to handle three men, Ruby? Seriously. You've barely dated!"

She was right. I was still a virgin. In fact, all three of us were. None of the guys in the warlock community were keen to mess with us, and the humans had a natural aversion toward our powers as well, so they steered clear. "I know, but..."

"Do you think that maybe the other two might be for us, though?" Tiffany asked, grabbing a can of Coke and casually popping it open with a *crack* and a *hiss*.

"Ooh... maybe!" Bella said with a sudden grin on her face.

"Dibs on the bad boy!" Tiffany called.

"I want the boy next door," Bella said, staking her claim immediately after.

Then they burst out laughing like it was the biggest joke on the planet.

I dropped my head and stared at the white countertop beneath my hands, trying to get control of the anger that had started boiling up inside of me. I couldn't contain it. It wanted out. *Fuck, this was bad.* My fingers turned into claws and a sinister green smoke billowed from under my palms. My stomach was in knots, and the anger I felt was rooted deep in my soul and was unlike anything I'd ever felt before.

"Ruby... whoa... are you okay?" Bella asked, reaching out to touch my arm.

I groaned at her touch but forced myself not to react. Not to slap her hand away as I wanted to. *Calm down.* I closed my eyes and forced myself to take deep steadying breaths. *Surely they were just joking. They wouldn't take my men. They're my best friends.* "They..." I cleared my throat, the tone of my voice strangely deep and uncharacteristically dark in its intensity. "They're mine. All three of them. They're mine."

I didn't know where the rage came from, nor the unfamiliar voice I heard coming from my own mouth. But the possessiveness I felt toward all three of them had me wanting to rip my friends' heads from their damn shoulders.

It didn't make sense. These girls were my best friends. I considered my sisters. These feelings were insane and marginally frightening.

"We were joking, Ruby. We promise. We're sorry." Bella's contrite voice penetrated the seething red cloud inside my mind.

With no small effort I willed the feelings away. Finally, when I could speak normally again, I staggered toward the family room. "I have to sit down." I managed to make it to the couch, but magic still pulsed chaotically through my veins, heavy and strong, overwhelming me. I needed to use it, quickly, so I pulled it inside myself and turned it around to make positive choices. I whipped my hands through the air and all the food from the kitchen magically appeared in front of me, spread out on my mom's large coffee table.

"Come join me!" I called out.

My friends sneaked into the family room, trepid and wary.

Bella was chewing on her lip.

Tiffany had crossed her arms over her chest in a defensive pose.

"I'm sorry," I said. "I don't know what came over me."

Tiffany slid onto one of the opposite sofas facing me.

Bella knelt on the floor and reached for some candy. "It looks like these bonds are going to be stronger than we ever imagined," Bella said, popping a red sweet into her mouth.

I nodded, feeling a little more sobered. "Yeah, I think so."

Tiffany laughed and shook her head, breaking the tension in the air. "We probably should have done a little more investigating before we dived into the deep end of such complex magic. But we didn't care at the time, did we? We all just agreed that it couldn't hurt..."

It had been a lot more than that, but we all liked to play down our abandonment issues.

I forced out a laugh, myself, retrospectively amazed at our foolishness. "And using Halloween magic probably increased the spell's strength and potency."

Bella giggled, enjoying her sugar. "Well, so what? You got three husbands for the price of one. I wonder what we're going to get?"

I couldn't help it, I cackled at that one. I felt better now the darkness had passed. "I guess only time will tell."

Tiffany relaxed and picked up the bowl of popcorn, placing it on her lap. "Do you really think all three of them are yours, Ruby? For real?"

I nodded, more certain than I'd ever felt in my life. "Yeah, I do." I knew it the way I knew I loved these girls in front of me. The way I knew I was a natural born witch. The way I knew my mother would die for me. Things that were all perfectly true and I knew instinctively. This was exactly the same feeling.

"So, when do you think you're going to see them again?" Bella asked, reaching for a drink to wash down her snacks.

I shrugged and settled back into my chair, letting the last of the tension in my body dissipate. "They'll find me. I told Darren that I'd be around tomorrow, being All Hallows' Eve, so we'll see what happens."

Tiffany grinned. "Leaving it up to Fate, huh?"

I matched her smile with my own grin. "Don't I always? It seems to have a mind of its own and there's no point in trying to fight it."

She rolled her eyes, then laughed. "Okay, so, what are we going to do for the rest of the night?"

The conversation changed to movies and work, our moms, and food—which I was grateful for—but that didn't mean that I could forget about everything we'd already discussed. The spell we'd worked last year on our birthday had called on the Universe. Magic. Fate. And it was pretty obvious that Fate had no intention of making any of this easy on us. Especially if my lovers were any indication of what Tiffany and Bella had in store for them.

But one truth remained and niggled at me as we enjoyed the rest of our evening... since when did three men get along well enough to share one woman?

Especially shifters...

CHAPTER 5
BILLY

I woke up on Halloween morning with a raging, nasty-ass hangover. Having found out my Fated mate was not only a witch, but a woman I'd have to share with my cousin and the part-warlock-wolf? I'd needed a stiff drink. And more than one.

Darren had gone home soon after dropping the truth bomb. He hadn't even finished his drink.

Then Jackson and I consumed every beer in his house and moved on to my stash. It took a lot to get drunk as a wolf-shifter, and even more to be hung over from it. Our metabolisms were abnormally rapid and to even feel the effects of alcohol took more than most humans could consume before passing out cold.

"Oh... God..." I moaned from my place on Jackson's couch where I'd crashed for the night. I tried to get up but found no strength in my legs and instead, kind of rolled onto the floor. I groaned as the floorboards seemed to rise up to smack me in the face.

"Yeah, I know," Jackson said from somewhere in the kitchen. "You want hair of the dog or water, cous?"

I tried to lick my dry lips and found I had no moisture to even wet them. I was dehydrated as fuck. "Water," I managed to croak out.

Jackson walked over and placed a glass down on the small table next to me.

When I finally sat up, my stomach lurched at the movement and my head pounded with the rhythm of my own heartbeat. "Fuck." I ran my hand through my tangled hair, then brought the glass to my lips and sipped at the cool water. My queasy stomach threatened to revolt but I swallowed harder and pushed through the pain. I would *not* vomit.

Jackson collapsed into the armchair opposite me, his hand wrapped around a bottle of some sort of vitamin water. He looked as pale—and as shit—as I felt. "We hit the sauce a little hard last night, don't you think?" Jackson said.

I rolled my eyes. *Talk about a rhetorical question.* Pushing myself to my feet, I staggered back over to sit down on the couch I'd fallen asleep on last night. "Can you blame us?" I said, sipping on the water and wincing at the feeling of how fuzzy my tongue felt in my mouth. *Gross.*

Jackson laughed, laid his head back against the headrest, and closed his eyes. "No, I don't. And part of me still doesn't believe it."

I stared at him. "Which part? That you finally found your mate and she's a witch? Or that you have to share her ass with two other guys?"

Jackson put his drink between his legs so it wouldn't topple over and scrubbed both hands over his face. "Why do you have to put it like that, Billy?"

"Which part? *Oh.* The ass part." I was partial to a tight ass, so if we were allocating body parts… I took another sip of the water before putting down the glass. "I don't know if it was my imagination but… did she smell like a virgin to you?"

It seemed almost impossible. A virgin at her age. Especially when she was so fucking beautiful! But she'd smelled like innocence to me, which had made my damn wolf shifter practically dance with glee. It had been nearly impossible not to shift in that flower shop. I'd had to clamp down my jaw and fight with every cell of self-preservation in my body.

Jackson sighed and didn't even look up. "Yep."

I grinned, unable to help myself from teasing him a little further. "Then you'll only have to share her ass with us. Never anyone else. There's comfort in that, surely?"

That got him to look at me, his lips pulled tight and down. "Yeah, thanks for that. It's not reassuring at all."

I had to smile at that one.

Jackson was from an Alpha bloodline, one of the few in our pack. But we didn't give the Alphas any real importance anymore, nor extra responsibilities. We considered ourselves to be above that ancient hierarchical bullshit, and yet, Jackson still had the genetics of an Alpha. The size of one. The need to claim, protect, and dominate. The mere idea of sharing his mate sexually must be frustrating the shit out of him.

"Not a great time to be an Alpha, huh, cousin?" I quipped with a smirk.

Jackson got to his feet. "Just shut up, okay? I need breakfast. You want to come to Milly's?"

"Yeah, I think I need to." I forced myself to my feet and dragged my sorry ass out of the house and after him.

Milly's was one of the few retail establishments we had. Due to the fact the main town was a solid fifteen-minute drive away, we only had the essential four businesses—a gas station, a clothing shop, a doctor's office, and Milly's. Milly's was a café that served the best, greasiest burgers and heartiest breakfasts around. If the folks in town knew how good Milly's was, I was sure they'd come and eat out here rather than put up with whatever diners they frequented.

We walked the two blocks in complete silence. Once inside the diner, we found a booth and ordered the biggest, heaviest breakfast available.

"You guys sure are hungry this morning," Toni, one of the older ladies who waitressed there, commented. She ran her gaze over both of us and frowned. "You look like you could both use coffee, too."

I nodded. "Yeah. Thanks."

Toni picked up our menus and left to ring up our orders.

I sighed and glanced at Jackson. "So, what are we going to do about Ruby?" I tried to stop myself from shuddering with tingling pleasure at the sound of her name, but if Jackson's annoyed look was any indication, I hadn't achieved it.

Jackson sighed. "I don't know," he said honestly. "Obviously, we have to claim her, but then what? I don't want her living out here with us. The pack will have an absolute fit. And I doubt she'd want to, anyway. All the witches stay in town. They have their own community and we have ours."

My jaw dropped. *Was he serious?* "Are you saying you want to live in town?"

Jackson shook his head and huffed out a laugh. "God, no."

Hang on a second. Was missing something here? He surely wasn't actually suggesting that he wanted to live separately from her after we were mated? That couldn't be right. No wolf could do that. We'd never want her out of our sight.

"And you expect that she'll want to stay in town?" I repeated.

He nodded.

The reality of my cousin's stupidity hit me like a ton of bricks. If he thought that he was going to be able to just walk away from this woman, like he had every other woman he'd taken into his bed, he had another thing coming.

I rolled my eyes at him incredulously. "You really don't want her to be your mate, do you?"

Jackson looked down at the table and ran his finger over some invisible crack he could see and I couldn't.

I groaned and ignored the impulse to reach over the damn table and shake some sense into him. I needed to know what the real issue was, but communication wasn't my forte and it certainly was his. "What's your problem now, cousin?"

Jackson had always been a conundrum in our family, so strong, sure and capable, and yet he ran from responsibility at every turn, and had never shown the slightest interest in wanting to settle down— except when it came to building his house. That had come as a shock to everyone. He'd been the only one in our whole pack who wanted to build a big family home, just for himself. No mate. No children. And no plans to fill it any time soon if his screwing around over the past ten years was anything to go by.

"I don't have a problem," Jackson said, puffing up his chest at me.

Toni arrived with our food.

I sighed with relief, even though my stomach roiled at the sight of the bacon, fried eggs, and sausages. I knew I'd feel better once I'd consumed it all.

"Really?" I asked, picking up my knife and buttering a piece of golden toast. "You want to claim the virgin witch, who just happens to be your wolf's mate... but then you're going to leave her in town and just move on with your life out here? I don't think so." I certainly wasn't going to do that. If that woman was mine, she would be sleeping next to me every night, and I'd be sinking my cock into her as often as she'd allow. But that was just me.

Jackson dug into his plate of pancakes first, pouring maple syrup over the stack, before digging in like a man starved.

I glanced around the cafe, for the first time ever wishing the warlock-wolf would pop up. He had an uncanny ability to be in the right place at the exact moment he was needed. Not this time, though. *Damn.*

"Who are you looking for?" Jackson asked between mouthfuls.

I stabbed a sausage and put it to my lips, the greasy oil dripping off the end before I could take a bite. "Darren. I thought he may have a plan that might actually work."

Jackson growled at me, a deep, threatening noise.

It made the hairs on the back of my neck stand on end. And it horrified me to realize that every wolfy part of me wanted to submit to that sound. To kneel, expose my throat, and let the Alpha know that I was no threat. But I wasn't doing that. We weren't in animal form, and he wasn't my Alpha in this setting. He was my stubborn-ass cousin who needed to check himself.

So, I ignored my animal instincts and shrugged, looking down at my plate to distract myself from my inner wolf's feelings. It took a conscious and concerted effort to stand up against Jackson when he was in this sort of state. I cleared my throat. "I'll go find him after breakfast." Then I kept eating, quietly annoyed at the fact I could barely lift my head with the Alpha glaring down on me.

He shouldn't do that. He had no right to force me to submit to him. I wasn't doing anything wrong.

And the more I thought about it, the more annoyed I became. My hands curled into fists as my wolf barked in protest inside my mind. I clenched my teeth and lifted my gaze to glare at the Alpha sitting opposite me. And I was just about to tell him where he could shove it, when a hand landed unexpectedly on my shoulder.

"I was wondering where you guys were. Move over, Billy."

I'd never been more glad to hear Darren's happy voice. The tension eased out of me as I focused on his soothing presence. Hopefully Jackson would back off now. I nodded in response to Darren's request and moved over on the booth seat, pulling my plates of food with me along the table. Then, realizing I was being rude, I offered Darren a plate. "You want some?"

"Nah, I'm good. I already ate. What happened to you two last night? You look like death warmed up."

I glanced over at Jackson, who was still doing his Alpha trick, growling and glaring.

Darren didn't seem to feel it as he continued to smile and look relaxed. Another advantage to having mixed blood, I supposed.

I decided to answer his question, since Jackson seemed incapable. "We got drunk."

Darren stared at me and then at Jackson. "Seriously?"

"Yeah, why?" I asked, forking the fried eggs into my mouth. My stomach was mercifully beginning to settle, and the coffee was helping to ease my headache.

"Oh, nothing. I'm just surprised, I suppose. I thought you'd be celebrating at finding our mate, not drowning your sorrows."

I glanced across the table at Jackson.

He'd stopped glaring at us, and instead was now fiddling with the napkin in front of him, looking as uncomfortable as I felt.

Darren was right. We should have been celebrating, shouldn't we? Finding Ruby was a good thing. *The best thing.* "Yeah... well," I began, "both of us were a little shell shocked to say the least."

Darren turned to look directly at me. "At which part? The witch thing? Or the fact you have to share her?"

God, he's blunt! I just stared at him. Darren had more balls than I'd ever given him credit for.

Jackson growled softly in warning.

Darren stared at the Alpha for a moment, then... laughed at him. He laughed!

I looked from Jackson to Darren, then back to Jackson. *What the hell?* How did Darren ignore the Alpha stare like that? Regardless of how he did it, I wanted to know his trick!

"Both, huh?" Darren said, taking Jackson's non-verbal response as confirmation. Then he turned and smiled at the waitress as she walked past. "Toni, could you grab me a cappuccino to go, please?"

"Sure, hon," she said with a smile and a wink that bordered on flirting.

Since when was Darren so popular?

Darren turned to us, placing both hands on the table, palms down. "Look. I know you guys don't want a witch as a mate, and you certainly

don't want to share. And no offense, but I don't want to share, either."
He stopped talking and shrugged. "The witch thing is an advantage as
far as I'm concerned, so I suppose I've only got one thing to worry
about and not two."

I swallowed hard. He was taking this way better than we had.
"Yeah, I can see that. So, what are we going to do about it?"

Darren grinned at me. "What do you mean? What are *we* going to
do? This is Fate's choice. There's no question here. There's no fight to
the death or asking her to choose. It just is what it is."

Jackson stared at him like he'd lost his mind, and finally managed
to find his tongue. "What are you talking about, Darren?"

Darren turned to accept his takeaway cup from Toni and stood up,
shaking his head at us like we were bloody simpletons. "You guys
really don't understand the concept of Fated Mates, do you?"

I glanced at Jackson, who looked distinctly annoyed at being told
he didn't know something that was at the core of wolf shifter society. I
tried not to laugh as I turned back to the warlock-wolf. I was liking this
guy more and more by the minute. "Explain it to us, then," I countered.
"Since you're the expert."

Darren smiled. "We have all been, quite literally, designed for her.
She won't be happy with just one of us, and we will never find happiness without her. If you guys think you have a choice about all this,
you're dead wrong. So, I suggest you wrap your heads around it and
fast, because I'm going to see her tonight."

"Where?" Jackson barked out, his wolf slipping, bristling at the
challenge.

Darren's gaze slid over to the Alpha, then he grinned, white teeth
flashing against his lips. "She's a witch, and it's Halloween. All
Hallows' Eve. The most powerful night of the year for the witches.
She'll be out in all her glory tonight and personally? I intend to find out
just what she can do." With that, he walked off, leaving Jackson and I
to wonder what the hell had just gone wrong.

CHAPTER 6
RUBY

My mom had made me an epic little black dress with her magic for Halloween. It was meant to be "modern witchy" with some gothic flare. It was cut low in the front and clung tightly to my waist and sported an incredible Pentastar halter neckline. But personal doubts niggled at me, and I wasn't sure. The dress itself was stunning, but did my tummy look too big? I was a bit on the voluptuous side... Did my ass stick out too much at the back?

"Hey, Mom, do you really think this outfit is flattering on me? I'm not sure about the length. It's pretty short."

My mother laughed at me from her place on my bed. "You look

incredible, honey. You are the embodiment of youthful perfection. And the LBD style was practically designed for women who have tiny little waists like yours! Plus, with the classic black witch's hat?" She made a kiss in the air. "Magnificent, darling."

Hmmm... if you say so. I turned once more and stared at my reflection in the mirror with disappointment. The image I had of myself in my head was never quite what I ended up seeing in the mirror. I sighed, not entirely satisfied, but not unhappy either. Mom had made this outfit with love. She knew what the modern fashions were, and she had really nailed it. I was just feeling more self-conscious than usual.

There was a pause, then Mom said, "Why do you ask? You don't usually care so much about what you wear—especially on Halloween when most of your friends will either be in full gruesome getup, or not dressed up at all. Is there someone special you're trying to impress tonight?"

My heart fluttered as I felt the pull of my mother's words, the undercurrent of an enchantment I couldn't fight. Since I was a child, it had been hard not to tell her the truth. The whole truth, and nothing but the truth. I just felt compelled to be honest with her. Whether or not she actually put a spell over her words, or whether it ran deeper, more ingrained than that—like a natural mother-daughter-bond—I wasn't sure. I'd never had the courage to ask, and I'd never had the strength or true need to fight against her. She always had my best interests at heart, after all.

"Yeah," I said, hedging my bets with something general. I didn't have to get too specific. "I met someone yesterday at work, and he said he might pop by tonight." I turned to the left, then the right, inspecting myself in the mirror one last time. *I looked okay*, I supposed as I pulled on the finishing touch—the matching witch's hat. But all I could see were my faults. The things I would remove if I had the choice.

Witches weren't supposed to use their magic to permanently alter their bodies. It was one of the few rules we had in the community. Transformational magic was meant to be for short-term use or only in a dire emergency. Not because you thought your nose was too big or you didn't like the way your ass looked.

My mother's head popped up and her eyes widened with sudden curiosity. "Oh, really? What's his name? Do I know him?"

I turned toward my mother, who was sitting on my bed like any friend of mine would. I wanted her advice on the odd situation I'd found myself in, but I was unsure how much I should reveal all at once. We hadn't told any of our mothers about the spell we'd cast last Halloween. And after my mother's failed attempt at one relationship—my father—she'd given up on romantic love entirely. She'd never even hooked up with anyone else again ever since. She was one and done.

What would she say about the fact I had three men vying for me? And even worse, how would she react to the fact that I wasn't sure I even wanted to choose between them?

My stomach dropped and my chest tightened with anxiety at the mere thought of telling her. She'd think I was some sort of... loose woman, when the complete opposite was the truth. How could I make her understand the pull of Destiny and Fate? "His name's Darren, and I don't think you would have met him. He lives out of town."

My mother stood up from her spot on my bed and smiled. "Darren. Well, that's a nice name. I can't wait to meet him."

She was so beautiful, trying to play the "cool mom", best friend-type of role. And I loved her so much for it. I knew she wanted to ask a thousand other questions but was holding back, letting me divulge what I felt comfortable with in my own time.

I laughed. "Yeah, maybe not just yet, Mom. Maybe wait until I've spent more than five minutes with him first?" And not before I worked out what I was going to do about the whole *three-men* thing, and the wolf shifter issue. A lot of witches and warlocks didn't like the wolf shifter packs. I'd never been sure why, beyond the fact that they were obviously different from us.

But I trusted the magic that had brought them to me and was fully prepared to find out everything about them that I needed to. We'd make this work—somehow.

Mom ignored my comment about not wanting her to meet Darren and changed the subject. "So, what are you party girls planning on doing tonight?"

You mean on our joint twenty-second birthday? Not much. I shrugged. "Not a lot. We said we'd dress up and walk around town. See what was going on. How about you, Mom? What are you doing tonight? Something with the Coven? Or just Rebecca and Kathy?"

Rebecca and Kathy were Bella and Tiffany's moms, and the three of them were almost as close as we were.

"We're going over to Kathy's later, thought we'd cast a little magic," my mother said, waggling her eyebrows as though it was naughty or taboo that they could throw a spell or two together.

Our mothers were all powerful witches and probably could have trained to become healers or teachers. But instead, they'd raised us, putting their time and energy into our well-being, while working menial jobs to pay the bills.

It made me sad and feel a little guilty sometimes that my mother had missed out on so many things. A good job. A husband. More kids. But hopefully, my mom's time would come where she'd feel truly free to be happy without worrying about me. Perhaps now that I'd met my soul mate—well, *mates*—I'd be able to move out and she could move on with her life. Maybe even start dating again? Start over!

I grinned at her and shared in her silliness. "Enjoy, Mom."

All Hallows' Eve was the most powerful night of the year for witches like us. If my mother or any of her friends wanted some special power for a spell, it would be available to them tonight.

Mom walked out of the room and headed down the stairs, clearly in a good mood.

I ran my hands through my hair, arranging the long red waves around my face before giving up on attempting to make myself look any better. Grabbing my bag, I checked its contents. Cell phone. Keys. Lip gloss. *All good to go.* I bounced down the stairs and stepped toward the front door. "See you later, Mom!"

"Have fun!" she called but didn't come out to see me leave. Normal behavior for mothers of twenty-two-year-olds all over the world. Not so normal for me.

I opened the door and hesitated, one leg lifted to take a step outside. Was she hiding something? Should I go investigate? My cell phone beeped in my bag, and I rolled my eyes. That would be Bella. I was late. I *had* to go now. No more dawdling. I went out the door and headed down the street. Tiffany lived one block away and Bella, two.

We often joked that our mothers should have bought one large house and raised us together in some sort of single mothers' commune. But with all our strong personalities, it was probably a good idea to put a block or two between us.

I crossed the street and waved at our neighbors, who were heading out to trick-or-treat with their kids. *How sweet.*

"You look awesome, Agnes!" I called out to the little girl who lived directly across the street from us.

She had red hair too, something she loved having in common between us. But her hair was tied up in cute pigtails and she was dressed as a zombie, with fake bloody gashes over her face, and a weird, home-made white sheet costume. She grinned at me and waved back, her front teeth still missing, making her look like some sort of ridiculously adorable gummy shark.

I smiled to myself as I kept walking to Bella's house. We lived in a normal community of humans, but there was a witch family on every street. The Coven kept their dealings and meetings strictly secret, and if we needed to perform a ritual of or gather, there was an old church with extensive grounds as well as an abandoned school outside of town that we used.

I liked being part of a community within a larger community. I didn't want to be isolated like the wolf shifters. Setting up your own town and excluding everyone else seemed unnatural, somehow.

As I turned to stroll up the sidewalk to Bella's house, I giggled to myself as I drank in the delightful and entertaining sight before me. Bella had decorated the house as she always did. There were cobwebs and spiders, skeletons, as well as a large plastic witch out the front.

Why she wanted to copy the humans that much when the effect was so comically tacky was beyond me. I mean, it was fun, but so cliché!

The door swung open before I could even knock.

"You didn't dress up," Bella said, her accusatory tone as obvious as her narrowed gaze.

"You know that if you used some of your magic to decorate the house, it would look a thousand times better." I motioned to the human decorative crap around her front yard and grinned in return.

Bella rolled her eyes and pulled me inside. "You *know* we can't do that."

I laughed at her purple wig and hat. "Are you seriously wearing that?"

"Yes. Why not? We said we'd dress up."

"Yeah, but..." I whispered a few words of magic and conjured up a broom to go with my black velvet witches' hat and complete my outfit. Now, my look mimicked every witch's outfit from every popular movie ever made about your kind. "You could at least try and make it look good."

Bella huffed at me.

Tiffany walked into the room, her zombie-nurse outfit on display for another year running. It was super short, white, and splashed with special effects blood.

I grinned at her. "Didn't want to make another costume this year, Tiff?"

Tiffany shrugged. "Why would I? It's not like I'm out to impress anyone. Speaking of which... what's with the new dress, huh?" Tiffany pointed her painted fingernail at me.

I twirled around.. "Mom made it. What do you think?"

Tiffany nodded approvingly. "It's nice. Your mom has a good eye for fashion that suits you."

I laughed. "Well, I do look just like a younger version of her, so she's kind of cheating, don't you think?"

There was a knock at the door and Bella rushed off to deal with the trick-or-treaters.

Tiffany closed the distance between us, her arms outstretched. "Happy birthday, Ruby."

I hugged her tightly. "Happy birthday, Tiff."

We'd been messaging each other from the moment we'd woken up this morning, but now we could eat, chat, hug, and laugh. All the things I loved to do with my best friends.

When she pulled back, she had a thoughtful look on her face. Her eyebrows were tugged down, and her lips were twisted.

"What's going on?" I asked, a little perturbed.

Tiffany wasn't the sort to have significant, deep thoughts, generally. She was always pretty easy going. She bit her glossy pink lip. "Nothing, really. I just... I was thinking about your guy problem."

"Guy problem?" I repeated with a playful nudge and chuckle. "Which part? The number of them or the wolf thing?"

Tiffany grinned at me. "I sort of like the idea of you having three guys fighting over you."

I pushed her with a grin. "Shut up, okay. I've never even had *one* guy interested in me. This is going to be insane." My breath caught in my throat, and I exhaled quickly to expel the stress building up. I hadn't even thought about that part until this morning, really. What on earth was I going to *do* with three guys? How did that even... um, work? I blush stole over me, and I tucked a red wave behind my ear.

Bella came back to join our circle. "So, what did I miss?" she asked, still holding the massive bowl of candy her mom had bought for the kids in the neighborhood.

All my favorites. *Yum.* I reached out and snagged a wrapped mini-Snickers and twisted the end to open it up. "Tiff was just telling me she's worried about my guy problem but hasn't elaborated yet."

We turned back to Tiff as one.

She rolled her eyes. "Yeah, thanks Rubes. Way to put the pressure on," she said.

I shrugged. "Just tell me? It's okay."

"Well, I was talking to my mom about the wolf shifters who live outside town..." She hesitated dramatically.

My heart skipped a beat. "Yeah? And?" Not that I'd wanted her to seek out information on my behalf, but Tiff had always been terrible at keeping secrets.

"I didn't tell her about you, don't worry," she added quickly. "I just mentioned some of them had come into town and asked what she knew about them."

"What did she say?" I certainly hadn't had the guts to ask my mom anything like that. I wasn't quite ready to reveal that much about my situation just yet.

"She was a bit shocked, actually. That I'd noticed them, I mean. But then she said, well... that they don't like us."

I stared at her. "What do you mean?"

"I mean... they're pretty much anti-witch. She said that they have a hierarchy of people they think are acceptable. Obviously, in their opinion wolf shifters are the best, then they'll tolerate humans, but witches...? Nope."

I put both hands up to stop her from talking, annoyed to even hear such things. "Hang on a second. You're telling me they just don't like us. That there's no good reason behind it? No explanations? We're just the bottom of the food chain as far as they're concerned?"

Tiffany nodded and grimaced. "Sorry, but yep. That was the gist of it."

Anger tightened my gut. It didn't make sense. "Then why does Darren have warlock in him? I could sense it. Maybe not a parent, but definitely a grandparent. It's there."

Tiffany shrugged. "I don't know, hon. You're going to have to ask him yourself."

Yes, I will, I resolved.

Bella's mom, Rebecca, walked into the room, dressed in purple and orange and other god-awful colored spots. She was a mixed bag, that one. "Hello, girls! Happy birthday and Happy Halloween."

Tiff and I smiled and thanked Bella's mom. She was the oddest of the mom group but had always been lovely to us.

"I'm heading over to Kathy's house," she said. 'If you girls decide to go into town, can you leave the bowl of candy out front, Bella?"

Bella nodded. "Of course. Hey, Mom?"

"Yes, hon?"

"Do you know much about the wolf shifters who live outside town?"

I almost smacked her for asking the question right in front of me. What was she thinking? What if Rebecca figured it out before I had a chance to tell my mom? But instead of hitting Bella, I plastered a smile on my face and concentrated on whatever her mom was about to tell us.

Rebecca picked up her woven hippy bag and turned to frown at us. "Why are you asking about them?" She twisted the strings of the bag around her fingers and pulled tight, as though anxious about the question, which was weird.

"Ruby met some of them the other day, when they came into town to see their grandmother or something. Do you know much about them?" Bella asked, keeping her tone relatively normal considering she, like all three of us, was terrible at keeping things from her mother.

Rebecca slid her bag up onto her shoulder and moved toward the door. "I don't know much about them, I'm sorry," she said, but there was something off about her tone. Then she laughed nervously and swallowed awkwardly.

I glanced toward Tiffany, brow furrowed. Had she noticed it, too?

Rebecca continued. "They don't like witches very much. We were always just told not to have anything to do with them."

I had to step forward and ask, my curiosity winning out over my sense of caution. "Do you mean we've fought with them in the past? Is there some kind of paranormal war going on we don't know about?"

Rebecca chuckled. "Oh, goodness no. There's no war. No fight. It's just that..." She sighed. "The elders of the wolf pack think we're beneath them, and the old High Warlock who died last year didn't like them either. But that's all in the past, now." She shrugged, kissed Bella on the forehead, and headed out the door a little too quickly for my liking.

As soon as she was gone, I turned toward my "sisters" bubbling with renewed agitation. "I don't think we got the whole story there, but this just got even more complicated."

CHAPTER 7
JACKSON

Going into town on Halloween was like walking into a nightmare and not being able to escape. Humans, witches, and warlocks all intermingled and dressed up in costumes. And unless I was close enough to smell them, I couldn't tell which was which.

Or which witch was a witch. "Fuck. I hate Halloween," I said to no one in particular.

Billy chuckled from the passenger seat of my truck.

Darren said from the back, "You and me both."

I frowned; surprised Darren felt the same way we did. "Huh? I thought you'd like all these... shenanigans?" I slowed my truck as we passed through the town looking for a parking spot. There were people everywhere. Children in elaborate costumes, shops decorated with ghastly black and orange displays. A skeleton here, and a hundred carved pumpkins there. *Yuck.*

Darren chuckled. "God, no. Why would I? There's nothing respectful here about the power of witches and magic. If anything? It's a mockery of our culture. I can't believe the witches in town condone it."

Ha. I hadn't thought of it like that.

"There's one," Billy said.

I swung into the spot outside a restaurant with a large fish painted on the window. We didn't eat much in town, but this place looked decent with its trendy tables and nice white tablecloths. I turned off the truck and tried to ignore the tension and stress radiating through my body. I didn't want to do this. Any of it. I didn't want to be walking around town at the height of Halloween, and I certainly didn't want to go in search of our little shared mate.

Darren reached over and squeezed my shoulder. "Hey. If you've changed your mind, it's all good. I can find my own way back at the end of the night."

And give him free rein to bond with my mate? *Not a chance in Hell.* My teeth clamped down and I shook my head, that stupid Alpha growl rolling in my throat. I couldn't control it and I didn't like it, but it came out, nonetheless.

Darren laughed.

Impudent pup.

"Yeah, thought so. Let's go." He jumped out of the truck and slammed the door behind him.

I glanced over at Billy, who was staring at the busy streets, a grimace on his face. "You sure you want to live with him for the rest of your life?" I asked, only partly joking.

Billy looked over at me as he unfastened his seat belt. "The better question is: you sure you want to live without her for the rest of your life?"

I frowned as Billy shrugged and got out of the truck.

I'd been joking about living with Darren. *Sort of.* Because the truth was, I wasn't sure I could share my house—my space—with anyone for the rest of my life. There was a reason I'd built a big house and never invited anyone to come live with me. I liked my own company. And yet suddenly I was being compelled to not only accept one mate, but another two guys on top of that?

And that wasn't going over well with the lone wolf part of me.

You're not a lone wolf, you have the genes of an Alpha. "Yeah, yeah, yeah." I stepped out of the truck, locked it, and pocketed the keys. "Which way?" I had no idea where we were headed, nor what we were going to do with the night besides hopefully locate our mate. But Darren probably had a plan, so for once, I was following him.

"Let's just have a wander and see what's on offer. I'm hungry," Darren said.

I shrugged. Sounded like as good a plan as any, and I followed the two other men down the street.

A variety of food trucks were parked along the road and colorful food stalls lined the pavement. Even the restaurants were open, no doubt hoping to score some extra business. The fear on some of the human faces when they saw me made my stomach churn. They shouldn't be instinctively afraid of me. I'd never hurt any of them. *Never.*

I shook off the uncomfortable feeling of being silently judged and instead focused on the scents of the food and candy all around me. The tightness in my shoulders lifted and my tense muscles relaxed. I sighed. Yeah, that was better. *And you know it's not their fault they're afraid of us,* I reminded myself. *It stops them from wanting to mate with us.*

"Jackson!"

I glanced up when my name was called out and spotted a familiar woman standing with Darren and Billy on the sidewalk. Warmth spread through my chest. "Grandma. What are you doing here?" I walked up and gave her a hug, her body small in my arms. *I missed her.* I really had to make more time to see her like I had yesterday. I owed her that much.

She chuckled in my ear. "I think that's my line, Jackson. I live in town, and I happen to enjoy Halloween. What are *you* doing here, tonight?" She was standing next to a stall serving cold drinks and cotton candy.

"We... ah..." How was I even going to begin to explain what had happened in the past twenty-four hours?

"Come to see if the pretty red head from the florist is around?" Grandma asked with a knowing wink.

My gaze slid to Darren and Billy, and I sucked in a deep breath. "Yeah... we did."

Grandma's eyes widened as she glanced from me, to Billy, to Darren, then back to me again. "No! She's... all your mates?" she asked, sounding shocked but also, not. "Goodness."

I frowned, amazed by her intuitive understanding. "How did you put that together so quickly?"

She shrugged. "It makes sense, in a way. And Fate is never wrong. The last generation of the pack has produced three to four times as many males as they have females. I told your grandfather years ago that the only solution was to breed outside the pack, or to partner off the females with multiple mates. He assumed, of course, that you would just partner up with women from neighboring packs, but they don't have an excess either. But in this case... it seems like you're doing both."

I couldn't believe she was being so calm about it. I'd noticed the lack of females but had always assumed my Fated Mate would turn up one day. A wolf shifter, of course. A single woman to myself. I'd never thought *this* would happen. "I—"

Darren butted in and claimed my grandmother's attention. "I'm not sure if you remember me, Mrs. Davis. I'm Darren."

Grandma took the hand Darren offered and shook it with a warm smile. "Of course, I do, young man. Please, call me Rose. Your grand-mother was one of my best friends before she passed on."

Darren's mouth dropped open. "I... I didn't know that."

I didn't either but wasn't surprised. They were the only two non-wolf-shifter women in our whole pack of their generation. It would have made sense for them to bond and become friends. They would have found a sense of unity in their shared differences.

"Oh, yes. And she was a truly good-hearted woman. I can see you have inherited a lot of her." Grandma stared at Darren for a long moment then smiled. "You must be happy to find out that your Fated Mate is a witch as well?"

Darren grinned. "Well, yes. I am."

Grandma beamed, taking the news of our situation better than any of us. "Well, I can't wait to meet the girl. I came into town hoping she'd be working, but Andrea said she isn't rostered on until tomorrow."

"We're hoping to find her tonight, as well," Darren said. "She told me today that she'd be around."

"Well, I can't help you there, I'm sorry. I wouldn't even know whom to point you towards or ask. The witches are secretive in town. Most of the humans don't even know they exist."

I frowned. "How do they hide themselves so well?" Surely there would be too many unusual things about the witches for a human to ignore.

Grandma waited a moment, smiling as a group of teenagers walked past, then continued. "Well, for one thing, they look as human as I do. And they have a church outside of town that I believe they use for Coven meetings."

"Could she be there tonight then?" Billy asked, jumping into the conversation.

Grandma shrugged. "Who knows? Your guess is as good as mine."

Darren shook his head. "No. She said she'd be around town. She made a point of mentioning it. I think she wants us to find her."

"Then go look for her!" Grandma said, fluttering her hands at us with a big smile on her face.

I bent forward and kissed my grandmother on the cheek. "Thank you."

She cupped my cheek in an affectionate gesture, her eyes twinkling, then headed off in the opposite direction.

We turned as a group and surged into the crowd once again.

"She's so lovely," Darren beamed as we made our way down the street between the stalls and the humans dressed as demons, witches, and ghosts. "I wish my grandmother was still around." He shook his head with a note of sadness.

I glanced at a guilty-looking Billy. We both knew we were lucky to have her in our family, and we didn't give her the respect or time she deserved. We'd have to change that.

"I think I see her," Darren said, stopping dead in his tracks.

"Where?" I demanded, looking around and inhaling sharply. I couldn't smell her over the top of all the Halloween festive nonsense, and my senses were the most heightened of the three of us.

"There! In the little black dress... Look, just follow me." Darren took off through the crowd and across the street, homing in on our mate like a trained bloodhound.

Billy and I chased after him.

I found myself quietly annoyed that I wasn't the one taking the lead. A stupid thought, but even so... Then I saw her, and my damn heart stopped. *Damn, she's beautiful.*

Darren walked right up to her.

She turned to smile at him and her whole face lit up. She stared at him the way I yearned for her to look at me. With happiness and shyness, and healthy dose of desire.

Then she said something, and Darren pointed toward us.

Ruby's gaze flicked straight toward me, and our gazes met with the nerve-jangling clash and raw heat of a new sword being forged.

My wolf howled inside of me, dying to bust out—to meet his mate in the flesh. My skin tingled and I locked my jaw down to stop myself from shifting on the spot. *The pack elders would have my head for revealing our kind.* I closed my eyes and froze where I stood, fighting to keep my ravenous and excited shifter under control. The last thing I needed was to wolf out in the middle of town, in front of my mate and every human around on Halloween. That would break several of our laws, not to mention probably terrify my mate.

I clamped down on my shifter hard, though he fought me every step of the way. But when I finally managed to shove him way down with the promise of a long run when we got home tonight, I opened my eyes again and found everyone staring at me. Heat flushed up my cheeks and I shoved my hands into my jean pockets as I walked forward to join the group. "Hey," I said, tilting my head up at Ruby in greeting.

"Hey, Jackson," she said back, her face as flushed as I expected mine to be.

She wore a spectacular short black dress that highlighted every curve of her body. Every twist and turn called to me, begging me to run my hands over them, and sink my teeth into...

"Guys, these are my friends, Tiffany and Bella," Ruby said, calling me back and away from my fantasies.

"Hey," I greeted them.

Billy just nodded. Was he having trouble speaking again as he fought down his own inner wolf? Probably.

Darren jumped in, the only one who had his head about him. "Hey. I'm Darren. This is Billy and Jackson. It's nice to meet you both."

The girls grinned at each other.

When I was finally able to drag my gaze away from Ruby, I looked over her friends. One of them was a gorgeous blonde whose outfit was a little too risqué for my tastes. The other—the brunette—was super cute too but dressed in the weirdest Halloween costume I'd ever seen.

My mate was by far the most attractive and most serene. But I wasn't biased. *Not at all.*

"So, do you guys come in for Halloween every year?" the blonde one—Tiffany, I thought—asked.

I shook my head, unable to answer properly. *God, this was embarrassing.*

Darren chuckled, saving the day yet again. "Nah. We're not the biggest Halloween fans to be honest. We just came in to see Ruby again." Darren stared at our mate.

She smiled at him then glanced up at me.

That was the moment I knew that she *knew*. That all three of us were hers, and she was ours. I stepped closer, my tongue loosening as my wolf retreated at my command. "The humans around here are a little freaked out by our presence here. Can we go somewhere a little less... crowded, maybe?"

Ruby glanced at her friends, "Well, um..."

Tiffany grinned and linked arms with the brunette, Bella. "No problem at all. We're gonna grab something to eat. We'll catch you later, Ruby."

Bella looked like she was about to protest, her eyebrows drawn low over her eyes in a frown. But when she opened her mouth to say something Tiffany hauled her away and we were left standing in the street with Ruby, shining brightly, her Fated wolf pack clustered protectively around her.

I stepped a little closer.

Ruby had to tilt her head back to look at me. She was a tiny thing.

I could tuck her up and carry her around with me if she wished it.

"Where do you want to go, Jackson?" she asked, then licked her lips, staring up at me with her huge, emerald, green eyes.

I shrugged. "Any where's good, although someplace quiet would be best."

Ruby pressed her lips together then tilted her head as she offered a solution. "How about we walk for a bit and see where it takes us?"

A growl rolled through my throat at the suggestion. *Hell, yes!* But I swallowed hard, trying to force the sound down.

She didn't so much as flinch at my natural reaction. Instead, she just smiled as she started to walk away.

All three of us fell into step and began to follow her.

CHAPTER 8

RUBY

My *Fated Mates!* Frenetic energy buzzed through me unlike anything I'd ever felt before. I wanted to squeal and scream; to jump up and down with excitement. But that would have appeared juvenile. And I didn't want the three gorgeous men who were following me—literally following me—to think I was a child. I was a young, but grown woman, regardless of fact I was still a virgin.

It was already plainly obvious that all three of them were older than me, but by how much? And how much experience would they have? Because mine was practically non-existent.

We cleared the edges of the shops on Main Street and the crowds began to thin out and disperse.

My plan was to walk the three wolf shifters the long way back to my house, and if I wanted to invite them in for a drink or something, I could. If I didn't, if I wasn't comfortable inviting them into my mother's house for any reason, I could just keep walking and do the loop back to the shops. But I wasn't going to tell them that was the plan. For now, we were just walking. "Hey, how old are you guys?" I asked, tossing the question over my shoulder as I waited for them to catch up.

Darren jogged up to my side with a grin on his face. "You want the four-one-one on all of us?"

I laughed. "You can do that?"

He shrugged. "Sure. It'll save some time."

I nodded. "Okay, great. Go for it."

We stopped at the edge of a road.

Darren turned to the other two men, both of whom were frowning at him but not speaking.

Interesting...

Darren gestured at Jackson, the biggest of the three. "Jackson's twenty-eight, a jack of all trades, and an Alpha wolf. Did you pick up on that already?"

I nodded. "Yeah, it's a bit hard to miss."

He grinned. "Your instincts are in good shape then." Darren tilted his head toward the third of my Fated Mates. "And this is Billy. He's Jackson's cousin. He's twenty-seven and a plumber."

Out of sheer curiosity, I had to ask. "And a... beta wolf? Do you guys still use those terms?" I'd done a little reading today about wolf shifter packs, but the internet had little on what true paranormals were like, so I wasn't sure I could trust it as a good and true source of information.

Darren shrugged. "Kind of. We're not a traditional pack in that sense. We don't really have a hierarchy where one member is higher than another, unless there's an emergency or an attack. Then we would revert instinctively to the natural pack hierarchy. And yes, Billy would be there, fighting right beside Jackson."

I wanted so desperately to reach over and touch Darren. My fingers itched and ached, so I twisted them together in front of me as we walked to stop myself from doing exactly that. He was so warm and vibrant. But I didn't dare just yet. It felt too early. Not to mention I'd have no way of knowing how the other two would react to my initiating physical contact. I definitely didn't want to instigate a pack fight.

"And how about you?" I asked Darren.

"Me?" he said, his dark eyes twinkling with mischief. "Guess."

I bit my bottom lip. "But I might be wrong."

He shrugged again. "Doesn't matter."

Okay... "I think you're probably a tradesman too, though I'm not sure which kind. You're closer to my age, so maybe something like twenty-three? And as far as your wolf origins go, I know you have witch in your genetics, but it's more distant than parents. So maybe a grandmother or grandfather?"

Darren laughed and grabbed me about the waist, hugging me against his body and swinging me around so that my feet lifted off the ground.

I squealed in shock as much as delight, unable to hold the sound in, until he finally planted me firmly back on the ground.

"You're awesome," he said, with a big smile. "Yes, my grandmother was a witch, actually. I'm twenty-five and a sparky by trade."

I glanced at the other two men who were now growling softly in their throats. I didn't really like the sound—it made my skin crawl—but I was also pretty sure the sound wasn't directed at me. I stepped closer to Darren. "Why are they doing that?"

He grinned. "They're just jealous I touched you, but it's okay. They'll get used to it in time."

I took the opportunity to ask the glaringly obvious but rather embarrassing question. "So... it's all three of you, right?" I couldn't bring myself to spell it out. How vain would I sound to just come out and ask if all three of them wanted me?

He lifted one eyebrow. "All three of us *what?*"

"You know..." I said, gesturing between him and me, and the other two men and me.

He laughed again, the sound putting me at ease. "Are you asking me if all three of us are here for you? If we all want you?"

I nodded, trying to stay calm, though a heated brushfire stole up my cheeks.

"Of course, we do," Darren said. "All three of us believe you're our Fated Mate. Do you feel the connection with us too?"

I nodded, though the terminology was not entirely familiar to me. "Fated Mate?"

"Yeah. It pretty much means that Fate designed us for you, and you for us. We're a perfect balance of personalities and strengths."

"Ah, okay," I said. *Soul Mates.* Destined Lovers. Something like that, anyway. So, our spell had truly worked after all! Tiffany and Bella would be thrilled to know. "So, is this common in your pack? To have three men and one woman, I mean? Because I can tell you, now, for the witches, this is highly unusual."

My mother was going to flip out when she found out.

Jackson growled louder and shook his head.

I looked over at Darren and scrunched up my nose. "How come they can't talk to me, and you can?"

He chuckled. "I think it's the witch in me? I don't respond to my wolf shifter in the same way they do. And much to his annoyance, I don't respond to Jackson's Alpha dominance thing either." He shrugged as though his differences were no big deal, then continued. "But to answer your question, no, it's not common to have three men to one woman in our pack. I've never heard of it, actually. And the reason they can't talk is because they're fighting their shifters back. At least, I think. I'll ask them later when we get home."

I glanced over at the two huge men and saw the strain in their jaws, the inherent anger in their gazes. "Are they mad at me?" I asked quietly, my stomach dipping strangely at the idea of them being disappointed in me.

Jackson and Billy both shook their heads and Jackson managed to growl out a garbled, "No."

Darren took my hand in his.

A frisson of excitement danced along my skin.

"Let's keep walking," he said and pulled me across the street.

I held his hand tightly and directed the group up the street around the block, and down my street. As we walked closer to my house, *my mother's house*, nerves began to creep in. My gut tightened and the hairs on the back of my neck stood up.

"So, tell me more about you guys," I said, not sure what I needed to know, but wanting to hear Darren speak all the same.

"I think we'd like to hear about you, Ruby. Tell us about your family, work. College, anything? Personally, I want to know more about your magic, too," Darren said with a grin.

I took that to mean that the other two probably wouldn't want to know about my witch abilities. "Oh... sure, but can I ask you a question first?"

He nodded. "Of course."

"How come wolf shifters don't like witches?" I asked, desperate to know. "I mean, it's obvious from your grandparents' marriage that not all witches are shunned by your pack. But from everything I've heard today from my friends and their moms, you guys generally have an issue with us. Is that true?"

Darren glanced over at the other two walking behind us.

I stopped, making the other men stop also. I turned to look at the big men behind me and raised my eyebrows in query. "Well?"

When they didn't respond, I crossed my arms over my chest and stared at them.

"I want you to speak, too, not just Darren," I said. "It's not fair. How am I supposed to get to know you all if you can't talk to me?"

"Ruby, they can't..." Darren tried to excuse them.

But I was getting annoyed. If they'd come into town to see me, to court me or whatever the expression was, I wasn't going to get a good feel for them with those ridiculous wolfish glares on their faces all the time. I may as well just choose Darren and be done with it. Release poor Jackson and Billy to date someone they could talk to.

The mere thought made my heart ache. Letting them go? *God... I really didn't want to.* I put those feelings into my voice, my disappointment and frustration rolling through my tone. I flicked my gaze at Darren. "Well, they can go home then, can't they? We're away from the crowds, and I'm not touching you, so they have no reason to let their animal half take over and rob them of their ability to speak. It's not fair on any of us. So, if they're not going to talk to me, they might as well go home, and you can come with me."

I lifted my chin in challenge, hoping it would be enough to drag them out of their wolf-bound isolation.

Still, neither Billy nor Jackson said anything. They simply continued to glare at me.

I threw up my hands. *This is insane. This can't work!* "Fine. Keep ignoring me." I turned around. My house was about five fences down. I could see the bells hanging on the front porch, swaying in the slight breeze. Enough was enough. Clearly Fate was drunk on spiked pumpkin juice. "I'm going home."

A hand snaked out, grabbed my arm, and whirled me back toward the group.

"Oh..." I gasped as I slammed into Jackson's chest and his arms wrapped around me.

I should have been terrified by his strength, his intensity, the way he was looking at me like he wanted to literally devour me alive. But I wasn't. Far from it. I wanted him to do everything to me that his look said he craved.

"Don't go," he said, and his teeth extended past his lips now. They were pointed and his jaw had changed. It was more angular. Stronger.

I blinked up at him. "Then tell your wolf to back off." I cocked my head in thought. "Unless you want me to work a spell to put him to sleep? I'm sure I could." I lifted my hand and wiggled my fingers. I didn't call on my magic, nor conjure anything. I was just teasing and bluffing *mostly* but was interested in seeing his reaction.

The growl that Jackson released shivered through me. One of his hands swept down to grab my ass and haul me against his body even tighter, fitting me into the cradle of his hips.

I gasped, frozen in place.

The other hand moved up to the back of my head, gripping my skull so that I was staring into the stormy blue eyes of an Alpha wolf. The focus of his gaze shifted when my lips parted so that I could breathe, my heart pounding in my chest like a runaway train.

He dropped his head and pressed his lips to mine more gently than I'd anticipated.

I moaned in my throat as a wave of heat swept through me. I could feel the veiled strength and wanted so much more of him than this kiss. His passions ran deep, I could sense them. This was only the tip of the iceberg. I ran my hands up his huge arms, over his neck and into his thick hair so I could grip his head and pull him closer. *Damn, he's big.* How hot and muscly would he be under this sweater?

Jackson groaned and pressed open my lips with his, using his tongue to sweep inside my mouth.

I shivered with desire, my belly tightening with liquid heat.

The hand that cupped my head moved lower, grabbing my other ass cheek so that he was holding my whole lower body firmly in his grasp.

I gasped against his mouth, stifling the wanton moan that rose.

"Ruby!" I heard my name being called as though from very far away.

Jackson froze against me, like a statue. His startled groan was not one of pleasure, but of pain.

I ripped my lips away from his and frowned toward the direction from which my name had been called.

My mother and her friends stood on the other side of the street, the anger in their faces a blazing mass of fury.

Oh shit! I couldn't extract myself from Jackson's tight grip. He was frozen, like a popsicle.

My mother raced across the pavement and reached out for me.

I glared at her as she stood in front of me. "Mother! What did you do?"

"What the hell are you doing with a pack of wolves?" my mother demanded, her eyes glittering with the silver of living magic.

If I wasn't so angry at the sudden intrusion, I'd be terrified of what she was about to do to my mates. "Unfreeze him, Mom. *Now*. I can't get out of here." I was bent backwards and at a rather awkward angle.. My gaze darted to Darren and Billy, who were both also frozen in place. "Mom!"

"Okay, okay," she said, and snapped her fingers.

All three men jolted forward in a strange way as though falling, then caught themselves as they came out of their stupor.

I managed to get my feet under me so that I didn't fall on my ass but stumbled a few steps away.

My mother grabbed my arm and pulled me to her side in a defensive and protective manner.

The guys took a moment to regain their faculties, then came together with a growl, redirecting their ire at my mom.

"Back off," my mother warned, conjuring a ball of fire with one hand and brandishing it toward the wolves—a very real threat.

"Mom! Stop!" I said, pulling down her arm. "You can't use your magic out in the open like this."

My mother finally seemed to hear me and dropped her hand down, though her best friends stood on either side of her like a military guard.

She barked at my men, "Go home. Now!"

Jackson glared at her, the Alpha in him standing strong. "We're not going anywhere."

Uh oh. Mom won't like that.

My mother glanced at her two best friends and as one, they spoke a single word, flicked their right wrists in the air, and then my men were gone.

Gone! Just vanished into thin air. I gaped at the space where six hundred pounds of wolf shifters was just moments before. I pulled my arm out of my mother's grasp and glared at her. "Where the hell did you just send them?"

CHAPTER 9

BILLY

One minute we were standing on the sidewalk in town, glaring at the cluster of three older witches who'd interrupted our moment with Ruby—the hairs on my arms and legs had been standing on end as my shifter howled to get out—then the next moment, light flashed before my eyes.

I staggered like a drunk, legs weak, heart pounding, sweat rolling down my back.

I grabbed for anything to stop myself from falling to the ground. My hands found nothing to grasp, and I bit the dust. Hard. My vision cleared as my head whirled, and my fingers dug into the dirt beneath my hands.

We were back in our town. Or at least I was. I glanced around. *Where were the others?*

Jackson's groan sounded a few feet away.

I pushed myself to roll over onto my back, breathing heavily.

"What the hell happened?" Jackson asked, coughing up a lung, his anger already on edge.

Darren staggered over, the only one of us to remain still standing; no doubt a boon of being part warlock. He took a deep breath and moaned as he straightened his spine and stood up, blinking rapidly. "They, uh, sent us back."

I pushed myself up using what little core strength I had left. "Who sent us back? And where the hell are we?" I blinked, my vision slowly clearing. I recognized the dirt I lay in now, the fence and the trees. We were just outside the wolf shifter community gates—discarded like trash.

Darren's lips kicked up at the sides into an amused smile. "Ruby's mother and her friends. When we refused to leave—or Jackson said we wouldn't leave—they cast a spell together to send us back here. Pretty impressive," Darren said, his tone indicating he was absolutely enraptured with the witches.

I tried to growl and glare at him, to share my displeasure, but it came out weak and half-hearted. It felt like she'd sapped every bit of strength from my body. "Why do I feel like such shit and you're standing there looking okay?" I asked. It certainly wasn't due to physical fitness or strength, obviously, because Jackson and I were three-fold stronger than Darren as full-blooded wolf shifters.

Darren shrugged, nonplussed. "I assume my own magic gave me some measure of resistance to theirs. Obviously not enough to stop them, but to handle the impact of their spell better. You guys probably haven't had a spell cast against you before."

"And you have?" Jackson asked from where he sat with his head in his hands, nearby.

Darren nodded. "Yeah, a few. My grandmother used to teach us to use our magic a little when we were kids. And she used her magic on us, even if it was just to make some new clothes or food. It wasn't anything nasty, just common, day-to-day stuff."

I stared at Jackson, then back to Darren. I hadn't realized witches used magic for everything. Simple stuff like clothes and food? *Was he serious?* Why hadn't I been told about that? It could have come in handy.

Jackson hauled himself to his feet.

I followed suit, forcing pure willpower into my muscles to make them hold my weight. It was painful, but not unbearably so.

"Well, what do we do now?" Jackson asked, dusting his hands off on his jeans.

"We need to go get your truck, for one thing," I said, annoyed that we'd have to drive back into town and get it. *Fuck it. It can wait until tomorrow.*

Jackson stared at me, one eyebrow raised. "I don't know about you, but I could really use a run to get my blood pumping again."

My mouth dropped open. I couldn't remember the last time we'd shifted into our wolf forms and run through the forest bordering our community. I grinned. "You know what? Me, too." My wolf had been flexing his strength inside my mind since we'd found our mate. "It might make it easier to control them around Ruby." I hated the fact I couldn't even talk to my Fated Mate because I was too busy clamping down on my jaw and keeping my shifter in check.

Jackson nodded in agreement. "You want to come, too?" he asked Darren.

I assumed he offered simply out of politeness, because everyone knew Darren didn't shift.

Darren grinned. "I'd love to."

My eyebrows flickered with surprise. *I'll be damned.*

Without further discussion, we all started walking the mile back to our actual town.

I had assumed that Darren simply *couldn't* shift, but then again, he was three-quarters wolf... so why I'd even assumed that, I didn't know.

It took us ten minutes to walk back, but by the time we got to Jackson's house, I was absolutely buzzing with energy.

The sun had dropped below the horizon, darkness had settled and spread its star-spangled shroud across the land. It was still Halloween, which meant it would be the perfect time to scare some local kids.

We dropped all our clothes at Jackson's place and let the magic of our inner wolves rip through us. There was nothing like it.

When I let go of my humanity my skin burned like I was standing too close to an open fire. Then the fur began to sprout, and my bones began to bend and break, reforming to accommodate the canine form. It had been painful the first few times, but like all shifters, I'd soon learned to embrace the feeling. A growl rumbled through my chest as I changed into a large, black wolf. Not quite as big as Jackson's, who stood half a head taller than me, but still big enough.

Darren shifted too, though his transformation was slower, and his wolf form was smaller than ours.

We took off into the woods, running as hard and as fast as we could, howling through the trees and rejoicing in this strange new adventure we were on. *Together.* And for the first time since we'd met Ruby, I was glad I wasn't alone.

Ruby

I waited for my mother to reply to my question and when she didn't, I threw up my hands in frustration and stalked back across the street toward home. She wasn't allowed to use any magic—let alone transportation magic—out in the open. Anyone could have seen her! *And where the hell had she and her friends sent my men?*

I stormed inside the house, not bothering to shut the front door because I knew they'd be following in a minute, anyway. My veins buzzed with adrenaline and anger, while my heart banged against my ribs in rebellion as my hands shook. I couldn't sit down. Couldn't stay still. Not for the life of me. I grabbed a bottle of water from the fridge and drank half of it in a few gulps.

"Ruby! What were you doing with those men?" my mother demanded as she raged into the kitchen, her best friends hot on her heels.

"I was kissing them!" I yelled back, flinging my arms around emphatically so that water from my bottle sloshed across the room, splattering the cabinets.

Bella's mom flicked her hand and the water splatters disappeared.

I rolled my eyes. She hated mess.

My mother's gaze narrowed at me. "You were kissing the big one. Why?"

I crossed my arms over my chest and glared stubbornly at her. She had no damn idea, and it was none of her business. "Because I wanted to. Because he kissed me!" *And because I'm their Fated Mate,* but I'm not sure I want to say that out aloud just yet—especially with tempers flaring so hot.

My mother paced around the kitchen and her friends fell back.

Kathy rested against the wall.

Rebecca leaned against one of the cupboards.

We all knew it was better to give my mother room when she was mad.

"How do you even know a group of wolf shifters?" she asked me, narrowing her gaze.

"I met them at the flower shop yesterday," I admitted.

"All three of them?" Her brows quirked in what I guessed was disbelief.

I nodded.

Mom gestured with her hands in a rolling motion. "Well, go on then! I know there's a story behind all this."

Of course, there was, but how much did I really want to tell her? I closed my eyes, weighing the pros and cons of exposing all of it now versus later. No matter what, my mother would find out everything eventually.

The tug of her magic pulled at me. She wanted to know the truth.

I was going to struggle to hold back or omit anything, let alone lie.

"Ruby..." My mother's tone held a dangerous warning edge.

I groaned, opening my eyes to face the music. "Fine. Here's the truth, Mom. Jackson, Darren, and Billy say they're all my Fated Mates. And I feel the same way... I think. So, yeah, there's that." I added, before I threw up my hands and shrugged.

Mom fell into one of the kitchen chairs. "Holy shit."

My eyebrows rose. *Holy shit?* That was her response? That's all she had to say?

Bella and Tiffany's moms began slowly backing out of the kitchen as one.

"We'll call you later," Kathy said.

Rebecca flashed an uncertain smile.

Then they hightailed it out the front door.

Smart move.

My mother jumped to her feet and began flicking her wrists and waving her hands around, magic zipped around our kitchen like a chaotic, roiling storm.

I stood as still as possible. This happened on occasion, and although my mother's magic now was simply for baking bread, making food, and changing the colors of the cabinets, it wasn't wise to get in the way. I could be painted purple or mixed in with the cookies if I wasn't careful. So, I waited to see what would come out of my mother's mouth at the end of it all. And what, exactly, she was so upset about. I knew that the three-guy thing was a lot to handle... but my mother was usually more composed than this.

Finally, the white sparks stopped flying and my mother halted, turning toward me, her green eyes blazing with light. "You're going to... *mate* with three men?" she asked, her expression aghast.

I sat down at the kitchen table and ran a finger up and down its white surface. She made it sound so sordid when all I'd managed so far was one single kiss! "I... don't know. I've barely spent any time with them yet. I just..." I shrugged, momentarily lost for words. I didn't want to fight with my mom about my mates. Finding them was meant to be a good thing.

My mother collapsed onto the chair opposite me. "This is all my fault."

My mouth dropped open. Her fault? How did she figure that? I was the one who'd conjured a Halloween spell calling for my one true love to find me. *Perhaps having Bella and Tiffany work the spell with me tripled the strength and called three men instead?* I had no ideas, truthfully, but this definitely wasn't on my mother. "Your fault? What the hell are you talking about, Mom?"

My mother ran her hands through the long strands of her red hair highlighted with streaks of natural gray. She wasn't talking and that was always a bad sign.

"Mom. What is it you're not telling me? Talk to me," I said. This didn't look like good news. Anxiety began to replace the frustration and bubbling anger within me. What was going on?

"Your..." She cleared her throat with a rough cough. "Your father wasn't a human. And he certainly wasn't a warlock."

My chest tightened and my breath stuck in my throat. "What do you mean? You always said he was a warlock passing through town. That you didn't know much about him. That it just kind of happened." I'd always hated the idea that my mother had procreated with and conceived of me with a stranger. It made me feel unwanted... lost, unplanned. Which I had been of course, but it was so much worse thinking that I'd been a pure mistake and one my mother had probably regretted.

"Well..." My mother inhaled deeply, stalling whatever terrible fate she was planning on revealing to me.

"Well, what?" I demanded. "You're freaking me out, Mom. We've always been honest with each other when it comes down to it. So, please, just spit it out!"

"I did know him," she finally admitted. "We dated secretly for almost a year before I fell pregnant with you. Then he just disappeared."

"Disappeared? Like vanished?" This was new information. Since when had *shooting through* after she got pregnant, turned into *disappeared?*

"Yeah, well, at first, I assumed he'd just left me. Abandoned me when I needed him the most. But no one's seen him at all since the night., And well, there are some strange things that happen to wolf shifters when they mess with witches.... And you know my parents weren't the kindest of people." My mother sighed.

I put both hands out in front of me, halting her next words like a traffic warden. "Hang on just a second. What did you just say?"

Mom blinked at me, clearly overwhelmed with the weight of her truth. "Which part?"

"Did you just infer that my father was a wolf shifter?"

My mother nodded and swallowed hard, running her fingers through her hair in anxiety. "Yes, Ruby. Yes, I did."

Suddenly everything in my world made sense—especially the fact that I had three wolf shifter Fated Mates. But how were they going to feel about my mixed bloodline? And the secrets I carried too...?

CHAPTER 10

RUBY

I jumped to my feet, my magic whirling through my veins, making it hard to sit down for even a moment longer. I wanted to fly to my three men. I wanted to blow the roof off the house. And strangely, I wanted a pizza. *Yes. Definitely a pizza.* But instead, I stayed put in my mother's kitchen and simply paced around the room. "How could you not have told me this sooner?" I asked. "I feel like I've been living a lie, Mom."

"I didn't know how to."

I grimaced at her and sighed. "You mean you didn't *want* to."

My mother slumped in her chair, defeated and crestfallen. "No, you're right. I didn't want to, Ruby. I didn't want this information to influence you in any way. I didn't want you to worry about your magic developing or where you fit in society. Or if you were going to, you know..." She gestured helplessly around us.

I groaned. "Going to what?" I asked.

She bit her lip, her brows raised plaintively. "You know... *shift*."

I stopped pacing then and stared at her. Shocked.

No wonder I felt like I didn't have a place in the witch community! All of this explained everything. Like why I was powerful *enough*, but had always ached to run, to be free, and not be rooted to this community that everyone else felt was integral to their survival. But to shift into an animal? *Crap balls.* "Is that even possible? I mean, how would we know?"

"Oh, it's not going to happen now," Mom said with a shake of her head and a relieved smile. "Now that you've reached full maturity, you've gone past the time when it would have been. I was told that we would realize a lot earlier if your wolf genes were going to be dominant, which, considering how powerful your magic is, would be unusual."

I didn't want to sit down, but I didn't know what to do with all the excess energy bursting away inside my body. My hands were shaking from the stress of this life-altering revelation. "Okay. So, you're telling me I'm half wolf shifter? Which is probably why the men I'm meant to be with turned out to be wolves?" That part at least made more sense, which truth be told, was a relief.

"I'll give you that. But three?" my mother said, looking skeptical as her gaze darted back to me.

I shrugged. "That wasn't my choice. It's just... how it is. It's Fate. I can feel it, and so can they. I couldn't stand to be without them now, Mom. We're connected."

My mother sighed, glancing down at the table, seemingly trying to gather her thoughts. "So, what are we going to do now?"

I crossed my arms over my chest and stared down at her. "Well, for starters, you can tell me where you sent them. And I can go sort all this mess out."

She nodded and sighed in a resigned way. "I'll drive you out there if you like?"

"You don't want to just zap me to the same spot?" I asked.

She stood up and shook her head. "They could be anywhere by now. I'll drive you to the outskirts of their township, and you can decide what to do from there."

I stared at her. "You're going to just drop me off? No more fighting? No arguing with Fate?"

My mother shuddered, as though letting me go off into the big world at age twenty-two was an ordeal she'd never thought she would have to endure. Then she nodded. "Yes. I'll behave. I owe you that much as least. Let's go."

～

Jackson

AFTER A DECENT RUN, Darren decided to return home.

But Billy and I weren't ready to stop. So, we ran through the woods and instinctively moved toward the human town, the complete opposite direction of what I had planned. And in direct opposition to Council recommendations.

The closer we ran to the human town, the more likely we were to be spotted or hunted. So the Council had rules in place to prevent us from being hurt. They told us the story of a group of cousins, of three men who'd gone missing over twenty years ago, when we were young. Most of the pack assumed they were dead. Shot most likely and perhaps mounted on someone's wall.

But I didn't care what the humans had done in the past or would do to me now. I was in my wolf form, and I could feel the unbridled strength of the mating bond we shared with Ruby. It was like something fundamental had changed deep within me. I was no longer adrift. A lone wolf. A man who could be happy just spending the rest of his days alone.

There was something tying me to the earth now — calling me home. And home was now Ruby. I jumped over a log with ease, dashed around a tree like it was nothing, and focused on my inner wolf. I felt a tickle on the back of my spine, feeling the crescent moon's power in the sky, the dirt beneath my paws, and the scent of pine and earth and magic in the air. Wait. *Magic?*

I slowed down, tilting my head toward the strange feeling. I peered through the woods and its dappled shadows, deeper into the trees and past the town. Was that where the church was? The Coven's hallowed grounds? I longed to run that way, to explore and spy on what they must be up to on Halloween night. But I didn't have time for that tonight.

There was something else calling me now. An itch like a bolt of lightning on the back of my neck made me stop, turn, and howl instinctively to the moon.

Billy stepped up and howled alongside me. He felt it too.

Our mate was on her way. She was traveling, and she was heading toward our town. We ran, our paws churning up the dirt in the dark. We galloped along the border of the town, and I could smell her, distantly. She was coming. We finally made it back to my house. We jumped the fence and shifted back into human form.

My black fur disappeared, and I was able to see color once again with my human eyes. I panted from the run; my skin slicked with sweat.

Billy transformed next to me, his eyes shifting back to their normal color. He looked straight at me. "You sense her, too?"

I nodded. "I do."

We rushed inside and pulled on our clothes.

I should have had a shower, but I didn't want to waste a single moment in case I missed out on seeing her. "Where do you think she is?" I asked aloud.

Billy shrugged as he tugged on his shirt. "No idea. Would she even know where to come? Who to ask for?"

"Not sure. But considering it was her mother's magic that sent us back here, maybe she can follow it?" I couldn't stop myself from grinning at the thought of her being so near to us again. We didn't know anything about witches or magic. The crap we'd been told came directly from our Council and our parents, who encouraged us to keep everything pure. Untainted. Which was so hypocritical it wasn't even funny.

Plus, Fate had different plans for us. I pulled on my boots and grabbed my phone. "Let's go."

We went to the front door.

A tremor of unease worked through my belly. What was my father going to say when he learned that my mate was not only a witch, but that I would have to share her with two other men? I shuddered at the thought. My father had always hated the fact he wasn't a full wolf shifter. He'd worked hard to make up for his lack of strength and speed by breeding with my mother, a daughter born to an Alpha wolf. It had meant that my brothers and I were strong in ways my father never was. He'd hate that I was diluting our bloodlines once again, even if it was because of the call of my Fated Mate.

We headed into town.

I lifted my nose in the air, searching for the scent of the red-haired witch who I knew would soon capture my heart forever. But what sort of future was there for us?

CHAPTER 11
DARREN

After I returned from my short run, I went to my parents' house. I wanted to tell them what we'd discovered and who we'd met.

"How was your night?" Mom asked, putting on the kettle to make a hot tea for my father before they went to bed.

I sat down on the couch, grinning at my father while Mom did what she needed to do in the background.

"It was amazing. I found my Fated Mate. She lives in town."

Shocked silence.

My father's gaze lifted to stare behind me.

I turned around to see my mother's mouth had dropped open. "The elders have prepared us for this," she said. "With so few females born in the past twenty years... your mate could be a human. Or a wolf shifter from another pack."

My father smiled at me, though it didn't reach his eyes and I knew he was disappointed that my mate wasn't also a wolf shifter. "So, she's human?" Dad asked. "What's her name?"

I inhaled sharply, surprised at how much I didn't want to disappoint my parents. My mother would hopefully be accepting of Ruby's heritage, but my father... I wasn't so sure. I forced a smile and spilled the beans. "Her name's Ruby. She's a witch."

My mother walked forward and sat down on the couch next to Dad. "A witch?"

I nodded. "Yes. I think it's great. Our children will be so much more powerful than me."

Mom looked down at her hands. "Well, this is a surprise."

"Why?" I asked. "You're half-witch, yourself, Mom."

"But I never developed my powers..." she began.

Dad slid his hand across her leg, taking her hand in his in a show of comfort and unity. "So, you felt the Fated Mate pull?" Dad asked, which was the only reason he'd married my mother. He hadn't wanted to marry a half-witch, but Fate had other plans for him. And if nothing else, he understood the importance of trusting Fate.

I nodded. "All of it. But... ah, I'm not the only one." It was my turn to glance away. This part was going to be even more difficult to explain to my parents. It would mean that they would know more about my sex life than I'd ever wanted them to know. I sighed. There was no avoiding it.

"What do you mean?" my dad asked.

"Well, you know how there's like... no females in our pack to mate with?" I said, leading them toward the conclusion.

"Yes?" Mom said.

"You don't mean..." Dad said, his bushy eyebrows drawing together to frown at me.

"I do." I nodded and took a deep breath. "Jackson and Billy are her Fated Mates as well. So, I suppose... if she accepts us all, we'll be a big family."

My mother's mouth dropped open again. "Ah... I've never heard of such a thing."

"You're going to share a mate with Jackson?" my dad asked, raising an eyebrow.

I knew what he was asking. How was an Alpha going to share with me? It went against their very nature. It stood in the face of his very bloodline. "Well... uh..."

Mom smiled at me. "I think Ruby will want someone like you, sweetheart. Part warlock and all heart. She's lucky to have you."

I stared at my mom for a moment, then grinned, a weight lifting from my shoulders. "Thanks, Mom. I think you're really going to like her." A sudden prickle of unease washed over me, and I frowned as a premonition flowed over me. She was coming. She was almost here. I got to my feet fast. "I've got to go. I think she's on her way here."

"Here?" my father demanded, his brow lowering as he jumped up from the couch.

My mother grabbed his arm. "Calm down, sweetheart." She looked at me. "Go ahead, sweetheart. We'll catch up with you later."

I smiled my thanks at my mother and raced out the door. Where would Ruby be coming from? Would she be in a car? Or would she be traveling on foot? Would she magic herself the same way her mother had forced us back here? I had so many questions and no answers.

I started walking along our road, around the block, and down the main street. If I were her, I would head for the few shops in town since they would still be open. I sniffed the air, the faint scent of Ruby's distinct smell on the breeze. I kept walking toward the edge of town. There were no sounds to betray the approach of any vehicle. No engines, no lights heading toward us. Then I saw her, and my heart began to pound.

She was still wearing that gorgeous little black dress, and her long red hair flowed down over her shoulders as she walked down the street toward me.

Adrenaline coursed through my veins, and I jogged toward her. I got within touching distance of my beautiful mate and couldn't stop the smile that stretched shamelessly across my face. "Hey."

Ruby smiled back, her green eyes lighting up even in the darkness. "Hey, yourself."

"So, you found us." I grinned, reaching over to grab her hand. "Do you want to walk into town?"

She nodded and pressed her body close to mine as we strolled back toward the light. "I'm so sorry my mom sent you guys back here," she burst out, as though she'd been holding it in and desperately wanted to apologize.

I chuckled. "It wasn't a big deal for me. I've traveled by magic before, when I was younger at least. But Billy and Jackson were pretty sick afterwards." I tried not to grin too much. Part of me enjoyed seeing the two powerful wolf shifters wiped out by something as small and innocent as a transportation spell.

"Yeah, I can imagine." She sighed heavily. "Mom and her friends really shouldn't have done that. They were all cast first, ask questions later."

"Why did they, anyway?" I asked. "Was it because we're a pack of wolves? Or was it more that your mom didn't like seeing her daughter kissing strange men on the street?" I chuckled at my own joke but found Ruby freezing up.

"Hey, I was kidding," I said, squeezing her hand to try and soothe her nerves.

She laughed nervously. "Well, she's never seen me kiss anyone, I don't think. I don't date much. And yeah, she was pretty freaked out by you guys being wolves and all."

Don't date much. I was pretty sure that was an understatement judging by the unmistakable innocent scent surrounding my mate.

"Does she have a history with wolves? Or is she like half the paranormal population and just doesn't like others who are different?" I asked, then realized how judgmental I sounded. I quickly backtracked, "I didn't mean for that to sound harsh. My own parents are firmly against any outside breeding." *Despite the fact my mother is half-witch. The hypocrisy...*

"Even though you're part warlock?" she asked.

I grinned down at my mate. "Yes. Even though my mother is half-witch, my father seems to think we need to breed it out of our line."

We were almost at the first streetlight in town, so I could see the emotions flickering across my mate's face.

She was chewing on her lip and looking anxiously at the ground, then up at me. "Is that how you feel, Darren? That me being a witch is a negative thing?"

I stopped, feeling the time dwindling away that I would have her to myself. The other two would be here soon, and I wouldn't be able to do this with her. I unlinked our fingers and slid my hands around her waist, pulling her close so that our pelvises were connected. "Not at all," I said, answering her question while attempting to squash the need to shiver at the deliciousness of the contact. "I love that you're a witch. Any children we have in future will be powerful and thanks to you, extremely beautiful, too."

Ruby glanced down, straight at my shirt where her hands now lay, near to my heart. Her beautiful pale skin pinked up at the compliment or at the idea of children. I wasn't sure which.

"May I kiss you, Ruby?" I asked, feeling the prickle of premonition on my neck. Jackson and Billy were closer now.

She nodded, her lips turning up in a genuine, if not slightly shy smile.

I leaned down and pressed my mouth to hers. She was as sweet and sensual as I had hoped. I breathed her in, tasting only the tiniest amount of her lips. I tried to keep it gentle but when her tongue flicked out to lick my lips, a groan rose up from my throat and my hands tightened on her waist.

I slid my hands down to her firm ass and pulled her into the cradle of my hips. I used my lips to press deeper and met her seeking tongue with my own.

She moaned.

Every part of me rejoiced as I recognized my one true mate. In my arms. For the very first time. It was everything I'd ever dreamed it could be, and more.

Her hands slid up my chest to my neck, then moved through my hair, holding me to her as she pressed her breasts against me.

A surge of lust plowed through me. I wanted to snap my fingers and have her naked in my bed, beneath me. But my magic wasn't that strong and as I inhaled sharply, I could sense that the other two men had arrived. I heard a loud gasp and then the ripping of clothes.

Scratch that. *The wolves had arrived.*

I broke our kiss but held her tight.

She swayed, her eyes closed, and a moan still trembled on her lips.

I pulled her to my side and turned toward the road where two large black wolves stalked toward us. They must have just shifted because a pair of jeans was still attached to Jackson's leg. My heart pounded with exhilaration and a touch of fear. I whispered into my mate's ear. "When you open your eyes, don't be afraid. Jackson and Billy are in their shifter forms." I held her tighter.

Ruby yelped as her eyes flew open. She stared at the men, who prowled forward as wolves. She slammed her hand over her mouth, a frightened squeal emerging, though she tried valiantly to stifle it.

"It's okay," I said. "They are in complete control of their wolves. Don't be afraid."

Ruby nodded, though her eyes were as big as the now full moon above our heads.

Jackson moved closer.

I waved at him. "Hey, Jackson." I knew him by his pure size. Despite the fact that our pack tried to be modern and not judge a person by rank, the shifter genes still determined our size, our strength, as well as our leadership skills.

Jackson was an Alpha through and through, with his massive body, his ability to handle any situation, and his stare that could turn even the most pureblood wolf submissive. He stopped moving and began to shift back to human.

I squeezed Ruby's waist. "He's shifting back. Watch."

Before our eyes, the black fur melted away. The four short canine legs became two long human legs, and two muscled arms; and the man began to grow into his own huge form. When he was done, Jackson stood before us in full light, naked as the day he was born.

I struggled not to stare, and almost laughed.

Ruby's hands moved up to cover her eyes. "Oh my God," she breathed.

"Hey, Billy," I called out to the second wolf as he also transformed back to human form.

They were both huge and muscular and had obviously forgotten that humans and witches alike weren't as comfortable with nudity as wolves were.

"Shall we take Ruby back to your place, Jackson?" I called out. "Maybe grab you guys some new clothes?"

Ruby peeked through her fingers, then as she dropped her hands, her gaze found the ground.

"You okay with that, Ruby, or would you prefer to come back to my place where my parents can chaperone?" I asked.

She inhaled sharply and lifted her head.

I could only imagine what she was thinking.

"No. It's okay. Let's go back to Jackson's house."

Jackson nodded and turned away to march up the street toward his house.

Billy followed.

I took Ruby's hand to lead the way. "This way, beautiful."

CHAPTER 12
RUBY

Oh. My. Fucking. God. They were naked. Naked as a babe... naked! I clung to Darren's hand and stumbled into town after the two men walking in front of us.

They bent over to scoop up some clothes on the street, which I had to assume were theirs.

Had they shifted when they'd seen Darren kissing me? Probably, silly jealous things that they were. "Aren't they cold?" I whispered to Darren, unable to take my eyes off the flexes of Billy and Jackson's muscles.

They were magnificent to look at. So much bigger, stronger, and more defined than any human man I'd seen in real life. And most probably the reason my mom fell for a shifter. The thought made me frown. *What happened to my father?*

Darren chuckled beside me. "No. They're not cold. Shifters run a few degrees hotter than humans, so the temperature doesn't bother them. And as far as the nudity thing goes… sorry about that. Shifters aren't worried about exposing their bodies at any time of the day. It's just not a thing to be embarrassed by. With us shifting in and out of our wolf forms so often, a person's body just doesn't have the same… taboo."

I nodded. "That makes sense." So, I had to get used to a world where this was normal? *Whoa. Bella and Tiffany are going to freak!* "Why aren't you in shifter form, Darren?" I asked, my gaze dragged back to Jackson's body. His ass was perfection—round, sculpted, and strong. And his back. Jeez, could the guy be any bigger? He had huge shoulders, massive arms, and a perfectly muscular back. There wasn't an inch of fat on him, and I began to worry about what they were going to think about my body.

I wasn't big by any stretch of the imagination but compared to these two? I was a frumpy sack of potatoes.

"Me?" Darren repeated. "Well, I shifted this evening and went for a run with Jackson and Billy, but I came back early. I don't shift a lot to be honest. I'm not that comfortable in wolf form, personally."

I got the feeling that for Billy, he was more comfortable in wolf form than human form. "So, you don't like to shift then?" I asked, just to make sure I understood what he meant.

He pressed his lips together as though thinking about my question before answering. "I'm three quarters wolf shifter so I can, obviously. But I'm much more comfortable in human form, and if I could, I'd perform a hell of a lot more magic than I do."

"Oh?" I asked, excitement racing through me. "Can you perform many spells?"

He sighed. "Unfortunately, no. My grandmother has been gone for a long time now, and my mother refuses to practice any magic. So, maybe you or someone from your Coven could give me some point-ers?" He sounded so hopeful.

I laughed. "I'm sure we could." I wasn't sure just how much magic a one-quarter warlock with little training would be able to perform, but why not try? It could be fun.

We continued to walk through town, or what little of a town there was.

"Are these all the shops?" I asked, glancing up and down the road.

"Yep. Pretty much. A café." He pointed at a small eatery. "Clothes and gas station. We go into town for all the big things."

If that was the case, then why hadn't I seen them more often? Did they shop during the night or something? "So, um, what's going to happen when we get back to Jackson's place?" I asked, chewing on my lip.

Darren glanced at me and squeezed my hand. "Those two can get some clothes on and we can chat some more, if you'd like?"

I nodded, swallowing the lump in my throat. My heart was hammering in my chest and if I hadn't been holding onto Darren's hand like a proverbial lifeline and pressing myself into his warmth, I would have been shaking all over. I'd never been so nervous in my life!

"Why? What would you like to happen?" Darren asked as we turned left off the main street and headed down a road with new houses.

I shrugged. "I don't know." But I did. Of course, I wanted them to kiss me. I wanted my senses to be overwhelmed. I wanted to find out if this was the mating, the relationship, and the love I'd prayed for, and called upon in the spell we'd cast last year on Halloween.

Jackson turned down a sidewalk.

Billy followed.

They headed up to the front door and disappeared into the house.

"Wow. Is that really Jackson's house?" I asked, staring up at the modern two-story abode that looked like it could hold a family of ten.

"Yes."

We stopped in front of it.

I stared up at the second floor. It was beautiful, with pretty shutters, big windows, and a welcoming, blue front door. "Does he live here alone?"

"He does," Darren said and then added with a grin, "for the moment."

I lifted an eyebrow at him. Was he saying that all four of us would live here one day? I certainly wouldn't mind. What an amazing house! And only fifteen minutes from my mom and town. Ideal, really.

"Come on," Darren said, and tugged my hand.

I followed him along the sidewalk, up the two steps and into the house. The inside of Jackson's place was as impressive as the outside, though it was kind of soulless. There were crisp white walls and flawless wooden floors.

Darren flicked on the lights.

As we walked farther into the house I was greeted with a fantastic modern kitchen, but it was devoid of color, warmth, or... feeling. Although, what should I have expected from a bachelor? My mother would have turned this place into a mess of purple and family pictures in mere minutes.

And if I were honest, my fingers itched to do the same. To splash the walls with red, to add appliances to the countertops, and pictures to the walls. Maybe some fresh flowers in vases artfully arranged around the place. I dug my nails into my palms and reminded myself to calm down. This wasn't my house, and even if it was... I wasn't sure my magic would be welcome here.

"Hey."

The deep voice behind me made me jump. I twisted around with a smile on my face.

Jackson stood by the kitchen counter, now dressed in jeans and a black shirt, and wore a sheepish smile on his face.

"Hey," I said, twisting my fingers together in front of me, nervous as all get out.

He took a breath and pressed forward. "I'm sorry you saw us like that. We *were* dressed but then we saw you and we both shifted again.

It wasn't intentional, and I didn't consider that you may be scared of seeing us in wolf form."

Oh, he was sorry about the shifter thing, not about the fact that I got to see them completely naked within two days of meeting them. "Oh, it's fine," I said, trying to brush off the fact that he'd caught me out. I'd definitely been scared. "It's something I have to get used to, right?" At least he was managing to talk to me now. That was definitely a plus.

Jackson nodded, agreeing with my question. His eyes darkened as he stared at me.

Billy stepped into the great room, his gaze going straight to me.

"Hi," I said, feeling strangely awkward and excited at the same time.

Billy nodded back, but once again was completely mute.

I wasn't sure I'd even heard his voice yet.

"Well..." Jackson said.

"Well," I repeated, and we all began to laugh at the absurdity of the situation.

Darren grabbed my hand. "Let's sit on the couch."

Jackson charged forward and took my other hand possessively. "My turn, Darren."

Darren reluctantly let go of me, ever the gracious one.

I had a moment of despair as my hand dropped away from him. I didn't want to disconnect from my part-warlock love.

But then Jackson was dragging me to the couch and those feelings were temporarily forgotten. Especially when he sat down and pulled me right onto his lap. It was strange, this huge man whom I barely knew, holding me. His breath was on my hair, his hands on my waist.

But soon—too soon—I began to melt into his heat. Into the feeling of familiarity, although I'd never known such a thing before. I sighed and rested my head on his shoulder, turning over a little so I could listen to the beat of his strong heart beneath my ear. *This must be what love feels like.*

A soft growl like a contented purr rolled through Jackson's chest as his arms came around me and held me even tighter.

No one spoke, so I closed my eyes and took a second to memorize the moment. To retain what this felt like, so I could remember and cherish it for all time. When I told the story of how I met my triad of men and fell in love with them, I'd be able to tell my grandkids about this moment. About just how right everything felt. How safe I was. How warm. How aroused. *No*, I wouldn't tell the grandkids that last part!

Jackson stroked my arms lazily, one hand still firmly on my waist.

I could feel tendrils of heat curling through my blood, inside my belly. Lower down, even. I felt a blush heat my cheeks and I sighed, giddy, nervous, but relaxed all at once.

"So," Darren said, who seemed to be the only one able to speak to me with any sort of casual ease. "Are we as much of a surprise to you, as you are to us?"

I opened my eyes and turned toward him, not lifting my head off Jackson's chest. His hands on me were tight, and I could feel the Alpha possessiveness in him. His need to hold me, touch me.

It was thrilling to be wanted so much by such a beautiful and impressive man. What was Darren's question again? Oh, yeah... "Surprised? By the fact that there's three of you? Or that you're wolves?"

Darren grinned.

Billy even smiled.

"Well, both, I suppose," Darren answered.

I nodded. "Same for me. I never expected three... mates. And I never thought I'd marry a wolf shifter. Well..." I cleared my throat and glanced away from Darren.

"Well, what?" Darren asked.

I shifted off Jackson's lap and settled on the couch next to him.

Jackson, unwilling to give up his claim, pulled me close.

"I never thought I had anything except witch blood in me," I said. "That's what I'd always been told, anyway."

Billy coughed, clearing his throat as he moved closer and took a seat opposite us. "And now?"

My eyebrows flickered up. His voice was even deeper than Jackson's. "Tonight, after my mom magicked you all back here, she finally confessed to me that my father wasn't a warlock, like I'd been told. See, I grew up with just my mom. She told me my father left before I was born. That he abandoned her. Abandoned both of us, really, I guess."

Billy leaned forward on his chair, his brow lowered and fierce. "What was he?"

I swallowed hard. This would be the first time I'd actually said it aloud and it terrified me. "He... was a wolf shifter."

Billy gasped, his eyes suddenly wide with curiosity. "Who was he? Do you know? Is he still around?" he asked with a heady mix of excitement and intensity.

Jackson pulled me in tighter, closer to him if that were even possible. "That makes sense. It fills in the blanks of why we want you and why you'd be our mate."

"It made a lot more sense to me, too," I agreed. "Though, I'm still kind of pissed at my mom for lying to me all these years."

"Why would she do that, though?" Darren asked, leaning forward like Billy.

"And did you get a name?" Billy added. "We should really make sure none of us are related to you."

Darren rolled his eyes. "The Fated Mates magic wouldn't be that stupid, Billy. Honestly."

I grinned at him. I liked that. "That's a cool way of looking at it. Like you guys have magic too."

"Well, it is magic of a sort," Darren said with a smile. "Even if the wolves don't want to call it that. Fated Mates is something that can't be explained in any other way, and the best part about it is that it's always right. Always perfect."

I wasn't sure I wanted to touch that one. I certainly wasn't perfect, even if they were. Instead, I looked over at Billy. "Um, to answer your question, no, I don't know who he was. I never got a name. Mom just said that he disappeared before I was born, and she never heard from him again."

A sudden, quiet stillness filled the air, the three men around me freezing as still as statues.

"When was this?" Jackson managed to ask.

"Well, I just turned twenty-two." *Like literally, today.* "So, it would be twenty-two years ago, or a little bit longer."

Jackson went completely rigid beneath my hands.

I glanced from one wolf to the other, watching their shocked expressions. Worry began to seep into my veins, dark and intrusive. "What's wrong?" I asked.

Jackson cleared his throat.

Billy stood up and clenched his fists.

I sat up straighter beside Jackson and stared at Darren. He would tell me the truth if there was something horrifying to reveal. *Wouldn't he?* "What is it, Darren?" I asked. "What are you not telling me?"

Darren ran a hand through his hair, looking uncomfortable. "There were three cousins who went missing nearly twenty-two, maybe twenty-three years ago. They went running in the woods one day and never returned. If your father was really one of those three, then you are the missing piece of a puzzle our pack has been trying to solve for over two decades."

Jackson sat up, breaking the constant contact with my body. "And according to my father, that was when everything changed for the pack."

"What do you mean?" I asked apprehensively.

Jackson turned back toward me. "Well, for one thing, ever since that night, only three females have been born to our pack. Every other birth has been a male wolf."

My mouth dropped open. Was that why I was Fated to these three? Because of something that had happened to my father. Or was there something much more insidious and sinister going on in this town?

CHAPTER 13
JACKSON

Suspicion oozed through my mind like an inky, dark cloud. Were the witches the reason we couldn't mate within our own pack this generation? Had they even gone so far as to put a spell on us to make ensure we would die out? That we could no longer breed more wolf shifters? Such a prospect seemed too terrible, too absurd to possibly be true. And yet everything pointed to it. I opened my mouth to ask her, desperate for the truth.

Billy pinned me with a stare. His dark eyes blazed, the hint of his wolf showing in his pupil shape and the flash of yellow coloring in his iris.

It was a warning. *To me.*

When he shook his head ever so slightly, my suspicions were confirmed. My cousin didn't want me questioning our mate. Not about this topic.

She was so young and only just starting to accept our Fated Mate bond. Besides, what would Ruby really know anyway? She was conceived around the time it had all happened. She wasn't the one responsible.

But those who were should be punished.

"What's wrong, Jackson?" Ruby asked quietly.

I moved my focus to the beautiful girl who had slid off my lap and was now sitting beside me on my couch, in my home, and within touching distance. I could smell her arousal. Her need for m—for us. That was what I needed to focus on, and not the mystery of the "wolves versus witches" feud that had been going on for generations.

I shook myself and forced a smile to my lips so that she wouldn't know how deep my apprehension ran. "Nothing, sweetheart. Sorry. I just got to thinking about those three men that went missing, that's all. But I shouldn't be focusing on that. I should be focusing on you. Now, come back here."

I reached out to her, and she came into my arms willingly. Happiness soared through my veins as I pulled her safely back onto my lap. As soon as she settled, all my dark thoughts, my insecurities and misgivings, disappeared, as though they'd never even existed. How was it possible that she already affected me so much? I sighed and breathed in the delicious citrus orange scent of her hair. "God, you smell good."

She moaned softly. "So do you. How can I feel so safe and happy here with you all? After such a short time?"

Darren grinned ear to ear. "Because you're our Fated Mate, Ruby, which means you were designed for us, and we were designed for you."

"All of you?" Ruby asked, as though she couldn't fully wrap her head around the idea.

And if I were being frank, I couldn't quite either. I'd never even heard of something like this happening before. Why this one witch—who I now knew to be half wolf shifter—needed three mates was beyond me.

Darren nodded and grinned in response.

Billy just stared at her. It seemed he was as consumed and compelled to be near to her and focused on her—like she was the new moon of our lives—as Darren and me.

She turned her head and glanced up at me with her eyebrows raised high in query. "Tiffany said that wolves are notoriously possessive and wouldn't like to share a mate. Is that true?"

Talk about getting straight to the point. I cleared my throat and swallowed hard. "Well, if I'm honest, yes. We are. Our animal instincts and wolf natures are strong."

She shuffled in my lap, sitting up a little straighter. "So, you're not happy about this... relationship then?"

"Well..." How could I be honest with her about this and keep her happy? When I didn't answer right away, she twisted around and looked at the other two and sighed. "It seems like Darren's the only one who's actually happy about us." She sounded hurt and crestfallen —lost.

And it killed me. I hated myself for not having the right answer for her.

Billy glared at me but didn't speak.

Darren jumped into the silence that hung like a blade above our heads, just waiting to fall and sever what precious happiness we might be able to have together. "It's not that they're unhappy. And I'm beyond happy, Ruby. It's just, with their stronger wolf genetics, as your friend suggested, they're really struggling with the jealous streak that makes it hard to share a mate. I think my mixed warlock genes make it easier for me, but I'm only guessing. I never thought I'd share a mate either, but I'm willing to if that's what the Fates have decided."

"The Fates? Is that what you think this is truly?" Ruby asked, her voice taking on an oddly high-pitched tone that echoed with worry.

"Well, yes. That's what we call it," Darren answered succinctly.

Ruby slid off my lap again.

I let her go without a fuss, feeling the pure anxiety suddenly pulsing through her.

"I hope you all know that I didn't plan for this," she said. "I didn't mean to make you feel jealous or possessive, or any of those things."

I frowned at her. Why was she trying to take on the responsibility for all of this? "Of course, you didn't, Ruby. This isn't your fault. It's no one's fault."

She twisted her hands in front of her, looking more nervous by the second and strangely guilty.

Did she really feel that badly about this situation? *Our* situation?

"Do you think it would be better if I just... dated one of you?" she asked.

None of us answered, we couldn't. Instead, we just gawped at one another, stupefied. *Was she serious?* How would she even begin to choose?

"Which one..." I began to ask, then realized that wasn't a question I should ask or wanted answered. If we stayed together—the four of us as it was intended—for the next fifty years, I didn't want her answer haunting us.

She turned toward Darren and gestured to him. "Since Darren is the only one who doesn't care that I'm a witch, I suppose it would make the most sense to—"

"No!"

The pained roar didn't come from my throat, like I'd expected. It came from a place to my left. *From my cousin.*

Billy was on his feet, staring straight at Ruby, his hands clenched into fists by his sides. He looked angry and defiant. But I knew that wasn't a true depiction of his feelings. He was frustrated as all hell.

I jumped to my feet too, not wanting our mate to be afraid of my cousin—one of her three men. "Ruby, don't mind Billy. He—"

Billy growled at me in warning, the sound as threatening as I'd ever heard from him. "Don't you dare make excuses for me, Jackson. It's not your place."

Ruby took a few steps forward, toward Billy.

It made me nervous. If he shifted now, he could do a lot of damage to our mate. "Ruby, be careful. He's..."

She put her hand out to me to stop me. "It's fine, Jackson," she said carefully, keeping her attention squarely on my cousin. "It's all right Billy, you can talk to me."

I took a breath and readied myself as much as I could to jump in if everything turned ugly. I would have to be faster than fast. I'd have to be super-human to save her from Billy's wolf.

~

Billy

As Ruby moved closer to me, my anger combined with everything else I was feeling. Jealousy and possessiveness, just as she'd said, but worse? The fear of rejection was the most prominent. It blinded me and made me feel weak—inadequate.

That was why I called out to her. To stop her from choosing Jackson, the obvious choice. The Alpha. The strongest and very best of us. Or who she said she'd choose. Darren, the warlock-wolf, who was cool and calm and... a nice guy, really. I was never going to be the one she'd pick out of the three of us. In fact, I would be the last one she would choose.

She didn't know me. Hell, I'd barely spoken to her! But that didn't mean I was wrong for her, or that I didn't want her. Because I *wanted* her. Despite her witch blood, and the fact that I'd have to share her with two other men forever. I wanted her more than any of that. I had to be a part of her life. I had to be with her. The mere thought of any other option ripped through me with tangible pain.

"Why shouldn't I choose just one of you, Billy?" Ruby asked me quietly.

I struggled to push forward with the conversation, through my wolf's hold on my throat. He wanted my humanity to be second to his animal control. It was often safer that way. But at that moment, I didn't agree with him. Not one bit. My mate needed to know how I felt. Verbalizing that would take everything I had, But I would damn well try.

I swallowed hard, clenching my hands so tightly that my nails nearly cut into my palms. I physically forced my wolf back down, and out of my mind. I would let him run free later tonight if he behaved now. He needed to relax, get back to his place. I was my own master. "I don't want you to choose... them." I exhaled sharply, relieved to have gotten the main message out. The rest should be easier.

Her eyebrows flew up. "You want me to choose you?" She sounded surprised.

And I realized suddenly that my insecurities indeed had merit.

She had no idea that I wanted her.

I shook my head. "I don't want you to choose at all. That's not what's meant to be."

And it wasn't. I knew that with a brutal and startling clarity that shook me to my very core. If Jackson and Darren could wrap their heads around sharing Ruby, then so could I.

Ruby bit her lip. "But if I was going to choose then you'd want me to choose..."

I shook my head again, refusing to answer her question, and instead pushing forward with what needed to be said. "I want you. Just as much as Jackson. And as much as Darren. I want you, too, Ruby." My words sounded rough, like I wasn't sure how to express my feelings.

But then she smiled at me and when she did, I saw the relief and happiness in her green eyes.

And right then, a part of me melted. And I knew I would die for this woman. My mate. *Our* mate.

"I'm glad," she said. "I mean, I wasn't sure. But—"

I charged forward, all pretense and frustration gone. I grabbed her, needing to kiss her more than anything. To show her that I desired her, too. That my feelings were real and just as valid as Jackson's and

Darren's. I slid my hands around her tiny waist and pulled her into me. I paused for just a moment, staring down into her huge green eyes to gauge if she was going to rebuff my advances.

Even though she'd kissed Jackson right before her mother had interrupted and blasted us back to our own town, and she'd been kissing Darren when Jackson and I had found her half an hour ago, a rather large part of me thought that she would stop me. No matter how growly or strong my wolf was, I was still afraid of rejection. And if she looked even remotely pressured or uncomfortable, I'd not only stop, but I would also leave.

But instead of looking afraid her eyes grew a little wider, as though she were surprised, and then she lifted her chin to meet my gaze and offered me her lips.

A satisfied growl rolled through me as I moved my hands up to her beautiful face, cupped her pink flushed cheeks, and kissed her. I poured every bit of desperation and love and frustration into our connection, and I was rewarded for my efforts.

Ruby kissed me back, her arms wrapping around my waist, holding me to her as she opened her mouth and swept her tongue against mine.

I groaned and lifted her up in my arms, her legs going around my hips as our bodies came together. I grabbed her ass and held her tightly to me, plundering her mouth with my tongue while marveling at the taste of her. The perfection of how she felt in my arms was everything and more.

Her hands went for my shirt buttons, and she pulled at my clothes.

I dragged my mouth away from hers to stare into her lust-filled eyes.

I didn't put her down—I couldn't— instead, I held her tighter and turned to my cousin. "Where are we going?"

"Bed," Jackson said, and charged toward his room off the living room.

I didn't bother checking with Darren. I was sure he'd be onboard anyway. I just followed my cousin into whatever came next.

CHAPTER 14
RUBY

I could barely keep my eyes open. All I could see were fireworks and flashes of white light inside my mind. My skin was on fire. Everywhere Billy touched was alight, and everywhere he hadn't yet visited was screaming out for attention.

Billy was my bad boy. Trouble. The one that ignited things in me I'd tried to ignore, and sometimes hoped weren't even there. He made me want to explore what it meant to be naughty, and he made me feel irresistible.

My bad boy carried me into a darkened room where he set me down on my feet, keeping a hand on my waist and holding me close.

I sagged against his strong body, my knees weakened and ridiculously wobbly. I forced my eyes open, though I felt drunk on pleasure, positively drugged out on one of my wolves.

We were in a bedroom. A large, dark, male bedroom. Jackson's I had to assume, since we were in his house.

This was it. It was really happening. The moment I'd been dreaming about for so long. The night I would lose my virginity and learn what true pleasure was. Hopefully.

Darren stepped into the room.

I shivered, anticipation and nervousness rippling through me. Would I make love to all three of them? And would it be all at once or individually—like taking turns? How would this work? I waited, full of nervous energy, expecting them to show me how to start, where to begin, but no one moved.

"Um, are we going to..." I gestured to the bed, feeling suddenly awkward. The heat in my blood was beginning to cool. I felt more sobered and anxious, and I didn't want that. But I wasn't going to be the one who initiated anything. I wouldn't even know where to begin!

I grabbed onto Billy's arm, desperate for an anchor or guidance. "Why has everyone stopped?"

He growled, in that soft, pleasing way. "I think we all want you to tell us that you want this, too."

I nodded quickly. "Yes, I do. Very much. But I don't know how to—."

"You're a virgin, then?" Jackson asked, his voice deeper and darker than before.

I pursed my lips and nodded. "I am."

All three men made a strange rumbling, purring noise in unison.

I clung harder to Billy's arm. "I don't understand. Is that a bad thing?" I whispered, not quite comprehending their response.

Billy shook his head.

Darren laughed, breaking the intense atmosphere. "No. It's the best news any of us have ever heard," he said. "It's perfect. *You're* perfect."

A smile tugged at my lips. "Then why am I still standing here? And why are you all still fully clothed?" I was shocked I had the guts to say that, but I honestly didn't understand why we were all still standing around doing nothing. I expected to experience a whirlwind of passion, to feel swept off my feet and breathless.

They thought I was their Fated Mate, and I knew they were my true loves. My magic had called them to me and now that I had them, I didn't want to waste any more time. But they certainly didn't seem to be in much of a rush to get me naked, considering their constant and ardent declarations about desiring me. Then the spell snapped.

The Alpha took the lead. Jackson pulled his shirt over his head, unbuttoned his jeans, and stepped out of them.

I gaped at him naked, aroused and standing in the middle of the room.

Billy's hands slid down my body from behind. They moved over my waist, down my thighs, then grabbed the skirt of my new little black dress.

"Arms up," he said.

I did as he asked.

He pulled the dress up over my head and tossed it to the floor without a second thought.

I should have magicked up prettier underwear.

Then Billy made that strange, purring noise and tore at his clothes until he was naked too. Maybe sexier undies weren't really that necessary.

Their gazes were hungry as they moved over my body.

I stared at Darren, who was still completely clothed. "Aren't you going to join in?" I asked with a shy grin. I needed him to be a part of this, my sweet warlock-wolf.

He nodded but didn't say anything.

Was he going to watch? Wait until the end? Was that his plan? The questions flew around my mind unanswered.

Billy's arms wrapped around my body and pulled me into his heat.

I gasped and put my hands back against his thighs, his skin burning beneath my palms.

"Damn, you feel good," Billy groaned into my ear as he nipped at my neck and his hands came up to cup my breasts, before he began to knead them, teasing my hardening nipples.

"You do too," I said, my throat tight with wanting.

Jackson walked over and knelt before me, tugging at my underwear and slipping it down my thighs.

I giggled aloud as I stepped out of my panties.

Jackson's hands came up to cup my bare ass cheeks.

I gasped at the strength of his grip; the way it made me feel owned and desired.

Then his mouth went to the juncture between my thighs.

"Holy shit!" I cried out as I reached for Jackson's head.

His tongue flicked out and caused a cacophony of pleasure to echo through my body.

My knees turned to jelly. I felt like I wouldn't be able to support my own weight much longer at this rate.

Jackson scooped me up and threw my legs easily over his shoulders, using my ass for an anchor.

I was completely exposed, my pussy open for him to devour.

Billy held my upper body tightly in his grip.

I turned my head to protest what they were doing to me, to cry out that I couldn't possibly handle so much pleasure.

A heartbeat later Billy kissed me, swallowing my moans and gasps, silencing my protests.

Jackson pleasured me in a way I'd never even dreamed of with his lips, his tongue, his hands. They were everywhere. Inside me, on my thighs, and all over my clit that pulsed with longing. His tongue manipulated me mercilessly.

Until my back arched up and I begged him to end the torture.

Billy unclipped my bra and it fell away, my aching breasts free to the air, bare to their hands and fingers. "Let's get her to the bed," Billy said, and I was lifted and taken over to the mattress where I was laid down as if I weighed less than a feather.

Damn, it felt incredible to be manhandled. To feel tiny and delicate in their grasp.

Billy and Jackson stood over me.

Their huge, muscled bodies made my mouth water. I wanted to touch them, to kiss them, to explore each crevice of their raw and unapologetically sexy masculinity.

Jackson slid on top of me in one precise movement, his hot, sweaty body gliding against mine in a familiar rhythm as old and timeless as love itself.

I wrapped my naked thighs around him, my body aching for more pleasure. For the completion that I knew would soon be mine to hold on to.

Jackson stilled, then pushed up on his arms and stared down at me. "Are you protected? Or should I..."

I blinked. *What did he mean?* Then it hit me, and I blushed. "Oh. Yeah, I'm on the pill for other issues." My mother's line had notoriously terrible monthly pains and wicked irregularity, so I'd been using the pill to regulate my cycles for years now.

"Fantastic," Jackson growled as he swooped down and captured my lips with his.

I moaned into his mouth, throwing myself into the kiss wholeheartedly.

He moved his body closer, fitting us against one another like puzzle pieces that were always destined to be.

Then I felt his hard cock pressing against me, seeking, searching for the way inside my virginal body. Which was exactly what I wanted, too. I arched my back, our lips disconnecting from our intense kiss. I dug my nails into his shoulders, a gasp hitching in my throat. Was this going to hurt? Excitement, adrenaline, and desire roared through me at the thought.

"Damn, you're perfect. So beautiful," Jackson whispered into my ear, stopping all the worries that might invade my mind.

He pressed his hard thickness into me, so slowly, and so sweetly.

I choked on my sob as he forged his way inside of me. To feel such tenderness and care from such a huge man was humbling and revealed to me a side to Jackson I hadn't expected or really experienced yet.

There was a sudden twinge of pain but then the feeling was gone, replaced by a deep, dull ache as his body buried itself inside me.

"Are you okay?" he asked, one hand stroking my hair as he paused.

For what, I wasn't sure, but I was glad he'd stopped. Everything was overwhelming and strange. I don't know what I was expecting, or what I'd imagined, but I needed just a second to adjust. "I think so," I said tentatively. I allowed myself to relax under him, enjoying the heat and weight of his immaculately fit form. He made me feel small, protected, and desired.

He began to move his cock inside of me, slowly at first. He thrust in and out in small increments that made me gasp and cling to him; to make sure he came back every time.

Just as I began to fall into the rhythm of the new sensations, he picked up speed, thrusting harder. Our flesh slapped together.

I rose to meet him, lifting my hips to greet his body with each desperate connection.

Jackson grunted and pushed even harder, seeking to plunge ever deeper.

I bit my lip, stifling the moans and sounds of ecstasy. Soon, I couldn't hold it in any longer, and whimpered as the pleasure inside my belly built to maddening and impossible heights. Everything was tightening as the tingles of lightning worked all the way down to my toes. "Jackson, I—" I gasped and cried out as my first vaginal orgasm hit me.

Jackson stiffened, then thrust into me one more time.

Pulsations of heat burst inside my lower belly, my pussy spasmed, and tears leaked down the sides of my face as the beauty of the moment completely overwhelmed me. *Oh, my God.* The feeling was like nothing I'd ever known. It was an awe-inspiring perfect moment of completion.

He kissed me on the lips and withdrew slowly from my body.

And suddenly I felt... empty. Alone. It was almost painful in a sense. "Don't leave me. Please." I sat up and reached out for him with both hands. The panic was intense.

But Jackson just grinned. "What's wrong, baby?"

"I..." How did I explain the impossible sadness that came with our first time being over?

Then Billy came forward.

My heart melted. I put my arms out to him, finally understanding why I was feeling so incomplete. I needed all my mates. It couldn't be any other way.

"You aren't too sore?" he asked as he lay down next to me on the mattress.

I allowed myself to lie back down again, too. I shook my head emphatically, a second wave of desire already threatening to drown me. "No. Please, come to me."

Billy rolled on top of me and settled between my thighs as though he'd always belonged there. He kissed my lips and stared into my eyes with so much intensity it was as though he might never see me again. Like he needed to memorize every inch of my face forever.

Jackson stood up and moved away.

I felt the weight shift on the mattress as he left, and I focused all my energy on Billy—my bad boy.

He slid down my body, kissing my neck, then stroked my breasts. First with his cheek, rubbing his roughened jaw against my flesh, then with his lips, taking the tip of one aching nipple into his mouth and sucking deeply.

I gasped and grabbed for his head, arching my back while I kept my gaze fixed on him, enjoying a perverse sense of pleasure. The image of his mouth suckling me was one that aroused me more than I thought it possibly could, sending arrows of pleasure deep into my belly.

I tangled my hands in his hair and cupped his jaw, enjoying the intense visuals and the feel of his hot mouth on me.

He moved up, thrusting his tongue into my mouth as he slid his cock into me at the exact same moment.

I groaned against his lips, my newly over-sensitized pussy opening to accept him as my insides greedily wrapped around him. He was thicker than Jackson, and he moved much faster from the start.

The fire in my belly began to build a new, higher and faster this time. I bit down on my lower lip to stifle the strangled scream that was growing in my throat and squeezed my eyes shut tight.

Billy bit my neck and sucked on the skin at the confluence of where my shoulder began. That was going to leave a mark.

I loved the idea of carrying the evidence of Billy's possession on me for all to see. I slid my hands up his arms and into his hair, holding him to me, encouraging him to mark me more. Deeper. Darker.

His breathing soon became ragged and harsh, almost growly.

Gripping him tighter, I squeezed my legs around him desperately.

He thrust harder and faster, pushing me higher, and closer toward that exquisite pinnacle of release.

I shuddered in mind-melting pleasure for the second time.

Then he came inside me, the delicious heat moving through me. Claiming me.

I moaned aloud, clinging to him so that he wouldn't leave me, too.

He joined me in mutual ecstasy, shuddering over me.

I felt a pure wave of emotion move through him. His recognition of me, of who I was and who we were together was something so much deeper than just physical.

He rolled to the side, not leaving me, but instead shifting his weight so that I was comfortable. He lifted his hand and cupped my face lovingly.

And though I knew I was red-faced, sweaty, and disheveled, he made me feel beautiful.

"Wow," he said, breathless. "That was…"

"I know," I said, smiling blissfully. If this is what the Fates had in store for me, I was the luckiest woman alive.

He kissed me softly on the lips one more time then pulled himself out of my body, leaving me cold and aching again.

I groaned. I couldn't have that feeling tormenting me every waking moment. I'd go insane!

Billy rolled away.

The pull of my magic tugged inside of me. I sat up and glanced over to where Darren sat on a large chest propped against the wall.

He was still dressed, and staring at me with a hunger that was somehow different than that of his wolf brethren.

I slid to the end of the bed and got to my feet, though my legs were unsteady.

Darren's gaze slid over my body with appreciation and when he met my gaze, purple magic swirled in his irises like whirlpools of enchantment. He wanted me, that much was obvious.

But I was covered in sweat, and the possession of my other soul mates was evident all over my body. Would he still want to be with me tonight?

"Are you going to make love to me, too?" I asked him, though the desire to cover my nakedness was strong, I resisted. Despite our intimacies, standing naked in front of these men was intimidating, especially since they were perfect specimens of what men could look like. I had no way of knowing if they liked what they saw in me. Were my breasts big enough? Were my thighs too thick? And what was Darren thinking? I wished I knew.

Then Darren stood up, a delicious and intense conviction in his movement.

My breath caught instantly in my throat. This was going to be entirely different from what I'd just enjoyed with Billy and Jackson. It was going to be something else. Somehow, I just knew it.

CHAPTER 15
DARREN

My whole body was on fire, from the tips of my toes to the inside of my gut. Part of me was afraid that if I moved even an inch, I might explode. Right here, in front of everyone. When Ruby asked me if I was going to make love to her, all that heat, all that fire, shot straight to my groin like a bullet train.

Damn it... So much for hoping to last a long time for her. I would probably come the moment she touched me if she kept on being so sexy. "Only if you want me to," I answered. It really was that simple and that complicated. Of course, I *wanted* to make love to her. Well to be completely honest, the animal part of me wanted to slam her into the wall and ride her well into next week. But I could see how unsteady she was on her feet, and I could only imagine how sore she would be feeling her first time.

And what if I couldn't be gentle enough? Or worse, what if I disappointed her in that very first moment when we were finally joined together? I didn't want to cast a shadow over our lives together in what should be an incredible night for us both.

"Of course, I do. Come over here." She smiled at me, curling a finger suggestively.

I took a tentative step toward her and the air around us shifted and whirled.

Billy and Jackson backed up as though they felt the magic too.

I smiled at my mate. "I have no idea what this is going to do to either of us."

She laughed, the sound musical and delighted. "Let's find out."

I reached over my head and dragged my blue tank off my body, kicked off my shoes, and took another step closer.

She closed the distance between us and reached for my buckled belt.

"Can I do it?" she asked.

A pulse of longing shimmered through me. How many things had she not done, and would she like to do to me? Hopefully as many as I wanted to do to her.

I let my hands drop away with a smile. "You can do anything you like."

She grinned then spoke a few magical words, the belt unbuckling, the zipper sliding down, and the pants disappearing onto the floor with no more than a whisper of wind.

I laughed. "Not what I thought you were going to do." I'd kind of hoped she wanted to touch me.

She beamed. "Me neither, but..." She slid closer still, running her hands up my chest, then back down again, her gaze fixed on my cock. "Can I touch you?" she asked hesitantly.

I nodded. "Of course."

Her hot little hand wrapped around me. "Wow," she whispered as she moved her fingers on my shaft, up and down, before exploring the head.

I clenched my hands into fists on either side of me. Heat bloomed inside my gut, racing down the backs of my thighs and up my back. I wasn't going to be able to handle much more of that. Her touch was like magic. I grabbed her hand and gently took it away from me, shuddering as I did so. "You need to stop that, Ruby, or I'll lose it before we even begin."

Her gaze came up to mine.

And even though I could see embarrassment in her eyes she was still smiling.

"Back to the bed you go," I said, taking her hand and leading her to the mattress where I'd watched both of the other men take her in the same way. But I wanted to do something a little different.

"Kneel down on all fours for me." I guided her into the position that I hoped would give her the most pleasure. She would be able to reach her clit, or I could from this position. And it would hopefully feel completely different from what she'd just experienced with Jackson and Billy.

She frowned at me slightly.

I encouraged her into position, then stood behind her. "Damn, you're beautiful," I said as I ran my hands over her back, her hips, and her smooth, full ass. I grabbed my shaft and used my cock head to paint her pussy lips, spreading the wetness, and enjoying the feel of being an artist with the most perfect canvas.

She gasped and pressed back against me with urgent need.

My cock head slipped into her body easily and I couldn't help the moan that rippled through my chest as her delicious tightness. I considered pulling it out to spend more time enjoying her body.

Then she reached her hand back and grabbed my fingers where I held her waist. "Darren," she said simply.

My name on her lips was like a reverent prayer and made what little control I had been holding onto disappear. I threaded my fingers through hers and grabbed tight, sinking into the depths of her body with one long, strong thrust. I groaned deep in my throat.

And she met my moan with one of her own.

I'd only learned three spells as an adult and I was about to use my favorite one. I whispered the incantation and flicked my finger against her hip in a wicked rhythm to stimulate her clitoris; casting my magic around her body to arouse her in ways she likely never dreamed possible.

She gasped and pushed up with one hand, arching her back off the bed. "Oh, Darren, what are you doing?" She moaned again, more desperately this time.

I moved my fingers faster in response.

Her pussy clenched down on me.

My balls tightened agonizingly. *Shit... control. Control!* With a quiet growl I thrust in and out of her sweet, tight hole, moving my fingers while listening to her sounds of delight and pleasure.

She tightened more and more, her pussy rippling and squeezing me to unparalleled ecstasy.

I couldn't hold out any longer. Magic forgotten, I grabbed for her hips and fucked her as hard and fast I was able.

Her anguished and ecstatic cry pushed me right over the edge.

I let go, thrusting one final time and came hard. Heat swept up my back, pulsing raw pleasure through my balls, and along my cock to ripple out to every cell in my body. Exhausted, I pulled out and collapsed next to her on the bed, totally spent.

She fell to her stomach on the mattress and turned her face toward me. Her cheeks were flushed red and covered with sweat, and she was panting.

I'd never seen anything so beautiful.

Then she began to giggle and grin. "I thought you said that you didn't know any magic."

I shrugged, then winked playfully, before rolling onto my back, a broad smile painted on my face. "I might have a secret or two."

She laughed and moved closer. Laying an arm over my chest, she sighed. "You certainly do, Darren."

I wrapped my arms around her and kissed the top of her head. This was unreal.

Jackson and Billy stepped forward, wanting to join us.

I squeezed her tight, realizing that my moment alone with her was over "Let's move farther up the bed." I encouraged her to shuffle up the mattress until she was laying down with her head on the pillow.

The other two wolf shifters moved in, and we settled around her satisfied body; Jackson the closest, holding her tight, me on one side stroking her sweet belly, and Billy on the other, holding her thigh. The tension in the room was minimal, considering we were all naked and vulnerable. And Ruby's once virginal body now housed seed from all three of us.

"You feeling okay?" I asked our mate, our lover.

She sighed and wriggled as though she would love to get up and run around but couldn't.

"I feel amazing," she said brightly, flashing us a brilliant, big, and beautiful smile.

Jackson grunted and kissed the top of her head. "This is only the beginning, Ruby."

I knew what he meant, wholeheartedly.

All three of us had probably not been up to our "A" game when it came to our abilities as lovers tonight. But the need to bond with her, and the sheer intensity of her attractiveness had made it very difficult to last.

The heat she imbued had certainly made me feel combustible. And I was pretty sure Jackson and Billy felt the same way.

Ruby sighed. "So true." Then she laughed. "I just still can't believe there's three of you. I can't believe this is our life—our Fate! I just can't..." She shook her head, grinning.

I glanced at the other men, and for the first time ever, felt a sense of kinship rather than the competition or the intimidation that had been there before. "You're going to be very well looked after, beautiful girl," I said. "In every way conceivable."

Sexually, emotionally, physically. We would cover every base, and be everything she ever needed, wanted, or craved.

She laughed. "If I'd known you were here waiting for me all along, I would have arrived so much sooner."

Billy growled and shook his head. "And if we'd known you were only fifteen minutes away in town, one of us would have come and claimed you years ago."

She smiled serenely. "Oh, it probably wouldn't have worked until I'd used my magic to call for you, anyway," she said absently.

And just like that our passionate evening shattered into a billion shards like a broken mirror. The potent heat and desire gone, leaving a strange chill in the air. I froze in my movements where I'd previously been tracing intricate patterns on her hot skin.

I glanced up. "What do you mean?" *She'd worked a spell to call for us?*

Ruby's eyes grew big and round, then she swallowed hard, looking unmistakably guilty.

Jackson rolled off the bed and stood beside us.

Billy withdrew his hands from her body, though he didn't leave the mattress.

"What do you mean by that, Ruby?" Jackson growled, his eyes flickering visibly between human and wolf.

"Hey," I snapped at him, suddenly alert. "Back off, Jackson."

Ruby slid up the bed, moving the pillows so she could sit up against the headboard comfortably. Then she wrapped her arms around her chest to cover her breasts, to protect her body from our view. "It isn't like it sounds," she protested, sounding vulnerable and afraid.

I smiled at her and reached for her leg, squeezing her knee reassuringly. I hated to see her like this, especially after what we'd all just shared together. "They don't understand much about magic, sweetheart," I reminded her gently. "So, you may want to explain a little more." I was trying to sound calm and diffuse the tension of the situation, but my own magic had kicked in with the only thing I was ever good at: premonitions rolled over me. Something was about to happen. Bad or good, I couldn't tell just yet. But one thing was for sure... a shit storm was headed our way, and I didn't know that any of us were prepared for it.

CHAPTER 16

JACKSON

The witch better explain. I couldn't stop the way my wolf rose up in protest inside my head. It took all my humanity, and all my strength, to force him back down again.

Ruby needed to explain and quickly. Surely her explanation would make everything clear, and I'd find I was overreacting. I had to be. *Please,* I begged the universe. "Explain," I said more flatly than I intended.

Had Ruby seriously conjured a spell to make the three of us fall in love with her? And if she had, how would we know the difference between our own Fated Mate attractions to her and those she had manufactured with magic? Or was it possible for her to manipulate the Fated love as well? I had no real knowledge of how potent her casting abilities were.

My anger only escalated with each passing second and the more I thought about it. My teeth clenched and my fists tightened.

"Well, ah…" Ruby shivered as though she were cold or terrified.

Darren pulled the blankets up to cover her.

I didn't know why, but that was pissing me off as well. Why the hell was he coddling her when she very well could be the reason the three of us had to share a mate? I'd just gotten my head wrapped around the idea that this was all the design of Fate. That the lack of females born to the pack meant that breeding with Ruby—bringing her into our pack—was the right thing to do. That was what was needed and was meant to be.

Was it possible she may be just as hurtful and conniving as the witches who'd originally broke our pack? *If that's the way it went. We'd have something else to follow up on.*

Darren patted her leg. "Go on, Ruby."

She clung to the blankets that covered her perky, pink-tipped tits and bit her lip. Her eyes were wide and they kept darting to me, down and then up again. She really looked terrified—of me.

God damn it. Calm the fuck down. I took several measured breaths. "I'm sorry, Ruby. Please, explain it to us. I don't know anything about witches, really." I knew only what my parents had told me, and it was all bad. They hated the witches and warlocks in town. They said the Coven was power hungry, vindictive, and traitorous. We stayed away from them for a reason.

Ruby licked her lips. "Well, uh, I grew up without a dad. We all did… my friends Tiffany and Bella and me," she began.

"What does that have to do with us?" Billy asked, sounding offended.

I felt the same way but held my tongue. Had we landed a girl with major daddy issues?

She shook her head. "Nothing, specifically. I just wanted you to know that our past is the reason we did what we did. None of us want to make the same mistakes as our mothers."

"What? Get knocked up and abandoned?" Billy's tone was even, but his eyes flared with deep emotion.

Darren swiped out with his fist, knocking Billy across the arm with intent and more force than I'd anticipated. "Back off," he snarled protectively.

Billy growled.

But Darren held his ground and glared at him long and hard.

Billy backed the fuck down. Then he got up and grabbed his pants, huffing and puffing the whole time as he re-dressed.

Good idea. I grabbed mine also, feeling less exposed with my cock tucked firmly behind my zipper. "Go on," I said.

Ruby stared at Darren, her heart in her eyes. "Do you want to get your clothes on, too?"

He smiled kindly at her. "Not really. But feel free to cover yourself if you'd feel more comfortable."

A smile trembled on her lips as she closed her eyes and whispered to herself. A soft breeze swirled through the room, and then she was clothed. Or, at least from what I could see, she was. She pushed the blanket down to her waist and revealed that she was now wearing a black sweatshirt and dark jeans.

"Now, please go on," Darren encouraged her, before throwing a dirty look over his shoulder at us.

I glanced at Billy and nodded. "Let her finish." Both of us jumping down her throat was not getting us to the end of this story quickly. If anything, I could already see the wedge we were driving between the three of us, all the while forcing her even closer to the warlock-wolf.

Ruby took a deep breath, then exhaled all at once. "Okay. Long story short. On our twenty-first birthday, which was last Halloween..."

"You were born on Halloween?" Darren asked, sounding happily surprised.

She nodded.

"What does that mean?" I asked, not wanting to slow the pace of the conversation, but it seemed like I knew nothing about this world and feeling stupid was new to me. The unfamiliar ground was unwelcome, to say the least.

Darren glanced at me, though his gaze was annoyed when he did. "It's very lucky, and usually means the witch born on that day will have her powers naturally amplified."

I pressed my lips together and exhaled sharply.

He turned back to Ruby. "Which is probably why you've never known you were half wolf shifter. Normally that would reduce your powers considerably, but with a powerful mother, and the power of All Hallows' Eve..."

"Anyway," she said with another sigh. "Last year, the girls and I went away together and performed a spell that would call our soul mates to us. None of us wanted to waste time sleeping around with the wrong guys. We didn't want to endure the endless break ups, and bad marriages... you know, all that crap. We just wanted the person who was right for us, to find us. That's all."

It sounded all well and good, and her intent was innocent enough, except for the fact that she had probably messed with our entire lives. I began to pace as the thoughts whirled around my head. "So, really, you thought it was okay to use magic to call your supposed soul mate to you?" Anger tightened my gut. So, this was it, then? I'd been tricked, fooled... duped! And by magic, no less. What a fucking fool I was.

She blinked at me, hurt. "What do you mean?"

"I mean, how can you think that any of this is okay? How will we ever know if what we feel for you is real? If you're truly our Fated Mate, or if we simply got twisted up in your magical avoid-pain-plan. Your... spell."

Ruby threw back the blankets, clambered off the bed, and rose to her feet. She glared at me. "You're blowing this completely out of proportion!"

"Me?" I laughed without humor, anger settling heavily in my chest. "I don't think so, Ruby. I think it's you that's not realizing what you've done here."

Darren shuffled off the bed too and went in search of his own clothes, being the only still naked person in the room.

Her lips trembled and she glared even harder, her green eyes glittering with flecks of emerald. "What have I done that's so terrible? I thought you were happy about finding me!"

"I was when I thought you were truly my Fated Mate!" I was panting too hard. If I didn't calm down soon, I'd shift again. "But now, how the hell do I know if any of this is real? If it really was what Fate intended?" *Breathe. Just breathe.*

"Can't you feel it?" she cried, throwing her hands up in the air in frustration and despair. "I can! When I look at you. When you kiss me. I feel it! It's real."

I clenched my jaw and refused to answer her. I didn't know what I felt now, and I didn't trust any of my instincts.

"Jackson!" she said, her eyes brimming with tears, then she turned to Billy. "Billy? Aren't you going to say something? Anything?"

He shook his head and came to stand to my right, just behind my shoulder. We were obviously united in our questions about her using magic to influence our lives.

"I... I can't believe this," Ruby said, shaking her head as tears overflowed and spilled down her cheeks.

I tried to harden my heart against such a human trick. I told myself she wasn't upset about anything other than being found out. It made it easier to ignore her tears. Even though the wolf inside me howled in protest at my denial. If we'd formally mated with her tonight, truly given ourselves over to this woman, there would be no going back— irrespective of the fact we may have wanted to.

I crossed my arms over my chest, the ramifications of having to live with a dishonest mate plowing through me. I had to do something to deal with this unacceptable situation. I was an Alpha. I would have truth and honesty from my mate or nothing at all. "I think we need to talk about where we're going to go from here," I said. "I don't know if it's possible to undo what we did here tonight. I'll need to speak to one of the elders."

Ruby gasped in horror.

But I was already busy inside my head wondering if there was a way to reverse the bonding we'd achieved tonight. I could already sense the mating feeling building inside of me, growing like a damn flower. After I'd made love to her—no, during it—I'd sensed our connection, my wolf being willing to lay down his very life for this woman.

"Don't go, Ruby," Darren said.

I snapped my attention back to the room.

"I think I need to," she said, her voice quavering with emotion. "These two don't want me. They don't even believe that I didn't do this on purpose! I never meant to hurt anyone or play with Fate! I just wanted to find my soul mate, that's all." She was sobbing between each sentence, and each breath.

This time the wall around my heart cracked just a little. "Ruby..." I began, but I didn't know what I was going to say afterwards, and it didn't matter.

Her attention was wholly focused on Darren.

"Well, I believe you," Darren said sincerely. "I need you, Ruby, more than I need air. And I don't care if you used a spell to call out to me. I'm just grateful I found you."

A growl rose in my throat as Darren said everything she wanted to hear. The opposite of everything I'd said. *Didn't he realize that this could all be fake?* Our true mate, *my* true mate, could still be out there. A woman without traitorous magical blood. One I wouldn't have to share with anyone.

The wind of Ruby's magic began to whirl, and a strange white light glowed around her as if she were an angel. She looked radiant.

"I want to come with you," Darren said and reached for her hand.

She nodded and smiled at him with all the affection and intensity I'd seen in her eyes when I'd made love to her just an hour ago.

My heart broke as she glanced back at us, her gaze cold and distant. And then, just like that, they were gone.

"Holy shit," Billy said, rushing forward into the space where

Darren and Ruby had been. He looked left and right like a confused pup. "Is that what her mom did to us? Just made us vanish into thin air?"

I nodded and locked my knees to stop myself from staggering for the bed. I felt completely adrift, with no foundation of strength left to speak of. "Ah... yeah, I suppose," I muttered. I changed my mind about needing to sit down. There was only Billy here to see me collapse, after all, and he was my blood, my cousin—my family.

I staggered backwards, toward the large chest against the wall that not long-ago Darren had sat upon, watching us have sex with Ruby as he patiently waited his turn.

"We did the right thing, Billy. Didn't we?" I asked, dazed.

He shrugged, pacing the carpet where Ruby and Darren had stood. "Yeah, I hope so."

"You hope so?" I repeated. Didn't he know?

Billy laughed, though the sound was dark and didn't hold even the slightest hint of amusement. "You're kidding, right? If she *is* our mate, if she is the one we're meant to spend the rest of our days with, we just royally fucked up! She'll never forgive us for tonight. So, then what? Are we supposed to just hang around forever without her? Not fucking likely. We couldn't endure it!"

I could hear the wolf in Billy's voice, the deep, guttural sounds between each of the clipped human words. "What do you mean, she'll never forgive us? I just questioned her magic and her motives. I had every right to. This is *my* life, Billy. *Our* lives." I heard the words, but found they were sticking uncomfortably in my throat.

Billy turned and stared at me, unspeaking.

"What?" I challenged, sitting up straighter. "If you didn't agree with me, then why stand by me? Why didn't you question her?"

"Because you're my Alpha," he said. "And my cousin."

"And I hope because you agreed with me," I shot back in heated frustration. We didn't follow the Alpha-Beta rules in our pack. And I hated to think that I'd made the wrong choice, and my cousin would pay for it.

Billy sat down on the rumpled bed; the scent of sex still heavy in the air. He shook his head. "I don't know, Jackson."

I snorted. "Well, we can fix it, I'm sure. if we find out I'm wrong... which I might not be. If I'm right, then we'll have our very own real mates just waiting to be found. Ruby's magic could have wholly fucked everything up."

Billy sighed. "I know. But if you're wrong and we *are* destined to love a half-blood witch—all three of us—do you really think she's going to forgive you after tonight?"

I frowned. "What do you mean?"

Billy shook his head and a strange smile pulled at his lips. "You really weren't listening, were you? First of all, it was her very first time, and she had sex with all three of us."

"Yeah..." *So?*

"And it was her *birthday*, today. Halloween, remember?"

My throat suddenly got tight and thick, and my words slowly came back to me like I was watching a film. I assessed everything again, from an entirely new angle now that I was calmer. I swallowed hard. "So, tonight was her birthday and her first time ever, and I accused her of deceiving us into mating with her?"

Billy nodded. "Yeah, that pretty much sums it up."

"God fucking damn it." I stood up and ran a shaky hand through my hair. "We better go speak to some of the elders then. I need to know if I did the right thing, Billy. I have to know if my instincts were right. Or if I just fucked up our whole lives."

Billy grabbed his shirt from the floor and threw mine to me. "Let's go."

We headed out the door and made a beeline straight for the elders. If I'd let my pride—and my temper—get the better of me tonight, I was pretty sure I would live to regret it for the rest of my life.

CHAPTER 17

RUBY

The tears wouldn't stop running once I got home no matter what I did. So, I just sat on the carpet in my bedroom, wrapped my arms around my knees, and sobbed until I could barely breathe.

But Darren couldn't abide my sorrow, so he picked me up and held me on his lap, wrapping his arms tightly around me. And he kept me there until the worst of the storm of emotions had passed.

But the pain around my heart wouldn't stop. I didn't think it'd go anywhere soon.

"It's okay, beautiful girl, I'm here," he murmured in my ear. "Everything will turn out all right, you'll see."

"But how can it?" I asked him, forcing myself to look up into his face.

He wiped my cheeks with his thumbs. "Because we're meant to be together. If those stupid assholes can't see that yet, they will. In time."

My lips quivered and I bit down on the bottom one. I wasn't so sure about that. I'd given Jackson my virginity, and Billy every bit of passion I could. I didn't have anything left to offer them. My heart was already theirs for the taking. If what I'd given wasn't enough to convince them that I was right for them, what more could I do? Wallowing certainly wasn't going to help, no matter how much it hurt. I had to be proactive. I had to do something...

I glanced up at the funky purple clock on the wall. I'd magicked us safely home to my house, and to my bedroom. It was 11:30 PM exactly, Halloween night. *I still had time to fix this!* I jumped to my feet and grabbed Darren's hand. "Come on. We've got to get out to the witch grounds before midnight."

"Where?" he asked, standing up with a slightly puzzled look on his face.

"The old church," I clarified, and turned to leave the room.

"Why?" he called out, following me as I ran down the stairs to the front door.

My mother was still out, which was good. Where she'd gone after she'd dropped me off, I didn't know. Probably Rebecca's or Kathy's. She was always with one of them, but usually both. Just like me, Bella, and Tiffany.

"I'm going to undo the spell I cast last year," I called back to him, the plan already forming in my head as I ran. I just needed the spell and some luck. I could do it, surely. Just like Darren said, I was born on All Hallows' Eve, I had naturally amplified magic! I wrenched open the door that revealed the closet under the stairs and I grabbed my mother's ancient spell book that she hid there. The very book that had started this whole saga—where all this Fated mess began.

"If we take my car, we'll make it," I said to Darren as I tucked the book under my arm, holding it tight. I could get us there quicker via a transportation spell, but it wasn't smart to expend any more magic unnecessarily tonight. I was probably going to need every drop of it for the reversal.

To be honest, I wasn't even sure I could do this spell by myself without my friends, but I had to try for the boys, or they'd never forgive me. And I couldn't ask Tiffany or Bella for help. Not now. It was too late. There wasn't enough time before midnight. And besides, I'd never ask them to give up their portion of the spell just because my lot had gone to hell in a handbag. They could still find their happily-ever-after... well, as long as their soul mates didn't include two bull-headed wolf shifters!

Darren ran with me.

I grabbed my car keys from the buffet and jumped into my beat-up little hatchback, Darren close behind.

We drove along our street, toward the witches' hallowed grounds. The earth there was steeped in history and had special, sacred powers; and if there was ever a need for a boost to my own strength, it was tonight.

"Are you sure about this, Ruby?" Darren asked, his tone told me that he was worried about my sudden decision.

"Yes." I nodded fiercely. "It's the only way to prove to Billy and Jackson that I haven't befuddled Fate by putting some spell over them. They'll feel the same way after I lift it, I'm sure of it. I believe it."

Darren didn't reply.

I glanced over at him, fear coursing through me. "Unless you believe what they do, too? That my spell somehow actually managed to alter the Fated Mates bond? Made you think you could love me when you really don't?"

He laughed and slid a hand over the console between the two car seats and squeezed my thigh possessively. "Are you kidding me? I've never counted myself as lucky until I met you, but I do now! And I don't care what brought us together. Your spell, or the wolves' version of Fate. All I know is that I want you, Ruby. And if you're crazy enough to want me back, then I'm taking that as a win and going with it."

I reached my hand over his and squeezed his fingers with mine. "I'm the lucky one."

We shared a smile, then I concentrated on the road. We had about twenty minutes until Halloween was over for another year. The clock was ticking, quite literally. Then I'd have to wait another twelve months for the right night, and for the strength to reverse the spell. I couldn't wait that long. I didn't want to be without Billy or Jackson for a whole year. I wouldn't survive it. I knew in my heart what we had was real, and I was willing to fight for it.

I drove carefully, but as quickly as possible, and pulled over into the church parking lot. Dust spun up in a cloud around the car as we flung open the doors and I grabbed the spell book. Together, we hurried toward the church.

"Why here?" Darren asked.

"This church is abandoned now," I explained as I ran. "Well, for religious purposes, anyway. My Coven owns it, although it was once a Catholic church. It was built on sacred ground." I headed around the rear of the church and made my way into the graveyard, to the tree that was planted at the very center of our power.

There was no one around anymore, although I was pretty sure that this place had been frequented all day. I looked up at the full moon and closed my eyes and focused on the waves of intense power permeating my skin and body.

"But why here? Why now?" Darren persisted, the warlock in him wanting to better understand.

I opened the book I'd carried from the car and found the page my friends and I had conjured from last Halloween. A thrill shot through me at seeing the words once more. I had to take a deep and steady breath to calm my nerves.

"It must be here, because the power in the earth will help amplify my magic. And why now? Same reason. It's Halloween, my birthday, the very same day we conducted the spell last year!" I explained hurriedly. I placed the spell book at my feet and flicked to the next page.

Now to reverse it.

"But why do you need more power, Ruby?" Darren asked, and once again, I could hear the worry in his voice.

I closed my eyes and raised my hands out in front of me. I was lucky that Darren wasn't trained in the art of magic, or he would no doubt realize that this spell was too much for me alone. "Because last year I had Bella and Tiffany with me to carry some of the weight of the spell. This time I'm doing it on my own. It's all me. Now *shhh...* I need to concentrate."

Raising my voice to the night sky, I began to chant until the wind around me picked up. I opened my eyes to witness the spell book rising off the ground in front of me, open to the page I needed, the words highlighted magically for me to read.

The magic of Halloween coursed through me from the ground up. I felt the earth move, heat, and strengthen me. I began the spell to reverse what I'd done last year. And it wasn't easy. I was asking the laws of attraction, of Fate, and of love, to no longer be in play. I was actively asking them to step away. To let go of what magic they'd already worked for me.

Last year, I had yearned for this spell to give me what I needed. Now, my heart was full to the point of breaking. I couldn't have this magic be the only reason my men stayed with me. They had to love me on their own. It was the only way any of us could truly know how we felt. And what was right mattered more than even the possibility of losing them.

Tears coursed down my cheeks as I said the spell in reverse, uttering it from the last line to the top. Pain charged through my body, starting from the soles of my feet, weaving up through my legs and into my core—like a poisonous vine climbing up through the earth and spreading it's coiling branches within my body. I wouldn't give up. I couldn't. The spell was seeking payment for what I had taken, and I would give it in my blood if that's what was needed.

My gaze clung to the words, to the lines on the page. I had to finish it no matter what. My arms shook with the strain, my back cramping up as I tried to remain standing upright. The pain soon blossomed from an unbearable ache into something much more tangible and sharp. Fire, like a raging inferno, lit up my muscles, and my belly heaved as my body rejected the spell I was trying to cast.

I groaned and retched, but still the book managed to stay suspended in the air, somehow helping me finish what I'd started a year ago. I didn't want to give up. That simply was not an option. This was the only way I could prove to my soul mates—to my men—that what they felt for me, and me for them, was real. *It truly was Fate!*

The pain raced down my arms, then seared up my spine, and would soon reach my head.

Darren was calling out to me, but he couldn't reach me.

Even behind my barely open eyes I could see the white light of All Hallows' power, feel the unnatural wind swirling all around me. I was enveloped in magic. And there was only one line left. One line of the spell to finish—to fix what I'd done. With all the strength I had left in my soul, and with my very last breath I uttered those few words, falling to my knees on the final one. And then everything went black.

Darren

WATCHING Ruby conduct her spell was one of the scariest things I've ever seen. My mate... my powerful, beautiful woman, surrounded by a magic vortex that had swirled around her like a tornado. It held me at bay while she'd conducted her spell, then as I was just about to charge into it, uncaring of what it would do to me, it dissipated.

I raced forward and dove as Ruby fainted, my heart leaping into my throat. I reached out and barely managed to get a hand under her head before she hit the ground.

"Ruby? Ruby! Wake up."

She didn't stir.

I swung her up into my arms and glared at that huge tome of a spell book we'd lugged out here. I was tempted to leave it on the ground, lifeless and dark, in the dirt.

But I knew that Ruby would be furious when she woke up, and the warlock part of me recognized an ancient, powerful spell book when I saw it.

So, I grabbed the book and put Ruby in her little car, then drove us back to her mother's empty house. Luckily the front door was unlocked when I tried the handle, and I brought Ruby straight in and lay her on the couch.

Then I sat on the worn-out love seat opposite the couch, staring at my mate, and waited for her mother to come home. Or for Ruby to wake up. Whatever came first.

I watched my beautiful mate and felt sick to my stomach. I should have found a way to prevent her from doing that spell. I should have convinced her that I would be enough for her. But deep inside, I didn't feel like I ever would be. She'd always miss Billy and Jackson, and I needed to do everything possible to make sure she had her heart's desire.

The front door opened suddenly and female voices chattering away burst into the silence surrounding me. Ruby's mother was home with her two friends.

I jumped to my feet, my heart pounding against my ribs. Part of me wanted to run away, but I forced my feet to stay put, to deal with whatever came out of this moment.

The three women stepped into the room, smiling and laughing together.

Then the laughter stopped.

"What the hell are you doing in here?" Ruby's mother growled at me, her eyebrows drawing together.

I indicated to Ruby, lying unconscious and supine on the couch. "Well, ah..."

The atmosphere switched instantly to one of concern.

"What happened to her?" Ruby's mother asked as she rushed to kneel beside her daughter. She put a hand to Ruby's forehead and looked at both of her palms as though inspecting the lines. Then she gasped. "She's in a magical sleep."

Ruby's mother, who looked uncannily like my mate, jumped to her feet and scowled at me, hands on her hips. Obviously, the red hair and temper ran in the family.

"What did you do to her, wolf?"

I'd never heard the word *wolf* used as an epithet before.

I swallowed against the feeling of being overwhelmed, bullied by a woman with red hair and fiery green eyes. "I didn't do anything. Ruby wanted to conduct a spell and I went with her."

"Where did you go?" she demanded.

"To the church."

There was deathly silence as the three older witches looked at each other.

Ruby's mother lifted her gaze to me, swallowing hard, her eyes shadowed with worry. "And what sort of spell did she cast?"

I inhaled sharply. "You don't know what they did last year?"

"Who?" one of the other women asked.

"Ruby and her two friends..." I began to tell them, then found my instincts flaring up saying to stop. I flicked my wrist. "Doesn't matter. Anyway, Ruby said that she and her two friends cast a spell that would make their soul mates find them. And when she told us about it tonight, Jackson flipped out and Ruby decided she wanted to undo the spell."

Her mother's eyes had gotten wider and wider, then she turned to her friends. "They did what? Holy shit on a stick... what are we going to do?"

"It's not a bad thing, is it?" I asked. "Surely..."

A cold dread washed over me as the witches turned to me.

Was Jackson right? Had Ruby and her friends messed with Fate? Or had they done something worse?

I glanced down at Ruby, lying unconscious on the couch.

Her mother bit her lip, tears forming in her eyes. "That spell is banned for a reason. It has brought heartache to anyone who's ever performed it, and it's an extremely difficult spell. I don't even know how the girls managed to pull it off in the first place."

I knew the answer to that. They'd used their birthdays, Halloween, and the pure strength of three witches who didn't want to be abandoned by their husbands the way they had been by their fathers.

But I didn't say that. Not here, to the three women at the core of their daughters' problems.

I only wanted to know one thing. "Is Ruby going to be okay, Mrs...."

"Uh, it's Sherie." Ruby's mother answered, but she didn't respond to my actual question, instead going back to assess Ruby on the couch once again, and then the three older witches began whispering amongst themselves.

I collapsed onto the love seat, my throat tight and my heart breaking. How cruel a world would it be to both find my mate and lose her in the same week?

CHAPTER 18

BILLY

We went to find Jackson's dad to ask him some questions, and we'd located him in a casual meeting with the elders.

Our news turned the meeting on its head.

"What?" Jackson's dad demanded, his temper flaring instantly.

Jackson glanced over at me.

I just stared back. I wasn't dealing with these guys. All three of them were Alpha born and my wolf didn't like going up against them.

"Our mate is..."

"What do you mean, *our* mate?" Tony demanded, one of the

other elders. "It's impossible for a woman to have more than one mate. It's... unnatural. Wrong. An abomination to the order of things."

I looked away so they didn't see my anger at that statement. There was nothing abnormal about our love for Ruby, nor hers for us.

Jackson went on. "Billy, Darren, and I all feel the same way about her. And believe me, I wish it wasn't true, but it is. We *all* feel the Fated Mate attraction to her."

"Then something must have gone terribly wrong!"

Jackson swallowed hard. "We think Ruby is half wolf shifter. Her mother told her that her father disappeared twenty-two years ago—before she was born."

Silence filled the room as the men looked at one another.

"The Manterri cousins," Jackson's grandfather said ominously.

"Those fucking witches!" Tony seethed. "I knew they did something to our men. No wonder our pack is dying out now."

"Calm down," Jackson's dad reasoned. "Our pack is not dying out. We have dozens of strong men. This is simply an opportunity to breed with other packs. To strengthen the purebred lines by introducing new blood."

Jackson glanced over at me; his jaw tight. "I don't want to share a mate," he managed to say.

My heart sank. I thought my cousin had wrapped his head around the idea of sharing Ruby with us. Didn't he realize that we would be a bigger, stronger family with her at the center? She'd be the radiant moon of our eternal night.

His dad looked at him. "You won't have to, son. The witch's magic won't work on you, not forever. We'll find you a wolf shifter mate, even if it means we need to travel further than the local packs. We'll make this right, boy."

I had to ask, to say something. I pushed my Beta wolf's natural submission away and forced the words from my throat. "But what of the mating bond? What if we bonded with Ruby tonight? How can such a thing be undone?"

Jackson turned to glare at me. "She cast a spell to make us fall in love with her, Billy. Surely that sort of bond can be broken."

"She *what*?" Jackson's father asked, his tone strained.

Jackson gave a quick rundown to the elders about what Ruby had said, and three of the elders exploded with anger.

I backed away toward the door and waited for Jackson to calm them down. If my stupid cousin was in denial, I didn't want to hear any more of this crap.

Finally, the growling and shouting about magic and witches died down, and Jackson began to back up toward the door. "Thank you for your time. I knew you'd have the answers," he said.

I tried not to roll my eyes as I inclined my head and followed Jackson out the door.

He marched back toward his house at speed.

"You know the elders are biased, right?" I called out to Jackson as I lengthened my stride to keep up with him. I didn't want to go back to my own bed in my parents' house, not when all I felt was turmoil and frustration. I'd rather sleep on Jackson's couch than be anywhere else right now. *Why was that?*

Unfortunately, I knew the answer. I'd mated with Ruby tonight, and therefore had bonded to the men she was mated to, as well. My home was now with the four of them. With Ruby the witch, Jackson the Alpha, and Darren the warlock wolf.

"They told us the truth," Jackson grunted. "That's more than what we got from her. And I was right. There's no such thing as three mates for one woman. We've been duped, cousin."

I sighed as I walked alongside him. There was no reasoning with him while his pig-headed, blustery Alpha was in control.

We entered Jackson's house, and he went straight for the refrigerator and beer.

"You want one?" he called out, already grabbing one for me.

I shook my head. I still hadn't recovered from our drinking session a few nights ago and despite this being one of the most stressful nights of my life, it was also one of the best. I wasn't joining him in commiseration drinks. I wanted to be sober and feel everything, the good and the bad. "Nah. I'm okay. I think I'll just go to bed. You still all right if I crash here?"

Jackson took a swig of his beer and nodded absently. "Yeah. But you know there's three bedrooms upstairs. I've set one of them up for visitors. You don't need to sleep on the couch. Help yourself."

I frowned at him. Visitors? Weird. Since when did he get visitors? "Okay. Thanks." I took a step toward the staircase. The ground shook. "Whoa." I darted for the banister, grabbing onto it as the whole house rocked on its very foundations.

"Earthquake," Jackson declared, gripping the countertop for stability.

I braced, waiting for another tremble. But nothing happened. "Damn." I ran a hand through my hair and shook myself. "What the hell was that?"

"I don't know, but—" Jackson clamped his hand suddenly over his heart and grimaced, gritting his teeth as though in pain.

I inhaled sharply, finding it harder to breathe. "What's happening? This isn't normal." *Something was wrong.* I met Jackson's confused gaze. "Do you think something's happened? With Ruby? Or Darren?" I asked, panic rising within me.

Jackson straightened up with a belligerent set to his jaw. "What do I care?"

"What do you care?" I repeated with a growl, getting to my feet so I could squarely glare at my pig-headed cousin. "You're not serious, are you?" *He couldn't be.*

Jackson frowned. "Billy, what you're feeling isn't real. It's just a spell. It's a lie."

I shook my head, my wolf tearing up inside me hard and fast. Something was wrong. *Very wrong.* I could feel it. Ruby was in trouble. "Ruby needs me. I'm going." I charged for the front door.

Jackson grabbed my arm, halting me. "Stay here. There's no reason to chase after her. She's not our mate. Not mine, not yours. She's just a witch, Billy."

I could feel the command in his words and my wolf wanted to submit to my Alpha. *No.* I wrenched my arm out of his grip. Not today. Not when Ruby could be in real danger. "Get this straight, Jackson. I don't care if she cast a spell on us. And I don't give a flying fuck if what I'm feeling isn't real. It feels like it is! And there are only three wolf shifter females of breeding age in the whole pack, cousin, so although you may get one of them, I sure as hell won't."

Jackson winced.

I knew none of the three available females were his mate. He'd never shown interest in any of them past a night or two in his bed.

"Yeah, see? You don't want any of them, do you?" I challenged. "Your father and all the other Alphas have their heads in the sand about this problem. Grandma is right. We either group up or breed outside the pack. Or both! Otherwise, we're going to live out our lives alone. A week ago, I thought I was okay with that. Now... I'm not. And if Ruby will still have me, I'm going to beg for forgiveness and hope she's gracious enough to give it."

Jackson frowned at me; conflict clear in his gaze. "You can't do that."

Once again, I felt the weight of his command on me. But I laughed at him. I laughed in his damn face, just as Darren would have. "Get over your ego, Jackson, and your pride while you're at it, or you're going to end up miserable and alone. I'm going to get our mate with or without your help. So, are you coming or not?"

I could see the warring emotions on his face, the worry, fear, and ego fighting one another. Then finally Jackson shook his head. "No. No way."

Stubborn idiot. I shrugged. "Fine by me." With my keys in my pocket, I jogged out the front door, ran all the way to my place, and jumped into my truck. It was late, well past midnight, now, so if nothing was wrong and Ruby was simply asleep, I would wait in the truck until morning. I wouldn't leave her side again. And then I would beg for forgiveness.

If something was wrong... I might need to beg for more than that.

~

Darren

I GLARED at Ruby's mother from my place on her sofa. "For the last time, I am not leaving," I repeated, for what felt like the thousandth time.

Sherie lifted her hand.

I growled in my throat. "Don't even think about it." If she dared to take me home again, I would only return. Again, and again. As many times as it took for the damn message to sink in. *I wasn't going anywhere.*

She looked me squarely in the eye, seemingly taking my measure. Then she nodded and went back to reading the ancient book that Ruby had been casting the spell from when she passed out.

After being unable to rouse her with any of their magic, Tiffany's and Bella's moms had gone home for the night. There was nothing more they could do.

I began to pace the living room, hands behind my back. "Could Bella or Tiffany help, do you think? They were, after all, part of the original spell from last year."

Sherie bit her lip, deep in thought. "If I can't find a way out of this by morning, then I'll contact them. But I don't want to endanger them if it's not necessary."

"I still don't understand why this was dangerous," I said. I knew only a little about magic, and this was well outside my sphere of knowledge.

Sherie sighed and looked up at me. "Because Ruby didn't have the magical ability to perform such a powerful spell on her own in the first place. I'm amazed they managed it at their age at all. But to take it back, to take that energy in on herself...? That would take more power than the original spell, even. And she didn't have it." Tears welled in her reddened eyes.

I swallowed hard. This was bad. "So, what are you saying? Does that mean she won't come out of this?" I gestured to where Ruby lay magically comatose on the sofa. Had the spell seriously leached her strength? Like, *all* her strength? As in… would it eventually wear her down and take her life? I didn't have the courage to ask Sherie straight out. Even thinking it was unbearable.

A tear slipped down Sherie's cheek.

My heart broke at the sight—a mother lost, and out of options, dutifully keeping vigil over her only child.

"It's possible," she said, a quiver to her voice. "It's possible. This was big. Far too big. It was too much…" she trailed off, stricken.

I couldn't stand it. "No. That cannot happen." I argued. I refused to believe it.

Sherie sobbed, no longer able to hold back the floodgates of her emotions. She closed the book on her lap as she leaned forward, finally consumed by tears. "Yes, it can." She whispered as she placed a hand over her mouth to stem the sobs.

I shook my head, frustration and impotence making my muscles shake. "No. No! We need to do something. Anything." All I could think of doing was to take her back to the church yard. To where her magic had imploded and ask whoever was out there and responsible for this, to give her back to us.

"You can't do anything," she choked, drying her eyes.

I stared at Sherie, then at my mate. "Yes, I can." I said resolutely. I walked over to the couch and scooped up Ruby with ease. "Let's take her back to the church. I'm sure the power there will help her." I had to do something. I wasn't just going to sit here and watch my precious mate fade away. I wouldn't.

Sherie jumped to her feet. "It's the middle of the night."

"I don't care." I carried my witch to the front door and nodded toward it. "Open it up, please."

Sherie hesitated momentarily uncertain then did as I asked, probably assuming I was doing this with or without her.

I stepped out into the cold night air.

She ducked around me and hurried down the driveway for her own car, then opened the back for me to put Ruby inside across the bench seat.

Another truck pulled up outside Ruby's house. One I instantly recognized.

Billy jumped out of the vehicle and when I glanced to the other side of the truck, there was no one.

"Where's Jackson?" I called out as I carefully lifted Ruby into the car.

Billy jogged over to me. "He's not coming." He frowned at me and looked over my shoulder at our comatose mate. "What the hell happened?"

"Get in and I'll explain." I jumped into the back of the car with Ruby.

Sherie slid in behind the steering wheel and glanced over at Billy in the passenger seat. "So, you're one of the three?"

Billy nodded. "Yep. I'm Billy."

"Sherie," she said, and the introductions were done.

We took off to the churchyard and Billy glanced over his shoulder, a look of worry on his face. "What happened?"

I stroked Ruby's magnificent red hair where her head lay in my lap. Her skin was even paler than normal and frighteningly cool to the touch. She was fading fast. "She reversed the spell they cast last year."

Billy's mouth dropped open. "But... why?"

I glared at him. "What do you mean, why? You know exactly why! To prove to us, and to herself, that we want her because she really is our Fated mate, and not just because she put a spell on us."

From the look of unmuted shock on Billy's face, I was pretty sure he still felt the same way I did—totally and utterly mated with her.

"How'd you know to come here, anyway?" I asked.

Billy grimaced. "Something strange happened when I was at Jackson's. The whole house shook like there was an earthquake or something. It practically knocked us on our asses."

"That was Ruby, or moreover, the effect of her spell. You should be completely cured of it now if it was the reason you wanted her," Sherie said.

I glanced at Billy.

He looked right back.

"Well?" I asked him, lifting my eyebrows with a mocking grimace of a smile on my face. "Feeling cured?"

Billy turned back around, ignoring my verbal jab, his face hard. "What do we need to do to wake her up?"

Sherie turned the car onto the gravel road that would take us to the church and shrugged. "Ask Darren. This is all his idea. I have no clue what we're going to do when we get there."

Billy waited for further explanation.

I didn't answer, I just clung to my mate. I didn't know what we were going to do when we arrived, but I knew we had to do *something* before the sun rose again and this Halloween night was officially over; taking any and all chance of saving Ruby with it.

JACKSON

After Billy left, I couldn't sleep. I couldn't even finish my damn beer. I paced my large, empty house, feeling sick to my stomach, my father's words whirling around in my head like a maelstrom.

He'd said that it had to be the magic that caused the three of us to want Ruby. That couldn't be real. That it was impossible for all three of us to mate with her, love her, and want her.

But damn, Billy wasn't wrong... it sure as hell felt real. I missed her so much that my heart hurt. My ribs felt like they were crushing my lungs, trying to squeeze the life out of me. I could barely breathe. I shook my arms and growled out my frustration. Maybe I needed to shift and go for another run. That usually sorted me out. But two in one night? That would be a first. *Nothing else to do.*

I began to strip, feeling the unstoppable and irrepressible urge to go. To shift. To escape the incessant voices in my human mind telling me that I was going to regret my decision tonight. That Ruby was my truly mate... My wolf missed her.

I dropped to the ground and let my wolf take over, his massive body ripping through mine. Fur sprouted through my skin, and my eyesight turned to black and white night vision. I growled loudly, feeling the prickle of premonition on the back of my neck. *What the hell?* I had to go. Now. I ran for the back door, bursting through it, and headed for the woods. From there I followed my nose and went straight to town. When I reached the edge of town, I sniffed the air again. My wolf bristled.

Wrong way. Keep going. I turned toward the woods once again, and in the direction of the church; the hallowed grounds of the witches' Coven. But why would I need to go there? Would I be lured into a trap? Put under another spell? Was this how the three cousins went missing those twenty-two years ago? Were they called to the sacred place of the witches only to fall prey to their enchantments?

Despite my misgivings and worries, I followed my heart. Every instinct in my wolf body told me where I needed to go. When I finally arrived, my paws slid to a halt on the gravel parking lot. There was a single car there but no one around. I stalked closer to the large family sedan. It wasn't a car I recognized, but the scents around the vehicle, were very much familiar to me.

Billy. Darren. Ruby. And another.

I crept around the car and followed their scents, my heart pounding in my chest. I refused to step into a trap. The witches would not get me. I was no one's prey. But then I saw them, out in the middle of the graveyard, surrounding a large tree: *my family.*

I pushed my legs to greater speeds, closing the distance between Billy and me before he even noticed my presence. As I skidded to an inelegant stop, and shifted back without thinking; wanting to be able to speak and communicate with them, to find out what was going on. I rose out of my animal state, standing on my two legs once again, naked as the day I was born.

A shocked gasp came from my left. "Do you mind?"

I glanced down to see one of the older witches that we'd met earlier in the night, glaring at me while she kneeled next to Ruby. She snapped her fingers, and I was suddenly wearing jeans. Faded, ripped, old, comfortable jeans.

I couldn't help smiling at her in gratitude. "Thanks."

Ruby lay on the ground, eyes closed, red hair fanned out around her. She wasn't moving.

"What the hell..." I dropped down to my knees in the dirt and grabbed Ruby's hand. "What happened to her?"

The woman kneeling next to her had to be Ruby's mom. She had the same red hair and a similar green angry gaze. "She reversed the spell she cast last year to appease you, and it almost killed her. Happy now?"

Fuck. Her words shot through me like molten bullets. I reeled back, pain pounding through me. "What do you mean?" I jumped to my feet and whirled around. "No. That's bullshit. She can't have. I still feel completely in love with her."

Darren took a step toward me, his eyes blazing in the darkness. "Yeah. Funny that, huh?"

I frowned at him. "So, this is all my fault?" It was. Of course, it was. She would never have attempted to reverse the spell if I hadn't questioned her motives—if I hadn't accused her of trying to manipulate Fate and our very lives.

The men around me didn't respond.

But I felt the crushing weight of responsibility fall heavily on my shoulders. "I didn't mean to hurt her. Not like this." I couldn't believe it. Had she really lifted the spell for me? To prove our love was real? "Why'd she do it?" I managed to ask, needing someone else to give voice to the thoughts plaguing me.

Darren crossed his arms over his chest. "To give you the choice. To ensure your free will. Taking the spell away would prove that it wasn't the reason you wanted her. She was trying to show us that we are meant to be together."

Heat prickled my eyes and my throat strained with emotion. "Really?"

"Yeah, really."

Ruby had neutralized the spell, but nothing at all had changed.

I still wanted her with every fiber of my being and my wolf still considered her his mate. Was that because we'd already mated that first time? Perhaps that was what was irreversible? I shook myself. To hell with it! I didn't fucking care anymore. This woman had sacrificed her wellbeing and risked her life just so I didn't feel trapped.

You idiot. I inhaled sharply against the pain and the feelings of betrayal that I'd caused. Then pushed the guilt aside. Recriminations would have to wait. I had to focus on Ruby. She's all that mattered now. "What can we do?" I asked the group, plaintively seeking their guidance. *My Alpha be damned!*

"We don't know," Darren said.

I walked toward Ruby's mother. "Can you use us?" I asked.

She stood up. "What do you mean?"

"I mean…" What *did* I mean? "I know nothing about magic, but it's still Halloween, technically. At least until the sun comes up, surely it still counts? This is a church on hallowed grounds, and you have three wolf shifters who love your daughter and are willing to die for her. Can't you work some sort of spell to coax her back to us?"

Ruby's mother looked from me, to Darren, and to Billy, then back again. "You don't mean…"

"We do," I stated, as the other two men rushed up to stand beside me, their silence a sign of their willingness to do anything for Ruby, just as I now knew I would. "Take whatever you need from me. From *us*. Just bring her back."

Ruby's mom searched my eyes for whatever answer she was looking for, then finally nodded. "All right. The three of you surround her. I'll see what I can find." She picked up a book from the ground and began flicking her hands around and speaking in a language I didn't understand.

Lights erupted around us, floating in the air, giving us all the ability to see.

The book lit up, the pages flipping by themselves now.

I turned away from the witch mother and stared down at my mate. She was as pale as milk, her lips as red as Snow White's. My heart squeezed tight, and my knees trembled beneath me. *What have I done?*

"Okay, I think I've got something," Ruby's mother announced. "I don't know if it's going to work, or honestly if it will harm you three, but are you willing to try?"

Darren and Billy looked at me, their jaws set. They nodded as one.

"Yes," I answered for all of us. "Do whatever you can. We're in this together. No matter what."

She began to chant, and the wind picked up, whirling around us as if it were alive.

I couldn't see anything in front of me, nor any changes in Ruby, but prickles of awareness moved up my spine like ants marching relentlessly up a hill.

Darren flinched.

Billy arched his back.

They were experiencing the same strange magical torture as well.

I closed my eyes against the pain that began to thread through my body like a needle and thread piercing my flesh, weaving up the backs of my legs, until it reached my spine.

Darren cried out in the haze of darkness and light, collapsing to the ground with a resounding thud.

I wanted to reach for him. To pull him up and take some of the pain for him. But he was too far away, and from what I could tell, he'd already passed out. I squeezed my eyes shut and clenched my hands into fists. The magic wouldn't break me. I refused to drop. I refused to fear it any longer. I would not give in. Especially not after what I'd done tonight; finding every damn excuse under the sun to try and sever the bond I'd created with my mate. And not after everything Ruby had gone through for us.

The pain moved around my waist.

Ruby's mum's voice quivered despite the powerful vortex as she called out. Was she still working the magic? Was the spell over yet?

I didn't want to open my eyes in case I broke something. This whole stupid mess we found ourselves in was my fault. If only I'd kept my stupid mouth shut. If only I'd thanked my lucky stars to have found a woman as beautiful, strong, and brave as Ruby.

The pain wriggled into my chest as though searching out my heart. Seeking my intentions and weighing my love. I roared at the fire inside of me, at the sheer, unrelenting intensity of it all.

Then Billy fell, the distinct *thump* of him landing next to me sounding loud in my ears.

I clenched my hands into tighter fists and hardened my jaw, hearing my teeth crack. My heart pounded faster. I wanted to vomit. To give in. To open my eyes and see if I could make the pain stop. Sweat rolled down my forehead but I refused to let up. *Pain is only temporary*, I reminded myself. *But Ruby is forever.* I opened my mouth, desperately panting for breath.

The witch's voice continued to call out, louder and louder seemingly commanding the very earth itself to hear her plea. If any of it was in English, I didn't understand a word of it.

Blood started to pour from my nose and ran over my lips. The metallic taste spilled into my mouth, and I shut my lips against the familiar tang. I swayed on my feet, then locked my knees by sheer force of will, to stop myself from falling. I wouldn't give in. *I wouldn't...*

And then it stopped, like someone just switched off a tap.

I went from spilling blood and feeling pain and prickling hot needles through my organs, to... nothing. Absolutely nothing. I was fine. My eyes sprung open; the maelstrom gone.

Darren and Billy remained on the ground in heaps. Neither moved, other than the slow rhythmic rise and fall of their chests. They'd passed out hard by the looks of things.

Between them lay Ruby, blinking her lovely green eyes.

"Ruby. Oh, my God. You're okay!" I moved toward her and fell to my knees, my exhausted body finally giving out. I crawled over to her, headless of the grass and cold dirt beneath my hands.

"Jackson... what are you...?" Ruby tried to sit up.

I pulled her into my arms, unable to hold back a second longer. I kissed her head and squeezed her tight, a lump forming in my throat. "I'm so sorry, Ruby. I should never... I don't..." I buried my face in her hair and inhaled the sweetness of her scent. I couldn't speak anymore. The words didn't matter right now anyway. She was alive.

Ruby's hand came up to stroke my hair.

Around us, the others roused and padded over to us.

I didn't let go. I wasn't sure if she would ever forgive me for what I'd said tonight, but I'd beg her for the chance to prove I could change. Billy had been right all along. The Council was bigoted and biased against witches, and I had to carve out my own path now—with my new family, and the woman Fate had chosen to be my mate. *No*, I caught myself. *Our mate.*

RUBY

I'd been dreaming about the weirdest things. Of wolves and a graveyard and flying. I think I'd been flying? But to where... I wasn't sure. I woke up suddenly, as though being shaken. I blinked my eyes open and lifted a hand to rub the sleep from my face.

"She's waking up!"

I heard a male voice and I gasped. *Who was that?* I tried to sit up, but my body wouldn't cooperate. "What the..." I opened my eyes fully, blinking rapidly to clear them as light poured in. Where was I? I glanced around, seeing all three of my mates, as well as my mother, all standing together. All in my living room—that was if I was correctly identifying the funky red wallpaper. "What are you guys doing here?" I asked, trying to sit up again, groaning with the strain of lifting my head.

"Here. Let me help you," Darren said, picking me up gently and sitting down so that I could lean against his chest.

I looked around at the anxious faces hovering over me.

Mom collapsed into the armchair, her hair wild and tangled.

Billy and Jackson stood nearby; their faces lined with stress.

"What happened?" I asked, then looked straight at my mother. "Mom? Are you okay?"

"Yes, honey. I'm okay," she said, though her voice trembled and there was an unmistakable sheen of tears glazing her eyes.

I glanced over at Billy and Jackson. "When did you guys get here?"

They didn't answer.

I began to feel frustrated. "Would someone *please* tell me what's going on?"

Mom jumped to her feet and frowned down at me, clearly at her wit's end. "What's going on is... you almost bloody died!"

"How?" I asked, my brows scrunching as I glanced around for a clue. "I don't remember anything."

Jackson stared at me, his eyes pools of sorrow. "What do you remember about last night?"

I frowned, searching my memory. "I came to your house..." *And we all made love.* "Then you told me that you..." *Didn't want me.* I trailed off and swallowed hard.

Jackson had told me that he didn't think I was his mate. That the magic I'd used to call him to me asking for my soul mate to find me had tricked them. He'd said that my magic had played with Fate. That what they felt for me wasn't real.

Jackson fell to his knees in front of me and crawled over the dark gray carpet, before grabbing one of my hands in his as he went up on one knee.

I stared at him. Why did he look like he was about to propose marriage or something? "What are you doing, Jackson?"

"I'm apologizing profusely for being such a jackass."

I tried not to smile, but he seemed so earnest. I knew how much it took for an Alpha to admit they were wrong. "So, you don't think I fooled you into mating with me anymore?"

My mother gasped and then flinched.

I purposely ignored her. I would deal with all the ramifications of *that* later.

He shook his head. "No. And I can't tell you how stupid I feel. That you would put your life in danger to prove to us that you're the right one for us."

I frowned. "I..." The memories came flooding back. Of me wanting to reverse the spell. Of taking Darren to the church yard, of the power and the pain I'd felt. My gaze shifted to my mother. "What happened?"

She smiled sadly. "You went into a magically induced coma, Ruby. You took too much on yourself. You know that don't you?"

I nodded, admitting to the truth. "Yes, I do. I knew the spell was too much for me, but I didn't want to risk Bella or Tiffany. They're my best friends. My Coven sisters."

"But you were willing to risk yourself?" Jackson asked, his tone accusatory.

I turned back to him. "I was trying to prove to you that I hadn't tricked you. And now you know. I removed the spell, and you're still here. So, I'm assuming it wasn't my spell that made you love me in the first place. It just helped us find each other." I glared at the big, stupid Alpha.

Jackson grimaced and nodded sheepishly.

Mom got up wearily from her seat and yawned. "You seem yourself again, so I'm going to bed. The sun will be up in about an hour, and I haven't slept a wink tonight. But you and I need to have a talk, Ruby. Later."

I swallowed hard. "Yes, Mom."

Mom smiled to the three men and left the room without another room.

My men gathered around me, stepping closer, becoming more protective.

I glanced up at Darren, who was holding me, but not speaking. "So, I pushed it a bit far, then?"

He kissed my hair and shook his head. "Way too far, baby. We almost lost you."

"But what brought me back?" I asked. "I'm starting to remember a little about going to church, but nothing after that. How did I even get back here?"

Darren sighed and twisted his fingers into mine. "Well, we drove back here after the church. But what got you to wake up is a whole different story. Your mother cast a spell to bring you back. She said you were in some sort of coma—that you'd drained yourself."

"What kind of spell?" I didn't know anything that was strong enough to return a person's soul after they'd gone burned out past the point of no return.

Darren answered. "I don't know. But she used us."

"*Used* you?" I repeated. Did he mean as anchors to this world? Or did she tap into their own magic? Their love for me?

Darren nodded. "Yeah. I'm sorry to admit that Billy and I passed out. But Jackson held out to the end. One advantage to being an Alpha, I suppose."

He said the words with a teasing tone, but I could hear the stress and admiration for Jackson's strength behind the words. Whatever they'd gone through together last night had not been pleasant. In fact, it sounded like it was downright horrendous, a real struggle of life and love triumphing over death.

I glanced toward Jackson. "So, does that mean that you still want me?" My gaze flicked to Billy. "You all do?"

Billy grabbed my hand and nodded fiercely. "Yes, I do. We all do."

Darren kissed my ear and whispered almost inaudibly, "Billy came back first. Then Jackson."

I swallowed hard, pain gripping my heart as I prepared myself to ask the next question. Their answer would determine so much about our future. I glanced back at Darren, the only one who'd stuck by me through it all, and the who would tell me the truth no matter what. "After they found out what had happened to me? Or..."

Billy shook his head, speaking for himself. "No, I could feel that something was wrong. Or maybe it was just my conscience eating me alive, I don't know. But I came back on my own. I had to. For you."

"And Jackson did, too, when it mattered most," Darren added. "I didn't have to call either of them. They both came looking for you."

Tears filled my eyes, blurring my vision. "You really want me as your mate, forever?" I asked, reaching out and gripping both Billy and Jackson, Darren's arms still around me.

"Yes. We do. We all do," Darren said, and began to kiss my face, then my cheek... then my lips...

Warmth swamped me and I closed my eyes, allowing myself to be dragged into the heated vortex of love that Darren, Billy, and Jackson had come together to create just for me.

EPILOGUE
RUBY

A month later.

I stared at Jackson as I slid my silk nightgown off my shoulders, letting it slide sensually down over my hips to whisper soundlessly to the ground.

"Are you sure about this, Ruby?" Jackson asked as he swallowed hard, his gaze intense as he drank me in.

I glanced around the large master bedroom and at my three men. "Yes. I'm sure."

We hadn't had sex since that first time on Halloween night, a month ago. We'd kissed and petted, and done things that made me wild with desire, but my men had patiently and nobly wanted to wait until I was fully healed before we engaged in anything more adventurous again.

And I loved them for it... but *damn*, was I desperate now—I needed them fiercely. I walked over to the huge bed we'd jammed into Jackson's house when we all moved in here a few weeks ago. It was two king-sized beds joined together, and I slept in the middle: the tasty meat in our proverbial shifter sandwich.

Crawling over the mattress, aware of their hot gazes on my naked ass, as I lay down on the pillow I'd occupied since moving in. "Please. Come to me," I begged them. "I need all of you." I wasn't sure exactly how this was going to work, but I'd been having a hazy recurring dream since the day after Halloween. Of all three men in my body at the same time. Mating with me. Completing me. Sealing our Fated connection.

There was no other word for it. I didn't feel as connected to them as I yearned to be, and tonight I would make it so. I'd been practicing my magic, and I had ways of helping them enter all of me.

The three men undressed quickly, jeans, shirts, and boots falling away in a tumbling pile of clothes. Then the three of them looked at one another.

And I saw the wolf flash in their eyes. My stomach tightened as my own wolf shifter genes, those that I was only beginning to recognize, called out to its mates.

They crawled onto the bed to join me.

Billy on my left.

Jackson on my right.

And Darren slid up the middle and lay on his belly, pushing open my thighs to stare down hungrily at my pussy.

I gasped and squirmed under his gaze, wishing the lights were off. Even now I still felt self-conscious, though I was slowly learning to accept that my beautiful harem of men loved me just the way I was.

He grinned at me and caressed the inside of my thighs with his thumbs. "Nuh-uh. No hiding now, my beautiful one," he coaxed.

Darren moved up, turning his head to kiss a trail of fire up the inside of one thigh, before licking a glistening path to my throbbing clit.

I grabbed his head and cried out as pleasure shot straight through my core like a flaming arrow.

But he didn't stop.

Then Jackson joined in, kissing my shoulder, and cupping my breast.

It was too much, and I cried out again, part of me fighting the erotic assault to my senses. It was positively impossible to process it all at once.

Billy ran his hand over my cheek and lifted my face, sliding in closer to press his lips against mine. Softly. Gently.

I groaned at the feather-light touch of his kiss, wanting more. Needing him to kiss me harder. I instinctively let go of Darren's hair, reaching up instead to entwine my fingers in Billy's hair. This was what I wanted. All three of my men surrounding me, loving me, all at once. Now it was time to let go of all control and to surrender completely to the flow of the storm surrounding me.

Darren suckled on my flesh and swiped his tongue across my sensitive pussy lips.

I broke free of Billy's kiss to moan aloud, tendrils of pure pleasure swirling through my legs toward my center. "Oh, please. Come up here," I said.

But the men seemed to ignore me as Darren pulled back to stand at the edge of the bed before he grabbed my ankles and dragged me down the mattress to meet him.

I giggled at the playfulness and the smile from Darren that came with it. "You guys have this all figured out, don't you?" I asked, noting the confident and coordinated way they were moving.

Billy crawled over to suckle my nipples, the unexpected heat of his mouth taking me by surprise.

I gasped as renewed fire spread through me.

"Yep. We've been planning this for a month," Darren said.

Jackson lay on the mattress next to me, then rolled to grab me around the waist. "Jump up on me, beautiful."

I rolled with him, squealing with delight at being tossed around. My pussy was soaking wet and as Jackson's hard cock jutted up beneath me. I tilted my hips and rubbed myself along his shaft, up and down, loving the feel of him against me.

He groaned suddenly.

I looked down, catching sight of the yellow wolf in his irises.

He lifted up and pulled me down, attaching his wet mouth over my nipples as my breasts spilled over.

I moaned, arching my back and thrusting my breasts so that he would suckle harder. Fingers explored me from behind and I found myself arching my back further to encourage the contact. I glanced over my shoulder and groaned.

Darren ran his hand over my searing flesh, circling my clit, before dipping inside me.

I cried out, every inch of me filled with greed and an insatiable need for their touch.

"Hurry up!" Jackson called.

Billy suddenly reappeared, coming back from the bathroom holding a tube of something.

"What's that?" I asked, squirming over Jackson.

Billy smiled. "It's lube. You wanted all three of us at once and I don't want to hurt you."

"So, you're going to..." *Fuck me in the ass.* I couldn't bring myself to say it. My cheeks flared with color.

Billy grinned and nodded, but thankfully didn't verbalize it.

I moaned as arousal swept through me once more and a soft wind rustled my hair. I looked up to find white magic swirling in the air around us. It moved in a leisurely circle, drawing us closer and closer together.

"I don't know what's going to happen," I panted.

Darren slid two fingers into my pussy, making my body ache for more.

"Neither do we," Jackson growled from beneath me, laying back on the bed, then grabbing hold of my hips. "You ready?"

I nodded with complete trust and let my men lead me.

Jackson grabbed hold of his cock and slid the large arrow-shaped head along my quivering pussy lips, then thrust up, joining us in one single, long stroke.

I gasped, sucking in breath, as lights exploded inside my mind. He was so big, and the sensation of fullness was beyond incredible.

I panted and moaned, feeling his body quake beneath my hands.

"Lean forward," Billy encouraged, pressing on my back so that I was forced to lean closer to Jackson.

I did as he directed, exposing my bare ass to him.

Billy moved his slicked-up fingers over me, the oil running over my skin and down my legs.

I tried not to focus too much on it, instead closing my eyes and enjoying the sensation of Jackson's cock inside me, thrusting in and out.

Then I felt Darren's hand on my chin, lifting my face.

I opened my eyes and stared at where he knelt next to Jackson on the bed, his cock in his hand, outstretched and waiting for my pouty little mouth. My stomach tightened with excitement and desire as I leaned forward, my tongue darting out to lick the hot, pink head of his cock.

He groaned and thrust his hips forward.

I parted my lips and welcomed him into my mouth, exploring his hot flesh with my tongue.

Billy rubbed his cock against my asshole.

I closed my eyes, consciously sending my magic down to the tight area he was about to enter. With time, I was confident I'd be able to enjoy taking all three of my men at once, without magical assistance. But tonight, I was going to cheat a little, and use my magic to stretch me, lube me up, and dull the pain.

Billy said to me, "Are you really sure about this, baby?"

I tried to nod, but my position made that difficult. I couldn't speak with a mouth full of cock, and I sure as hell wasn't letting Darren go. A thumbs-up seemed too ridiculous of a gesture, so I just wriggled my hips a little and pressed back. *Surely, I was being direct enough?*

Billy pressed forward, his hard, thick cock plowing my ass, stretching me, and completing my trifecta.

I closed my eyes on a moan as a wave of pleasure rolled over me, drowning me alive in ecstasy.

"Fuck... I'm not going to last long," Jackson groaned from beneath me, squeezing my hips and thrusting in and out in short, sharp, powerful bursts.

I let my mouth slip from Darren's cock momentarily. "You don't have to. Please. Come inside me. All of you." My cheeks flushed with a fiery blush at saying those words, but I didn't hesitate to re-open my mouth and get back to sucking on Darren's gorgeous, hard cock.

Billy growled from behind me, thrusting harder, deeper, and faster.

My magic mercifully held firm, so I relaxed into Jackson's grip and let my men ride away with me. My body became a living conduit of my love for them, and theirs for me. I could feel the wolf inside me rise, stretch, and howl to the moon. And then there was my magic. Weaving us all together, for all time.

I gasped around Darren as he began to thrust into my mouth and deep into my throat with a frenzied purpose.

Jackson and Billy groaned from beneath me and behind me.

"I'm going to come," Jackson growled.

"Me too," Billy snarled.

I squeezed them tightly with my pussy and ass, my pleasure rising and cresting within my belly, just waiting for the moment I could plunge and join them in mutual release.

Darren tried to pull away from me at the last moment.

I grabbed his shaft with my hand possessively and held him in.

"But..." he rasped.

I shook my head and sucked him deeper into my mouth, creating a tight seal with my lips, wanting absolutely all of him.

"Oh... God!" Jackson cried out, grabbing hold of my hips and thrusting up into me.

I waited for one soundless, timeless moment, and then it began. Jackson's seed pulsed into me, and I groaned as my own orgasm raged through me like wildfire. Pleasure swept through me, and I shuddered and shook over the top of him like a leaf.

"Fuck!" Billy swore, thrusting deep and releasing his seed up my ass.

Another round of orgasmic spasms hit me, and I would have screamed in ecstasy except for fact Darren's cock was still in my mouth.

"I'm..." Darren began to shake and stiffen.

I took him to the back of my throat and valiantly swallowed down his seed, making my body a vessel for all three of my mates at once—just like in my dream.

Finally, when the groans and gasps began to quieten, I let Darren's cock slip from my mouth and collapsed on Jackson's chest, panting and whimpering as the aftershocks of pleasure continued to rock through my body.

Billy retreated and rolled onto the bed next to me.

Jackson slipped free of my body a moment later as well.

I sighed happily, though I felt strangely empty now. I closed my eyes and reached for my men with both hands, needing contact.

With one hand on Billy, one hand on Darren, and my body resting on Jackson, I gathered and focused my happiness and magic and sent it out in a wave that rippled over my men.

I heard a moan and two gasps and smiled. "I love you. All of you. Thank you for making my dreams come true."

The men drew closer, and I let myself drift off into that magical place between wakefulness and sleep, to just float in the love all around me.

These beautiful, sexy men were my Halloween miracle for a Halloween-born witch.

Now, it was Bella's and Tiffany's turn to find theirs!

PACK MAGIC

PROLOGUE

Halloween night. One year and one month ago.

The day had come, the day I'd dreaded for so long. My twenty-first birthday and the night I'd promised my friends I'd join them in a spell that could destroy us all. Not that they knew it.

I was the reliable one. The witch that read the labels, looked into the warnings, and heeded the wisdom of the generations that came before us. Not Ruby and Tiffany. They were just excited, eager to see results; whereas I felt ill at ease with the whole situation.

I loved them to death—they were the closest things I'd ever had to sisters—but they had to know there was a reason this spell book had been hidden from us. The magic inside was powerful and payment would be demanded if the spell was ultimately successful.

"So, are we going to do this, or not?" Ruby asked, staring at Tiffany and I in turn. "Because there's no going back after this."

Her grin made my stomach drop.

Don't I know it.

Growing up fatherless, the only children of three heartbroken witches, had been hard on all of us. So, years ago, when Ruby had found an ancient spell book belonging to her mother hidden under the stairs, we'd read it. Of course. What kind of teenage daughter wouldn't?

In its pages we'd found an incantation that guaranteed we'd be able to avoid the heartbreak of our mothers before us. Like my best friends, at the time, I'd readily agreed to cast it with them, when we were old enough to want our soul mates to find us. And were powerful enough to pull it off.

After that night, I'd done my due diligence and dived into research, only to realize that terrible things happened to witches who dared to use this particular spell. It was a complicated incantation and required a significant well of power to bring to fruition. Which was why all three of us would need to do it. *Together.* There was no way that any of us could work this spell alone.

My friends believed the benefits far outweighed the risks... but I had my reservations.

The wind moved through the trees around us, rustling the leaves. A fall storm was well and truly on its way and if we were out here too much longer, we'd be caught in the rain. I'd asked my parents if Tiffany, Ruby, and I could use the cabin for our birthday. It was my grandparents' old house, and conveniently in the middle of nowhere.

It was perfect for secret nights like this one. No one would be able to see us here. And as long as we never uttered a word about our activities tonight, nobody would ever know that on our joint twenty-first birthday we'd conducted a spell to call our true loves into our lives.

Tiffany nodded fiercely, agreeing that it was time to start the spell.

I bit my lip as anxiety raced through me. *Shit.* I couldn't be the one to pull out and disappoint my two favorite people in the world.

Ruby rolled her eyes at me. "Come on, Bella. You know we can't do this without you."

She meant that quite literally, unfortunately. Despite my personality falling toward the quieter, more bookwormish type, I was a decidedly powerful witch and without my magic, Tiffany and Ruby couldn't manage a spell of this magnitude.

I frowned and swallowed hard against the worry that tightened my chest. I narrowed my eyes at her, mimicking her expression.

Ruby pouted at me, her gaze becoming plaintive. "Come on, Bella. *Please.*"

I sighed internally. We'd been talking about this spell for years, planning every part of the complex incantation. Waiting until the night we were old enough, powerful enough, and gutsy enough to pull it off.

Despite my better judgement a stubborn resolve settled over me. I couldn't disappoint my two friends. Not now. "Okay, Ruby. I'm in. Let's do this."

Ruby grabbed our hands, and Tiffany followed suit, reaching for my free hand to form a perfect triangle of strength.

We were three witches born on the same day, the most powerful and sacred day of the year for our kind: All Hallows' Eve. We'd literally grown up together, strong, bonded, and loyal to a fault. Our mothers always said we were Fated—blessed—and I believed it.

We clasped hands and glanced down at the ancient book that lay spread open on the ground between us, the spell book Ruby had found years ago, hidden amongst her mother's things.

Fear whistled through me, but I pushed it down and away. This spell would take everything I had, and for these girls—my sisters—I would give it.

As a small coven, a trio of witches, we began to chant in the ancient language of the warlocks and witches that had come before us, a dialect long lost to time and memory.

I concentrated hard on my lines, reading from the book. I hadn't memorized the spell out of fear. I spoke my part and my friends said theirs. Each verse of the spell was a call to the magic that rippled in our veins—to Fate—and most of all, to the unconditional love that we so desperately desired and craved.

Over and over, we chanted our words, our rhythm growing, while the magic in our blood, in our very ancestry, simmered, ready to burst at the seams.

The stress of the spell pummeled down upon us, and I glanced at my best friends.

Tiffany's lips were turned down into a frown.

And Ruby had sweat rolling down her face.

I couldn't stop the spell now, and I wouldn't. In fact, I pushed harder, channeling more of my own power into it. I could feel the words draining my energy at a frightening rate, but pressing my heels into the grass beneath me, I grounded myself and pushed back.

With my strength I knew I could handle more than my fair share of the load. So, I did. I just hoped that Tiffany and Ruby would make it to the end of the spell if I successfully carried most of the pressure. We couldn't stop now, even if we wanted to. There were far too many risks associated with this spell, and not finishing it was just as treacherous. The spell must be completed!

The power of our combined magic swirled around us, alive and violent like a hurricane. I clung to the hope that this spell offered us. It would change our destinies. After this night, we'd never end up like our mothers—abandoned and alone. That in itself had to be worth whatever payment the spell demanded, surely?

The ancient book floated in the space between us, glowing and powerful. I watched it defy gravity with a growing sense of dread.

Ruby opened her eyes, her gaze locked on the book, too.

Tiff grinned.

Relief shot through me. Obviously, what I was doing was working! They were handling the smaller parts of the spell they were carrying.

Buoyed on, we chanted louder, the words in our hearts building naturally as the spell came to a great crescendo. I stared in awe at our joined hands as a bright white light shone between our clenched fingers.

There was a sudden surge of power, and a growing sense of urgency filled the air. We were almost there! We uttered the final words of the spell as a group. The white magic we'd conjured shot into the air above our heads with a cosmic *boom*, exploding in a spectacular eruption of color, like fireworks, sparkling against the dark night sky.

The impact of the explosion blew us back with surprising force. I landed with a heavy thump on the grass, my magic draining away like sand through an hourglass until I could barely open my eyes. I closed my eyes and permitted myself a moment of rest. *The spell had worked.* It must have. I definitely wouldn't have felt so terrible and weak, if it hadn't.

I just needed another minute to collect myself.

"Is that it?" Ruby asked.

Before I could answer, the spell book that had been hovering in the air dropped and landed in the dirt between us with a heavy thump. The front cover closed by itself, all signs of magic, gone.

Tiffany jumped up, groaning as she brushed the dirt from her tight pants.

I took a deep breath, readying myself to stand. I didn't want my friends to know just how much of the spell I'd taken on myself. They'd feel guilty if they knew, and it wasn't their fault that they weren't as naturally strong I was.

Ruby began to rise.

I forced myself to my feet, too. I staggered a little, but recovered quickly and the other two didn't seem to notice. Relief filled me. The moment I'd been dreading all these years was finally over. Now, all we had to do was wait for the spell to come to fruition. For the men—our men—to seek us out.

"So... back to the house for a celebratory drink?" Ruby asked.

I sighed. I seriously needed sleep, but I couldn't be a spoilsport. *It was our twenty-first birthday after all.*

"Sounds like a plan," Tiffany said, flicking her long blonde hair over her shoulder.

Then together we turned and trekked our way back to the cabin.

Once inside, we flicked on the lights and used our magic to mix up cocktails with the colors of the sunset—red, orange, yellow, and a splash of dusky purple.

"Perfect," Ruby said as she picked up her glass that had been resting on the counter.

Tiffany and I plucked up our drinks as well and clinked them with Ruby's.

"Happy birthday," we chorused.

I'd always personally loved sharing a birthday with my two best friends. I never fancied being the center of attention, but Ruby and Tiffany sure did.

We all took a sip of our first legal drink and mutually grimaced at the sheer amount of liquor Ruby had poured into the mix. I gasped, my throat burning.

"Wow, that's strong," Tiff said, blinking rapidly as if to clear her eyes of the burning vapor.

I gulped awkwardly and couched, shuddering before I set the drink back down firmly on the counter. I needed something to eat and soon. My energy was about to burn out completely like a spent candle.

With what little magic I had left, I took a quick breath and waved my hand over the table in front of us, conjuring up a whole feast of savory and sweet snacks to celebrate. Chips, chocolate cake, cookies, and crackers with cheese littered the surface in front of us.

I slumped, exhausted, then slid onto a stool at the kitchen counter. I was done.

"Oh, perfect. Thanks, Belle!" Ruby said, grabbing a handful of chips and stuffing them in her mouth without an ounce of shame.

I sighed and forced myself to pick up some candy and suck on it. I needed the sugar hit in a big way.

"What's up, Bell-Bell?" Ruby asked me.

I glanced at my friend. Her brow was furrowed. She was worried about me.

"Do you think it worked?" I managed to ask, the only thing I could think of to say.

Ruby shrugged. "I don't know. I hope so. I mean, I guess we'll find out."

We certainly would...

"I hope so, too!" Tiffany said, her tone exasperated. "We've only been planning this since forever."

Ruby summoned some extra stools, and then the other two sat down with me, around our tasty birthday spread.

We chatted and ate, drank and laughed, celebrating the fact we had our whole lives ahead of us. I was at college, the only one of the three of us, but still wasn't sure what I wanted to do with my degree just yet.

I leaned forward and rested some of my weight on the counter, happy to let Tiffany and Ruby carry the conversation while I rested a little.

It was kind of strange to think that somewhere out there, our magic was finding its way to our soul mates. I'd never even dated a guy before, so what was I going to do with the one that wanted to marry me? Would I know him on sight? Would he recognize that I was the right woman for him straight away, or would the normal laws of dating apply? Would it just give us the opportunity to figure it all out once we'd met? Or would it be an instant, Fated love kind of thing?

I had a ton of questions, and not a lot of answers or information to go on. But what I did know for sure was, I wasn't dating anyone at all until my soul mate showed up. I would trust in our magic and wait for the spell to manifest. I wouldn't end up like my mother; sad and alone, and still desperately pining after the man who had abandoned her over twenty years ago.

I wouldn't. This love spell was powerful and off limits for a reason. I had to believe that it would see to it—that it would fulfil its promise. All I had to do, just like my friends, was be patient and endure the waiting game. No matter how long it took.

CHAPTER 1
BELLA

A few days before Thanksgiving.

I glanced around Kathy's lounge room, looking from Ruby to Tiffany, then back at our mothers lined up on each side of the room. I could have cut the tension in the room with a knife. Although, seeing as we were all witches, a relaxing spell would probably have been better for the stress.

"Girls, you have to understand that what you did was dangerous," Ruby's mother began to lecture.

I stifled the sigh that rose in my chest. I knew what was coming.

We'd been called to Ruby's house under the pretense of having 'a chat' but really, our moms just wanted to yell at us for the love spell we'd cast last year on Halloween.

Sherie pushed up from the couch where she'd been sitting and moved to the front of the lounge room, standing before the cold fireplace. "Every person who has ever worked that spell has had to endure dire consequences. Just look at what happened to Ruby." She pointed to her daughter as though our friend's happiness—having found not one, but *three* Fated Mates—was a bad thing.

I wanted to refute her claims that we'd done something terrible, but I kept my mouth shut. I wasn't ready to jump into the fray of this lecture yet. I needed more information before commenting.

Tiffany, on the other hand, never thought twice before butting in with her opinion. "You're blaming us for what happened to Ruby?" She said as she jumped to her feet to confront our moms. "Rubys happy! She found her soul mates. But if you really want to blame someone for us casting that spell, how about we blame you three for the fact we had to do it in the first place!"

Damn, we got there quick. I grimaced. This was not going to be pretty.

Sherie dropped down onto the couch next to my mom and their faces drained of color.

My mom glanced over at me. "What does she mean, Bella?"

All five witches turned to me.

A flood of heat coursed up my face and I felt even more uncomfortable—if that was even possible. I shrunk back into the sofa. I didn't want to have this conversation. It was one I'd avoided all my life. I gestured at Tiffany with anxiety. "She can explain." I said quickly.

Tiffany put both hands on her hips and stared down at our moms. "How can you not put two and two together? Seriously? All three of us have grown up without fathers. We've had to grow up seeing you all single and miserable our whole lives and it's been hard! We don't want that for ourselves or our children. We want..." Tiffany stopped, her voice stuttering to a halt as she swallowed hard, a sheen of tears in her eyes as anger gave way to sadness.

Ruby wasn't moving a muscle, and I could see how close to tears she was as well.

Damn. It was my turn to speak. I had to explain and try to salvage this shitty situation we'd found ourselves in. I stood up and reached for Tiffany's hand, threading my fingers in between hers and squeezing tight. "We found the spell book a few years ago," I began. Well, technically, Ruby had, but there was no way I was laying the blame on her. "And it said that the spell would attract our true soul mates to us. None of us wanted to date anyone else except the men we're meant to marry. And after watching the three of you survive the past twenty years heartbroken and alone, we wanted to avoid that, if it was possible."

Mom stared at me; her mouth open. "But, Bella, you know how much power is required for a spell like that. It was dangerous. How did you even pull it off?"

"There's three of us," Ruby said, standing up and joining in the conversation. "We did it together."

My mom's gaze slid to Ruby, then back to me as though Ruby hadn't spoken at all. "Bella? How'd you do it?" she repeated.

I bit my lip. "Um, I just helped as much as I could."

"You mean, you shouldered more than your fair share?" my mother accused, her mouth twisting in a way that showed both concern and a measure of pride.

I shrugged and licked my lips, trying to brush the accusation aside. "We all did the best we could, Mom."

Ruby reached out and grabbed my hand, the one that wasn't already holding Tiffany's. "What did you do, Bella?" she pressed, her brow furrowed.

I shook my head. "Nothing special. The spell just required a lot more power than I'd originally estimated, and I needed to throw in a little more than I expected. That's all."

Ruby stared at me, then the light of comprehension dawned in her eyes. "No wonder I didn't have a hope of undoing the spell without you."

I squeezed her hand, offering her my support in return. "But you did! You managed it without any help at all."

She chuckled awkwardly. "Maybe, but it almost killed me."

I inhaled sharply, pain squeezing my chest at the thought of losing one of my best friends. "Please don't do anything like that ever again. You could have asked me. I would have helped you with anything you needed then, and I still would, now."

"I know, but there wasn't time. Well, I didn't think there was anyway." Ruby turned back to our mothers again. "Does that mean that Bella is going to cop more of these so-called 'consequences' for using the spell?"

I bloody hope not.

The three mothers exchanged glances, worry clear in the lines on their pale faces.

My heart dropped. "Great."

Mom looked to me. "Not necessarily. I'm more interested in the fact that you have more power than Ruby and Tiffany. I mean, I've always known of course, but..."

"Does this have something to do with the fact that my father was a wolf shifter?" Ruby burst out, shocking the whole room into silence.

I gasped and turned to stare at her. "Seriously? When did you find that out?"

How could that be? *None of us could shift.* We were all full witches... weren't we?

"Mom told me, the night of Halloween," Ruby said, then grimaced in apology. "Sorry I haven't caught you up on that. My brain's been a bit scrambled with everything's that happened." She made a whirling signal next to her head with her fingers.

I nodded, a shiver of premonition sliding down my spine. I turned back to our parental units. "Mom..."

She gulped visibly. "Yes, Bella?"

"Was my father a warlock?" I'd been told he was, and it had always made sense that he would have been. Even now. I was more powerful than Ruby, and Tiffany too for that matter. My magic gave me the sense that I wasn't going to like the answer that was about to spill out of my mother's mouth.

Tiffany seemed to understand why I was asking and rounded on her own mother as well. "What about my sperm donor, then?" she asked boldly.

I flinched at her choice of words, but Tiffany had always used humor to deflect from anything serious or hurtful.

Mom, Sherie, and Kathy looked at each other, their eyes wide and wary.

Oh no, this was a secret they all shared, which could only mean...

"Mom," I said, adopting my serious tone of voice. "Please answer the question. Who, or more likely *what* species, were our fathers? You all led us to believe they were warlocks."

Mom waved her hands at us. "Girls, sit down, or we'll stand up. But please don't stand over us. We aren't the ones in trouble here."

I raised my eyebrows. *We'll see about that.* I tugged at Tiffany and Bella. "Come on. Let's sit."

Tiffany's barely leashed anger vibrated through the room in response.

"Let's hear them out." I tugged harder and managed to get both of my friends to sit their butts back down onto the sofa beside me. I knew beyond a shadow of a doubt that the answer to this question was going to change the course of our lives forever. "Okay, we're listening. So, tell us," I said, clenching my teeth in preparation for what was to come.

Sherie stood up and paced to the front of the room again. "I'll go first," she said. "Because Ruby already knows about her parentage. Her father was a wolf shifter and a pure blood from what I understand, which is why I was worried that she might have exhibited signs of being part wolf when she was younger. But as it turns out, she never did, and won't now that she's reached full maturity. But when she brought home a wolf shifter for a soul mate, it made sense to me."

Sherie's lips kinked up at the sides. "I didn't expect three of them of course but considering the curse—I shouldn't have been surprised."

"What curse?" I asked, narrowing my eyes.

Sherie slapped a hand over her mouth suddenly as though she'd revealed more than she was meant to, her eyes wide and panicked.

"Great, even more secrets," I muttered under my breath.

My mom stood up, directing Sherie to take a seat. "We can talk about that later. First things first."

Mom took a deep, steadying breath and stared at me, then Tiffany. "I think the easiest way is to explain is that all three of your fathers... were first cousins."

Ruby jumped to her feet. "They were what?" She whirled on us. "Do you know what that means?" she said, her face pink with excitement and wonder. "We all have wolf shifter dads, which means we could all have soul mates from the pack! Or you guys might even have three like me." Ruby sounded positively elated by the idea and clapped her hands.

My own immediate reaction was quite different. My stomach twisted and lurched, upset by the new revelation. How I saw myself, my genetic makeup, had been turned on its head in a heartbeat. I was part wolf shifter. I wasn't a real, pure-blooded witch. *Damn it.*

Tiffany stood up, grinning like a loon. She obviously didn't mind the idea of mixed blood. "Three wolf shifter mates sounds good to me."

I could only see one silver lining to this dark cloud. "You know what it also means?" I said to them, getting slowly to my feet.

Now our sister-like friendship made more sense than ever before. No wonder we loved each other so much and felt so connected, even though we weren't related. *Or we hadn't thought we were, anyway.*

"What?" Ruby asked, her expression bright.

"We're related," I said. "If our fathers were all first cousins, then we're officially second cousins, all of us." I'd always thought of these two girls as my soul sisters, my best friends. Now, they were more. *They were literally family.*

Tiffany cried out happily and hugged Ruby and me to her.

I let my cousins, my best friends, hold me tightly, but inside, my heart was aching. I felt betrayed. My mother had lied to me all these years. I had wolf shifter in my blood.

A rough cough made us break our embrace. It was my mom.

"I'm glad you're all happy about your relationship because it's a very special bond, even without the blood link. We always believed that the three of you were meant to be. Your linked birthdays meant that you were supposed to be born together."

"But...?" I led her to continue. I had a feeling there was more to it.

Mom smiled at me. "But your father, Bella, *was* part warlock. He was related to..." she desperately glanced at Sherie for help.

"Darren," Sherie offered.

Ruby's mate! The one with one quarter warlock genes, and three quarters wolf shifter.

"Yes, thank you. Darren, I believe," Mom finished.

Ruby looked at me. "Really? Well, that's kind of cool. Our kids are going to have all sorts of crossed over relationships at this rate."

I swallowed hard. We weren't finished yet. "So, tell me the real story of my father then. Did he actually abandon you like you always said?"

Sherie stood up next to my mom. "All three of us were dating your fathers in secret. We knew the Coven wouldn't understand. The high warlock hated the wolf shifter packs in the area. We weren't allowed to go anywhere near them."

"Then how did you even meet?" I asked. Then I waved my hand. "No. Forget that part. I don't care." I shook my head, angry. The details didn't matter. What mattered was that everything I'd been told all my life was a damn lie. "So, you were actually dating my father. You weren't abandoned by some random stranger?" I lashed out. Which in retrospect was a much better tale and made more sense as to why my mother had never dated anyone else.

My mother shook her head slowly. "No. I was totally in love with him. He was half wolf shifter and half warlock. His mother was a witch the pack had taken in, so I don't know why our high warlock hated wolf shifters so much when they seemed to be accepting of us at the time."

I filed that piece of information away for another day. Maybe the witch who'd married the shifter all those years ago had been related to the high warlock? Or was meant to marry him and chose a shifter instead? Who knew at this point? They were all gone, or dead. I wouldn't be able to ask them.

"So, what happened? Why did they disappear?" That seemed to be the most pertinent part of the story for me. I wanted to know what had happened to our fathers. All three of them.

Tiffany grabbed my hand. "Hang on. Can we back it up? Can I just ask if my dad's a half warlock too?"

I smiled and nodded, but I already knew the answer. There was a reason I was more powerful than Tiffany and Ruby. It was because of my father's mixed blood—he had the most warlock in him.

Tiffany's mom turned to her. "Your dad was a full wolf shifter, honey. Similar to... Billy, I believe. He was Ruby's father's Beta."

The spell and the people involved were all turning full circle. Our three fathers were just like Ruby's triad: two full wolf shifters and a half breed. Now Tiffany and I had to wait to see what men were sent our way. Would we get three as well? Or just one?

My stomach clenched. I wasn't sure I could handle three. That seemed... unmanageable. I still wasn't sure how Ruby did it.

"And you two dated as well?" Tiffany asked.

Tiffany's mom nodded, though her cheeks flared red.

"Mom!" Tiffany said. "Don't lie to me."

"I'm not lying!" Kathy retorted earnestly. "It's just that we'd only just started dating when he disappeared. And I conceived you the very first time we slept together, so I always felt like you were meant to be, Tiffany. Always."

Tiffany slumped toward the couch.

I sighed. There was just too much information coming at us. Too many emotions. And yet I couldn't stop now. I needed to know every-thing—at least all the major stuff. I focused on my mother once more.

"Mom, tell me what happened when our fathers disappeared. *Please.* Has it got something to do with the curse Sherie mentioned before?"

Our three moms joined together again presenting a united front, as though afraid of what was coming next.

I stood firm. I needed to know this. What had happened to my father? Why had my mother spent twenty years alone? Why had I never met him? Or heard his voice? Was even he alive?

When they didn't answer, I persisted. "You all told us that they abandoned you. So, all our lives we've assumed that you had one-night stands with some random assholes who didn't care about you. And those supposed realities drove us to perform the soul mate spell." I glared at each mother, letting the truth of that sink in. "But it seems that was all a lie. You loved them and they loved you. So, our misery was all for nothing. We deserve the truth. So, tell us what happened. Are they still alive? Did they die?"

Ruby gasped, grabbing hold of Tiffany and me as though we were her lifelines or anchor points. "Oh my God, I know who they are! Or were... or whatever."

"Tell me," I said instantly, since my mom didn't seem to want to be honest or more forthcoming.

Ruby's eyes were alight with excitement. "They're the cousins who went missing twenty-two years ago! Jackson and Billy told me about them. Ever since that night, not a single female has been born to the pack. They have all these strong males and no-one to mate with!"

I twisted around to stare at our three mothers, who all looked guilty as hell. I met my mother's gaze defiantly and crossed my arms over my chest. "Sounds like a bloody curse to me."

CHAPTER 2
BELLA

I tapped my foot impatiently and waited for my mother to tell me I was wrong. But I wasn't wrong. I had a feeling for these sorts of things, and although I was never arrogant about my magic—after all, it was a gift, not something to take for granted—I could feel the premonition and the rightness of my claim.

"Who cursed them?" I asked. "The high warlock?" That sort of spell, especially one big enough to spread through an entire town of people, could only be performed by someone much more powerful than your everyday witch. Then another thought occurred to me. "Or was it the elders? The whole Coven? Tell me."

If my father, Ruby's father, and Tiffany's father had been taken from us because of some misguided curse, I wanted to damn well know about it. I, scratch that, *we* had the right to know!

Ruby slid her hand over my arm. "Calm down, Bella."

I shook her off. "Don't you realize what this means? Our fathers could still be alive!" I twisted back around to stare at our mothers. "Where are they?"

My mom pulled the other moms to their feet, so all six of us were now standing in the small lounge room. It was squashy, and hot, and tempers were flaring.

But we needed to know this.

I needed to know.

"We don't know. When we found out we were pregnant, all of us, we were terrified. We knew the coven would hate it, so we..." Kathy trailed off.

"You went to the high warlock, didn't you?" I accused, knowing exactly where this conversation was going. "Oh, no."

The high warlock, when he came into his role, was given the power of the Coven, the land, and the centuries of magic that was naturally instilled in our people. He could have done anything to us—or our fathers. Literally *anything*.

My mom grabbed my hand, her brows furrowed. "We didn't know what was going to happen, so we went to him seeking help. He'd always been like a father to us, old and wise."

I swallowed hard, strangely aware that I was the leading this conversation. Ruby and Tiffany had faded into the background, observing and listening in relative silence. This was certainly not a role I was used to, or remotely comfortable with, but I pushed on, determined to get to the bottom of this—to the truth, no matter how painful it might prove to be. "And what did he do?" I asked calmly, though I wasn't feeling it at all.

"He offered to help," Mom said, biting her lip the way I did when I was nervous. "He said we could perform a spell to suppress your wolf shifter genes so that you would be accepted by our Coven as full witches."

I could imagine our mothers believing that—they'd been young and scared after all—but obviously something else had gone on.

I clenched my teeth together. "Then what happened?"

My mom's hands shook as she ran her fingers through the tangle of her long hair. "The high warlock conducted his spell, calling on our magic to help him finalize the incantation. We didn't think much of it, to be honest. We just wanted our babies to be healthy. But when we went looking for our secret lovers to tell them about you three, our little miracles... they were gone."

"Gone?" Ruby repeated. "Gone, where exactly?"

Sherie shrugged. "We don't know. We spent months looking for them, and waited, hoping they'd come back—but they never did. And the high warlock never really explained to us what his spell specifically did beyond suppression, or if it did something more than he'd claimed."

Kathy jumped into the discussion. "When none of you shifted during your teenage years, we assumed the spell had done just what he promised, but the timing of the men disappearing... It's always worried us."

"So, then, did you ask him if he did something else?" Ruby asked.

"Of course, we did. Many times, hon," Sherie said. "The high warlock only reiterated that the spell simply stopped our babies from shifting; and if our men had disappeared on us, then that was merely a reflection on their character. But it was..."

"Too coincidental?" I asked, frustrated.

"Especially for all three to go missing at the same time," Ruby added. "What are the odds of that actually happening?"

I shook my head. *Too small to calculate.* Especially considering they were all wolf shifters, paranormal beings renowned for their pack behaviors and lifestyle. Family was integral to their very genetics, to their hierarchical structure. I felt sick. My father had been taken from me. A man who could have loved me and helped guide me through life.

He could have continued to love my mother. Our lives would have been so entirely different if he'd been around.

"Do you think they might still be alive?" Tiffany asked quietly, the usual humor and heat behind her words, gone. If anything, she sounded sad. And genuinely more so than I'd ever heard of her being before.

I glanced over at our moms, not wanting to weigh in myself.

Sherie began to speak, *umming* and *ahhing* in a way that told me she had no actual idea of how to respond, probably because she didn't know the truth.

"Hang on a second!" Ruby said, her green eyes glittering. "Did you say my father was an Alpha wolf, Mom?"

Sherie nodded, her lips pursed. "I think so. Like Jackson. Why?"

"Because I saw one, once. When I was little. In the woods near the church. He was big, and gray, and I knew he was an Alpha from the way he moved and his smell. Don't ask me how—I just *knew*. Then, when I met Jackson, I picked up on the same scent coming from him, because he smelled the same. Just like an Alpha."

The whole room fell quiet, not one of us daring to breathe in case the spell around her words popped like an ephemeral bubble.

"You..." Sherie was peering at Ruby as though she'd never laid eyes on her daughter before. She swallowed hard, then tried again. "You saw a wolf in the woods and never told me?"

I shivered, feeling the magic of the truth weaving through the room. We'd always suspected our moms used a spell to make us tell them the truth. And now it was just a habit for us to always tell them. They didn't need to command it anymore.

Ruby shrugged. "I wasn't scared or anything at the time. He seemed strong and nice, in a way. And I knew there were wolf shifters just outside town, so I guessed that he was one of them, and went on my way. I was only like, six or seven. I didn't think it was important."

We were all staring at Ruby now, our gazes locked on her like she was a tasty hot chip, and we were starving seagulls.

Why wasn't she freaking out? Didn't she realize that she probably met her father? The good news was he was probably still alive, or at least had been fifteen years ago. And if he was still alive, then maybe there was a chance that my dad, and Tiffany's dad, were too!

"What?" Ruby demanded, looking around our group as though we were the ones that had gone insane, and not her.

"I've got to sit down," Sherie said, staggering backwards before half falling onto the couch behind her.

"We always thought it was possible, Sherie. You know that," Mom said.

"You always thought what was possible?" I asked my mom. "That they were alive? Or..."

She shook her head. "No, that they had shifted into their wolf forms and weren't able to shift back again."

"What do you mean?" Ruby asked, folding her arms.

"Well, that explained how they were suddenly gone, and how no-one could find them," Kathy said.

"Although, if that was the case, why wouldn't they go back to the pack, or us?" Sherie went on. "Why would they leave?"

"Hang on a second," Ruby said, holding up her hands suddenly, obviously having finally clued into what we were all thinking. "Could that gray wolf I saw when I was little... could that really have been... my father? I just thought since I was related to an Alpha, and that I could recognize their genetics... It never occurred to me that it could have actually been my..." Her eyes shimmered with unshed tears.

It made my throat clog up to see my friend struggle to speak and find the words to say that she may have met her father and not even known it.

"But they didn't know about us, did they?" I repeated to our moms, checking that I had my facts right. Then I turned to Tiffany and Ruby. "Sit. Sit."

They did, exchanging glances with each other.

With everyone sitting again, my brain whirled with information. I popped up and began to pace around the small living room. "Let me get this straight. Our fathers were related. First cousins. And they were all varying degrees of wolf shifters?" I glanced at our moms, who nodded in response. I turned and headed back the other way, trudging along the worn carpet in thought. "They didn't know you were all pregnant, but disappeared after the high warlock did some sort of spell on you guys?"

Mom nodded. "Pretty much."

I looked toward my best friend, Ruby. "And you said the cousins were never heard from again?"

Ruby chewed on her bottom lip. "I think so. I only heard Jackson and Billy discuss it once or twice. They thought the missing cousins might have something to do with the lack of females born into the pack."

Shit. I'd forgotten about that part. I twisted around to face our moms again. "So, our fathers disappeared, and the pack they're from have no women to breed with? You don't think that sounds like a legitimate curse?" I eyed our mothers one after another. They had to *know* that this sounded suspicious beyond feasibility.

Mom nodded. "Yeah. It does when you put it like that, but we always just kind of..."

The three moms glanced at each other; guilt etched into their faces.

I sighed and pulled the elastic from my ponytail, letting my hair fall around my shoulders. "You chose to ignore it. You had babies to raise, and your men up and disappeared. I guess I kind of get that." I didn't want to judge our moms too harshly, but they could have done something more to find our fathers. *Surely?* I collapsed on the couch between Ruby and Tiffany. "I just can't believe it."

Ruby chuckled. "Which part, Tiff?"

"Well... all of it, really."

Tiffany grinned at me. "I like the part about us possibly having three wolf mates each, though. That'd be pretty cool."

I swallowed hard. *Three men?* "Speak for yourself," I said.

Tiffany laughed. "Don't worry! I am."

"I know." I rubbed my eyes, a headache pulsing along my temples. "I don't know what to do with all this information. It's just too much."

Mom slid to the edge of the couch. "This was supposed to be a conversation about responsibility and magic, but you three managed to hijack it."

I glanced at her, annoyed beyond words. *Irresponsible? Us? Compared to them?* "Mom. You can't be..."

Mom waved her hands at me. "I know, I *know*. You don't have to say anymore. Maybe we should go and give Ruby and Sherie a little privacy? It's been a long night for them."

She glanced at Tiffany's mom who nodded. "Yeah, good idea."

I stood up and hugged my friends—my cousins—my chest aching and tight with unresolved emotion and tension. "I'll message you guys later."

Ruby pulled back and grinned at both of us. "Sounds like you two might need to spend some time at my new house. Your mates could be casually hanging around at the pack... just waiting for you to show up!"

I tried not to flinch. "I'd love to see your new house," I said. But I'd deliberately stayed away from visiting Ruby at Jackson's house, fearing the pack politics and, well, the wolf shifters, themselves.

Tiffany sighed, looking dejected. "I've been out to Ruby's loads of times, and I've never met my guys."

I shrugged. "There's no way of knowing if our soul mates are part of the same pack," I reasoned. "They could be human, or even a wolf shifter from another pack entirely. Surely there's more than just Jackson's pack in the state?"

Ruby nodded. "Yeah, there's at least three within driving distance that I know of."

"See," I said to Tiffany, my stomach clenching at how real this was suddenly all getting. "Don't stress so much. Fate will send your guys to you when they're good and ready."

We said our good-byes and parted ways.

I wandered out the front door with my head hurting.

Mom walked beside me, silent.

Our house was only down the block, but I appreciated the quiet as we walked. *So much had changed.* I looked at my mom. "You know, if we'd known the truth about our fathers and your relationship with them, we would never have cast that spell in the first place."

Mom sighed as we walked up our path and opened the front door. "I know, Bella. And that's something I'm going to always regret." She went inside.

I turned back to look out toward the horizon. To the pack's town within the forest in the distance. Inhaling deeply, I shivered with premonition. Something was moving. *Something was changing.* And whether I was ready for it, it was coming.

CHAPTER 3
BELLA

Come by after you finish classes for the day.

Ruby's message came through on my cell phone as I walked to the car.

Just finished, I typed back. *You okay for me to come now? I can be there in 20 mins.*

Yay! I'll put on some lunch. See you soon.

I laughed to myself as I climbed into my little red beetle and turned the ignition on with a touch of anxiety. I was tempted to ask her what sort of lunch she had planned for us. Was Ruby going to just make some sandwiches? Or would I get there to see her wave her hands around and magic up a feast? I honestly didn't mind either way, though it would be interesting to see what the wolf shifters permitted in their home and town. Would she be able to do magic within the pack's territory?

I drove away from classes and toward my house, but instead of following the highway into town, I made a quick left toward the pack's land. My stomach dropped as I indicated, and I became sicker and more trembly, the closer I drove. Now that I knew this was where my biological father was from my nerves were on high alert. Did I have more cousins in the pack? Grandparents, maybe? *Did I even want to find out?*

When I reached the small set of shops that comprised the wolves' town, I glanced around. There were people about, but it certainly wasn't what I would call busy. Busy or not, Ruby was right about one thing, that's for sure—there were a lot of men. Walking across the road, hanging out at the restaurant, and filling up their vehicles at the local gas station.

Where were all the women? *Oh, that's right. The high warlock cursed them because of us.* All the females would be twenty-three, or older. I wouldn't spot any little girls with pigtails around here.

I followed my phone's map directions, making a few quick turns, before coming to park outside of a large, two-story house. "Whoa. Nice," I said to myself as I grabbed my backpack and climbed out of my car.

This was Jackson's house? This new, family-sized home on a nice street? I nodded approvingly as I clutched my cell and walked up to the front door. I checked the message from Ruby again to confirm the address. The last thing I needed was to come face to face with a wolf shifter I didn't know. I wasn't sure my nerves could take that.

With my heart in my throat, I knocked on the door and a moment later, it flew open to reveal my red-haired friend. Relief swept through me like a tidal wave. *Thank goodness.*

"You came!" Ruby cried excitedly, pulling me into a hug.

"Of course."

She glared at me as she stood back with a dark note of humor. "What do you mean, *of course*? I've asked you to come visit at least ten times over the last month and you've never been able to make it." She pulled me inside and shut the front door behind us.

I glanced around the large living room and new kitchen. "Yeah, well, I was a little intimidated by it all," I said. I still was.

There was a classic spread of crusty, fresh bread rolls, a colorful salad, and some delicious smelling cold chicken on the counter.

I smiled at my friend. "Did you make all this?"

She waved a hand at our lunch dismissively. "Well, I bought the bread rolls from the bakery this morning, chopped up some veggies, and the chicken is from last night's dinner. Though you're lucky I cooked four chickens or there wouldn't be any left for lunch today! Those guys eat so damn much, you have no idea." Ruby shook her head with a secretive, self-indulgent laugh.

I slid onto one of the kitchen barstools with a coy smile. "Want me to make us a drink? Or maybe some dessert?" I lifted my hand.

Ruby reached out to stop me. "No, thank you. It's okay," she said. "I'm trying not to do too much magic around here."

My heart sank. "Yeah, I assumed the wolves wouldn't like it."

Ruby laughed. "Oh no. It's not like that, I promise. The guys are fine with my magic. It's just that ever since Halloween, I've been struggling with my health a little, and Darren's been watching me like a hawk. If he found out I used my magic for anything other than a lifesaving operation? He'd flip out."

I slumped on the stool. "I can use mine though, right?"

"Oh, yeah. Sure. You're good. Go for it." Ruby grinned, excusing herself.

But all the fun had gone out of it now, the moment deflated like a dead balloon. "Nah, it's okay. This is great."

"What's wrong, Bell Bell?" Ruby asked, picking up plates as she began to put together salad and chicken rolls for us both. "You want all the stuff?" She gestured to the lettuce, tomato, shredded carrot, and sliced cheese.

I nodded. "Yes, please. I'm starving."

"So," Ruby said, stuffing our rolls full of all the trimmings. "Talk to me. I've known you long enough to know when something's up."

I sighed and pulled out my hair tie, then ran my fingers through my tangled locks. "I don't know, it's just that... I don't know." How I was feeling at the moment was too hard to put into words.

"You're worried about everything we found out yesterday?" Ruby asked, handing me a plate. "Let's go sit on the couch and you can magic me up some Pepsi Max. The supermarket here doesn't sell it."

I laughed at the simple request and flicked my hand, conjuring up two tall glasses and the bubbly drink. I settled onto the couch and took a bite out of my roll, the soft white bread and crunchy salad making me salivate. "Yum. Thanks. I needed this." I glanced around the white, rather sterile-looking room, then stared at my friend. "It's a really beautiful house, Ruby."

My friend grinned. "I know exactly what you're thinking. It needs some color, right? My mom hasn't visited yet. I'm holding her back. I'm honestly terrified about what she'll do when she sets foot in the place. She's chomping at the bit to come over, but I don't think the boys would appreciate her eccentric sense of style."

I laughed out loud. "Oh my God, she'll have this place whipped into perfectly witchy shape in three seconds flat."

Ruby groaned. "I know. She's coming here for Thanksgiving tomorrow and I've banned her from doing any spells outside of food, because I know what she's like. She'll totally re-paint the whole damn house if I so much as look the wrong way."

I nodded. "She totally would."

Ruby sighed as she looked around. "I like it like this to be honest. White, and clean, and new. Don't get me wrong, it needs a splash of color, some throw blankets and cushions, and maybe even a few choice photos or paintings for the walls; but it's nice to live somewhere so completely different to the house I grew up in."

I blinked down at the sofa and realized it was just as plain as the rest of the house. It had no personality of its own. "Do you mind?"

She shook her head. "Not at all."

"What colors were you thinking?" I asked, conjuring my magic to the tips of my fingers, ready to create.

"Nothing too out there. Maybe purple, black, and silver?"

I cracked my knuckles and wove a spell, creating a throw rug for the back of the sofa, and three cushions, matching the colors Ruby had requested. Then I wiggled my fingers in Ruby's direction and made more cushions for her chair, as well as the one next to her.

"Awesome!" Ruby said, clapping her hands and sighing. "That's great. I love it, thank you."

I glanced at the plain white wall behind her and had an idea. "What color wolves are your guys?"

Ruby tilted her head curiously. "They're black. Why?"

I spoke a soft spell and behind Ruby a framed canvas formed. My beautiful, red-haired friend stood at its center, flanked by three majestic black wolves.

"What do you think?" I asked.

Ruby twisted around and gasped. "Oh, my God, Bell, that's beautiful." When she turned back around to face me, her eyes were shining with unshed tears. "Thank you so much."

I smiled in embarrassment and went back to eating my lunch. When I was finally finished, I picked up my drink to wash it down. "So, you're happy then, Ruby? You look it." I'd never seen my friend so vibrant. So bouncy. Even after the spell that had almost ended her life.

Ruby nodded, pushing a stray piece of shredded carrot into her mouth. "Oh, yeah, the guys are amazing. They're everything I ever wanted. Passionate and funny, loving and affectionate, but tough too."

"Yeah, I can imagine they would be pretty strong." Wolf shifters were part animal after all. Surely that translated into them being rough and even feral at times.

"Not in a bad way, Bell," Ruby assured me. "All I mean is that they seem tough, you know? They're muscly, big, and gruff, but underneath it all, they're total sweethearts."

I lifted an eyebrow at her. "Always?"

Her face turned the color of her hair. "Well, ah, the bedroom stuff can get pretty intense, but in the best way. I want them to be dominant there. I certainly didn't have any idea what to do at the start."

It was my turn to flush red. "I didn't mean like that..."

Ruby laughed at me. "Well, what else did you mean? Surely, you're a tiny bit curious about it all?"

I shook my head. No. I really wasn't. "What you do in the privacy of your own bedroom is your business, not mine."

Ruby opened her mouth to say something, but the front door burst open and the sounds of rumbling, loud men exploded into the previously quiet room.

I jumped at the noise. "What's that?"

"Ruby! We're home. Have you eaten yet? Or... Hello."

I turned around. Three beautiful men stood in the lounge room. I recognized them from the one time I'd met them at Halloween in town, but my heart still hammered in my chest at seeing them again.

"Hello," I managed to say and waved awkwardly.

"This is Bella. I think you guys met once on Halloween," Ruby said. "I invited her around for lunch since she hasn't seen the house, or where I'm living, until now." Ruby got up off her chair with a bounce in her step and went to greet her triad of men.

I watched, unable to look away.

The biggest guy, Jackson, scooped her up and pressed a hard kiss to her lips.

Then they passed her between them, each of the three men kissing and hugging her, not a sign of jealousy or worry.

Seeing them did weird things to my insides, so I looked away, not sure if I was turned on, or stupefied by the turn of events.

"You're Bella. Hey, I'm Darren." The smallest of the three men approached me and held out his hand.

I got to my feet, not wanting to be so far below his eye level. "Yeah, I am," I said, noticing the swirl of purple in his eyes. "You're the part warlock one."

He chuckled. "Yeah. My grandmother was a witch."

I looked over at Ruby. "So, he's technically related to… me. Wow." I glanced back at Darren, to his stubborn chin and elegant nose.

Darren's eyebrows rose. "I'm sorry, what?"

Ruby tugged Billy onto the lounge with her since he didn't seem to want to let her go. "That's right. I didn't get to tell you guys everything I learnt yesterday. Bella's mom said that the reason Bella is more powerful than me and Tiffany in magic, is because her dad was a wolf who was half witch-half wolf. I think it was your mom's brother, or something like that." Ruby grinned at Darren.

Darren turned to stare at me, his gaze roaming over me in a strangely assessing way, then he grinned, his white teeth flashing. "Nice to meet you, then, cousin."

I chuckled, feeling abashed and put on the spot. "Um, yeah, likewise."

"The Council's going to flip when they find out there's more Manterri daughters," Jackson said, walking over to the food in the kitchen. "Ruby, can we make up some rolls to take back to work with us?"

"Yeah, of course," she called. "Though there's not a lot of chicken left, now."

"Oh, I can fix that," I said and flicked my wrist in the direction of the chicken platter without a thought.

Jackson's sharp gaze snapped to mine. Then his face lit up. "Thanks!" he said appreciatively.

"That's a damn handy trick to have up your sleeve," Billy quipped, joining Jackson in making himself some lunch.

Independent guys. I liked them already.

Ruby glared at them and crossed her arms with a dramatic sigh. "You know, I could magic you up some food too—if you'd let me."

"Don't you dare," Darren said, reaching for Ruby and drawing her into his arms for another kiss. "You can't afford the energy at the moment. Wait until you've fully recovered, then you can do all the magic you want, baby."

A wave of sadness hit me again. "I still can't believe you almost died, Ruby. I'm so sorry I didn't tell you how much strength that spell truly needed. But I couldn't have known you were going to attempt it on your own..."

"What do you mean?" Darren asked quizzically.

I sighed. "Basically, when we performed the soul mate spell, I took on more than my third of the burden to ensure the spell was successful. It was too big for the two of them, Tiffany and Ruby, but it was just as dangerous to stop and let the spell fail as well. So, I..."

"Bella basically took on the full force of the magic. Because she's more powerful, and braver than us," Ruby finished for me with a grin. "But that meant when I went to undo it, I wasn't just tripling the need for my own share of magic. It was in fact way more."

"And yet you still managed it!" I said, a smile flitting to my lips.

She shrugged. "Ultimately, I don't care if my magic's really gone for good at the end of all this. I've got my soul mates. I don't need anything else."

I watched my friend as her men descended on her for more hugs and kisses, this time to say goodbye.

I frowned as Ruby's words registered in my mind. *Was she serious? Was her magic acting up? Did she really think she'd never fully recover? And was that the payment the spell would ask of all of us?* Because I wasn't sure that my magic was something I would be willing to part with.

CHAPTER 4
JONAH

I made my way over to my cousin Jackson's house, looking for my older brother Billy. I'd been told they'd headed home for lunch from the work site, but I needed his help sooner rather than later. So, instead of being afraid like half the pack was of his witch mate, I jogged over to his new house and boldly knocked on the door. Ruby was cool. They all needed to get the hell over their prejudices and meet her—just give her a chance.

"Coming," came a female voice from inside.

I smiled to hear her sounding so happy. The lack of females in the pack was really starting to affect the whole mentality of the town. It was getting tougher, rougher, and harder to live like this. We needed more women. And children. Like... *now*.

The front door opened and my greeting froze on my lips as a wave of pure perfection overwhelmed my senses. I inhaled deeply and closed my eyes on a moan. *Who, or what, was that?* I wondered.

"Make sure you come over tomorrow. Bring your mom too," Ruby was saying to someone inside the house as she pulled the door open wide. Then Jackson's mate turned toward me with a smile. "Hey Jonah. Which of the boys are you looking for?"

If it had been any other day, I would have smiled at Ruby's easy way of talking about her pack of men. But today, all my wolf senses were on high alert, and I struggled to talk. "Billy," I managed, though my teeth had begun to shift, and my inner wolf was howling like mad in my head. And then, looking past Ruby, I got my first look at the woman responsible for my wolf to going bonkers on me.

She stared directly at me.

My heart squeezed tight in a way I've never felt before and I swallowed hard. She had long brown hair, spectacular dark eyes, and beautiful lips.

"Jonah, this is my best friend, Bella. Bell, this is one of Billy's brothers," Ruby said, her happy tone bouncing between us as we were introduced.

"Hello," the beautiful stranger said to me cautiously. "It's nice to meet you."

I tried to talk, but the only thing that came out was a garbled load of crap. Then a growly bark. "Fuck," I spat out, shaking myself.

Bella backed away from me, and closer to Ruby, clearly taken aback.

I didn't blame her one bit. I was acting freaking insane, and there was only one possible reason for it. One entirely all too simple explanation. She was my mate. *Fuck...* There was no other sane excuse as to why I just wanted to grab her, kiss her, shift into my wolf, and run howling through the forest—all at the same time.

"You okay, Jonah?" Ruby asked, stepping in front of Bella like a physical shield and frowning at me.

I stumbled backwards, putting distance between us. My wolf calmed down once I wasn't quite so close to her. I could breathe again, if I couldn't smell her. *God, she smells amazing.* "Um, my shifter is kind of having a hard time around Bella."

Ruby's mouth dropped open and her eyes went wide. "No way!" she gasped. "Does that mean she's your...?"

I looked straight at Bella, noticing the unmistakable purple swirl of her magic and my stomach dropped. Another witch. Of course, she was. *Damn, the elders are going to hate this.* I straightened my spine. *Fuck the elders.* I wanted my mate. Someone to love. Someone Fate chose for me. I didn't care if she had magic or not.

I coughed to clear my throat. "Bella, I need to shift and run. I'm sorry I can't stay and chat. But I don't want to freak you out, so I have to go. Now. Can we have breakfast tomorrow at Milly's? Will you come back?" My gaze slid to Ruby's. "Will you tell her where?"

Ruby nodded excitedly. "Yeah, of course. You don't want to make it dinner tonight, maybe?"

I hesitated. "I want to, but I don't know how my wolf is going to handle this or how long I'll need to shift for. Maybe I should ask Billy—"

"I need to get back home," Bella interjected, her beautiful eyes finding her feet. "My mom's already expecting me for dinner."

Ruby beamed. "Well, that's that then. Breakfast it is. Go on, Jonah. Run!"

I thought I'd at least make it to the end of the street before my wolf ripped through me.

But Bella stepped over the threshold and called out, "Wait! I don't understand."

The wind picked up her scent and sent it spiraling toward me. I inhaled her sweetness like a drug, my eyes rolling back in my head as I practically gagged trying to drag the scent in faster and my wolf whipped up inside me like a hurricane.

One moment, I had full control of him, and the next I was shifting. I staggered further away but couldn't get far enough before my wolf burst forth. I dropped to all fours. My skin sprouted fur, my face morphed and elongated, and my limbs grew shorter. When I was fully transformed and my eyes had shifted to black and white vision, I turned my head and glanced back toward the front door.

Bella stood next to Ruby, clinging to one of the porch balustrades. Her mouth had dropped open in awe and she was staring at me like she'd never seen a wolf shift before. Which she probably hadn't. *Poor girl.* I whined a little, unhappy to be leaving her so soon, but seeing as her nails digging into the wooden porch like she was holding on for dear life, I needed to get going.

I took off, running down the street and away from my mate—away from my future. Billy had said that his mate Ruby had three wolf mates, not just one. And he should know, he was one of them. *Would Bella be the same?* Would I be hanging around just waiting for her number second and third mates to show up? I shuddered as I hit the forest edge and picked up my pace. I didn't want to share my mate like Billy did.

Then again, as a Beta wolf, surely I could cope with an Alpha in our family as well? We only had a few of those in the pack, though I wasn't sure who I wanted to share my home and hearth with. *Hopefully none of them*, was my last thought for a long time as I raced through the forest, hope swelling in my heart. I'd beaten the curse! Despite there being no mate born for me in our pack, Fate had found a way to bring her to me.

Bella

I turned around to Ruby, my mouth hanging open. "Did you just see that?" Or had I imagined a gorgeous young man turning up to see Ruby, before turning into a white wolf and running away?

Ruby covered her mouth with her hand and nodded. "Yep."

"He was white!" I said. The most magnificent white wolf I'd ever seen. Not that I'd seen any in my time, not in real life, anyway. "I can't believe it."

Ruby reached out a hand to me, slowly, as though I might spook. "Are you okay, Bell?"

"I..." I placed a hand on my chest, my heart pounding beneath my palm. But I didn't think it was from fear. I felt strangely excited. "I think so..." I said, my gaze still focused off in the distance.

"What is it?" asked Ruby.

I swallowed hard, trying to sort out my jarred thoughts. "I'd assumed that seeing them in wolf form would be crazy scary. But it's not. It's..."

"Exhilarating, isn't it?" Ruby finished for me.

I nodded and swallowed hard again. Adrenaline zinged through my body like lightning or bursts of energy, making me want to run. Which for someone who didn't exercise a hell of a lot, was a truly strange sensation.

"It's weird," I said. "Though I didn't realize they changed like that. I don't know what I imagined. But..."

Ruby chuckled in good humor. "The first time I saw Jackson and Billy in wolf form I almost died. So, you're taking it much better than me."

I really couldn't believe it. I felt alive for the first time in, well, forever. I don't know what had lit up inside me, sparking in a way that changed everything—but I didn't want it to stop. "Well, it's exciting, really," I said. "And now that I know we're related to these... shifters, it makes sense as to why we would feel more connected to them."

I'd honestly been terrified to come here. To meet a shifter in the flesh. Now, I wanted to race after Jonah to see him again. Maybe watch him shift back to human. *What would that look like?* Speaking of which... "Jonah's Billy's younger brother, you said? He's not directly related to me, though, is he?" I bloody hoped not, but with my bad luck he probably would be.

Ruby frowned. "I don't think so, but we could check. Did you feel anything when you saw him?"

I tilted my head at her. "You mean other than terrified by the growling and all those sharp teeth?"

Ruby nodded. "That's normal. He couldn't control his shifter around you."

I laughed at that. "Yeah, he said that his shifter liked me. I thought the shifters hated us witches, and I'm three quarters witch." *And a quarter wolf shifter.* A fact I was still growing accustomed to thanks to Jonah showing me that wolves were beautiful, powerful creatures. And ones that the men could control, because he ran for the safety and wilds of the forest, and not toward another person in unchecked aggression.

Ruby took my hand. "Look, you may want to come back inside for a bit."

I pulled my cell phone out of my pocket and glanced at the time on the screen. "It's past four, Ruby. I really need to get home."

Ruby's lips twisted. "Um, you're going to need to hear this before you go, Bell."

"Why?" I pressed.

Ruby sighed.

I didn't budge. I needed to go, and I hated being late for my mom. She worried too much already. I'd been her everything for twenty-three years... "Are you sure this can't this wait until tomorrow? I agreed to come back in the morning and see Jonah for breakfast." Why? I had no idea. "Maybe I could pop in afterwards and we could catch up again? Let me know what your guys think of the painting and stuff."

Ruby pinched the bridge of her nose. "Bella, this is serious. The reason Jonah couldn't control his shifter around you, and he went all growly and strange..."

"Yeah?" That had been weird, but what was even more weird was that I wasn't scared of him at all at that moment. If anything, I'd found it intensely interesting.

"It's because you're his Fated mate."

CHAPTER 5
BELLA

My mouth dropped open. "I'm sorry, what?" *Impossible.* Surely, I would have known something as important as that instantly. "He can't be," I reasoned.

Ruby stared at me, then crossed her arms firmly over her chest before cocking an eyebrow at me. "Why not? Found another soul mate recently?"

"No! But..."

"But what?" she pushed.

I didn't have an answer because there was no answer that would have satisfied Ruby. I hadn't met anyone I'd thought was the one for me—including the man I'd just met. "But... he's Billy's cousin?" I asked, skeptical. That sounded somehow almost incestuous to me.

"And what's wrong with that? Jonah's cute! And I'll put money on that you're safe on the direct relation front."

Oh, he was more than cute. He was damn hot, with bright blue eyes and his funky, spiky hair. Although I hadn't seen him naked while he was shifting thanks to his clothes covering his human body, then the wolf appearing, I could see how lithe and strong, and sexy he must be underneath it all. I shook myself. "I know, but..."

Ruby sighed. "Obviously, you aren't feeling it all just yet. I mean, we're all different, but when I met Jackson, I knew straight away. He was the Alpha. But Jonah's a Beta, like Billy. So, maybe you just need to meet your Alpha as well?"

I gaped at her. "You've got to be kidding. I don't want more than one!"

Ruby laughed at me and rolled her eyes. "And why not?"

"Because..." *How could I say this without offending her?* "I wouldn't even know what to do with one man, Ruby, let alone three. I grew up with no brothers, no father, no uncles..."

"Neither did I, and I'm doing just fine with my boys, Bella."

"But we're different Ruby!" I huffed. "You're vibrant, and fun, and exciting. And I'm... well, *me*." I liked books and reading, and college for the learning angle, *not* the wild parties.

Ruby grinned at me. "Go on, go home, and have dinner with your mom. Just let me know if you find out anything more about our dads, or anything like that."

I grabbed my keys out of my bag and shot back. "You, too! Especially about the curse. That's the most interesting part of all this for me. I can only imagine how much power it took to curse this whole town."

"Shhh..." Ruby hissed at me. "Don't say that too loudly."

I slammed my hand over my mouth and whispered, "Sorry." It probably wasn't the best idea to advertise to the wolf pack that we thought our old high warlock cursed them all. We needed proof before we said anything, and even better, a solution.

I waved to Ruby and headed to my car. Glancing back as I got in the door, I couldn't stop the strangely hysterical laughter that bubbled up in my throat. What had been a simple lunch with my friend had turned into something so much more. "What the hell was that?" I asked the car interior and shook my head.

When I arrived back at my mother's house, the home I'd grown up in, I couldn't shake the strange feeling that something had changed. But was it in me? Or something in my environment? I couldn't tell yet. But something beyond my control, something... truly magical was going on.

Once inside the house, I looked around as though I might discover something different. Perhaps sense the thing that had changed. But there was nothing new. Nothing at all. My house was still the same old mix of ordered chaos and the over-the-top injection of rainbow of colors that my mother enjoyed so much.

"Mom, I'm home," I called out.

"Hey Bella! How was your day?" She called back from the general direction of the kitchen.

"Ah, good thanks." *Overall, I suppose.* "Yours?" I put my bag on the floor and went straight for the bookshelf against the wall in the lounge room. I needed some answers. I had far too many questions at this point, which never sat well with me. And today, I wanted to know more about my future... and whether Jonah was in it. I didn't want to turn up to breakfast like an ignorant half-wit, tomorrow. Which, if I was honest, was probably half the reason I was feeling so unsettled.

I'd never been the kind of person who flew by the seat of their pants through life. I wanted to know what was going to happen today, tomorrow, next week, and next year if possible.

I grabbed a scrying book off the shelf, sat down on the couch cross-legged, and opened the massive tome. I'd looked in this book before, and I had a natural affinity with premonition spells—the ability to see into or predict the future. Unfortunately predicting the future and looking too far into your own future was frowned upon by the Coven. So, I tried not to do it too much.

"Dinners in the oven. It'll be about an hour," Mom said, walking into the room while drying her hands with a colorful towel. "What are you up to, sweetheart?" she asked curiously.

I flicked through the future-telling book and found a page I'd used before. It was a relatively easy spell, but it was limited in what you could see or feel. There was a lot of interpretation required, as well as a skilled witch's hand. I glanced up at my mom as she stared at me.

There was no point lying to her about what I was doing, or even trying to avoid the truth for that matter. For some reason, I couldn't lie to my mom. *None of us could.* Ruby and Tiffany, either. We were pretty sure our mothers had put a spell on us to conjure the truth at some point in our lives. It was subtle, but even now I could feel the warm pull at the back of my neck. *Pity the spell doesn't go both ways*, I mused.

"I had lunch at Ruby's new place, and met someone," I answered. "A wolf shifter named Jonah. Ruby said that I'm his mate. But I didn't feel the same way he did. Or, at least, I don't think I did. Honestly, I'm not even sure what I'm meant to feel."

My mom staggered forward as though she was unsteady or suddenly and inexplicably drunk.

"You okay?" I frowned, reaching out a steady hand toward her.

"Yeah, yeah. Fine, fine." Mom waved me away as she fell into the armchair opposite me. "What do you mean, he thinks you're his mate?"

I frowned at her. "I think it means that our soul mate spell worked on him, too. But I'm not sure."

My mom made a strange, choking noise.

I grimaced and looked back at her.

"Doesn't that mean anything to you, Bella?" she asked, her eyebrows high on her forehead as though she was surprised by my lack of reaction or excitement.

I shrugged. "I don't know, I guess." I slid to the floor, kneeling beside the coffee table and placed the book on the surface of the table.

"I didn't feel the same things Ruby said he did. He was cute and everything, but I want to know for sure." There was no way I would even see him again unless I had a direction.

I'd always been quite good at scrying, though my mother would never allow me to look into the past, though I'd been tempted. What father-less daughter wouldn't want to know more about the past? Especially her mother's past, specifically.

Mom had always kept a priceless crystal ball in the middle of the table, sitting on a black ring pedestal to keep it from rolling away. Most of the time the crystal was a colorless, pretty orb. Nothing more than a New Age decoration to non-magical onlookers. But as I placed my hands on either side of its smooth, flawless surface and spoke the ancient language of the warlocks, the crystal ball began to swirl with smoke inside its depths, and flickers of bright green light appeared.

I mentally asked the scrying spell a question, then conjured up a feeling, an image of my future. *Was Jonah a part of my future? The answering call of the soul mate spell I'd cast last year with my friends?* The crystal orb glowed and hummed with a silent vibration. I couldn't see him in the mystical smoke, but the feeling I got was, *yes*, he was part of my future. But he wasn't the only one. There was more. More people. *More men.*

I dropped my hands away, letting the spell go. The smoke and intangible tendrils of magic faded away. I slumped. "Damn." Not the answer I'd been hoping for.

"What is it?" Mom asked.

I pushed myself back until I was resting against the couch and flicked the stray hair out of my face. "I have more than one soul mate, too."

My mom stilled, not uttering a sound.

I sighed and ran my fingers through the tangles of my long hair. I didn't want three mates like Ruby. *I didn't.* I hated being the center of attention! I looked up at my mother.

She was frozen in place and her eyes were wide, as though frightened.

"What?" I asked, my brows furrowing.

"I don't know quite what to say, Bell."

Well, at least that was honest.

"Me neither," I said, and sighed. "I'm not sure what to do."

She slid to the floor and joined me on the carpet, crossing her legs and sitting opposite me. She hadn't done that since I was a child.

I smiled at her, feeling like I was kindergarten age all over again and she was about to do a puzzle with me. "I'm impressed you can still sit like that," I said, indicating her crossed legs.

She grinned at me. "Yoga."

"Hmm..."

"Sweetheart, you know the soul mate spell is going to drag the man you're meant to love, meant to marry, out of hiding, don't you? I mean, it sounds like you're disappointed that Fate has sent you a person to love, which is exactly what you asked for."

"Oh, it's not that. It's just ..." I stopped, not sure how to finish the sentence. *What was the problem?* I stared down at my lap and flicked a piece of fluff off my jeans. "I suppose I was hoping I'd get a few more years before they found me. I don't feel ready. Tiffany hasn't met her guy yet, or guys, and she's so much more ready than I am. Even Ruby was! I haven't finished college yet. I..."

"There's never a perfect time to meet the man you're supposed to fall in love with," Mom said softly. "When I met your father..."

I stared at her, watching the way she swallowed hard and glanced down at her multilayered, multicolored skirts. She'd never mentioned my father before, not like this. And certainly not in such soft tones.

"When I met your father," she repeated, "I was half-way through college, living at home with my parents. Very similar to you, actually."

"And what happened?" I asked, my heart aching with the need to know.

She chuckled. "I met him at a friend's party. These three hot boys showed up wearing leather jackets. On motorbikes. They were the coolest guys I'd ever seen."

The Manterri cousins. The shifters.

"What did my father look like?"

Mom smiled. "A lot like you. He has beautiful dark hair, perfect skin, and a stubborn jaw."

I ran my hand over my cheek, and cupped my chin, trying to imagine a man that looked like me. "And you knew he was for you? Did you experience the soul mate feeling?"

Mom nodded. "I didn't know it at the time. I honestly just thought he was cute. And I couldn't keep my eyes off him. But the more time we spent together; it became obvious that he was meant for me. And I for him." Mom fell silent.

A wave of pain washed over me. I reached out and grabbed her hand. "You still miss him?"

She smiled and for the first time in my whole life, I saw my mother cry real tears of sadness. Not like those from a movie, or the sort you get while chopping onions. Two large, single tears slid down her cheeks, and with them came a heavy cascade of true sadness.

She squeezed my hand. "I know you're scared, Bella, and I know I haven't set a good example for you in regards to marriage, or even a relationship. But to this day, I don't regret the time I spent with your father. I never will. Not even for a moment. So please, *please*, don't be afraid. Love and relationships are what life's all about. They're what make life worth living."

My voice hitched in my throat, but I swallowed the pain. "Even if they break your heart?" I asked quietly.

She nodded, genuine honesty in her gaze. "Even if they break your heart."

CHAPTER 6

JONAH

I drummed my fingers along the table at Milly's, nervous energy making every part of me practically vibrate.

"Can I get you anything, Jonah?" Tania, the waitress, and one of the last females to be born to our pack, asked as she smiled at me. She was twenty-three years old, like me, and had been mated since the day she turned eighteen. She'd been snaffled up by one of the older guys, desperate for a wife, after it became obvious that our pack was never going to have another daughter born to it again.

"No, thank you. I'm waiting for someone," I answered.

She quirked an eyebrow at me, curious as a cat. "Anyone I might know?"

There were only three unmated females of fertile age born in our pack, and they'd all frequented the beds of most of the guys in town. Not a problem if you liked that—but none of them were my style.

"Afraid not."

The bell above the door chimed. We turned as one toward the sound.

My heart began thumping madly in my chest when I laid eyes upon who'd arrived. I stared at Bella, my little witch mate, as she slid inside the loud café.

She cast her tentative gaze around the room.

Tania laughed and hurried over to where Bella stood, looking utterly beautiful but nervous as hell, in her blue denim jeans and bright purple tank.

I didn't bother trying to stop Tania from going up to her. Tania was a force of nature. And it was nice to just sit back and watch them for a minute.

Tania grinned and chatted amiably to Bella, then gestured to where I sat in the back.

Bella glanced my way, pursing her lips, and nodded.

Our gazes clashed in a heat that stole up my back and tingled along my neck like flickers of flame. My wolf leapt inside me in joy, instantly recognizing my mate in the beautiful young witch who walked toward me. *Calm the hell down*, I commanded.

I'd purposely run all afternoon yesterday, and all night, trying to tire my wolf out just so I could get some control today and be able to speak to her. But as I swallowed hard and forced my wolf down once again, I realized it was going to be way harder than I'd initially thought it would be.

Bella stepped up to my table.

I jumped to my feet, grinning at her. "Hey."

She bobbed her head a little, appearing shy. "Hi Jonah." She had beautiful long dark hair that shone in the light and fell across her shoulders as she stared at her shoes. When she finally managed to look up at me, despite the dark brown color of her eyes, purple magic swirled in their depths.

"Let's sit," I suggested, forcing myself not to touch her, though I desperately ached to haul her to my body, to kiss her, hold her, and keep her safe. I curled my fingers into tight fists, slid into the booth, and firmly placed both hands on my knees beneath the table. I didn't want her to see how hard I was fighting my wolf. *Relax! Stay down. You can run again later.* I cleared my throat with a rough cough. "Sit down." I gestured to the seat opposite me. "Please. Join me."

Bella nodded and slid onto the leather booth bench.

"You're human again," she observed.

The softness of her voice surprised me. Ruby was confident and charismatic, a proud witch who suited her three strong mates. Bella seemed shy and reserved in comparison. Very different from her friend. And I liked it. With a smile, I nodded. "I shifted back last night before bed."

She tilted her head as if studying me. "Is that normal?"

"Which bit?" *That I shifted? That I skipped meals? What?*

The edges of her lips lifted, and she stared intently at me. "That you would go all afternoon and evening in your wolf form?" she clarified.

I shook my head. "Not really. I can go weeks without shifting at all, and even then, I tend to only run for an hour, tops. I prefer being in my human form."

A lot of the other guys didn't—my brother Billy included—they felt much more confident in their wolf bodies.

"So, what happened yesterday?" she asked.

I raised my eyebrows. "Honestly?"

She became serious, her mouth flattening into an unforgiving straight line. "Always. Please."

Mental note: has issues about being lied to.

"Well, I transformed so quickly when I saw you yesterday, I was sort of hoping a good run would sort my wolf out and afford me more control today."

She smiled again. "And did it?"

I checked myself. I was more relaxed now that she was close to me and paying me attention. "Well, the words are flowing at least," I answered with a smile of my own.

"And your wolf?" she asked, genuinely interested.

I grinned. "He's close to the surface, but I've got a handle on him."

She slid her hands over the table, moving slightly closer. "And is it true that you have complete control over your wolf? That your brain functions as though you were still human?"

Tania walked up and handed us some menus, temporarily interrupting our conversation. "You two ready to order?"

Bella scanned the menu quickly, then looked to me. "Any suggestions?"

"They make the best cooked breakfast around. And hamburgers."

Bella smiled at Tania and handed back the menu. "Eggs benedict and a chocolate milkshake, please."

Tania glanced at me.

"The usual, please, Tania."

She smiled briefly and headed off.

Bella looked at me. "So, you eat here often?"

I laughed. "It's the only eatery in town and I like a cooked breakfast."

"Fair enough," Bella said, and we lapsed into comfortable silence. Then my little mate looked up, her bright eyes sharp with interest.

"What do you do, Jonah?"

"I'm a brick layer," I said, shrugging. I wasn't one of those guys who defined themselves by what they did for a crust. It made me money, and it helped the community, but it wasn't my life. "It's physical work, and early mornings, but I like it."

She grinned shyly. "The exercise must be good, too?"

"How about you?" I countered.

She smiled shyly. "I'm actually at college at the moment, finishing up my degree in teaching."

I couldn't help myself. I grinned. "I would have loved to have had a teacher who looked like you back in high school."

Her cheeks turned a pretty pink color, then she glanced down at the table. "Thanks, but I'd prefer to teach at an elementary school. I like the little ones."

The bell above the door rang, as it had been all morning with people coming in and going out, but this time the sound caught my attention.

I glanced up as my oldest brother Thomas walked in.

"Hey, Jonah!" he called out.

I raised my hand to wave and sighed at the interruption. I should have assumed we'd be spotted.

Bella froze. Then she shivered, and turned around slowly, staring at the door of the café where Thomas, and his best friend Elliot, stood.

The two guys stared at my mate.

She stared right back. "Who are they?" she whispered, the desire in her voice impossible to ignore.

Damn it. I swallowed my need to question her about who she meant, and what she was feeling. It was painfully obvious. Her pupils were dilated, and her gaze was hungry. I could literally see the desire for them on her face, and their attraction for her was written all over theirs. It was all there. The attraction, the sizzle, the need.

My brother and his best friend stumbled forward, toward us. They didn't take their eyes off Bella.

I stood up, ready to direct them to the door the moment they needed to shift, which if they were her mate, they'd likely need to. *Shit. I was hoping I was her only one.*

Thomas began to say, "Jonah... ah..." But words failed him, and his throat worked as he swallowed hard.

I moved over to stand in front of my mate.

She sat still on the bench seat, just staring up at the two Alpha males in front of us.

I gestured to her by way of introduction. "This is Bella. She's one of Ruby's friends."

"She's a witch?" Elliot asked, shock evident in his tone.

I narrowed my eyes at them. "And she's my mate, though from the looks of you guys…"

Thomas visibly shook.

Elliot's eyes were practically popping out of his head.

"Your *what*?" Elliot asked as a low growl emerged.

Bella pushed herself to her feet.

I moved toward her protectively, shielding her.

She pressed into my side and grabbed onto my arm.

My wolf surged inside of me, pleasure zinging along my skin at her touch.

Bella gasped.

And I found myself hoping that she felt the same thing.

"What's wrong with them?" she hissed quietly at me.

I grinned, though part of me was devastated. Bella had more than one mate. Just like Ruby. *Pull yourself together, man. If Billy can be happy in a pack of three men sharing one woman, so can you.* I smiled down at her. "Same as what was up with me yesterday."

Bella's eyes widened, then she bit her lip. She knew what I meant, though I wasn't sure how she felt about it. At that moment, she seemed a little scared.

I turned to my brother and Elliot, both of whose eyes had shifted to those of their inner wolves.

"Go shift and run. It helps. I'll fill you both in later."

"But…" Tommy tried to talk, but he was shaking too much to get anything more out.

I sighed heavily. "Trust me on this. Go run. I'll catch up with you guys later." When they didn't move, I turned to my beautiful witch. "Tell them you're not going anywhere. I think they're afraid you'll leave, and they'll lose you."

Both men made strangled, grunting noises. They probably didn't like me revealing such things so openly, but she liked the truth, so she was getting the truth.

She bit her lip. "Well, I do have classes after lunch, but I could come back around dinner time?"

"Perfect," I said, overriding any sort of rejection of the plan the other two guys might have had in mind. "You'll meet us back here tonight then, yeah?"

"Yes." She swallowed hard, her gaze roving over the two Alphas, before returning to me. "Sixish?"

"Done." I turned back to the other two. "Now, go. Before you shift and make a mess of the diner. Tania won't be impressed."

Elliot grabbed onto Tommy's arm and pulled hard. "Let's go," he managed to say, though it came out all garbled and weird.

My brother planted his feet, not wanting to move, fighting against his friend.

But Elliot tugged at him harder, practically wrestling him almost all the way to the door.

I wrapped my arm around Bella's shoulders.

Her small body trembling beneath mine.

"Go. It's all good," I assured them.

The two guys stared at us, then they both fell out the front doors and shifted into their massive white wolf forms.

Bella's jaw dropped as she stared after them through the glass. "They're white, too," she whispered.

"Yeah." I didn't really get what that had to do with anything.

My mate shivered even more in response.

I tugged her back into the booth with me and wrapped my arms around her. "Now, tell me what you're feeling, because I want you to feel safe here." I expected words. I expected laughter. I certainly didn't expect what came next.

Tears rolled down her cheeks and she cuddled into my chest and sobbed as though her very heart was breaking.

Shit. What the hell did I do now?

CHAPTER 7

BELLA

No matter what I did, I couldn't stop shaking or crying. I felt utterly ridiculous.

But Jonah held me, and rocked me, and told me everything was going to be okay.

There was no choice but to go with the torrent of emotions buffering my senses, cuddle into the guy offering me a shoulder to cry on and wait out the storm. Finally, after it felt like my throat would break from the sobbing, the tantalizing aroma of eggs and bacon reached me through the haze of my pain, and I realized the waitress was serving our food.

"Thanks, Tania," Jonah said over my head.

"Is she okay?" Tania whispered.

I nodded, wiping my face. "Sorry. I'm okay."

Tania pressed some napkins into my hand, and I pulled away from Jonah's hot body—both the temperature and his rock-hard muscles.

"Sorry," I said again, seeing all the tear stains I'd left behind on his shirt. "I'll fix that." I waved my hand and got rid of all the evidence of my emotional trauma from his shirt. I didn't try and fix myself up. I knew my face was red and blotchy, but there was no point if I was just going to burst into tears again, which at this point, it felt like I was definitely going to.

"Have something to eat," Tania said. "You'll feel better." She walked away to serve another table, leaving me with one of my wolf mates.

One of three. I hung my head. "Three. I don't want three."

"Three what?" Jonah asked, picking up his knife and fork. "There's three rashers of bacon and three sausages if you want some of mine?"

Three sausages... Oh, my God. I should have cried again, but instead I burst out laughing, snorting so inelegantly I had to slam my hand over my mouth to stop the spit and snot flying across the table. I almost died. Okay, so maybe I needed a little magical clean up. I waved my hand over my face, drying my eyes and nose. I blinked at Jonah.

He was cutting and eating and drinking like a machine.

"Hungry?" I asked rhetorically.

He nodded. "Always. How about you?"

I stared down at my breakfast, and even though it looked and smelled amazing I was not hungry at all anymore. But I would be later, so I picked up my milkshake and took a long draw, filling my mouth with the icy cold drink and swallowing hard.

Three. I had *three*. That was three men. Three hearts to love. Three penises to... satisfy. Three different personalities to mesh with mine. This was going to be impossible. *Impossible!* My eyes began to burn with tears again.

Jonah reached across the table and squeezed my arm. "Hey, hey. It's okay. Whatever's upsetting you, I'm sure we can fix it."

I lifted my gaze to his. "I somehow doubt it."

"Try me."

I exhaled sharply. "I don't want three mates."

Jonah's eyes widened, then he grinned. "Sounds good to me. I can keep you all to myself. How about we run off together? Just you and me."

I opened my mouth to agree, but the words got so stuck in my throat and it felt like someone had squeezed my larynx shut or like someone had rubbed it raw with sandpaper. I swallowed furiously, then took another long sip of my milkshake through the straw. I tried to speak again, but this time my heart physically ached. My ribs squeezed and deep inside my chest, I hurt. I couldn't say it. I couldn't agree. It's like my entire body rebelled at the idea of abandoning my other two mates. I slumped. "I don't think that's a possibility."

Jonah sighed. "Yeah, I know... or at least, I assume that's the case."

"What do you mean?" I asked, finding my voice more easily now.

He scooped some of his eggs onto his fork, then stuffed them in his mouth. "Well, I kind of hoped I'd be your only mate, even though Ruby has three. After all, those four are the first of their kind, so none of us expected the pattern to repeat."

I nodded, slightly amused that Jonah had jumped straight to that conclusion.

"So, you think we're Fated too?" I asked.

He nodded. "There's no denying my wolf's response to you. What about you? How do you feel about me?"

I shivered, wanting to be honest with him. "I didn't feel as much yesterday as I thought I should, but when I touched you just before..."

"Yes?" he prompted, grinning madly.

"Did you feel it too?" I asked tentatively. "That... tingle?" The moment I'd reached for him, more in fear than anything else, my breath had been sucked from my lungs and my core had tightened and pulsed with longing. I'd never felt anything like it before in my life. I wanted to melt into his arms, press my lips to his bare neck, and taste him. Then the intensity of the other two had overwhelmed me. Distracted me from the moment.

"I felt *a lot* more than that." He grinned, then sobered. "Is that why you're upset? Because you felt the same thing for Tommy and Elliot?"

I swallowed hard, my stomach twisting. "Is that their names?" I hated that I could feel so much for men whose names I didn't even know.

Jonah nodded. "They're both Alphas. And Tommy's my older brother."

My mouth dropped open and a single word fell from my lips. "No."

"No, what?"

"I can't handle two Alphas!" I grabbed my head in my hands and squeezed my temples. I couldn't handle one Alpha male! Let alone the brother thing. I couldn't even think about that bit. "Oh, my God. This is such a mess. Okay. All right, let's run away." The moment I said the words, pain struck me in the chest like a hot iron. I pressed a hand to my sternum. "Stop that," I told myself, instantly frustrated.

Jonah laughed. "Stop what?"

I swallowed hard, picking up my knife and fork. *Maybe I was just hungry and it was heartburn?* "Every time I even try and talk about leaving the other two, my chest caves in and it feels like I'm going to die. It hurts." I stabbed my poached eggs, the yellow yolk running over my muffins and smoked salmon.

"Sounds like your body doesn't want you giving them up," Jonah said quietly, and this time a wave of sadness radiated from him.

"I'm sorry," I said, though I had no control over my response. "I don't want three mates, but it seems I have no choice." There was absolutely no denying the way I was attracted to them, though. When Tommy and Elliot had walked into the café, I'd shivered all over, feeling the magic—the draw of them from our soul mates spell. I'd wanted to throw myself into their arms... until they started growling and stiffening up as though they were angry at me.

"So that's why you're upset? You'd prefer just one partner?"

The hopeful expression on Jonah's face made my heart ache in an altogether different way. I didn't want to give him false hope. He seemed like such a sweet, good guy. Unfortunately, there seemed to be a feisty, hot female lying dormant inside of me. And she wanted, no, needed Elliot and Tommy too. "I've always thought I'd have one soul mate. A husband." I jabbed absently at my breakfast with my knife again. "But it looks like Fate has a different plan for me."

There was no arguing with that.

"Billy said that Ruby and her friends cast a soul mate spell. Was that you?" Jonah asked, shoveling the last of his greasy, awesome breakfast into his mouth.

I nodded. "To be honest, I wasn't that interested in conducting the spell, but Ruby and Tiffany talked me into it. At the time, I felt like I couldn't let them down. Those girls have always been like sisters to me."

He cocked his head. "Why weren't you?"

I glanced down. "Because there was a warning attached to the spell. It said there would be a payment taken for a successful result."

"A payment?"

I nodded. "It didn't say what sort, and considering how unwell Ruby has been since after Halloween, the spell obviously took its pound of flesh from her."

"At least she has her three guys now," Jonah said with a shrug, as though that was enough of a reward for enduring life possibly magicless.

I opened my mouth, then thought better of what I was about to say. "Yeah, well Ruby's happy, I guess." And she was. She'd outright said she'd be happy to pay the cost of finding her mates.

"And you're worried about what you'll lose?" Jonah asked, pushing his plate away and leaning back against the booth. As he did, he glanced at me and the sunlight caught the blue in his eyes, making them sparkle.

My breath caught in my throat. *Damn*, he was beautiful. I reached across the space between us and touched him, wanting to feel his skin beneath my fingers. I ran my hand down his forearm until I could intertwine my fingers with his.

He shivered and goosebumps prickled his skin.

"Does that feel good for you too?" I asked.

He gave me a wolf-like smile, all teeth and flashy grin. "If I didn't know that my brother would kill me for seducing you, I'd throw you over my shoulder and take you back to my place right now."

The smile fell from my face, and I pulled my hand back.

He reached out in spite of my sudden withdrawal and took my hand in his, interlacing our fingers.

Warm tendrils of heat curled in my belly. *Whoa. Yes, Jonah is my soul mate. This attraction is intense.*

"Hey. Chill. I was just joking," Jonah said, squeezing my hand gently. "I'm not a pushy guy, at all, I promise. We can sit here and talk all year if you like. Though I might try to steal a kiss or two." He winked with a charming smile.

I swallowed hard and licked my dry lips.

"What's wrong?"

How could I tell a guy that at twenty-two, I'd never been kissed? "Well, I..." I flicked my hair over my shoulder and looked him straight in the eye. If I couldn't tell Jonah, I didn't have a hope in hell of telling the other two. I opened my mouth to tell him, but the words simply failed me.

I decided to do something completely out of character for me and show him what I meant. After all, they said that actions speak louder than words. I leaned forward, tilted my chin up, and reached for his face—to pull him to me. Surely, he'd feel my inexperience when I gave him the world's worst kiss imaginable?

Jonah's eyes went wide, and I was pretty sure I saw a flash of yellow in his otherwise blue irises, before he surged forward to kiss me.

I moaned at the suddenness of it all, the pressure.

Then his lips softened, and he cupped my cheek.

I sighed, expecting him to back away.

Instead, he deepened the kiss, sweeping his tongue out to brush against the seam of my lips.

I opened to him and he tasted the inside of my mouth. Another moan erupted from my throat as I tried to get closer to him, feeling awkward in the booth, all squashed and sideways.

A soft growl rolled through Jonah's throat as I lifted my tongue to tangle with his. He tasted of heat and lust.

As desire curled through my belly, blazing to life like a wildfire, I realized I'd been kidding myself if I thought for even a moment that I wasn't really attracted to this guy. I was. Completely. If the table hadn't been in my way, I would have swung my leg over his waist and straddled him, just to get closer to his heat. To the *heart* of him.

He broke away, panting hard. "If you were trying to convince me *not* to seduce you, there are more convincing ways." He grinned.

My gaze dropped straight to his mouth. I lifted my hand tentatively and pressed my fingers to his lips. My mouth throbbed with blood and feel of Jonah's possession.

Jonah groaned and leaned close, his hot breath sweeping against my ear. "Are you sure you don't wanna go back to my place for a bit?"

God, I wanted to. I ached to find out more about the physical love side of this thing. But something stopped me. "Can I tell you one thing before we go anywhere?"

He pulled back from whispering in my ear to grin down at me. "Of course. What is it?"

"I'm a..." I swallowed hard. *Virgin* was such a strange word to say out loud, so I opted for a different choice of words. "I've never had sex with anyone before." The idea of having sex with all three of my supposed 'mates' was terrifying.

Jonah pulled a bit further back, his mouth dropping open in shock or awe, or perhaps both. "Are you serious, Bella?"

"Of course, I am. That's hardly something to lie about."

He grabbed my face in his hands so suddenly I gasped. The he started kissing me all over again, fast, intense, and all-consuming.

I closed my eyes and willingly went along for the dizzying, heady ride. Obviously my being a hopeless virgin wasn't a turn-off for this guy. Hopefully, Elliot and Tommy would feel the same way—though a part of me knew they wouldn't.

CHAPTER 8
TOMMY

Elliot and I ran until we were exhausted, then ran some more. Through the forest and past the town. When I was finally aching in every joint and all four paws, Elliot and I turned around and ran all the way back to our pack.

If that didn't wear out my wolf long enough to give me some breathing room to speak to Bella, I didn't know what would.

When we finally got back to town, we went straight for our shack, the small two-bedroom house Elliot and I shared.

I ran for the back door and closed my eyes, letting go of my wolf so that I could shift back to my human form. My back legs elongated, and

I lost my black and white vision so that I could see in color once again. It was still afternoon judging by the look of where the golden sun hung suspended in the sky.

Elliot shifted next to me and slowly stretched up to his full height.

I grinned at him. "We found our mate."

Elliot didn't smile back. "You really think she has two Alpha mates?"

I shrugged. "Why? You willing to give her up?"

Elliot growled, low and threatening.

Surprised by his aggression, I glared at him. "Back the fuck up. I was joking." I pushed at our back door, already annoyed. Storming into our kitchen, I pulled some energy drinks out of the fridge. I threw one to Elliot, then opened one for myself.

A lot of people had said that two Alphas couldn't be as close as we'd always been. Best friends. Living together. But we'd always made it work, until now.

"Listen," I said, "she's my mate. I know it in my bones. All the signs are there. The instant attraction. The scent of her drives me wild. And of course, my total loss of control when it came to my shifter." I stared at Elliot, waiting for him to say something. Anything.

All he did was grunt. "Yeah, and...?"

For fuck's sake... seriously? I grabbed my sports drink, chugged down the full bottle, then threw it toward the recycling. "So, did you feel the same thing? Is she your mate as well? Or did I read you all wrong when I saw you shaking like a damn leaf at Milly's?" I glared at him.

And he glared back.

I probably shouldn't have poked him about his reaction to our mate, but *hell*, he was being a dick about all of this.

Elliot didn't deign to answer me. He just stormed off toward the bathroom. "I'm going to have a shower."

I glanced at the time. "It's five already, so I'll be heading off to Milly's in forty-five. You coming?"

Elliot just slammed the bathroom door behind him.

"Wanker," I muttered under my breath with a sigh. I leaned back against the counter and ran my hands through my hair. Jeez. I'd never imagined my mate could be so beautiful or so young. And even in all my craziest dreams I certainly never would have guessed she'd be a witch. I laughed and shook my head. "Billy's going to give me bloody hell for this." I'd teased my younger brother for weeks over his mate, Ruby, being a witch. I had it coming now!

I headed upstairs to my own private bathroom to have a shower and a shave. I didn't care if my mate was a dark-haired witch. Or that she was younger than my youngest brother, which made her at least ten years my junior. She was beautiful. And she was mine.

Since I'd all but given up any hope of being mated, and having a family, this felt like a literal dream come true. If I had to share her, then so be it—my inner Alpha be damned. If Billy could do it, and if an Alpha like Jackson could too, so could I. But whether Elliot could share her with us? Well, that was a question I didn't know the answer to.

Once I was dressed in my best jeans and favorite black shirt, I headed downstairs.

Elliot was nowhere to be seen. He'd obviously decided he didn't want to see Bella again.

That was fine by me. If he wanted to give Fate the big middle finger, so be it. But I damn well wasn't going to. This was the opportunity of a lifetime. Everything I'd ever wanted, albeit a little different than I envisaged. I grabbed my cell phone and wallet and headed out the door. Elliot wasn't a child, and I wasn't his bloody mother. If he didn't want to see our mate again, then that was on him. It was his life, not mine. I wouldn't be the one living with regret.

Personally, I thought it was pretty ridiculous to leave her to Jonah and me, but I'd never bothered to try and figure out Elliot or his moods before. Then again, I'd never really cared before that he was a grumpy bastard. It didn't affect me when I was just his best friend. But as his co-mate, or whatever we wanted to call this new relationship dynamic we found ourselves in, it might become an issue that needed to be resolved in future.

I walked the two blocks over to the main drag, that only consisted of four shops, then stopped dead. There she was. I opened my mouth, forcing myself to breathe as my heart hammered like a drum in my chest. *God, she's an angel.*

Bella stepped out of her little car and looked around as though she was lost. Her eyes were big and her shoulders slumped.

I wanted nothing more than to go over there and kiss her worries away.

She bit her lip like she was nervous, and the breeze ruffled her long dark hair around her, making her appear even more sensual and inviting. She tucked the loose strands behind her ear, seemingly uncertain of what to do next.

My heart squeezed tight at just how right this all felt. And then I was walking across the street before I'd even decided to move. I stepped around a passing truck and grinned.

My mate whirled around to stare at me wide-eyed like a deer caught in headlights, as though she'd heard me approaching—which was almost impossible. She must have *felt* me somehow, as I moved like most shifters did—with perfect stealth.

"Hey," I managed to say, though my wolf rose within me like I hadn't run him for eight hours today. *Calm down.* I swallowed hard, willing my human self to stay attentive and strong. "We didn't officially meet this morning. I'm Tommy." I extended my hand, wanting to touch her.

She stared up at me with those dark, beautiful eyes.

All I wanted to do was reach for her so I could cup her face and press my lips against hers in a deep, possessive kiss. Then I noticed the swirl of purple, the magic deep within her and I decided that sweeping her up into a kiss, moments after officially meeting my witch mate, might not be the smartest move of my life. I didn't want to magically end up on my ass.

"I'm Bella," she said and reached for my hand.

I shook her hand and the second our skin touched everything inside me exploded with rapture. I gasped, gripping her fingers tighter to capture and hold onto the feeling.

She began to crumple.

I let go of her hand and swept her up into my arms before her head hit the concrete. "Whoa. I've got you."

She put her head on my chest and her hand on my neck. She panted as though she'd run a mile.

My skin tingled from head to toe in a similar way to what I feel before I shift. With knowledge. With power. With intense awareness. I shivered, suppressing the growl that rose in my throat. "Are you okay?" I asked her, not able to see her face.

She glanced down, her hair falling over her cheek. "Yeah, I'm okay. But that was a bit intense. Can we go maybe inside?"

People walking by looked at us strangely. It was a small town; everyone knew everyone. Which meant Bella stood out like a bulldog's balls, and the fact I was holding her in my arms was a strong testament as to my commitment to her.

"Sure. Let's go." I hoisted her up higher in my arms and made for the front door.

A heavy hand landed on my shoulder, stopping me in my tracks. "What happened to her?"

I turned to see Elliot frowning down at me. "Get the door, would you?" I said tersely.

Elliot glared at me but grabbed the handle and held open the door open for us.

"Couldn't stay away, huh?" I threw over my shoulder, unable to resist.

Elliot growled.

Bella shivered in my arms.

I grimaced. "You're scaring her. If you're gonna be like that, you can fuck right off."

Elliot's eyebrows drew together as he glared pure fire at me.

I could see he was about to spit back at me.

Bella's hand reached out for him unexpectedly. She touched his skin and squeezed his arm with need. "Don't go," she said. Two of the sweetest words I'd ever heard. My best friend didn't stand a chance against her.

Elliot's face changed from one of intense anger to one of complete passive helplessness. He swallowed hard, his throat working, then he nodded. "Okay."

I rolled my eyes. I didn't think she'd cast an actual spell on him, but she may as well have.

Jonah came rushing up from the back of the eatery. "What happened? Bella? Are you okay?" He cupped Bella's face and ran his hand all over her.

Every part of me wanted to scream at him that he needed to back off. But I didn't need to say anything.

Jonah seemed to get the message as he locked eyes with me, froze, then began to back away. "I've got a booth," he offered. "Come sit in the back, with me." He turned on his heel and walked away at pace.

I shared a glance with Elliot. I knew exactly what he was thinking. Were we going to have to put up with living with my little brother for the rest of our lives? *Oh fuck, heaven help us.* And him. I walked ten or so feet to where Jonah had slid into our booth.

Bella wiggled in my arms. "Um, you can put me down now."

I didn't want to, but what sort of man didn't put a woman down when she asked? *A sicko. So, put her down.* I tilted forward and let Bella slide out of my arms and to her feet.

She shuffled around the table and sat with Jonah, pressing right up against him. Hip to hip. Shoulder to shoulder.

I glanced over at Elliot. *Oh, crap.*

We were Alphas.

Jonah was a Beta.

Bella shouldn't be cuddling up to him like that. It went against traditional pack politics and the expected, normal female behavior. And yet our mate seemed to know him, and at the moment, she also seemed to like him better than she did us.

Acknowledging that apparent fact felt like trying to swallow a throatful of sawdust. I shuffled over the seat. "Thanks for coming back tonight, Bella. I know this morning must have been strange for you," I said to break the tension.

Elliot slid into the booth beside me, managing to not touch me despite the fact that we barely fit together in the seat.

She smiled. "It's okay. I know we probably have a lot to talk about."

"Yes, I suppose we do."

Her gaze slid up to Jonah, then across the table to stare at us. She took a deep breath, then began what sounded like a rehearsed speech. "I have to be honest with you guys, here. I'm not sure I'm cut out to deal with three mates. Honestly, I doubt I'll be a good mate for one of you, let alone all three, but if you want me..."

"I want you," Jonah said straight away, his hand sliding over hers, where she rested her hand on the tabletop. "We'll work it out, some-how. I'm sure. We'll just take it one day at a time."

Bella's gaze flicked up to mine.

I opened my mouth to say the same thing. But the only 'words' that came out were garbled growls of anger.

Bella turned to Elliot, her gaze hopeful, but he'd already slid out of the booth and was sauntering toward the exit.

Damn it. I swallowed hard and forced myself to focus, to speak bloody coherent words. "I want you, Bella."

An answering smile trembled on her lips. "Thank you, Tommy. But why do I feel like my heart just marched out on me?" she asked, watching after the other Alpha.

Elliot threw open the door to Milly's and left.

I sighed. Part of me had hoped that having two Alphas in this pack was going to be a mistake. But that was selfish, because from the look on Bella's face, the only mistake that had been made, was that we'd let the dickhead walk out the door in the first place.

CHAPTER 9

ELLIOT

Of all the stupid, fucking things to do. Anger surged through me at a phenomenal rate of knots. I couldn't stop the feeling. It was like the tide, or the moon. Gravity even! It was inevitable. My hands clenched by my side and my vision flashed from wolf to human. The urge to scream—to howl to the moon—was so strong that my throat ached.

I stormed down the street, my wolf rising into the outer edges of my subconscious. What was I going to do? My mate was here. *My mate!* I should be at Milly's still wooing her and seducing her, before I dragged her back to my bed to make love to her for so long, and so well, that she'd never leave me. Never even consider looking at another man. Except, this mate, my mate... *would.* No matter what I did. And she *always* would.

She had two other male mates. I'd never be able to convince her that I was good enough to be her one and only mate. Jonah and Tommy would always be there. In our life. In our... bed. A sick, twisted smile screwed up my face. *Tommy.* Of all people. I loved the guy. Truly. Like a brother. Even more than my own damn brothers, in fact.

I'd reconciled myself to the fact that I'd probably live with him for the rest of my life, if I couldn't find a mate. But I didn't want to share a woman with him! I didn't want to see him naked and fucking her. I shuddered. The very thought of watching my best friend fucking my mate almost made me lose it. A growl rumbled in my chest. My shifter called to burst free. To run. To get away from the pain, the anxiety, and the jealousy.

But one thing held me back, a single tendril of logic that my wolf couldn't fight. Despite the fact she looked at least ten years younger than me, and she was a witch—one of those that we had been taught to fear, to hate—she was here. In the pack grounds. And she wanted me! That is if I read her touch and her looks correctly.

I reached the edge of town, and ahead of me was a winding gravel road that would take me to the highway. My wolf itched to shift and run, to escape from the unpleasantness that came with being human. With being *me.* But as I stared down the road out of town, I realized I couldn't go. I didn't want to run away from my mate. I wanted to look at her. Touch her. Hear her voice. Protect her.

I turned back around and stared down the main street of our town. Could I do it? Share my mate? Probably not. Jonah would submit to me if it came to a fight between the three of us. But Tommy? A grudging respect swept through me at the thought of my best friend. *Hell no, he'd never submit.* Not on his life.

Although I was taller and heavier, Tommy had cunning and speed on his side, attributes that would serve our mate well if she needed to be protected. As that thought snaked through my consciousness, I sighed and began to amble back to Milly's.

Thinking about what my mate needed, and wanted, should be my top priority. My everything. It was where my parents' marriage had failed. They'd both been too selfish, only looking after their own needs. They'd had one of the only failed matings in the long history of our pack.

I groaned as I trudged forward, running two hands through my hair and squeezing my head with my palms like I was being held in a vice. I had both of their genetics. Selfishness was literally in my blood. Why else would I feel this way? And yet Tommy was quite happy to share with Jonah? Share a mate. A woman. *Her pussy.* I shuddered at the thought, and yet my feet kept dragging me back the way I'd come.

Jonah stood at the edge of the street staring at me.

I groaned aloud. Had the young pup seriously come after me? I didn't see Bella or Tommy anywhere else. I stopped where I was, about half a block away.

Jonah waited for a car to drive past, then jogged over the road toward me.

I crossed my arms over my chest. "Come to find me?"

He grinned at me, undeterred by my size or strength. I'd always admired the kid for that.

"Coming back to us because you realized you made a mistake?" he countered.

I growled at him.

He laughed. "Yeah, I figured as much. Are you going to come back? Bella's been saying she wants to go home, but I don't think she really wants to. It's more that she doesn't feel welcome."

He didn't say anything about the fact that *I* was the reason she felt so unwelcome, but I got the message loud and clear. "Okay," I said. "Let's go." I followed the kid back to Milly's to see Bella arguing with Tommy. I frowned and dashed over to them. "What's going on?"

They turned to look at me and Bella's eyes were full of tears.

I reached for her, and she came into my arms. I held her close, her face pressed tightly against my chest. I rested my chin on her head. She was the perfect height for me. A wave of undeniable longing passed over me, almost stealing my breath away. I wrapped my arms around her and just held her. *Oh, my God. I'm never going to let this woman go.* I forced my eyes open, even though I wanted to simply remain there and rock her forever. "What's going on?" I repeated.

Tommy shrugged. "She wants to go home. I was just trying to get her to stay for dinner."

Bella lifted her head and looked up at me, her heart in her eyes. "I really want to go. Can you take please me?"

I nodded. There was no way I could deny her. "If she wants to go, I'll drive her." I pulled back, though a wave of cold moved in the moment she stepped away from me.

"We'll all go," Tommy said.

"*No.*" The word shot out of me so fast I couldn't stop it. I glanced at Bella with a grimace of half-hearted apology. "Would you be okay with me driving you?"

She stared at me a second, then nodded. "Yes. I think we need to chat."

Yeah, we probably did. I grinned at her. "You could probably blast me out of the car if I do or say anything you don't like, right?"

She smiled slowly through her tears. "I could blast you out of this diner if I wanted to, but I'm not afraid of you Elliot."

My mouth dropped open. She looked sweet, innocent, and delicate, but there was steel in the petals of this flower. I liked it. A lot.

She turned toward the other two, who were veritably pouting. "I'll be back here tomorrow, with my mom, for Thanksgiving. We're having lunch over at Ruby's house."

Tommy went to say something.

Jonah put a hand out and stopped him, surprisingly commanding his silence. "We'll see you then."

I nodded at my fellow co-mates and took Bella's hand, a sizzle of awareness shooting up my arm. I swallowed the moan that rose in me with difficulty.

We exited through the front door.

I glanced left and right. I'd lived here my whole life, and yet in this moment, with my mate's hand in mine, all I could feel buzzing through my veins was my need to protect her. As if danger might come from anywhere.

"Where's your car?" Bella asked me.

"It's back at my place. You okay to walk a few blocks? It's not far."

She nodded. "I'd like that actually. I need to clear my head."

I intertwined our fingers so she couldn't go anywhere. "This way."

We walked across the road, down to the end of the shops, then turned right off the main street, heading toward my place.

"It's only another block or so," I told her, relieved that my wolf seemed to have quietened since walking with her. Or maybe it was the touch of Bella's skin on mine. But there was something substantial holding me anchored in my human form.

"Okay."

We strolled the rest of the way in silence, though I got the feeling she wanted to say something but wasn't ready. Not yet anyway.

We arrived at my place, and I tugged her toward my truck. "I don't assume you want to see inside?" I asked, indicating the house, and then fished my car keys from my pocket.

Bella turned toward the small two-bedroom house Tommy and I had built about five years ago, when both of us had realized we couldn't live with anyone else, and our fated mates were nowhere to be found. "Who lives here with you?" she asked.

"Just Tommy and me."

She turned again to stare at me, her eyebrows drawn down in a frown, as though confused. "You two live together?"

"Yeah. Why?"

"Because... I don't know. I guess I kind of got a strange, competitive vibe from the two of you."

I laughed. She read us well, which would hold her in good stead for the future. I leaned against my truck and crossed my arms over my chest. "We have an insane rivalry for best friends. But that's what kind of makes us work. You want to see inside?" I asked again.

She raised an eyebrow at me. "I wouldn't mind, but you seem ready to go, already. What's wrong? Haven't cleaned the place up in a while?"

I chuckled and shook my head. "We don't clean up. We're bachelors—or were," I corrected.

"Then what's the problem?" she asked.

How honest could I be with a woman like this? I could smell the innocence on her—something else that was driving my wolf absolutely insane!

I cocked my head to the side and stared at her. "The problem is that if I get you within ten feet of a bed, you're not going to stay vertical for very long."

She yelped and practically ran over to the car, her dark hair whipping behind her.

Yep. Far too innocent for me.

She hustled around to the passenger side of the car.

I stared over the top of the cabin. "Are you as innocent as you smell?"

"As I *smell?*" she asked, her voice going all squeaky as though she was offended or shocked by the question.

I nodded. Of course, there was one good way to tell: sink my cock into her and see how tightly she squeezed me. I shook the thought off. "Well?" I repeated.

"Well, what?"

"Are you a virgin?" *Please, please, don't be a virgin. I'm not sure if I have the patience, or control for that.*

Her eyes went strangely wide, then she nodded.

Damn it. I groaned. "Get in the car before I make a fool out of us both."

She jumped into the truck.

I closed my eyes and threw back my head. If I made a list of everything I didn't want in a mate, Bella was practically the epitome of it. Too sweet. Too young. A witch, for heaven's sake. And of all things? A fucking... virgin! How the hell was she ever going to handle someone like me?

I threw myself into the car and turned on the engine. There was one thing for certain though. I might fear her ability to handle my sex drive and strength, but my wolf loved the idea that she'd never been taken. I would be her first. I'd make sure of it. Perhaps not her only. Perhaps not her last. But I would stamp my ownership on this little witch so that she'd never leave me. She'd never want for anything while I was around.

If I had to share her with my co-mates, then so be it. But even as the thought spun around in my head, my stomach tightened like I'd taken a punch to the gut and my heart sank. This wasn't what I wanted. Not at all.

CHAPTER 10

BELLA

I wrapped my arms around myself, suddenly freezing. Anxiety skittered along my nerves like sparks along live wire. I was about ready to fling my magic around the car and transport myself back home. But as I bit my lip and glanced over at the guy filling the car beside me with his massive bulk, and obvious resentment, I couldn't do it.

Running away from him would be the worst mistake of my life. I knew it. I could feel it in every premonition, and magical bone in my body. The same way I knew my mother regretted nothing more than leaving my father alone long enough for whatever had happened to happen.

There was a difference in our situations, obviously, but I was drawn to this huge hulking Alpha more than anyone. *Why?* I had no idea. He was a mystery. That was for certain. "Are you angry at me?" I asked, though I was pretty sure I knew the answer already. He *was* angry at me. At the situation. At everything, if his demeanor was anything to go.

He turned onto the road and started driving out of town. "No. Why would I be?"

I lifted my hand and swirled my hand in his direction. "I'm getting a whole lot of angry vibes over here, for one thing. And you stormed out of the café without a word or explanation."

He sighed.

I waited for him to say something. I was more patient than Ruby and Tiffany, but damn it was hard to wait him out. I began to recite spells in my head, practicing, testing myself—to see how many I remembered by heart.

"I'm not angry at you," he finally said, breaking the silence. "Just, this whole *mess*."

"You mean your pack not having enough females for you to mate with?" I asked. That was something I really wanted to help the pack fix if I could. Without the ability to give birth to daughters, the pack's blood lines would soon be dead and gone. Once I'd sorted out my own situation, of course.

He sighed. "Partly. Hang on. What do you know about that?"

I swallowed hard and lifted my legs so that my feet were on the car seat, and I could hug my knees like a physical shield against my heart. "Just so you know," I began, "I have this... thing with being honest. I like to tell the truth as much as possible and prefer other people to be the same. Even if its uncomfortable or whatever."

I'd learnt that the hard way when I hadn't told Ruby about what I'd done with the spell last year. And now with my mom's lies about my dad. The truth was just better, no matter how hard it was to admit to.

Elliot nodded. "Fine by me. So, tell me what you know."

"Basically, twenty-three years ago, three cousins from your pack went missing, and ever since then, there's been no females born to your pack. Correct?"

Elliot nodded. "Pretty much."

"How old are you?" I asked. "Because there should have been heaps of females around your age born... or do I assume incorrectly?" He had to be older than me, by quite a bit if I wasn't mistaken.

"I'm almost thirty-five, so yeah, there were a lot of females for Tommy and me, in our years."

Thirty-five. Shit. He's so much older than me! I swallowed down the response that would point out just how young I was. My mom wasn't going to like this at all, despite her encouragement to chase love. "And you still didn't get married?"

Elliot shrugged. "I was waiting for my Fated mate. I wasn't going to just... mate some woman who wasn't meant to be mine."

His poetic and strangely possessive words fell around me like a spell and I shivered. Despite his huge, gruff, exterior, it was obvious this wolf shifter believed in the magic that drew two people together. Or in our case, four people.

He glanced at me as we drove closer to my house. "What's that got to do with the Manterri cousins?"

I sighed. "Long story short, one of those men was my father."

Elliot's arms flinched and he swerved.

"Whoa!" I yelled, grabbing hold of the 'oh shit' handle above the door, as Tiffany liked to call it.

He swerved back into the lane. "Are you telling me that you're half wolf shifter? That's why you're my mate?"

"Well, according to my mom, my dad was half warlock, but yeah, there's wolf shifter in me, too."

Elliot shook his head as if the puzzle pieces were finally falling together. "It's all making sense now."

I swallowed hard. "There's more."

"More what?"

"More you need to know."

Elliot gripped the steering wheel tighter, his knuckles showing white in the fading sunlight. "I'm game. Hit me with the truth, Bella."

If he hadn't been driving, it would have been laughable how intense this conversation had gotten. By the way my heart was pounding in my chest, my whole body knew how dangerous a situation I was in.

I drew my magic into my fingertips, ready to cast a spell to transport us both to safety if anything untoward happened. Like Elliot swerving the truck off the road entirely. My heart dropped, but I forced myself to say this next part in a rush. This piece of truth almost lost Ruby her mates, and I wasn't going to make the same mistake. "Last year, Ruby, Tiffany, and I cast a love spell that would bring our soul mates to us."

Elliot frowned. "Why would you do that?"

His reaction was unusually calm, so I relaxed a little. "Because all three of us grew up without fathers. Our mothers were, and still are, all single. Their hearts were broken. We didn't want that same fate for us. So, we all swore when we were teenagers to not date and wait for the right man to come along. Plus, the warlocks in our coven were always super suspicious of us and never wanted to date us anyway. In retrospect, it was probably the wolf shifter genes that put them off."

That was something I'd never really thought about before this minute but made sense now that I was hashing it out. Of course, none of the boys in town, human or warlock, wanted to date us. Our wolf shifter genes would have scared them all off!

"And when you say love spell, it doesn't make us fall in love with you, right?"

I shook my head. "Oh, no! It's nothing like that. It just encourages Fate to put our soul mates in our path, earlier. It can't make you feel anything that's not real."

Elliot slowed down the car as we drove down the main street of town. "You're going to need to give me directions on where to go."

I directed him left, then right, then over to where my mother's house was. "Just there. The house with all the flowers in the front yard."

My mom was a bit of a hippy. She wore bright colors, had long flowing hair, and liked flowers all around her. I for one loved how different she was.

Elliot pulled up and turned off the engine. He twisted around to stare at me from the driver's seat. "Okay, so, you're half wolf shifter, well, a quarter wolf shifter. Your father is one of the Manterri cousins who went missing twenty-three years ago, and that is somehow linked to the lack of women in our pack. And you cast a love spell that sped up our meeting. Anything else I need to know?"

I blinked at him. "How are you so calm about all of this?"

Ruby's guys had all but flipped over this very thing.

He shrugged. "I already knew most of it."

My mouth dropped open. "How?"

"Jackson and I are cousins."

I slapped my hand against my forehead. "Oh, my God. Why didn't you stop me then?"

"I wanted to hear your side of the story as well."

I nodded slowly. "Okay, well, that's good to know." *The strong and silent type. Never thought I'd get one of those.*

Elliot shifted in his seat. "Do you think the cousins' disappearance has much to do with our pack's population problem?"

I nodded. "I'm not meant to say anything yet, not until we investigate it more, but yeah, I do. It sounds like someone cursed your pack. Why? I don't know. How? Same. No idea." I bit my lip. I hated knowing so little.

Elliot stared out the windshield. "I suppose it doesn't really matter now, and it's not like you had anything to do with it. You weren't even born yet."

I dropped my feet to the floor and unbuckled my seat belt. "I can't believe you're being so calm." I opened the door to the truck and got out, a little in awe of the guy who'd driven me home. Ruby's guys had lost their shit over the fact that we'd used a love spell to find them. Was Elliot really that much cooler?

He got out of the car too, walked around the hood, and leaned against it.

I stared at him, drinking him in. He was hot. Too hot for me. Mature with a

huge body. Thick thighs. Massive shoulders. Then there was his face. *Damn it.* Those eyes were those of an angel and devil, mixed into one.

"Come here," he said, and held out his hand.

I glanced around. This was my neighborhood. What if someone saw and told on me? What if my mom saw me?

"Come here," Elliot repeated.

I walked forward and took his hand.

He pulled me into his body so that our hips were connected and he was staring down at me. "Have you kissed either of the guys yet?"

I nodded honestly. "I kissed Jonah yesterday."

Elliot grabbed me around the waist, spun us around, lifted me up, and put me on top of the hood of his car.

"Tommy?" I shook my head, swallowing hard against the nervous shivers coursing through me.

Elliot cupped my face with his huge, strong hands, his skin hot against mine. He tilted my face up to him.

I could hear the frantic hammering of my heart in my chest.

He was so much taller than me that even though I was sitting on the hood of the car, I still had to stretch up to meet his lips as he came toward me.

I wanted to get even closer. I slid my hand up his chest, connecting with hot, hard muscle.

Then he pressed his lips against mine so sweetly, hot tears gathered in my eyes.

I surged up to get closer, wanting a deeper contact.

He groaned in his throat and pressed open my lips with his, stroking his tongue through in search of mine.

I moaned in return, wrapping my arms around his neck to pull him closer.

His hands left my face and slid lower, grabbing a hold of my ass and dragging me hard against his body.

I gasped against his mouth, both terrified by the huge, hard lump between his thighs, and aghast at my body's reaction to it. My belly melted like a hot pool of lava, then began to tighten and throb with yearning. The desire for Elliot rose up so hard and so fast inside of me it felt like he was working a spell on me. My hands were everywhere, and I was moaning like a wanton in some porn film.

I was out of control. I didn't care if it was meant to be this way, or if, because he was my mate, this would be considered 'right'. It was too much, too fast. I wanted him too much. This couldn't be normal. I pushed my hands hard against his chest.

He lifted his head, staring down at me with eyes that had partly shifted.

"Please stop," I said, though my open thighs shook with the need to wrap themselves around his waist and pull him tighter to my body.

He growled softly in his throat, grimacing as he stepped back. "What happened? Did I do something wrong?"

I slid off the hood of his car and on trembling legs I walked over to my front door. "Nothing. You didn't do anything wrong." *Except remind me that I'm more of a woman that I realized.*

My front door opened, and my mother stepped out. She raised her hand as though to cast a spell.

Fear pulsed through me. I yelled out, "No!" and flung a protection spell around myself and Elliot, dragging him closer to me. I could hear his cursed complaints from behind me as he stumbled forward, ending up practically pressed against me.

"What the hell is that?" he asked.

My mom dropped her hand and stared at me; her eyes as round as the moon. "Who is this, Bella?"

I checked my mother's mood, and although she seemed stable, I wasn't ready to drop my shield just yet. Ruby had told us how the moms had magicked her boys back to the pack grounds when they'd seen her kiss Jackson. I didn't want Elliot to have any more reasons to distrust us witches. "This is Elliot. One of my soul mates."

Mom's eyes bugged out of her head. "So, it's true? You have three just like Ruby?"

I nodded. No point lying, not that I ever would to my mom. "Yes. I have three. Just like Ruby."

My mom's mouth opened and closed.

I felt her energy change, and I dropped the shield.

Elliot stumbled away.

I turned toward him.

His eyebrows were lowered and there was an angry glint in his eyes.

I didn't understand what he was angry about now. "What...?"

"Don't you ever do that to me again." Elliot growled, spun on his heel, then stormed off.

I stared after him.

He jumped in his truck and drove off without another word.

"But you don't even know what I did. Or why," I whispered, because I knew he'd never hear me, even if I yelled them.

Mom's arm came around my shoulders. "I don't think he liked being magically manhandled."

I glanced up at her. "What do you mean?"

She turned me toward the house and we started walking to the front door. "What you just did, wrapping him up in a protection spell and pulling him into you so I couldn't touch him? That's the magical equivalent of manhandling."

I sighed. "Seriously? I was trying to protect him!" *Stupid men.*

I spent the night tossing and turning, worrying about Elliot. At one point, around one a.m., I'd been super close to just transporting myself into his house so that I could check on him and see if he still hated me for what I'd done.

But then I realized that if he'd had such a bad reaction to the small bit of magic I'd worked on him, he was unlikely to appreciate me teleporting right into his house. It was kind of breaking and entering, technically. *Sort of.* Plus, what if he slept naked? The idea filled me with so much desire, I was horrified. So, instead, I stayed in bed, writhing with unfulfilled lust and no small amount of embarrassment.

By the time I'd gotten up and helped Mom prepare for Thanksgiving lunch at Ruby's house, I was practically gasping with unsatiated need.

"What's up with you this morning?" Mom asked as we got in the car, ready to drive over to Ruby's new place. "You're like a cat on a hot tin roof."

I sighed and glanced out the window, watching the town fly by. "I'm fine. Just worried about Elliot." *And the fact that I have no control when I'm around him.* What was with that kiss? I'd been ready to let him take me, in whatever way he wanted. And that scared me. How was it possible to want someone on that level? Someone I barely knew.

I'd never really thought about the chemistry that existed between two people. Or the sexual attraction and connection that would build between me and my soul mate. And yet here I was, smack bang in the middle of everything I didn't want. Three men. Sexual attraction galore.

I groaned and crossed my arms over my chest, my nipples tingling uncomfortably. This was ridiculous. Maybe there was a spell I could do to counteract this? Or at least tone it down? I felt like I was going to explode with desperation!

"You're going to have to direct me," Mom said. "I don't know where I'm going."

I shook myself. "Oh, yes. Sorry, turn into the pack's town, and drive right up Main Street."

Mom did as I told her, driving slower than the speed limit.

"Mom, you can go a little faster."

"I know. I'm just looking around."

Or looking for someone, perhaps? I smiled at her as she practically stuck her head out the window to see everything.

"Did you look for him, Mom?"

She glanced over at me, then turned back to the road. "Of course, I did. I even cast searching spells and did scrying for months—looking for him and the others. But nothing showed up. It was like they'd become ghosts and vanished from the face of the Earth."

Or cursed, I mused. "Turn left here." I directed Mom to Ruby's house, and we pulled up behind her mom's car.

"Looks like Sherie is here already," Mom said with a more relaxed tone.

I nodded, glancing around. Were my men here already? Would they come today?

"Let's go." Mom grinned and grabbed the food she'd made: a scrumptious pumpkin pie, a special, organic, hippy-style quinoa salad, and a seriously colorful fruit platter.

The latter was my request since my stomach was churning with anxiety and I didn't want to have to eat 'heavy' food all day. I grabbed the salad and the pie.

We headed across the road and up the garden path to Ruby's new home.

"Impressive," Mom said, glancing around at the quiet, clean neighborhood.

"The house is as well," I told her. "Haven't you been in the wolves' town before, Mom?"

She shook her head. "Not really. I think I came here and met your father once or twice, but it was so long ago. The memories fade with time."

I tilted my head at her. "It's strange to hear you talk about him so casually now." Unlike throughout my whole life, when my father was practically the only banned subject.

A pink hue flushed her cheeks. "Well, it's kind of nice that every-thing's out in the open, now."

Not yet it's not. Not until we know what happened to our fathers.

The front door opened, and Ruby burst out. "You're here! Come in!" She ushered us inside with a flurry of noise and commotion.

The lounge room was abuzz. There was rock music playing, and the table had been set for ten. I glanced around, noticing extra changes that I hadn't made. A silver gilded mirror, another rug, and a few more decorative throw pillows. Someone had clearly been busy. Was it Ruby? Or her mom, perhaps?

The painting I'd magically created was still the only hanging picture adorning the space. I walked over to stare at it, a smile full of pride lifting my lips.

"You did a great job with that," Billy said casually as he walked up next to me.

His voice sent a small shiver down my spine, and I rubbed my hand over one of my arms to warm the now-goose-bumped flesh.

"Thanks. I haven't seen you guys in wolf form yet, so I hope I got it mostly right." I glanced up at the picture. "I can change anything in it, really."

Billy shook his head. "No. It's perfect."

I turned toward him and found him staring at me. I lifted an eyebrow. "Yes?"

He didn't smile, but something lit up in his eyes that looked like amusement. "I hear we're soon to be related."

I groaned. I'd almost forgotten two of my mates were brothers. And that their brother was Ruby's mate.

"News travels fast."

He shrugged. "It's a small town."

"You're pretty close to your brothers, I assume?" I asked.

Despite Tommy and Jonah being quite different, I could imagine there was a certain, unbreakable closeness among people who grew up together in the same household, especially if they were related by blood.

I couldn't imagine having siblings myself, not now anyway. My best friends, my *cousins*, were the closest thing I'd ever had to sisters.

Billy nodded, glancing up at the painting again. "I could never work out why I was black, and my brothers were white wolves. Especially when both our parents shift into gray."

I shrugged. "Well, black and white make gray." It kind of made sense to me.

Billy turned to me with a look that told me I didn't get it. "Ruby's wolves are all black. Yours are all white. Including Elliot."

I stared at him. "You think our mates are, what... color coded or something?"

Billy laughed and the sound was a harsh barking, like he didn't laugh very often. "Yeah, something like that."

I looked up at the picture, then back at him again. "I wonder if Tiffany will have the same thing?"

Billy grinned. "The blonde?"

I nodded. That was how most people saw Tiffany, as 'the blonde' one of our trio. She was so much more though, strong in a way I wasn't.

He shrugged. "You've got white. Ruby's got black."

"What's left?" I asked.

He frowned. "The rest of the pack is mostly brown."

I tilted my head. "Didn't you say that both of your parents are gray?"

He nodded, though there were shadows in his eyes I didn't understand. "Yes. But the gray wolves are rare now."

I started to ask what he meant, but the front door opened, and I shivered. Not from the cold, but with awareness and premonition. *My men were here.* I turned to face the hallway that led to the front door. My breath caught in my throat, and I froze as all three sets of eyes zeroed in on me. I couldn't move.

The whole room seemed to be holding their breath in preparation for what would happen next.

Jonah stepped away from the two, hulking Alphas and moved over to me. "Hey, beautiful."

I managed to smile, though my knees were starting to give way. "Hey."

The room broke into a cacophony of noise as all the men greeted each other and Ruby was at the center of the hurricane.

My mom stood with Sherie in the kitchen, watching the maelstrom with a strange look of envy.

I frowned. Were they really jealous of us? What for? For finding these men? I stared, feeling for the vibe of our moms and yes, it came back the same. *Jealous.*

They must really miss their men, I thought, a twinge of sadness for them snaring inside of me.

"What happened last night?" Jonah asked, leaning close and whispering against my ear, all the while pressing a warm hand to the small of my back.

"What do you mean?" I asked. *Other than the hottest kiss of my life.*

He shrugged. "Tommy came back to the pack, mad as a cut snake. You two get into a fight, or something?"

I shook my head. "Not really, but I used some magic, and I don't think he liked it."

"Is that it?"

"Yep."

Jonah turned back to the group with a shake of his head. "Weird."

Ruby began to take control of the room, throwing her hands and voice about. "Lunch is served. Grab a plate. Help yourself. Sit wherever you want!"

The guys all grabbed plates, and single file, filled their plates with all the trimmings. Turkey and pork, pies and bread, salads and roast potatoes.

I stood back and watched, standing with the moms.

When the men were finally settled at the table, I got my plate, filled it with whatever I thought I could stomach, then slid into one of the only remaining chairs—in between Jonah and Ruby.

The conversation flowed well, and the food was beautiful. Ruby's mom magicked up more dessert when the first platters were empty; but I couldn't eat half of my main meal, let alone dessert. My stomach was in knots. What was I going to do about my men? I needed something to distract me.

I turned to Ruby who sat to my left. "I want to go speak to some of the Coven about the high warlock and try and find out what he might have done to our moms twenty-three years ago. You want to come along?"

Even though I'd spoken very quietly, the whole table of six wolf shifters stopped talking, and turned to look at me.

An embarrassed heat flushed up my cheeks and I stared at the wooden table, unable to take the pressure of all six men staring at me.

Ruby laughed. "Shifters have exceptional hearing. You'll never get away with whispering ever again."

I risked glancing up and was mortified to see them all staring at me still. My gaze shifted to my mom, who was sitting with Sherie and looking perplexed.

It was Darren, the part-warlock, who leaned forward and spoke to me first. "What do you mean, exactly? Ruby told us what your moms told you guys about the spell, and that you assume it's linked to the lack of females in our pack."

I looked over at Ruby.

She threw her hands up. "I don't keep secrets from them. Sorry."

I pressed my lips together, unsure how much to share.

Jonah's hand slid across my thigh and squeezed. "It's okay. Just tell us what you're thinking. Everyone here knows that you weren't even alive when it all went down."

"They're right," Sherie said, interjecting. "If anything, they should blame us for what happened."

I shook my head. "But we don't actually know what happened, and that's what I want to find out."

"Why?" Jackson asked, taking another slice of pumpkin pie and placing it on his plate. "I mean, there's nothing you can do now, is there?"

I tilted my head. "Well, it truly depends on what was done."

"What do you mean?" Darren asked, staring at me intently.

I took a deep breath, "Well, if my instincts are correct..."

"And they usually are," Ruby added with grin.

I continued as though she hadn't spoken. "Then the high warlock at the time created a spell that got rid of our fathers and cursed the women of this town so that they couldn't have any more daughters."

The whole table was listening to me, and although I kept staring at the table to avoid their gazes, I had to push through the uncomfortable feeling so that I could keep talking and share the truth as I knew it.

"Yeah, but the high warlock's gone," Ruby said from her place beside me. "He died what... two years ago?"

I looked at Jonah. "And there's been no girls born in that time?"

He shook his head. "None."

I nodded, running through the components of the spell. *What would have been required to harness that much power?* I tapped my fingers on the wooden table. "Then the curse has to be linked to either our mothers or us. If we can sever that tie, then maybe there's a chance we could lift the curse."

No one spoke.

I risked a glance up. I met Tommy's gaze because he seemed the least intimidating of all these virtual strangers.

"So, does that mean you might be able to fix the pack's problem?" he asked hopefully. "Make it possible for our women to have daughters again?"

"You might be able to save the pack," Jackson said from the other side of the table, his eyes wide.

I nodded. "That, and more."

"What more?" Jackson asked.

I swallowed, finding it harder than usual to be honest in this moment, but they deserved the truth. "I want to find out what happened to my father."

CHAPTER 12

BELLA

Ruby reached over and squeezed my hand. "They're gone, Bella. They've been missing for twenty-three years. For all we know they might even be dead."

I twisted in my chair to stare at her, anger flaring brightly in my chest. "How can you say that? You might've met your dad when you were young, and he was a wolf. What if the high warlock cursed them to their wolf forms, forever? Unable to communicate or shift back to human. What would they do? Where would they go?"

Ruby stared at me, her eyes wide and a little hurt.

I sighed. She wasn't the one I should be asking. I turned around to stare around at the table of wolf shifters. "Do you guys know? Would they hang around here? Would they go to another pack?"

Elliot and Tommy glanced at each other.

Then Tommy looked at me. "You need to speak to the pack elders."

"Why?" I asked. "Would they know?"

"Elliot and I heard them talking about the Manterri cousins, years ago, now. We were, I don't know, maybe fifteen at the time?"

Elliot pressed his lips into a thin line but didn't say anything.

They'd been fifteen, so assuming Tommy and Elliot were the same age, that was some twenty years ago.

"What did they say?" I pressed.

"That they'd run into a small pack of wolves that looked like the Manterri cousins. They were distinctive because they were the same size, same age, and all three of them were gray."

A sense of premonition shot down my spine like a bolt of lightning. *That was them!* "So, what happened after that?"

"They said that if the guys wanted to come back, they could. But they had to apologize to the whole pack first, for what they'd done."

My mouth dropped open. "What did they do?"

Tommy shrugged. "We don't know. They never told us. And we were kids, practically. We weren't part of the council."

I nodded, putting all the pieces together. "So, our fathers could very much be alive." I swallowed hard as emotion rose. What would my father look like? What would his voice sound like? And if the three men had been in wolf form for twenty-three years, would there be much of their humanity left?

"There's no way of knowing if they're still out there, Bella," my mom said softly. "I told you; we did so many location spells trying to find them, but we never could."

I ignored my mom. She'd been heartbroken and pregnant and had assumed my father had abandoned her twenty-three years ago. I didn't really believe her when she said she'd tried *everything* possible to find him. I looked at Tommy and Elliot, my Alphas. "Can you organize for me to speak with the elders?"

"Me too!" Ruby piped up.

I bit my lip. "We'll probably need to include Tiffany as well. She won't want to be left out of this, especially as her father was involved, too. Where is she, by the way?"

Ruby shrugged. "She said she had to work, but I think she didn't want to deal with us and all our mates. It'd be hard for her."

The words hung in the air, and I swallowed hard, trying not to blush. It was still so new, and such a surreal thing to acknowledge that I'd found my soul mates. *And Tiffany hadn't.*

"Yeah, you're right. She must be feeling left out." I tried not to look at my men, but my gaze swung with unerring accuracy toward Elliot and Tommy.

They stared back with an intensity that made my chest ache.

Tommy nodded. "We can arrange something."

I smiled at him, wanting to tell him how grateful I was for their help, but now wasn't the time to be super gushy. "Thank you."

With that sorted, Ruby soon moved the conversation into less fraught waters and the rest of the afternoon passed quickly.

I managed to follow along with the conversations, but inside my mind, I was consumed by questions. Mostly about my father, and where he'd been for the last twenty years. I couldn't even imagine having a father in my life now. Like I couldn't imagine having three soul mates. And yet, wanting Jonah, Tommy, and Elliot in my life was a lot more natural than I could have ever dreamed. *Perhaps having a father would be the same?*

When the kitchen was packed up and the festivities were over, Mom and I began to grab our bags.

Tommy and Jonah stepped forward and greeted my mom.

"We didn't officially meet," Jonah said, standing quietly by.

I smiled at my sweet Beta and turned to my mom. "Mom, this is Jonah and Tommy. They're Billy's brothers."

"Brothers? As in, you're both Bella's mates, and you're brothers?" Her shock relating to my situation had officially reached a whole new level.

I turned to Mom and whispered, close to her ear, "They don't touch each other, Mom." Then I turned to where Ruby had moved to stand beside me. "Do they?"

Ruby laughed.

Jackson slung a possessive arm over her shoulder. "There's no crossing swords around here."

I frowned at Jackson. "Crossing...?" *Oh, my God.* I turned to my mom, heat warming my face. "Time to go."

"Actually," Tommy said, interjecting. "We were hoping you'd hang around a bit and we could have some time with you. Alone."

"Alone," I repeated, assuming I would never be *alone* again. "As in, the four of us?"

I could feel Ruby practically vibrating with excitement, but she was holding herself together.

"Bella, I'm not sure about that..." Mom began.

I turned to her and gave her a stern look. "I'll be fine." A virgin I may be. But a child I was not. And these were the men that both Fate, and my magic, had decided I should be with.

Tommy cleared his throat and glanced at the floor. "Ah, it'll be the three of us. Elliot had some work to do on a house. But we could catch up with him later."

My gaze shot around the room. "Where is he?"

"He already left."

Disappointment washed over me like a tidal wave. I wasn't sure why. Two days ago, I would have been terrified about the idea of handling three men at all, let alone, at once. Now, I felt so rejected. My throat tightened and I had to force myself to swallow the lump that rose. "But... why? He seriously had to work?" *On Thanksgiving?* I didn't believe it.

Tommy glanced away.

Jonah grinned. "What's wrong, beautiful? We're not enough for you?"

His tone was light-hearted and humorous, but something behind the words made me stop and assess what I was about to say next.

Balancing all their needs was going to be a challenge, especially with the jealousy aspects of brothers and best friends. Not to mention the competitive nature of men to begin with.

"It's not that. I'm just worried about him." I said. "We had a bit of a fight, or something, last night. I know he's mad at me and I just wanted to sort it out."

Jonah's posture relaxed.

Tommy grinned at me. "Don't worry about Elliot. When he's got his back up about something it's better if you just let him be. He'll work through it."

I wanted to believe Tommy. After all, from what I'd gathered, they'd been best friends their whole lives. But something told me that more time apart was just going to tear us asunder. But how was I going to tell these two that? All I was going on was a gut instinct and premonition.

"Okay. I'll trust you know him better than me." I put my bag on my shoulder and kissed Ruby goodbye. "Thank you so much for lunch and it was great to catch up." I waved to Ruby's men, then kissed Sherie on the cheek. "See you all soon."

My mom walked me out, her nervous aura making me want to shake her.

"Stop it," I said when we were way down the path, elbowing her gently in the arm. "They're not going to hurt me."

"Just take this with you," Mom said, tugging off one of her bracelets and pressing it into my palm. "It's a locator and will bring you straight home if you need it."

I almost rolled my eyes at how protective she was being but tried to empathize. I tried to imagine what it would be like to be in her shoes, watching her only child walk away with two huge wolf shifters intent on seducing her. "Thanks, Mom. I appreciate that." I hugged her tightly. "I'll be home later, okay."

"Do you want me to come get you?" Mom asked, as she pulled her car keys out of her bag, the keys jingling a little more than normal.

"We can drive Bella home later," Jonah offered.

"I'll call you if I need a lift, Mom, thanks."

Jonah took my hand and pulled me into him.

We both watched my mom stiffly walk to her car and hop in.

Tommy stepped up next to me. He chuckled as she drove away. "She's so worried about us," he said. "I thought she was about to magic you back to your house just so she could save you from us big, bad, wolves."

I laughed as I turned toward the big Alpha, the only one I hadn't kissed of my three mates. "Well, compared to most witches, my mom is very open-minded. It's probably how she ended up falling in love with a wolf shifter in the first place, even though it was forbidden."

"Forbidden? Are you serious?" Jonah asked.

"Yeah, I read about it years ago. Marrying outside of the Coven has always been forbidden. Some human marriages were allowed, but they had to be approved." And that was another reason Tiffany, Ruby, and I had assumed our fathers were warlocks. They were the only ones that our mothers should have been associating with.

"Well, I'm glad your mom fell in love with a shifter," Tommy said, grabbing me around the waist and pulling me from Jonah so that I was pressed against him, staring up into his bright blue eyes.

"And why's that?" I asked, though Tommy's intent was pretty obvious, and it wasn't to continue the conversation.

"Because they made you, and your wolf shifter genes made you our mate. It's perfect."

"Perfect, huh?" I slid my hands up his chest until I could feel the pounding of his heart beneath my palms. "Wouldn't you have preferred a wolf mate?" *Surely that would have been easier for them?*

Tommy grinned, his white teeth flashing as his hands kneaded the flesh of my hips, drawing me even closer. "Who am I to question Fate? It knows what I need more than I do." He dropped his head.

I lifted my chin, wanting to know what it would feel like to kiss him. To know that everything was just as right with him as it was with Jonah and Elliot.

Before I could finish the thought, Tommy kissed me.

A sweetness stole over me that I hadn't expected. It was soft, and gentle. I slid my hands up and gripped his head, dragging him closer. Deeper. Wanting more.

Tommy growled, deep in his throat and grabbed my ass, hard.

There it is. What I was looking for. It's not what I'd experienced with Elliot, *thank God.* This was controllable and not scary. Just a beautiful, smooth, soft roll of desire through my body. I opened my mouth and let Tommy explore me, reveling in the kiss and wanting more. Needing more. I wanted to know what was behind this desire, this lust, where our mating would finally lead us.

I pulled away from the kiss and stared up into Tommy's lust-drugged eyes. I felt so safe with this Alpha. There wasn't the wildness in him that I felt with Elliot. With Tommy there would be safety and control. "Where are you guys taking me so we can spend some time together?" I asked. Hopefully, it was somewhere more private than the street outside Ruby's house.

Tommy kissed me once more, lightly on the lips, then gripped my hand and pulled me down the street. "Our house is empty for the next few hours. Let's go check that out."

Jonah hurried to catch up with us.

I squealed as excitement hit me in the belly. But closely behind it, a wave of doubt settled in. What would Elliot say? How would he feel if I moved ahead to the next stage of our relationship with Jonah and Tommy? I shook off the thought and allowed Tommy to pull me into the unknown.

Elliot was the one who had chosen to leave us today. He was the one who had to live with the consequences of that choice. Not me—*I hoped.*

CHAPTER 13

TOMMY

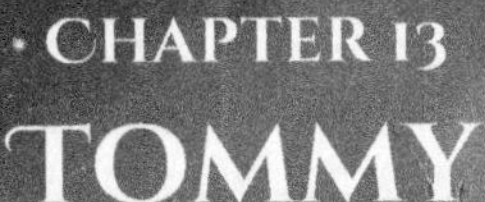

Having Bella's hand in mine was like walking in paradise, a place I'd never known existed. Just touching her skin, and knowing she was mine, settled my wolf to a level I didn't know existed. My wolf was no longer scratching at me to run, to fight, to be on the constant move.

He was still there, inside my chest, but with my mate's hand in mine, as I pulled her toward our house so I could finally make love to her, my wolf was calm. We would finally have the mate we'd waited for all this time.

Jonah jogged ahead of me to open the door.

I swept our mate up into my arms and crossed the threshold.

She squeaked and grabbed my neck, pressing herself against me.

Our house was simple. It only had one living room with a spacious kitchen and dining area. We had two large bedrooms, each with its own ensuite. One downstairs next to the living area which was mine. And one upstairs, which was Elliot's.

Elliot and I had designed it with the impression we'd always live here together, growing into two grumpy old men. Single. Forever.

How things change. I walked straight into my bedroom, still holding my mate, and set her down on her feet.

She looked around, her eyes wide. "You're not giving me the tour then?"

I pointed toward the living room. "Kitchen. Bathrooms behind you."

Bella walked over to the bedside table and placed her mother's bracelet down. Then she turned around to look at the ensuite as though she wanted a tour of the house.

Screw that. I was desperate to hold her, touch her. "Come here, beautiful." I walked over to where she stood by the bed and grabbed her hand, pulling her into me.

She pressed a flat palm to my chest. "We're going slow, right?"

I nodded. "Absolutely."

Jonah had said something about Bella being a virgin yesterday, which didn't surprise me. She smelled of purity, and sweetness, in a way that only virgin women did, not that I'd sensed one for a very long time.

I cupped her face and kissed her.

Jonah moved around behind her.

I glanced up.

My brother was kissing her neck.

Bella moaned luxuriously.

And at that moment, I decided this whole teaming up thing could work out well. She'd get so much more out of both of us working on her. Despite how much it was going to kill me to go slow,

I wanted Bella to remember this, always. "Lie down on the bed, baby."

Bella lifted her head and stared at me. "I'm not sure..."

I smiled at her. "We won't go any further than you want. I promise." I led her to the bed and reached for her blouse. "Let me show you how good you can feel."

She turned her head to glance back at Jonah.

He walked up behind her and kissed her hungrily.

While she was moaning softly with her eyes shut, kissing my brother, I tugged her skirt down over her hips and lifted the hem of her blouse. "Arms up, beautiful."

She broke her kiss with Jonah and lifted her arms so I could tug off her top. Then she was standing in her underwear.

"Damn, you're beautiful."

Bella glanced down at her body and began to lift her arms to cover herself.

"Oh no," I said, swinging her up in my arms, then walking the few feet to the bed and placing her down on the soft mattress. "There'll be no covering up this perfect body."

I glanced at my brother. "You go up. I'll go down."

Jonah grinned at me and crawled onto the bed.

"What does that mean?" Bella asked, glancing up at Jonah.

Hovering over her, my younger brother smiled at our mate. "It means I'm going to pleasure the top of you, while Tommy takes care of you down below."

She sat bolt upright. "No! I... I don't think I can do this. It's too much."

I hadn't been expecting that reaction.

Jonah stared at me, his eyes wide and panicked.

I got up and slid onto the bed next to her, lying down on my side. "Come here, beautiful." I rolled her onto her side and stared at her beautiful face, cupping her cheek. "I want to make love to you. Will you let me?"

She swallowed hard. "I'm not sure I want to do... everything."

I nodded. "How about everything else but sex? I'll keep my pants on. And so will Jonah."

Her eyebrows rose. "So, I won't be able to touch you at all?"

I laughed. "I thought you wanted to keep some distance between us?" *Goodness, this girl was contrary.*

She bit her lip. "No. Can we just go slow. Please?"

I nodded. "Yes. And if you say stop, at any point, we'll stop. Promise. Okay?"

She nodded. "Okay."

"So, you trust us to do the right thing?" I asked, wanting her full consent though my plan was to pleasure her and leave myself frustrated. Tonight was just about Bella.

"Yes."

I lifted her chin and kissed her lightly on the lips. "Then let me love you."

She nodded.

I slid off the bed, going down onto my knees, and reached out to grab her thighs.

She cried out in surprise.

I smiled and grabbed her ass, hauling her close enough to eat. Then I glanced up at my brother.

Jonah was repositioning himself so that he could lay down and kiss her at the same time.

Satisfied with our team efforts, I looked down at my meal. "So beautiful," I said, as I ran my hand up her silky thighs and stared down at her soft belly. I dropped my head, pressing a kiss to her belly button and inhaled her scent.

She was wet and wanting me.

Or us?

I couldn't be sure, and I didn't think it mattered. The scent of arousal wafting up my nostrils was making my wolf go insane. I clenched my teeth. *She wants slow. Settle down.* I grabbed her ass and began to knead her supple flesh, glancing up when I heard Bella gasp.

Jonah was tweaking her nipples and sucking her flesh through her lacy white bra.

I pulled back and grabbed the waist band of her pale pink panties. "These need to come off, beautiful."

"The bra too," Jonah growled softly.

I moved to pull them down, but Bella called out.

"Hang on, let me do it." She inhaled sharply and frowned.

How?

And then her underwear was gone entirely.

I stared up at her. *Respect.* "That is a neat ass trick."

She covered her face with her hands.

I chuckled at her embarrassment. She was so strong and yet so sweet. So naïve and yet so instinctual. Our mate was a lot of things, and not all of them made sense, but she was perfectly our Bella. I stared down at her pussy lightly covered in soft, dark hair. Natural. *Nice.*

I pushed open her thighs and began to kiss the insides of her legs.

She resisted at first, but then Jonah began to work on her and she was soon distracted.

He suckled her nipples and kissed her neck and face, smothering her in intense, but tender passion.

Her legs relaxed as she did.

I moved closer to paradise. My own body throbbed, my cock hard in my jeans. I staunchly ignored the need to rip off my clothes and free my aching shaft. Bella needed to know that she could trust us, and I couldn't think of a better way to prove it to her than this. We would give her the most amazing amount of pleasure possible and take none for ourselves. She was our focus.

I kissed a path all the way up to her inner thigh, then moved up and licked across her belly and down, tasting her pussy for the first time. *Oh, fuck yeah.*

Bella gasped and grabbed my head, gripping my hair tightly.

Although I sensed she wanted to, she didn't pull me away. So, I waited, just breathing against her soft flesh.

She didn't move or try further to stop me.

Satisfied that she yearned to continue, I flattened my tongue and stroked it over her swollen clit.

She gasped again, the sound like music to my ears.

I moved lower, tasting her lips and her sweet juices.

Her belly contracted tight, and she half sat up, gasping even louder. She writhed in pleasure, arching her back and throwing her head from side to side.

I wanted—needed—to get closer to her. Carefully I slid up next to her, running my hand down her sexy little body, over her mons, and slid my fingers lightly over her wet folds.

She turned her head toward me, her lips parted on a gasp and her eyes widened.

Without a moment's hesitation I slid a long finger inside her.

She moaned, her eyes closing as she arched closer to me.

I pressed deeper, loving how wet and juicy she was. How her pussy gripped my finger tight. *Damn*, that was going to feel nice on my cock. I groaned as I thrust my finger in and out. "Bella, you feel so fucking good."

She turned her head toward me again.

I took the opportunity to kiss her, tasting her lips and groaning as she thrust her tongue forward desperately to meet mine.

"My turn," Jonah said, shuffling down her body so he could kneel between her thighs.

I didn't want to withdraw from her body, but I took my fingers out of her perfect pussy and wiped my hand on the sheets.

Jonah began to kiss her thighs.

"How you going, beautiful?" I asked her, cupping her sweet little breasts. They were perky, and pink-tipped, and fit my palm perfectly.

"I'm... ah!" She arched again. "I'm... I don't know."

Jonah began to work on her.

She thrashed her head as she experienced the pleasures that a man —*or men*—could give for the first time.

I smiled to myself. My balls were practically blue, I needed release so bad. But as a virgin who knew little of her body, I could only assume that Bella had no idea what she needed. She trusted us to guide her, to go slow with her. I got up on my elbows and leaned over her body, cupping her breasts and sucking on their delightful pink tips. Her nipples hardened in my mouth, and I used my teeth and my tongue to lavish them with love.

"Oh! Ah... Tommy, I... Can you—" Bella managed between shallow, gasping breaths.

Jonah came up next to her again, putting a hand on her belly in a possessive caress I didn't expect of the younger Beta. "What's wrong, Bella? Did I hurt you?"

"No," she said, shaking her head from side to side on the pillow adamantly. Then her gaze landed squarely on me. "Tommy, can you put your hand back... inside me?" She tugged on my arm, need written all over her beautiful expression as she led me back down between her thighs.

I grinned. "Need to come, baby?"

She nodded in agreement, though I wasn't sure she fully understood what I meant.

I slid my fingers over the swollen bud of her clit, circling the flesh.

She grabbed at me with urgent hands, her nails pinching my skin.

Then I slid two fingers inside her, feeling her gasp at being stretched.

She tightened around me like a perfectly fitted glove.

"Come on, beautiful. Come for us." I flexed my fingers inside of her with years of practice, hitting all the spots I hoped she'd love.

Her eyes began to roll back, and she reached for Jonah, turning her head and lifting her chin to kiss him. She gasped against his mouth.

I watched as she began to tense up, her pussy tightening around my fingers as I continued to gently thrust them in and out. I heard the front door open and shut but didn't think much of it. I couldn't pay it much heed, not when Bella was about to have her first orgasm in my arms.

She screamed out in ecstasy, and began to pulsate around my

fingers, her belly shaking and trembling as she frantically rode her first ever wave of release.

I watched her face contort in rapture as she came down from its crest, then her eyes opened in wonder, and she looked up. Then she scrambled to sit up, her gaze one of shock.

I withdrew my fingers, worried I'd hurt her, and glanced toward the door.

There stood Elliot, taking up most of the door frame. With the light casting shadows around him, he looked like some sort of demon. He didn't so much as utter a single word, but as a growl rolled through his chest and his teeth flashed even in the dark, I *knew* we were all in trouble.

The hairs on the back of my neck stood up and I jumped to my feet, ripping off my shirt, putting myself between him and Bella.

If the Alpha wanted a fight, he was going to bloody well get one.

CHAPTER 14
ELLIOT

The sound of Bella's orgasm should have been the hottest, most amazing sound I'd ever heard in my life. But instead of getting to enjoy it, feeling it around me, and wanting to be a part of it—I stood practically a world away, in a doorway watching it happen. Cold and alone.

The rage of my wolf simmered deep in my gut. My mate was lying completely, gloriously naked, between Jonah and Tommy. Tommy had his fingers inside of her, juices glistening all over his hands. And Bella came for them, long and hard, her naked body writhing on the bed as she screamed for them in the throes of passion.

The sound was like a knife in my heart. The betrayal ran deep, antagonizing old wounds. My hands clenched into tight fists, and a dark, possessive growl rolled through my chest. She was my mate. *Mine!* What the hell were they doing here without me in the first place?

My wolf rose up inside me and fast began to take over my human body. I had no hope of stopping it. Not now. It was dangerous. Closing my eyes, I tried to push him down, tried to stop him from emerging. There was no-one to fight here except the men I considered family and the woman who was my mate. But there was no pulling him back. It was an exercise in futility.

Tommy jumped from the bed, an expression of determination in his features.

Fur began to sprout from my skin and I dropped down to all fours, my clothes melting away as my wolf emerged, rearing for a fight. Then I launched at my oldest friend, teeth bared.

～

Bella

I WANTED to scream but my throat closed up and the sound was lost forever. I stared, horrified at the scene unfolding before me.

Elliot transformed into a savage-looking, snarling wolf.

Jonah threw himself in front of me.

Tommy got to his feet, the Alpha in him rising.

"What do we do?" I gasped out to Jonah.

"Your mom's bracelet," Jonah said, launching across the bed to where I'd put the piece of jewelry down on the bedside table. He thrust it into my hand. "Go. Quickly. We'll find you later."

Tommy had shifted already, and the two huge, growling wolves stood in the room, facing off against each other.

I didn't think, there was no time. I clutched the talisman, said the transportation spell in my mind, and closed my eyes. The sounds of aggression and feelings of terror faded away, and I was suddenly in a quiet room. I opened my eyes and looked around, instantly recognizing the location. I was stark naked on my mother's bed, and she was nowhere to be found. *Thank God.* I jumped to my feet and raced to the bedroom door, but it opened before I could get there.

"Bella!" Mom stared at me aghast.

Both of my hands went to my boobs, covering them up, and I awkwardly crossed my legs over in an attempt to protect my lower modesty. "Um…"

Mom flung her hand through the air.

I was suddenly wrapped in her dressing gown. I smiled in relief at the small mercy as I slipped my arms into the holes and tied the belt. "Couldn't remember where mine was?"

Mom gave me a half smile in return. "I panicked. You're lucky you didn't end up wrapped in a sheet. Or worse, my underwear."

I grimaced, pulling the dressing gown tightly around my body, my heart still thundering inside my ribs. "Thanks, Mom."

"What happened?" my mom asked. "Are you okay?"

I nodded, thankfully still in one piece. "Yeah, I'm okay." But my eyes were filling with hot tears, and it became apparent that I was probably not as okay as I thought.

Mom wrapped her arms around me and held me tight.

I buried my head into the corner of her neck and sobbed, releasing the pent-up tension and shock of what just happened with my mates. *What a day.*

"Did they hurt you, sweetheart?" Mom whispered. "Because if they did, the girls and I will make them pay, don't you worry."

The vehemence in her soft words made my tears dry faster than anything else could. I lifted my head, wiping away the wetness that still clung to my cheeks. "Oh no. You can't do that. They didn't do anything wrong. It wasn't them." It wasn't me either. It was just nature. Wolves and witches weren't meant to get along, let alone mate. We were too different.

"What happened, Bella?" Mom asked more softly, taking my hand and leading me to sit on the large blanket chest at the end of her bed.

I sat and picked up a purple throw blanket, pulling it over my lap for something to hold on to.

"Please tell me," Mom pressed, her lower lip wobbling as though she may start crying soon too. "I'm imagining the most horrible things."

"Oh, please don't," I said, before sighing. "Long story short. I went back to Tommy's house with Tommy and Jonah, and they decided to... try some stuff with me."

"What kind of stuff?" Mom asked, narrowing her eyes.

I rolled my eyes. "You know, Mom. Kiss me, and touch me, and... stuff!" *Damn.* This was embarrassing.

"So... good stuff, then?" Mom asked.

"Yes!" *Why was she assuming the worst?* "You were in love with a wolf shifter, yourself, Mom. And I'm sure he wasn't horrible to you. Why are you assuming that my men are... rough or something?"

Her face turned as rosy as Ruby's red hair. "Oh, well, you're right. Your father never did anything I didn't want him to."

That sounded slightly strange. Had he been rough, and my mother had liked it?

Ugh! Too much information! I shook the thought out of my head and concentrated on the conversation at hand. "Well, they didn't do anything bad to me either."

"So, why did you transport back here naked?" Mom asked.

I shook my head. There would be no hiding anything from my mom now. "Basically, I was with Jonah and Tommy, then Elliot came home unexpectedly and saw us."

"And he got upset?"

I nodded. "Yeah. Very. It was like—rage. He shifted into his wolf. Then Tommy shifted into his. And Jonah told me to go. So, I did. It seemed like the best course of action."

Mom stared at me, then covered her mouth with her hand.

"What?" Was she horrified? Was she disgusted? "What is it, Mom? Tell me."

Then she began to laugh.

"Mom!"

"I'm sorry," she said through her laughter, a tear rolling down her cheek. "I just can't believe it. I've spent your whole life worried about you. Worried that you'd find out who your father was. Worried about who you were going to marry in future. And now? You have three huge, possessive, jealous wolves fighting over you... and it's just too much."

I pouted. "Well, according to the boys, Fate decided I was the best person for them."

"Of course, you are, sweetheart. The love spell has ensured that outcome certain as well. It's just, I never imagined it would be like this for you."

I sighed heavily. "Me neither. I wasn't even sure I'd have a husband, or children."

Mom cocked her head at me. "Why not?"

I shrugged. "I don't know. It was just a feeling." I *did* know, though. My mom was sad and alone. I didn't want that for myself. So, avoiding all sorts of romantic relationships and entanglements had seemed like the right way to avoid that.

"So why did you do the love spell in the first place, then?" she asked softly.

"Because Ruby and Tiffany wanted me to."

Mom groaned. It was a long, drawn-out sound. "You know what I've always said about those girls. Just because they're you're best friends..."

"And my *cousins*," I added.

"And your cousins," she amended, "doesn't mean you have to be like them, Bella. You're different. You're special."

"Well, it doesn't matter now. I did it, and now I have two Alphas fighting over me, and then there's Jonah, of course." A strange laugh bubbled up in my throat. "I can't believe it, really. I have two guys fighting over me. It's insane."

"Three," Mom corrected.

"No, not really. Jonah doesn't fight. He's a Beta. Things between

Jonah and Tommy are fine. They're happy to share me. It's just Elliot. He's possessive to a whole other level."

"So, maybe you need to choose just to be with them," Mom said.

The thought made my stomach swoop, and I forced down the bile that rose in my throat. "I'm not sure I can choose between them, Mom." The idea made me physically sick. Especially the idea of walking away from Elliot entirely. My connection to him seemed unusually strong.

Fate had sent me three men. The love spell wanted me to love all of them. Now that I'd started to fall for them, all for different reasons, I wasn't sure I wanted to give any of them up.

"Jonah seems like the sort of guy you should be with," Mom said. "He seems nice, protective as well."

Of course, that's who she'd suggest for me. The guy next door type. Sweet. Non-threatening. Nice and safe, but capable of taking care of her only daughter. "Was that what Dad was like?" I asked.

Mom's gaze zoomed back to mine, and I saw her carefully considering her words.

I raised an impatient eyebrow. "Well?"

Mom opened her mouth, then cleared her throat with a rough cough. "Um, no. Not at all."

"What was he like then?" I prompted.

Mom stared at her hands which were clasped in her lap. "He was strong. A lot more like Ruby's Billy, I'd say."

The bad boy. Damn, Mom. "I wish I could have met him," I said, and it was true. It always would be.

Mom reached over and clasped my hand. "Me too, sweetheart."

I stared at my mom for a long moment and felt her love squeeze me, wrapping me in a warm cocoon. Then I broke the look and stood up. "I better get dressed. Jonah said they'd come for me later—when they've resolved their wolfy issues, I guess." I began to walk toward the door.

"Bella?" Mom called out. "Think about what I said, yeah? Just because you feel attracted to all three men, doesn't necessarily mean you can be a family in the end."

I twisted around and stared at her. "But Ruby..."

Mom shook her head. "I told you, sweetheart. You're not like your friends. Perhaps three men is simply... too much. Just because Fate has offered you that many men, doesn't mean that you're meant to be with all of them. Maybe it's more about making the right choice for you?"

I straightened, feeling my stubborn streak flare. *No, that's not true. Fate sent me three men because I'm meant to be with all three!*

My mom put out a hand, obviously seeing the obstinance in my face. "Please, just *think* about it at least."

I nodded, conceding that it was something to consider. "I will." I left Mom's room and headed straight for the shower. I needed a moment to think and to wash away the scent of arousal that lingered on my body. Closing the door, I turned on the water, and shrugged out of the dressing gown. My nipples were tender, and my thighs were still slick with my own juices. *Ew.*

I stepped beneath the water and let the heat wash away Tommy's and Jonah's touch. If I had to, could I really choose between my mates? And who would I choose if I could?

Jonah was beautiful and young, like me. Happy and sweet. He'd be a good best friend for the rest of my life. I could trust him and rely on him. And kissing him was just heavenly. Surely, sex with him would be good, too?

Tommy was hot and dominant, which a secret part of me loved. He made me feel cherished. He'd look after me and perhaps encourage me to explore things and push myself in a way that Jonah and I just... wouldn't.

And Elliot, well, he made me want to strip off and mount him practically in the street. It actually frightened me how much I wanted Elliot. I didn't feel like myself when I was with him.

With Tommy and Jonah, I could be *me*—Bella the witch—without worrying about losing control. But with Elliot, a part of me was scared. I wasn't sure if it was the Alpha in him calling out to the wolf shifter in me, or if there was another reason for it. But our connection was... otherworldly.

Perhaps we'd been partners in a past life? Because a part of me recognized him; wanted to go down on my knees and serve him. And that went against everything else inside my rational mind.

I scrubbed my body and washed my hair, then finally got out of the shower and towel-dried myself. If I had to choose, Jonah was the safest bet. Jonah and Tommy, if I could choose two. We'd work well and easily as a little family. The guys, after all, were already family. Rationally, I would never choose Elliot as my one and only. He was all the things I wasn't. Passionate. Intense. And completely uncontrollable.

And then it hit me. *Elliot was my punishment for the love spell I'd cast.* Salty, hot tears stung my eyes. He was the curse and the gift all at once. To want someone so much who just didn't suit me, or the other men in my love triangle. My family. I sobbed softly as I brushed out my hair and wrapped a towel around my body so I could get dressed.

I hadn't been sure what my punishment would be for casting the love spell that took payment for its success, but the answer seemed to be staring me in the face. I couldn't have Elliot, no matter how much I wanted him. He would forever be the fire to my ice, and that would be my cross to bear. Even if it broke my heart to do so.

CHAPTER 15
TOMMY

I put an ice pack on my swollen eye and took a sip of the bourbon and Coke my brother had placed in front of me. Nothing like a drink to settle the stomach and take the edge off the pain of a fight—especially a losing fight.

"You need anything else?" Jonah asked me.

I shook my head and relaxed on the couch. "No, thanks."

Jonah collapsed onto the other side of the couch. "Where's Elliot gone? Do you know?"

I shook my head. "Nope. And at the moment, little brother, I don't give a shit." I would in the morning, though. Elliot and I had blown up at each other about shit in the past, but we always worked things out. It was one of the reasons we'd stayed friends all these years. We always put past grievances behind us, where they belonged.

"Do you think he'll forgive us for taking Bella to bed without him?"

I glared at Jonah, his question surprised me. "What do you mean, will he forgive us? There's nothing to forgive. We didn't do anything wrong."

"Didn't we?" Jonah asked, giving me a steady stare.

I took a long drink of my bourbon then rolled my eyes at my baby brother. "Listen, Junior. Stop getting all smart with me, okay? Elliot wouldn't have thought twice about us if he'd gotten to Bella, himself. He's just sore he wasn't the first."

And that was all it was. The stupid idiot was jealous as fuck, and being possessive over something that shouldn't have those sorts of rules. Loving our mate shouldn't be a competition about who could give her the most or the best. She wasn't a pie to divide and hoard in individual pieces.

"We've got our whole fucking lives to be with Bella. Why did he have to go all wolf and freak her out?" I said.

Jonah held up both hands. "Don't ask me."

I sobered, then took another drink. "That was good thinking, by the way. Getting her to, you know, magic out of here."

Jonah grinned at me. "Did you hear that bit?"

I nodded. "We're a good team. I was too focused on the threat to think about getting Bella to safety. So, nice job."

For a kid of barely twenty-three, Jonah had some guts about him. It made me proud.

Jonah shrugged. "As you said, we're a good team. It's probably why these witches need three of us. You know, to cover all the bases."

"Yeah. I suppose." I hadn't thought of it like that until now. "What do you mean, exactly, though?" I'd had a few bourbons now, and the pain in my head from the fight with Elliot was hammering away at what little thinking ability I had.

Jonah shrugged again and ran his hand over a nearby pillow. "Well, you know, we can be different things for them. Like, with Ruby, she's got a dominant Alpha, a tough Beta, and a part warlock who doesn't listen to anyone. With us, I'm the Beta, you're the Alpha. She gets fun, lighthearted me, and protective, strong you."

I frowned. "And Elliot?"

Jonah pressed his lips into a thin line. "I'm not sure where he fits, honestly."

I sighed, taking another swig. "Yeah, me neither."

Elliot had always been like a super-Alpha to me, and to most of the pack. No-one could beat him in a fight. He was angry almost all the time and had been since we were kids.

"Look, he'll come home later, and we'll sort all this out. Like you said, if Bella needs all of our different strength, we have to figure this out—or her."

Jonah glanced at his phone. "All right, well, I told Bella I'd find her later, just to check up on her. I don't have her number, though, so I might drive into town. You want to come?"

I shook my head. "It's probably best she doesn't see me like this." I indicated my bruised face. "Do you know where she lives?"

Jonah frowned. "No. Maybe I'll go ask Ruby."

"Get her cell number too, while you're there, let her know you're coming."

Jonah stood up and walked toward the door. "Will do. Be back in a bit."

I put my head back and closed my eyes. I needed a rest before Elliot got back. He'd already kicked my ass once tonight. I didn't want to hand him another victory on a silver platter.

Jonah

"Thanks for your help, Ruby," I said to the young, flame-haired witch, and headed to my car. "Appreciate it!"

"I'll text her and tell her that you're on the way," Ruby called back.

"Great!" I got in my car and headed into town, excited to see my mate again. After so many of my brother's generation had ended up single, I'd never assumed I'd be lucky enough to end up with a mate. Especially one as beautiful, smart, and talented as Bella.

I found her house easily enough thanks to Ruby's instructions and pulled up outside the quaint little two story.

Bella jogged out to greet me with a big smile on her face.

I jumped out of the car and grabbed her, wanting her lips on mine. "Hey."

I kissed her and she lifted her mouth to mine in greeting. A shot of triumph pulsed through me. *She wanted me.* Even as a Beta, and therefore the weakest of her three mates, she still wanted me.

She smiled up at me as she pulled back. "Thanks for coming to check up on me. It means a lot."

I grinned. "Of course."

"Do you want to come inside for a bit?"

I glanced toward the house. "Is it safe?"

She giggled, the sound gorgeous, light, and happy. "Yeah, of course. It's just my mom."

A full-blown adult witch. Yeah, nothing to worry about there. I let Bella tug me inside the small house and was overcome by how cozy it was. And colorful. There was patterned wallpaper and different types of carpet everywhere.

"Mom. Jonah's popped by to say hi," Bella called up the stairs.

"Hi Jonah!" her mother called down the stairs.

I smiled, though I couldn't see her. "Um, hi!"

"Kathy," Bella said.

"Hi Kathy!" Her mother didn't respond further, so I assumed I was allowed to stay.

"Come sit," Bella said. She wore a flowing pair of purple pants and a black tank that accentuated her tiny waist.

Lust hit me in the gut. Even with her hair half wet and hanging over her shoulder, she was still the most beautiful woman I'd ever seen. I sat on the brown couch littered with a dozen red cushions of varying hues.

"Come sit with me." I grabbed Bella's hand and tugged her down.

She half landed on me, then leaned closer.

I kissed the top of her head and inhaled deeply. "Your hair smells good."

"Thanks," she said. "My mom makes our shampoo."

"Really? That's cool." I pulled her closer, fitting her into my lap so we were eye to eye. "So?" I asked. "Are you okay?"

"I am," she said, nodding. "What happened with Elliot and Tommy?"

I shrugged. "You know, Alpha shit."

"Who won?"

I raised my eyebrows at her. "Who do you think?"

Her smile faded. "Elliot."

I nodded. "He's the strongest Alpha of our pack. No-one has ever beaten him in a one-on-one fight." Nor a two-on-one, or even a three-on-one with the Betas.

Bella bit her lip in the sweetest, most worried way. "What does that mean? Is Tommy okay?"

"Yeah, of course he is. A bit beaten up, but wolves heal fast. We have super metabolisms."

She grinned. "I noticed; you guys don't have an ounce of fat between you."

I laughed. "We'll still keep you warm in winter, don't you worry."

She nodded, but glanced down, avoiding my gaze.

"Hey," I said, reaching out to take her chin in my hand and lift her face until she was looking at me again. "What's wrong?"

Her dark eyes brimmed with unshed tears, but she blinked them away. "Mom thinks I'll need to choose between you guys. She doesn't think I can handle all three of you. She thinks that just because Fate presented me with three men, that it doesn't necessarily mean I'm meant to be with all of you."

I laughed. How could I not? "What does your mom know about that? Has she tried having three men and failed, or something?"

She giggled, the tears disappearing. "Hardly. She dated my dad, got pregnant with me, and hasn't dated anyone since."

I brushed her hair behind her ear, loving being able to touch her so freely. "Then I'd say she isn't an expert on the subject."

Bella nodded, but the sigh told me there was more to it.

"Hey, come on, what's really up?"

She looked down and away, then finally lifted her face to look at me again. "I don't think Elliot and I are meant to be together."

My mouth dropped open. "Um, okay." *I doubt that very much from what I've seen.* "Well, that's easy then. Just you and me and Tommy. That'll be... easy." If that's what she wanted. Easy.

She nodded, her lips tilting up into a smile. "It would be, wouldn't it? So easy. And calm. I think that would work best."

My gut started to burn like I'd swallowed acid. I didn't like discussing getting rid of one of her mates so casually. I'd been mostly joking when I said we could get rid of Elliot. We couldn't, and I didn't think she really wanted to. She was just scared. Even talking about the subject felt like we were betraying Elliot, and I didn't like that feeling.

The guy and I had never been close. Twelve years my senior, we hadn't ever 'hung out'. But he was a respected member of our pack, and my oldest brother's best friend. He was loyal, and fierce, it was as obvious as the day was long, that Bella was his mate.

I swallowed hard. "You know that if you reject him, he'll never have another mate? That's not how this works."

Her eyebrows flew up. "What do you mean?"

She really hadn't thought this through properly.

I sighed, not sure how to tackle this, but determined to give her all the information so she could make the right choice. "I mean, if you don't want Elliot, or believe he's not your soul mate, then that's fine by me. But Elliot's wolf has chosen you, or Fate has chosen you as his Fated mate. Wolf shifters only have one. If you reject him, then he'll always be single. Not that you should worry about that—it's not your fault if the two of you don't click. I just want you to know that it's not like he can just go choose someone else if you don't him."

I shut my mouth, feeling like I was repeating myself and sounding stupid. Bella was saying she wanted to reduce her mates by one. That would give me more, not having to share her so much. I should be encouraging her, not trying to talk her out of it. *Then why does it feel so wrong?*

She slid from my lap and started pacing around the tiny lounge room. "It's not that I don't want him, Jonah. It's just that I don't think I can handle him! Look at how he responded to seeing me with you guys. He wolfed out, and Tommy got hurt when they fought. I can't spend my life like that, and neither can you guys."

I grinned at her. "Wolfed out. I like that."

She groaned. "It's true. And look at me," she said, throwing her hands around. "I'm not equipped to handle someone like that."

I wasn't sure exactly what she meant but agreeing with her seemed like the most appropriate course of action. I stood up and walked over to her. "It's all right. Whatever you decide you need, we'll find a way to make it work. Okay?"

She took a deep breath, then finally nodded. "Okay."

I didn't know if it was going to be that easy—actually, I was certain that breaking that sort of Fated bond was impossible—but at the rate Elliot was going, he was driving a big enough wedge between him and Bella, he may never be able to remove it.

I reached out to her and grabbed her around the tiny waist. "I'm sorry, baby, but I've got to go, now."

I'd come to check on her, just as I said I would. Now, I wanted to get back home and check on my brother. Make sure Elliot hadn't come back and started another fight. Tommy wasn't up for another round. He'd been lucky to get away with only the few injuries he'd sustained as it was.

Bella stepped closer and lifted her chin to present her face to me.

I dropped my head and took her mouth in a kiss that had me hardening in my jeans.

She squirmed against me invitingly.

When I broke off, we were both breathing heavily. "I think you need to come visit us again sometime soon."

She nodded, her lips swollen and red. "As long as Elliot is all sorted out, I'd love to." She walked me to the door.

I took out my cell. "I'm going to get Tommy to contact some of the elders, by the way. Have you got college tomorrow?"

She shook her head. "No. It's a holiday after Thanksgiving. We go back Monday."

"Great. We'll organize something so you can talk to them about the Manterri cousins."

"Thank you, Jonah. I appreciate that."

I walked through the door and grabbed my keys out of my pocket. "No problem. If I was you, I'd want to know what happened to my parents, too."

She stood on the doorstep and grinned at me. "Do I get to meet your parents soon?"

I nodded. "If you want."

She smiled. "Do you think they'll wonder why all three of their sons have witch mates?"

I laughed. "Nah. They'll just be glad to get some grandchildren, I think. After all the issues the pack's had, and the worries about the next generation, they'll be fine."

Her mouth dropped open. "Kids. I hadn't even thought about that yet."

I stared at her, worry knitting my gut. "You want kids, yeah?"

She nodded. "I suppose so. One day." She bit her lip. "But I'm still in college. It'll be years until I'm ready for something like that."

I held up my hands. "Hey, I'm only twenty-three. There's no rush on my account."

"But Tommy..."

She didn't say Elliot's name, but I knew she was thinking about him, too. My brother and his best friend were already thirty-five.

They'd like kids now, I was sure. But that wasn't up to them. Bella's body was her own and they'd have to accept that one way or another.

I shrugged as I strolled over to my car. "They're lucky they've got you at all, Bella. Let them wait." I waved at her before I climbed into the car. "Call you in the morning."

She waved in return. "Okay, see you tomorrow."

I pulled the door shut and drove off, intent on getting to Tommy and sorting out this Manterri cousin puzzle, once and for all.

TOMMY

I set off for home, rubbing my shoulder as I walked. It still ached from where it had been snapped earlier by my supposed best friend. "Thanks, Elliot." *Jealous bastard.*

The elders had agreed to speak to Ruby and Bella, though I sensed some hesitation in the ranks. If it wasn't for the fact that Jackson had already made a stand about Ruby being his Fated mate, the whole 'witch mate' topic would still be too taboo to even speak about; let alone the possibility of having them accepted and living with the pack.

When I returned to our house, Elliot still wasn't home, and Bella had arrived.

She stood by her little beetle car and chatted happily with Jonah. When she turned and saw me, her whole face lit up and she smiled at me as though she hadn't seen me in forever.

My heart thumped hard in my chest, and I inhaled sharply against the wave of longing that passed through me. That was my mate. The woman meant for me and literally chosen by Fate. "Hey, beautiful," I said through the thick emotion clogging my throat. I grabbed her, pulled her close, and without hesitation planted a kiss on her soft, full lips.

She kissed me quickly, then pulled back. "Is Elliot here...?"

I shook my head. "The big idiot still hasn't come home yet." I growled to pretend I was outraged, but I was actually beginning to get a little worried.

He'd never *not* come back to the pack before, even when he was younger and had less control over his wolf. *Unless he'd made the mistake of climbing into one of the available beds in town?* None of the single female shifters would reject him if he'd wanted to be there. Hopefully he wasn't that dumb, though. Jealous and angry as he was, the last thing we needed was for Bella to see Elliot stumbling out of another woman's bed. Getting her to forgive him after something like that wouldn't be an easy task. Getting her to forgive him for yesterday's outburst was going to be hard enough.

"Great," Bella said, obviously a little more relaxed knowing Mr. Grumpy hadn't come back yet. "So, what's the plan?"

"The elders have agreed to chat with you and Ruby. Have you called... what's the blonde one's name again?" I kept forgetting.

"Tiffany."

"Right. Did you want to call her too? The elders want you guys there in the next half hour or so, so we better go tell Ruby."

"Let me check." Bella pulled out her cell and started tapping away. She waited a moment, then an immediate message came. "Tiff's caught up with doing something with her mom. I'll just tell her that we'll let her know what the council says, later." Bella typed back a message, then slid the cell into her bag again. "Shall we get Ruby?"

I nodded and took her hand, loving the feel of her fingers interlaced with mine. "Let's go."

We walked the few blocks over to Jackson's house, collected Ruby and Darren, then set off to the elders.

Hopefully the girls would find some of the answers they sought, because I got the feeling this mystery was a lot more complicated than any of us expected.

∽

Bella

NERVES TIGHTENED MY STOMACH, giving me the jitters. "What do you think they're going to say?" I asked Ruby as we walked along the street, grabbing her arm and linking my hand around her elbow.

Ruby pulled me closer. "I have no idea to be honest. Don't you think that if they knew where the cousins had gone, they would have tried to get them back by now?"

"I don't know." I grimaced. I really didn't understand any of this—but I wanted to. What was the likelihood pf our fathers still being alive? *Not a lot, probably.* But hopefully we were about to find out the truth, no matter how sad or ugly it might be.

The five of us—Ruby, Darren, Tommy, Jonah, and myself—made our way to a large house that looked like a rustic church. It had gorgeous stained-glass windows and a large, steepled roof.

"What is this place?" I asked, staring up at the impressive façade.

"It's the Council building," Jonah said. "It's where we hold mating ceremonies, and birthdays, and the council members have their meetings here."

"Oh. Cool." Sounded simple. Except for the fact that I was about to walk into a room with some of the most powerful and knowledgeable wolf shifters in the whole town. *Where's Elliot when you need him? I'd feel safer if he was here.* I took a deep breath and, with my stomach flip-flopping nervously, I gripped Ruby's arm as we made our way up the steps and into the council hall.

Darren opened the large door for us, and we stepped inside.

I gasped at the sparseness inside the hall. It was a little intimidating.

Three men sat on chairs upon a raised stage at the end of the room, but otherwise the space was empty.

"Come forth," one of the men said, his deep voice booming through the room.

I glanced at Jonah and Tommy, fear skittering down my spine.

Tommy smiled at me. "It's okay. Let's go."

Ruby and I shuffled up to the stage, trembling beneath the icy stares of the three older men. They looked well into their sixties, with graying hair, and wrinkled faces. But they still seemed strong, and confident beyond measure.

"Tommy. Introduce your mate," one of the men called, addressing the only Alpha in the room.

I narrowed my eyes at them. I didn't like that. What happened to them being a modern pack that didn't follow the traditional hierarchy? Jonah or Darren were perfectly capable of introducing us all.

Tommy took a step forward. "Elder Mason, this is Bella, mine and Jonah's mate. And I believe you already know Ruby."

The elder cleared his throat. "Yes, hello Ruby."

Ruby grinned up at them. "Hi." She didn't seem perturbed by them at all.

I lifted my chin and forced myself to be as fearless as possible.

"How can we help you today?" the loud one in the middle of the trio asked.

Ruby straightened up and spoke for us. "Our mothers told us the other night that our fathers were the Manterri cousins."

There was a shocked stillness in the air, and no-one spoke.

I stared closer and sent out a wave of premonition magic.

They weren't shocked by the news. *They already knew who our sires were.* They were simply shocked we'd finally found out—that the wolf was out of the bag, so to speak.

"You already knew," I whispered.

The man in the middle frowned at me. "Yes. We knew that three witches had fallen pregnant by wolf shifters belonging to our pack. The high warlock made sure we knew about that."

The men glanced at each other in anger.

I stared at Ruby, before turning my attention back to the elders. "He came here? Why?"

"To punish us," the elder said. "The warlock swore it was sacrilege, a mixing of blood lines that shouldn't exist."

My mouth fell open. We'd been taught as children that wolf shifters weren't to be trusted; that they were dangerous and baser animals. But this was a whole new level of discrimination and hatred. "What did you tell him?"

The elder shrugged. "That we welcomed anyone who was a Fated mate of our pack. If that was three witches, then we would bring them into our fold as equals."

I frowned. "That doesn't sound right." I glanced at Ruby who'd told me that Jackson and Billy had been horrified to find out their mate was a witch. They'd obviously been taught the same thing we had as children, that it was better to marry our own sort, or a human at the very least.

"Are you calling me a liar?" the elder asked.

His growly tone sent a shiver down my spine and I stepped back and away from his hatred.

Tommy came up behind me, putting his hands on my arms to steady me. "Bella was simply asking a question, elder," Tommy growled back. "We've told her that growing up, marrying outside of the pack was not encouraged. Especially not to the witches."

I glanced at Ruby again.

She nodded. "Jackson and Billy said the same thing."

The elders were lying. I stared back at the trio of older wolf shifters. I was tempted to send out a truth spell, but that was against our laws. Not that the wolves would know that, but for the moment I would wait and see if they could stomach telling the truth on their own.

There was silence as the three elders looked amongst themselves, then they turned to us and the man to the left said, "Well, it wasn't encouraged, but there are no laws against it. Darren's grandmother was a witch. Jackson's grandmother, a human."

"Then why—" I didn't even finish getting the question out.

The elder stood up roughly from his chair. "Because that damn warlock cursed us. He said that our pack's punishment would be to have our blood lines die out. That the last three females to ever be born of our blood lines would be witches."

I gasped at his ferocity as much as at the new information too. "We're the last of all females born to your blood lines? What about all the men who mated outside of the pack?"

The elders shook their heads. "None of the men who've mated outside our pack have been successful in breeding."

"What?" I demanded. "So, hang on. Those who were lucky enough to find their mate in this pack, from the girls born before us, they all had kids?"

One of the elders nodded. "Yes, but all have been sons."

"And all those who mated outside of the pack, to what... other wolf-born females...?"

"Have not had a single live birth between them."

My stomach dropped. "My God."

Ruby grabbed me and turned me to face her. "This is even worse than we thought, Bella."

"I know." We'd known that no other females had been born since we were, thus cutting off the mating ability of most of the pack. But we'd also assumed that those same unmated males could have just bred with women born of another pack, or even other humans.

"What are you talking about?" an elder called out to us,

But I was focusing on Ruby.

Her eyes were wide as she stared at me. "No girls. No children,"

I nodded. "Only males born to those of this pack, and if they breed outside the pack, then no children at all."

Ruby nodded. "This is more than punishment."

"This is revenge," I whispered. "It means that this pack will end up with dozens of lonely males, childless and miserable."

"Talk about torture. They have to watch their pack end with them." I shook my head. "The high warlock must have really hated them."

"What are you talking about!" an elder yelled at us.

I twisted around to glare at him. "You don't need to raise your voice at us! We're just trying to figure things out."

The elder blinked at me, as though stunned I'd answered back. "Well, we've been trying to work this out for twenty years."

I shook my head. "It doesn't make sense. Why would the high warlock hate the wolf shifters enough to curse you in this way?"

"We don't know," the elder in the middle said.

Despite his ambiguous answer, I felt another layer of truth beneath what he was saying. But I held back from pushing for more information because I was afraid of getting distracted from the real reason we'd come here today. I took a deep breath and squared my shoulders. "Do you know what happened to our fathers?"

There was another moment of still silence.

The elder to the left shook his head. "No."

I narrowed my gaze at them. "I don't believe you." I raised my hand and felt the fire of frustration burning within my heart. "Tell me the truth."

"Or what?" the elder in the middle said, standing up and staring down at me.

The wallflower inside me ached to shrink back from his gaze, but a new side of me had awoken since meeting my men. A new, stronger Bella. One that wanted the truth, at all costs. "Or I'll *make* you."

BELLA

Jonah grabbed my arm, a note of panic in his voice. "What are you doing?"

I didn't flinch, nor drop my hand. "Jonah, take your hand off me, please. I don't want to hurt you."

The elders laughed.

"Hurt him? You're not that strong, little witch," said Mason.

Ruby giggled from beside me. "You underestimate Bella, Mason. She's three quarters magical and the strongest witch of any of us."

He growled at me, his eyes flashing silver. "Don't threaten me. You're no better than the warlock who cursed us."

I dropped my hand, the tingle of magic I'd conjured still pulsing through my fingers. I turned and twisted the magical spark into something new, filtering a gentle truth serum through the room. It would only last ten minutes or so, but hopefully it would be enough to get us the information we so desperately needed. With a sigh I let my shoulders slump, feigning defeat. "*Please*, just tell us—is it true that our fathers could still be alive?"

The elders stared at one another, shock infiltrating through them.

Then the third man, the one who hadn't spoken yet, turned to me. "You're my son's mate, are you not?"

I stared at him.

He rose from his seat. Easily the largest of the three by far. He was broader, taller, and there was something familiar about his mouth...

"You're Elliot's dad," I said finally.

He nodded. "My son doesn't speak to me."

"Why?" I asked, hoping the truth serum was beginning to work.

"His mother and I embarrassed him when he was younger. He hasn't forgiven me for leaving her." The huge man swallowed awkwardly.

I ducked my head, some of Elliot's angry intensity making sense now. "It's nice to meet you. Can you tell me if my father might still be alive?"

Mason hit Elliot's dad on the shoulder. "Tony. Don't."

My magic seemed to be working better on Elliot's father than anyone. He jumped off the stage and walked toward us. He was as big as Elliot.

I had to crane my neck to look up and into his intense blue eyes. "Is he alive?" I repeated, curling my wrist and lending more strength to the magic of the truth spell. "Please tell us."

Tony nodded. "We think so, but we don't *know* for certain."

"What do you mean? What happened to him?"

"We believe they shifted into their wolves and then couldn't shift back. There have been sightings of them over the years..."

"Did they come back to the pack?" I asked. "Did they come here looking for help?"

"Ask Mason." Tony indicated one of the other elders on the stage. "He knows."

I walked around Elliot's dad with a quiet smile. He would be my father-in-law if Elliot and I managed to work things out. I stared up at the other two elders. "All right, who knows the truth?"

Mason stepped forward, opening and closing his mouth as though he was fighting the need to tell me.

"Is my father still alive?" I asked, feeling the strain against my magic.

The elders were fighting the coercion of my truth spell.

"When was the last time anyone saw him?" I pressed.

Mason opened and closed his mouth again. "About... ten years ago. He... his wolf. I saw him." Mason grunted and shook his head as though he was shocked with what he was admitting to.

"Can he shift back?" I asked. "Is he stuck like everyone believes?"

Mason's eyes opened wide as he fought the coercion.

"Tell me!" I demanded.

Mason gasped, then exhaled in a huge rush, speaking fast. "No. He can't shift back. None of them can! I don't know if they're still alive. We don't know where they are now."

"So, you've seen all three of them?"

Mason nodded.

"And did they come back here for help?"

"Yes, but there was no way to communicate with them. Even in wolf form, we couldn't speak to them. There was a barrier between us."

My heart fell. "So, they came here for help, but you couldn't do anything about the curse?"

The effects of the spell were wearing off a lot faster than I'd hoped.

The elders were soon looking at each other with irritation and suspicion. They began to argue amongst themselves.

"I thought we weren't going to say anything about the cousins."

"I didn't! You did!"

I glanced over at Tommy and Jonah. "Time to go."

Jonah grabbed my hand and pulled me toward the exit, with the other three hot on our heels.

"What did you do to them?" Jonah asked, as soon as we broke through the doors.

"You put some sort of truth hex on them, yeah?" Darren asked, his eyes gleaming with excitement.

"You did great," Ruby said, smiling at me. "But damn, I miss my magic."

I stared at her, sadness in my heart. "It still hasn't come back?"

Ruby shrugged.

Darren reached out for her in comfort. "You aren't meant to be trying to use it yet."

"I haven't," Ruby admitted. "Not really, anyway. It's just... whenever I reach for the connection? It's not there anymore." Tears dashed down her cheeks and she brushed them away, forcing a smile onto her face. "It's silly, I'm sorry. It really doesn't matter. I have everything I need in you three," she said, referring to her Fated mates.

I doubt that very much. I didn't say it aloud. Magic was a part of us, the same way the shifter was a part of our men. I couldn't imagine that any one of them would be happy about having their wolves taken away from them. "I think we should get home," I said, reaching for Tommy.

"Whose home?" he asked.

I didn't know, but my head was throbbing. I put my hand to my temple and grimaced. "I don't care. I just need a minute to think."

Tommy grabbed my hand and pulled me into him.

I sagged against his strong body in relief as the pain began to overwhelm me.

"Let's go back to our place for a bit. You guys' want to come?" he asked the group.

Ruby shook her head in the negative. "I've got to catch up with Tiff later. We're organizing to speak to the witch's coven tomorrow."

I nodded, feeling dizzy. "Um, I think I need to lie down."

Tommy swept me up in his arms and started walking down the street, throwing the words, "Catch up with you guys later!" over his shoulder.

"I'm fine. Really," I told Tommy, though my eyes were already closing, and my head rested comfortably against his chest as we walked through town.

"You hold on. We'll be home soon," he promised, lending me his strength.

~

Tommy

"Is she okay?" Jonah asked me once we reached my place and got her sleeping form safely inside.

"I'm not sure," I said honestly. Glancing around our small house, I sniffed the air. Elliot had been here. I'd know that testosterone-fueled scent anywhere. I wasn't sure if he was still around, though.

I was just about to place a sleeping Bella onto the couch when Elliot's bedroom door flew open, and he marched out.

I squeezed Bella tight to me.

Jonah stepped in front of us protectively. "What do you want?" he asked, puffing up to face the Alpha.

Damn, I was proud of the pup. Even if together, we'd lose a fight to Elliot, every day of the week, I'd be glad to have my little brother standing by my side.

Strangely, Elliot looked perturbed by Jonah's aggression and actually took a step back.

There's a first time for everything.

"What's wrong with her? Is she hurt?" he asked.

The first phrase to jump to my mind was, 'what do you care?' but I bit my tongue and pulled out my adult voice instead. "I don't know.

We went to talk to the elders about the Manterri cousins, and she fell asleep."

I moved over to the couch and gently lay her down, my shoulder killing me where it was still healing.

Jonah fussed over making sure she had a pillow under her head and pulled the throw blanket down over her.

I stood upright again.

Jonah stayed crouched on the ground, staring at our mate and stroking her face.

Elliot looked freshly showered, his skin still red from the heat and his hair wet. He looked thinner than he had a few days ago. So, he hadn't stopped to eat or drink anything.

The idiot. I stomped over to the fridge and started pulling out food and drinks. "Here." I threw him a bottle of sports drink and took out the fresh bread and roast turkey Mom had dropped over. "Make yourself a sandwich. You're no good to any of us if you starve yourself to death." I wasn't going to wait on the bastard, but he wasn't allowed to starve to death either.

"Thanks," Elliot said, shuffling over to the kitchen while drinking the blue sports drink.

I stepped back over to the couch and sat down on the end near Bella's feet. I reached out for her and touched her ankle, the skin cold between her long skirt and shoes. "Is she too cold, or is it just me?" I asked, unable to hide my concern.

Jonah put the back of his hand to her forehead as though checking for a fever. "She feels okay, but you're right. She is a little bit cold."

Elliot brought his plate over to the dining table, sat down, and began eating. "So, what happened?"

I sighed and crossed my arms over my chest. "We went to the council to ask them about Bella's dad, and the other Manterri cousins. The elders didn't want to divulge anything to Ruby or Bella."

"So, what did she do?" Elliot asked casually, almost in jest. "Put a spell on them or something?"

I shrugged. "Yeah. Pretty much."

Elliot froze, his mouth open and halfway to biting the sandwich. His gaze flicked to mine and connected. "Are you serious?"

I nodded. "But I don't think it agreed with her. She went all weak afterwards."

"What did she do to them?"

I ran a hand through my hair. "I don't really know. Darren said something about a truth spell."

Elliot took a bite of his sandwich, then shrugged, seemingly more at peace with the idea. "Fair enough, I guess. If they're hiding something, someone's got to make them tell the truth."

I swallowed down the need to tell Elliot what his dad had said. I'd never really talked to Elliot about the fact his parents were literally the only mated pair of wolves to officially sever their mating. It was generally unheard of. Divorce didn't exist in our community. But very occasionally there was a couple that couldn't sort out their differences and they officially dissolved their relationship.

Elliot's parents had been one of those rare couples, and since that day, Elliot's temper had been out of control. I'd never put those two facts together before, but now his anger made sense. As did his absolute doggedness about only marrying a Fated mate. Elliot had never once suggested he'd find a woman outside the pack to marry. *Never.*

"So, what did she manage to find out?" Elliot continued.

"Pretty much what they had assumed all along. Or at least what their mothers had. All three cousins had turned into their wolves and couldn't shift back. It's all linked to some curse that was set off by the High Warlock back then."

"And what are they going to do now?"

"We need to speak to the coven witches," Bella said, her voice a thready whisper from the couch.

I twisted toward her. "Hey! You're awake. Are you okay?"

She nodded and pushed herself to sit up. "I think I need to go home."

"Can't you stay here?" I asked hopefully, unwilling to be apart from her.

She shook her head, her gaze darting over to where Elliot sat, silent as a statue. "I think I did something wrong. That spell shouldn't have wiped me out. It was a simple spell to encourage the elders to just tell the truth. It's not even hard." She put a hand up to the bridge of her nose and closed her eyes. "But my head hurts. I think I need my mom."

"I'll drive her," Elliot said unexpectedly, standing up.

"No," I said, facing him. My black eye and swollen jaw had healed, but some of my cracked ribs were still sore, not to mention my shoulder. It wouldn't be fun to take another beating again, but I wasn't letting him anywhere near my mate alone.

"We'll all go," Jonah said.

I turned around as Bella staggered to her feet with Jonah's assistance.

"Don't fight," Bella pleaded weakly. "All three is fine."

"Jonah, take her to Elliot's car. It's the biggest." I turned to face Bella's third mate. "But *I'm* driving. And if I see even the smallest sign of you shifting, I'll stop the car and kick your ass to the curb. Got it?"

Elliot nodded. "Not a problem."

I frowned. *Giving in without a fight?* That wasn't like Elliot either. There was more to this change in his demeanor than he was letting on. "Fine, let's go."

We all got into Elliot's big truck. I drove, Elliot sat in the passenger seat, and Jonah was in the back cradling our mate tenderly, watching over her condition.

"Quickly please, Tommy," Bella whispered.

CHAPTER 18
ELLIOT

Sitting in the passenger seat of my own car while sober was a first.

"When'd you get back?" Tommy asked, his words clipped and short. He was still angry at me, and he had every right to be.

"About an hour before you got there," I said. I'd run all day and night, and then rested in some random forest almost a state away. I hadn't stopped to eat, and barely drank enough water to stave off dehydration. But I was back, now, and I had news. Though considering Bella's health, it was probably not the time to reveal all.

"And you're... okay?" Tommy asked.

A lump stuck in my throat. Even after what I'd done to him, he was still worried about me. "Yeah. You?"

He nodded. "All good."

I cleared my throat and prepared my apology. "I'm sorry I hurt you. No excuses. I was in the wrong." I'd heard ribs break. I'd seen blood. And yet the rage inside me had known no bounds. I'd hurt the one person who had stood by me my whole life. And if I didn't love Tommy the way I did, the shame of what I'd done last night probably would have driven me to just keep on running.

But my need to make amends—to check if he was okay—that was what brought me home. *And Bella, of course.* My shame on that front was intense as well. Enough to keep me away for a very long time.

Tommy shrugged. "Yeah, you were. But we're all good." His gaze flicked to the back of the car.

I twisted in my seat.

Bella had her head in Jonah's lap.

I swallowed hard against the self-disgust that rose, but I pushed down my damn pride and persevered. "I'm so sorry about yesterday, Bella. I shouldn't have lost control like that. It was unacceptable and I never wanted you to see me like that."

It was still early evening, so there was enough light in the car to see her face. She gazed up at me, meeting my gaze. "It's okay," she said, her voice a mere shadow of what it had been when we first met.

"It's not okay," I said, my chest tight with pain. "It makes me sick to think of it. I... was jealous. And fucking dumb. I don't know what else to say, except I'll make it up to you, somehow. I promise, Bella." And I would. I already had some ideas of how to do it.

Bella reached out and touched my arm. "You can't help how you feel, Elliot." Then she took her hand back.

The loss was as keen as a blade to my chest. There was no warmth in her touch. No tingle or awareness of me as her mate. I couldn't help how I felt? Did that mean she understood? Or just that she'd given up on me? I turned back and concentrated on the road in front of us.

Had I done irreparable damage to our connection with my jealousy last night? Or had Bella decided she was never going to forgive me? My stomach dropped and my throat tightened with grief. It was very clearly the wrong time to ask her if she still wanted me, but *God*, it hurt to think that one stupid mistake may have cost me my mate. *My only mate.*

"Almost there, Bella," Tommy said as he slowed the truck down and drove through the streets of the town.

I stared out the window. *Should I tell them all now what I found? Would it make Bella feel better?* Maybe she'd forgive me if I told her. "I met some wolves while I was running last night." The words fell into the quiet of the car like coins in a glass jar, shattering the silence.

"Who were they?" Jonah asked.

I turned around and stared at Bella. "I'm pretty sure I met the Manterri cousins last night. All three of them."

Bella's eyes widened, and even though she didn't try to sit up, a weak smile curled her lips. "Where? Where'd you see them?"

"Pretty much all the way over the state line. I got there last night and decided to turn back when I realized that I needed to come back and beg you to forgive me, rather than run away like some stupid kid."

Tommy snorted from the front seat.

Bella's smile lightened the pain in my heart.

It was hard being this honest. I stared at Bella. "You sure you aren't still casting a truth spell? I can't usually talk this much about my feelings."

She lifted her hand and twinkled her fingers. "Nothing left in the gas tank. Sorry. It's all you."

Somehow, I wasn't sure about that. *Maybe having a mate has its own magic?* I inhaled deeply, preparing myself to reveal all. "They were all gray in color. All of them were older, with whitening around their muzzles. And they were lean and dirty. Like they hadn't seen a good feed, or a shower, in a very long time."

Bella gasped.

The pained noise hit me in the gut. *Crap.* "I didn't mean it like that, I'm sorry. I've just been putting it all together in my head, and if they were any other wolf shifters, ones that flicked back to human often, they just wouldn't look like that."

"It's true," Jonah said, stroking her hair. "I think all Elliot's trying to say is that he thinks it could be your dad and his cousins, and not some other random pack." Jonah glared at me like I'd done something wrong, and to the young pup, I probably had.

I swallowed hard. "Exactly. I'm sorry if I'm not explaining this well. It's just... I wanted you to know that I think they're alive. And they're really out there."

"Where are they now?" Bella asked.

"I don't know. They wouldn't run with me, and I didn't know how to communicate with them. I stayed around for a while, but in the end, I had to leave, and they wouldn't come back with me." I'd tried to bring my mate's father home, and failed.

She closed her eyes. "At least they're still alive. Thank you, Elliot. It means a lot to me that you brought that home with you."

Tommy pulled the car to a stop.

I glanced outside at the little cottage-style house Bella lived in.

"Should I ring the doorbell, or..."

"No. Mom will know..." Bella said confidently.

Sure enough, the door burst open, and Bella's mom ran out, coming straight to the car.

Jonah opened the door.

Bella's mom pulled the door wider. "What happened?"

Bella smiled at her mom. "Hi Mom. I did a truth spell and it... I don't know."

"You did a truth spell on a wolf shifter?" Her mom gasped. "You can't do that! It screws with your magic."

Bella laughed softly. "Well, that's nice to know, now."

"I'll grab her," I said, getting out of the passenger door.. "Come here, beautiful." I reached for Bella.

She came into my arms willingly.

But once again, there was something missing. That *spark*, the instant connection I'd felt since the moment I met Bella. It wasn't there. Maybe it was because her magic was going haywire? Hopefully that was all it was.

"Bring her inside," Bella's mom said, waving madly at me and rushing ahead. "Put her on the couch and I'll make up a remedy." She darted inside the front door, purple skirts and orange ribbons flying in the breeze behind her.

"Your mom's... colorful," I said, smiling down at Bella to break the tension.

She smiled back, though it was weak. "She's eccentric, I know. But she's awesome."

Warmth pulsed through her words and envy panged in my heart. Bella loved her mom in a way that I'd stopped feeling about my own parents after the age of eight. I envied her that feeling. The ability to still admire her parent. Wanting to go home to her mom because she knew she'd be taken care of. I hadn't had that in a long time.

I rushed into the small house and placed Bella down on the couch amongst the fluffy cushions.

A sleek-looking black cat jumped up out of nowhere.

I stepped back, shuddering.

The cat opened its mouth, and through pointed teeth, hissed at me.

I couldn't help but laugh. "Um. Yeah. Nice to meet you, too."

Bella struggled into a seated position.

The cat walked over her legs, did a little circle, then sat down, glaring up at me.

I had to chuckle. "Is that cat a human you turned into a cat, or are all cats like that?"

Bella ran her hand down its black fur, and the cat arched into her caress. "Storm found us. She was meowing on our front step in the middle of the night. It was raining and she was completely drenched, the poor thing."

I sobered. "So, it was meant to be, huh?"

Bella nodded, and stared down at the cat, not looking at me. "Yeah."

Bella's mom rushed in and handed Bella a steaming beverage in a mug. "Drink this, slowly. It'll help replenish the magic you lost." She dusted off her hands and craned her head back to stare up at me. "You must be Elliot." She stuck her hand out

I shook it gently. "Yeah, I am. It's nice to meet you…"

"Kathy."

I inclined my head. "Nice to meet you, Kathy."

"Nice to meet you too. I saw you run off after Thanksgiving. Couldn't handle the competition, huh? Or…?" Bella's mom quirked an eyebrow at me.

Ouch. I couldn't help the answering smile that tugged at my lips. "I can see where Bella gets her strength from."

Kathy shrugged. "No shame in asking a question."

"True," I said, but I wasn't really interested in answering it.

"So," she said. "Is there any good reason why you left the other day?"

I thrust my hands into my jeans pockets and shook my head with a grimace of shame. "Nope. No good reason."

She cocked her head. "You're not dealing with the sharing part very well, are you?"

I rocked on my heels and shook my head again. "Nope. Not really."

She smiled. "It's good to see you can tell the truth. That'll serve you well. Now, I need to feed my daughter, then I'm going to put her to sleep for at least twelve hours. Then she should be good as new by tomorrow." She made a shooing motion with her hands. "So, all three of you. Out you go."

"Mom!" Bella complained, her eyes wide and annoyed as she stared at her mother.

"It's just one night, Bella. You need to recover properly. I'm sure your mates can survive without you for *one* night."

I managed to smile at Bella before Tommy, Jonah, and I were all unceremoniously ushered out the door.

Kathy waved us off. "It's Saturday tomorrow. No coming by before ten AM., got it?"

"Yes, ma'am," I said, waving back.

She shut the door.

Something inside of me shifted. A strange sort of peace stole through me. *Was that what it's like to have a mother who cares about you?* Someone who wasn't scared to go to bat for you, even against someone as big as, well, me. I got back in the truck and let Tommy drive us all the way home. Everything was going to be all right. *It had to be.*

As we got out of the truck, tiredness hit me like a steam train. I was definitely going to sleep well tonight.

We started walking up the drive to go inside.

"Can I crash on the couch tonight?" Jonah asked.

"Yeah, of course. Why?" Tommy asked.

I wondered the same question. Jonah had never stayed over before, and it wasn't like Tommy, and I were going to get into another fight. He didn't need to stick around to act as mediator or anything.

Jonah shrugged. "I feel like I should. And do you think we could put an extension on this house if I move in? Or do you think we should just build a bigger house somewhere else? Billy said that the four of them sleep in one bedroom, in one bed, but I can't imagine we'd be doing that."

I stopped walking and stared at the kid. "What are you talking about?"

Jonah frowned at me. "Logistics. Bella is our mate. More than likely, she'll come here and live with us, like Ruby did with her three mates. So, can we tack on an extra bedroom here for me?"

I glanced over at Tommy, who was staring at me, too. Tommy and I had never thought we'd ever share our home with anyone. It was our bachelor pad. Small, and often incredibly messy. "Not sure. I've never thought about it. Tommy?"

Jonah rolled his eyes at me. "Of course, you've never thought about it. You never thought you'd have a mate at all, let alone one you'd have to share with two other guys."

"How do you know that?" I asked the pup.

Jonah snorted at me. "Because when I was a kid, you told me that you were either going to marry your Fated mate, or no-one at all. You were drunk and probably don't remember, but I do. So, I'll sleep on the couch tonight, but once Bella moves in, I'm sleeping next to her, too." Jonah went ahead, opened the front door, and headed inside—into our home.

Tommy and I stood staring, in shocked silence.

I turned and stared at Tommy. "When did he grow up?"

Tommy's smile grew bigger and bigger, until he was practically grinning at me. "I'm not sure but it looks like we've got another room mate." Tommy headed inside.

I stared off into the distance, toward the town where my mate was being healed and pampered by her mother.

CHAPTER 19
BELLA

My mom was beginning to get on my nerves. I'd woken up in my bed, in my bedroom, to find her sleeping on a mattress she'd conjured on the floor. Then she'd sat on the toilet and chatted to me while I was in the shower—just in case I fainted. And now she was hovering over me, when all I was doing was sitting on the couch reading a book.

"Mom. Please." I groaned. "You need to relax. I'm fine."

"You weren't fine last night, Bella. You came home a mess," she reminded me for the umpteenth time.

I released the pent-up tension in my throat, sighing loudly. "I know. I made a mistake. But I didn't realize that working a spell on a wolf shifter would be any different to a human, or another witch."

"There's lots you don't know, Bella," Mom said, sinking down onto the couch opposite me and staring at me the way she did sometimes. Like a teacher at school teaching me something as basic as my ABCs.

I rolled my eyes. *Heaven help me.* "Mom, don't patronize me. Please. I'm not one of those girls who runs around making all the normal mistakes you're meant to do when you're young. I do well at school, I've never slept with any boys, let alone had the chance to sleep around. I don't drink. I don't do drugs..."

"Yeah, yeah. Okay. I get it, Bella. Yes, you've been a dream child. I admit it." Mom put up her hands in defeat.

I sighed again. "I didn't mean it like that. I'm not perfect, far from it. But you don't need to helicopter over me like I'm two years old. I made a mistake and I'm reading all about it now." I held up the book I was reading which detailed the different strengths and changes to spells that were needed if a witch were to cast them on paranormal creatures. Shifters included.

Then a thought occurred to me, and I shut the book, careful to slide the ribbon bookmark into place before I lost my spot. "If putting a spell on a shifter takes a lot more energy and magic than most, because they burn through the magic faster, how do you think the High Warlock put a spell on the whole pack? Wouldn't that have like... killed him to do something that immense?" Especially since the curse continued to exist, far beyond his death...

Mom tapped her fingers against her lips in contemplation, her brow furrowing. "You know, I've never really thought about it."

"Probably because you didn't have confirmation that there was a spell cast."

And there *was* a hex on the pack, I was sure of it. If the High Warlock had gone to the trouble to tell the pack elders that he was punishing them for our moms' getting pregnant, then he definitely followed through with the curse.

"Bella," Mom said, staring at me. "We don't know what he—"

The doorbell rang.

"Well, we're about to find out, Mom."

The front door opened, and Ruby and Tiffany called out. "Hello?"

"Come on in," I answered.

Ruby walked into the room, eating a packet of chips while grinning at Tiffany. "You are *so* jealous. Stop denying it! I can see you glowing green from here."

"Jealous of what?" I asked, putting the book down and getting to my feet.

Mom jumped up too, following me and what I was doing.

"Jealous of us," Ruby said, crunching on another chip. "Tiff wants her mates, like *yesterday*."

Tiffany rolled her eyes as though Ruby was exaggerating, but then crossed her arms over her chest. "It's not like *that*."

I cocked my head. It kind of looked like it was, but I wasn't saying anything yet.

Ruby groaned. "It has to be! Why else wouldn't you come to Thanksgiving even though you were invited?"

"Your house is tiny, Ruby. As if you were going to fit more of us in when you already had ten."

"Tiny? Oh, my God... you're kidding me, right?" said Ruby, frowning.

"Are you guys ready to go?" I interjected. They'd obviously been fighting about this for a while, and it wasn't going anywhere. "What time did you say the Coven wanted us there, Ruby?"

Ruby gave Tiff the eye, then flicked her gaze back to me. "About ten."

I picked up my cell phone from the coffee table and checked the time. "We better get going then." I turned around and grabbed my house keys and my shoulder bag, slipping my purse and my cell into it. "See you later, Mom. I've got my phone if you need me."

Mom smiled and waved. "Make sure you watch your energy today. You'll feel drained if you do too much!"

"What happened yesterday?" Ruby asked.

I shuffled all of us out the door. "Tell you in a sec." As soon as I managed to shut the door behind me, I blew out a sigh of relief. I needed some space.

"So, what's going on?" Tiff asked as we walked along the garden path.

We all jumped in my car so I could drive us to the Coven meeting which was happening at the old church.

"Basically," I said, as I reversed out the driveway then put the car in gear, "I worked a truth spell on some of the wolf elders yesterday, and it kind of wiped me out."

"You okay now?" Ruby asked as we drove towards the church. "You did look pretty exhausted yesterday."

"What did I miss?" Tiff asked from the back seat.

Ruby turned around from the passenger's side. "We went to the wolf elders yesterday and demanded some answers about our dads. I messaged you about it, but you said you had to work."

"What did they say?" Tiff asked, her voice unusually high pitched.

I answered that one. "They said that the High Warlock told them that the punishment for getting our mothers pregnant was that the whole pack was going to die out."

"Yeah! And I thought that it wouldn't matter if no females were born to the pack this generation, because there's so many other wolf shifter packs around, the guys could just mate with them," Ruby added.

"But?" Tiff asked.

"But" I continued, "they said that none of the men who *have* married outside the pack have had children. None of them. No living children, anyway. So, if they stayed and mated with a woman from the pack, born before us, they only had sons. And if they marry outside the pack, even now, then they don't have any kids at all."

Tiffany grunted. "Well, that sucks."

I nodded, turning into the gravel parking lot by the church. "It's a very effective, but cruel and unconscionable punishment."

The High Warlock had known what he was doing in that regard. He must have *really* hated the wolf shifters.

I parked the car and turned off the engine. I wasn't sure whether to tell the girls about what Elliot had said last night about our fathers being alive just yet. Mostly because I wasn't sure about what I was going to do about Elliot and me, so the information he'd brought home seemed kind of tainted.

He also didn't seem like the kind of man to lie, so at some point I was going to have to tell Tiffany and Ruby that our fathers were more than likely alive but were trapped in their wolf form... forever. That was, unless we could work out a way to unravel the High Warlock's insanely intricate, and obviously powerful, curse. Either way, it was far too much to think about right at this minute. "Let's go," I said, grabbing my bag and hopping out of the car.

Together we walked into the old church, for our meeting with the Coven.

We were greeted by Simone, a young witch like us, but the daughter of the current High Warlock, and a powerful witch in her own right. "Hello Bella, Ruby, Tiffany. How can I help you three today?"

I smiled at her, though something about her voice grated on my nerves every time I saw her. "We have an appointment with the Coven."

Simone's eyebrows flickered a little, then she said, "Have a seat. I won't be long."

We glanced around. There were only two seats in the foyer, and we weren't about to sit down.

Simone went through the stained-glass doors and into the main area of the church where voices could be heard and people moving about.

"Are you sure they're going to see us?" I whispered to Ruby.

She nodded. "They better."

I could feel her energy vibrating around her and could have sworn I felt her magic pulse. *Didn't she say that her magic was gone?*

Simone popped back through the doors; a large, fake smile plastered on her face. "I'm sorry, but the High Council are too busy to speak to anyone today. Can you make another appointment for next week, perhaps?"

I glanced at Ruby, who was growing redder and tighter in the face, and Tiffany, whose flashing blue eyes were not a sign of serenity.

Uh-oh. "And when would the next available appointment be?" I asked, not wanting the fight my premonition knew was brewing. "It's kind of urgent."

Simone conjured a diary out of thin air and began flicking through the pages. "Well, you see, Tabitha is away next week with her family, and the week after that they're completely full."

Tiffany glared at me.

I tried to ignore her, even though her look felt like hot daggers stabbing into my cheek.

She stepped closer. "Do the thing," she whispered.

I pressed my lips into a thin line. I knew what Tiff wanted me to do. They'd made me use a freeze spell on our mothers on multiple occasions, and every time we'd gotten into more trouble than it had been worth. But to do it to Simone... the penalty would be *a lot* worse than being grounded for a month.

"If you don't do it, I will," Tiff whispered, lifting her hands.

"Fine," I said, rolling my eyes and conjuring the spell I was far too good at.

"Fine, what?" Simone asked, lifting her gaze to me.

I cast the spell over her, and she froze, that 'bored stupid' look etched into her pretty features.

Worry smacked me in the gut. "I'm going pay for that one. I can already tell."

"Then let's hurry," Tiffany said, gripping my arm and pulling me through the huge church doors and into the inner sanctum of our Coven elders.

The three of us stopped short.

The two witches and two warlocks that made up our high council were sitting around on couches casually drinking coffee and eating cake.

Tiffany turned to me. "Yeah, they're *so* busy they can't even speak to us. Can't you tell?" she hissed.

When the four members turned to us, shock was plastered all over their faces.

I drew my magic into me and flung out a protection spell around all three of us. I didn't know what was going to happen in the next hour, but my tingling premonition senses were on fire. "Don't move too far from me," I said to Tiff and Ruby. "Both of you."

My friends knew me well and nodded.

Together, we walked toward four of the most powerful beings in our town. There was no going back now.

I held my magic tight to me, curling protectively around Ruby, especially. Tiffany was a good witch. She could handle herself to a certain degree, but if they decided to attack? Ruby wouldn't stand a chance.

"What are you doing in here?" Tabitha asked, setting down her teacup and standing up. "Where's Simone?"

"Simone told us to come right in," Tiffany lied.

Tabitha frowned and her lips twitched.

Pressure against my protection spell made me gasp. *Who is trying to hurt us?*

David, the current High Warlock, stood up and approached us, his shoulder-length black hair more gray than black nowadays. "What do you three want?"

"I told you," Ruby said, "when I made the appointment. We want to talk about the old High Warlock."

"What about him?" Rose asked from the couch. She looked relaxed, plaiting and re-plaiting her long white hair.

"We want to know what he did to our fathers," Ruby said.

My heart thumped in my chest, adrenaline zinging through my bloodstream. Something had changed in the room.

"What are you talking about?" Rose asked, sounding exasperated. "How do you even know who your fathers are? Weren't they just some warlocks from up north?"

Tabitha's eyes had become guarded, her demeanor taking on an even more frosty feel. "The high warlock is gone girls, dead. He took his secrets with him."

I didn't believe that for one second. I stepped forward, unwilling and unable to let this go. "Our fathers were, or are, wolf shifters. The High Warlock cursed them when he found out our mothers were pregnant with us."

There was a round of gasps from the others, except for David and Tabitha.

David narrowed his eyes and stayed silent.

Tabitha glared at me. "Lies."

I swayed, wanting to take a step back, but unable to back down without compromising my protection spell. I grounded myself and stayed exactly where I was. "I don't think so," I said, "but you're right —we don't know if it was *him*, or someone *else* in the community. So, perhaps you can help us solve a riddle? You are, after all, the four most powerful members of the Coven." I injected as much lightheartedness and sincerity into what I was saying, as possible. After all, it was the truth.

Tabitha lifted her chin. "What riddle?"

"Well," I began, "the puzzle is this. If my mother had gotten angry at my father and forced him to shift into his wolf form, and he was never able to shift back, how could she have done such a thing to begin with, and how would we undo it?"

The room went silent, and David and Tabitha exchanged glances.

"Sounds like a transformative spell to me," Rose said from the couch. "Though, to keep it going for twenty-years or more, would require an extreme amount of grounding."

"Grounding?" I repeated. "What do you mean?"

Horus, the other warlock in the room who hadn't spoken yet, turned to look at me from where he sat on one of the other couches. "Grounding is where you base a spell. Generally, we ground most spells in our own magic. But it is possible to ground a spell in a place, or a person, or even an object. Though that thing, whatever you chose, would weaken over time—eventually."

"Could I ground a powerful spell in something like a book?" I asked. *Could it really be anything? And if it was, how were we going to find such a thing?*

Horus shook his head. "No. Grounding a spell requires something of extreme power, and magic in itself. So, to ground a spell for twenty years, it would need to be grounded into a younger person, or a place to last. Like this church, for instance. Something with consistent longevity." He gestured to the building around us.

"And what if that person died?" I asked.

Horus shook his head. "Then the spell would be released."

Ruby stepped up. "So, you're saying that if someone put a spell on our fathers that still exists to this day, then the spell is grounded by something equally powerful?"

Rose nodded. "Yes, most likely."

I nodded, thinking about the elements of the spell and how much power it would have sucked off the High Warlock.

"How would we break such a spell?" Ruby asked.

"You'd need to destroy the element that it is locked to," Tabitha said, lifting her chin. There was something strange about her, about the anger she displayed around this subject.

I narrowed my eyes and followed the feeling of my premonition. "You know what it is, don't you?" The hairs on the back of my neck stood up.

"I don't know what you're talking about," Tabitha said, sauntering back to the safety of the other coven members and standing behind the couches.

I took a small step closer. "I think you do. Is it all linked? The infertility? The plan to destroy them all?"

"What's she talking about, Tabitha?" Rose asked.

"Nothing," Tabitha hissed. "She doesn't know what she's saying."

I looked at Rose, who was still sitting on the couch. "Whatever spell the High Warlock performed on our mothers when they were pregnant with us, seems to have made the whole local wolf pack infertile in a way. There hasn't been a single live female born to the pack since the day the three of us were born."

"Good," Tabitha snorted. "I hope they die off."

"They will," Ruby practically shouted with fire in her eyes. "Without females, the blood lines will be lost!"

"Is it possible?" Horus asked the group, his face showing nothing but surprise. "I know the High Warlock hated the wolf shifters, but I never thought he'd do such a thing to an entire town of people..."

"Horus, shut up," Tabitha said, then rounded the couches and started flapping her hands at us. "You all need to go. Now."

"Not until you tell us how to free our fathers," I bit out, anger swelling in my heart. "We've been without them our whole lives already. It isn't fair."

Tabitha stopped a foot away from me and glared. "There's no way of knowing if they're even still alive."

They were. Elliot had seen them.

"It doesn't matter," I said. "Just tell us how to undo the spell."

Tabitha rolled her eyes and huffed.

"Please," Tiffany added, her gaze more imploring than angry.

I considered throwing a truth spell at the witch before me, but that would mean letting go of the protection spell around me and my friends, and I didn't trust Tabitha one bit.

"Fine," she said, stomping her foot. "I'll tell you if you leave, immediately."

"We will," Ruby said.

"I'm not talking to *you*, traitor," Tabitha all but spat at Ruby. "You're not welcome here any longer."

Ruby blinked and shut her mouth.

Tabitha's gaze zeroed in on me. "I can smell them on you too, Bella, so make your choices wisely. If you choose to marry a shifter, you will never be welcomed back into the Coven. Never."

I swallowed hard, not willing to even contemplate what she was saying. "Tell me what to do," I pressed.

"The High Warlock hated the wolf shifters," she said. "He was in love with a woman once, a witch in our town. They were set to be married, but then the woman ran off and mated with one of the wolf shifters. Had his pups, too."

I swallowed hard. "What's that got to do with me?" *Though that does sound like my grandparents, and Darren's.*

She continued, and there was a vicious gleam in her eyes that made my stomach churn. "So, when your mothers came to the High Warlock and told him they were all pregnant to a bunch of wolves, he cast a spell to bind you all together. As the three of you grow—the pack dies. The spell is grounded to your very lives. As long as you're all still living, your fathers will remain wolves, and the pack will die out. It's that simple."

Her words hit me like a full-blown storm, smack in the face. I gasped and staggered backwards, holding onto my best friends and letting go of the spell I was casting.

Ruby grabbed onto me.

Tiffany pressed in close. "It can't be," she said.

Simone barged in through the doors. "What are you three doing in here?"

"We're going. We're going," I said, groaning as my legs gave out beneath me. I would have fallen to the floor if Tiffany and Ruby hadn't caught me. *Damn. I've run out of power. And we are in danger.* I could feel it. Someone very close by wanted to cause us serious bodily harm.

"Tiff," I said. She was the only one with any powers left to rely on. "The hallowed ground beneath us will help boost your magic. Can you get us home?"

"Your place?" Tiff asked.

I nodded and closed my eyes.

Tiffany grabbed hold of us, and magic whirled around me, then we were all falling to the floor in my mom's lounge, the softness of the carpet and the rugs beneath my knees a heavenly feel after the coldness of the Coven's headquarters.

"Damn, that hurt." I groaned, holding my belly.

"Bella, is that you? What happened?" Mom raced out of the kitchen and fell to her knees in front of me. "Are you okay? Look at me."

I stared up at her. "I need some more... of that tea."

Mom stared around at all three of us and staggered to her feet. "You three, don't move. Just stay there. I'll be right back." Mom ran to the kitchen to make her brew.

I leaned to the side, resting my head on the couch and cradling my aching stomach.

"You okay, Bella?" Tiff asked.

I opened my eyes and stared at my best friend who was also on her ass on the carpet. *Damn, that took it out of me.* "Yeah, thanks for getting us out of there. I couldn't stay a minute longer." Not to mention the fact that I'd used up all my magic. If I'd needed to protect Ruby, or myself, I would have been defenseless.

Ruby was gasping like a landed fish and struggling to get up.

"Just stay down, Ruby," I said, flapping my hand. "It's nice down here."

Ruby continued to struggle until she was up and sitting on the couch.

"No. I need to get up." She groaned, then collapsed against the back support. "That's better."

"What's wrong?" I asked her. "You seem more exhausted than me."

Ruby had gone deathly white, and I wasn't sure if it was the shock of what we'd learnt about our fathers, or her petering magic. "I'm pregnant," Ruby whispered.

Tiff and I stared at each other, then both managed to get to our feet and stumble over to the couch to embrace our friend.

It hurt to get up, and it hurt even more to launch myself at Ruby, but once I was sitting down again, hugging her, everything relaxed.

"Congratulations," I said, though I couldn't even imagine what that must feel like for her.

Tears tracked down Ruby's pale face. "I only found out yesterday, and I just... I can't cope with all this." She threw her hands up in the air.

I looked at Tiff, then up at my mom as she walked into the room carrying a tray of mugs. "All of you need this."

I took mine and handed Ruby hers. "Is this safe for Ruby to drink, Mom?"

My mom's eyes widened. "What do you mean?"

Ruby sobbed, wiping the tears from her face. "I'm pregnant, and I don't want anything to happen to my babies."

My mom's mouth dropped open. Then she set the mugs down and pulled Ruby into her arms, where my friend cried and cried.

I took a long drink of my mom's tea, feeling the heat and the healing spreading through my body.

Mom stroked Ruby's hair and said, "Nothing's going to happen to your babies, Ruby. Believe you me."

I shook my head, still in disbelief. *Babies...* What was going to happen next?

CHAPTER 21

JONAH

’d been busting to go see our mate from the moment we’d woken up, but Tommy convinced me to go for a run first. Then breakfast at Milly’s, followed by a shower. By the time we were actually ready to go, it was almost eleven A.M. “For fuck’s sake, Tommy. Hurry up!” I paced the lounge impatiently. “Or I’m going to leave without you.”

“You have your own car, you know,” Elliot said from the kitchen where he was eating a second—or was it a third?—breakfast.

I glared at him for being right. “Don’t you ever stop eating?”

He laughed. “Not really.”

"Thanks for the reminder I've got my own car." I charged for the front door.

Tommy came out of his bedroom just at that moment, his shirt still unbuttoned, and his shoes in hand. "Stop being such an old woman, Jonah. I'm coming."

I growled and shook my head. "Nope. Can't wait! See you there. I need to go." I ran out the door, jumped in my car, and took off. Everything in me this morning was buzzing with adrenalin and excitement. I could barely stay still. I'd slept on Tommy's and Elliot's couch, which hadn't been the best nights' sleep of my life, but I felt good this morning.

I felt alive, like I was *finally* where I was meant to be in my life. Maybe I was, now? I was meant to live with Tommy and Elliot, even if they hadn't come to realize it just yet. Without a thought I drove through town, turned into Bella's street, and barely managed to turn off the car engine before I was out and bolting for the front door.

It opened before I could knock, Kathy grinning at me. "I was expecting you at exactly 10:01."

I grinned back at her. "The other two convinced me to go for a run and eat first. Otherwise, I would have been here, believe me."

She glanced over my shoulder. "So, where are they now?"

"I left them at home. They were being way too slow."

Kathy laughed; the sound similar to Bella's. "I like your attitude, Jonah. Come in. They're all here."

I walked through the front door and into the lounge. "All...?" I queried.

And there they were. Five more witches.

My heart hammered in my chest. "Ah, good morning."

"Hey Jonah," Bella said, getting up from her place on the floor and coming over to greet me.

I grabbed her beautiful face and planted a kiss on her soft lips, enjoying the sweetness of her taste.

Then she turned back to her cousins.

I narrowed my eyes at the scene before me. "What are you guys up to?"

Ruby, Tiffany, and Bella were sitting on the floor, surrounded by books and crystals. While their mothers were sitting at a round dining table, also surrounded by a plethora of books. Empty cups of tea and mugs of coffee were strewn about the room.

"You look like you've been at it all night."

The women laughed.

"Not all night," answered Bella. "We had a break somewhere in the middle."

My mouth dropped open. "I was joking. Have you really been up all night?"

Bella settled back onto the floor amongst her nest of books. "We have. We're trying to find a way to undo the spell the High Warlock put on us."

I slid onto the couch, staring down at the three witches on the floor. "To you? I thought the spell was on the pack, and your fathers?"

Ruby screwed up her face. "Yeah, well, we went to the Coven yesterday and questioned them about what they knew."

That didn't sound so good. "And what did you find out?"

"Maybe we should wait until the others are here, too?" Tiffany said. "You don't want to repeat the story over and over."

I rolled my eyes. "They could be another hour. Bloody slowpokes."

Bella lit up. "Nope. They're just around the corner." She stood up and the sound of Elliot's truck hurtling down the street became obvious. Bella's breath hitched as she stared out the window and she bit on her lip as though nervous. Her eyes widened. "They're both here."

"Yeah. Why?" I asked, narrowing my eyes at the worry in her voice. "Haven't you and Elliot sorted your shit out yet?"

Bella smiled at me but didn't answer. Instead, she walked to the front door and opened it for their timely arrival.

I shook my head. "*I* didn't get a personal welcome."

Kathy laughed. "Yes, you did. I just beat Bella to the door."

I smiled at her. Was that a sign that Kathy liked me more than the other two? Or that Bella didn't like me as much? I wasn't sure I wanted to know at this point in time. Questions like those were laden with explosive possibilities like a minefield. It was probably best if the answers to such questions remained elusive and unspoken.

The guys came into the room and Elliot stood next to me. "We were one minute behind you."

I shrugged. "Only because I left when I did. You guys don't like being last."

They couldn't argue with the truth.

So, I turned back to the cluster of witches. "Bella was about to tell me about what the Coven said yesterday, but they wanted to wait for you guys. So, Bella?" I raised my eyebrows at my mate.

She smiled at me with a true, warm smile that made my heart leap. "The High Warlock hates wolf shifters because the woman he was in love with ended up married to a wolf shifter instead."

I frowned. "Do you mean...?"

Bella nodded. "Yeah, I'm pretty sure it's my grandparents on my dad's side, but let's leave that for the minute. The important part is that the witch we spoke to yesterday said that the whole spell, the pack being unable to have any more females, and our dads being wolves forever, it's all linked!"

"To what?" I asked.

Bella looked at Ruby, who stared at Tiffany. Then they all looked up at me, and the pain and intensity there was too strong to handle. "To us," they said as one.

Tommy slid onto the couch beside me, his hands curled into fists on his knees. "What do you mean, it's linked to you?"

Kathy stood up. "According to the witch the girls spoke to yesterday, and she isn't the most reliable source of information..."

"She's a nasty bitch, that one. Always has been," Sherie said, sitting at the table.

Kathy shrugged. "But if there's any truth to it at all, then we need to investigate how to unhook it."

"And if you unhook it, the spell might be broken?" I asked. "Would that mean the Manterri cousins might be able to shift back again?"

Bella nodded. "Yes, and the pack might have a chance of having daughters once more."

Elliot and Tommy looked at each other.

"That would change everything," said Elliot, speaking for them both.

I nodded. "It would. So, how can we help, ladies?"

Sherie stood up and stretched like a cat. "You can take the girls out for a walk into town. We need more tea, and they need a break."

"But Mom..." Bella started to say.

"No buts," Sherie said. "Ruby especially needs a break." She gave the girls a look that had them all standing and getting ready to go out.

"What's wrong with Ruby?" I asked, when no-one else looked as if they were going to question the logic. When again, no-one answered, I glanced at Ruby, and her gaze connected with mine. "Are you okay?" I pressed.

She nodded, though her cheeks were pink. "I'm pregnant."

My mouth dropped open, then a happy feeling washed over me. "Congratulations!"

"Another male shifter for the cause," Tommy said from beside me, a smile on his face. "Congratulations."

Ruby slid her hand to her belly. "I'm not sure it's going to be a boy."

I frowned at her. "It has to be, doesn't it? The spell isn't undone yet."

Ruby glanced at Bella, who looked at me. "It's too early to really be talking about it. She's only five weeks along. Let's go get some fresh air."

The six of us trundled outside and I managed to snag Bella's hand so I could walk beside her as we strolled toward the shops.

"Is Ruby okay?" I asked.

Bella nodded. "Yeah, but she's scared."

"Of what?"

Bella shrugged. "Of everything. Losing the baby. Of the sacrifice that may be needed to break the curse."

"The sacrifice?" I repeated, hoping I'd heard wrong.

Bella nodded. "Yeah. A lot of these very old, insanely powerful spells require a sacrifice to break the spell. And since the three of us are the ones linked to the spell, it's possible that if we gave up our lives, the spell would be broken."

My mouth dropped open. "No."

"It's true," Bella said.

I shook my head. "That's not what I meant. I'm sure it is true, but *no*. You can't do that. We just found you, Bella. I can't lose you, and Ruby's mates can't lose her either. It would kill us all."

Bella smiled. "Don't worry. I'm not intending on giving up my life anytime soon."

"I hope not," I said. "You've got too much to live for. We all do now." Bella had given my life purpose, and I intended to see us both through to a ripe old age.

We turned the corner and began weaving through the townspeople who walked up and down the street on their daily errands.

Bella turned to me. "Tiffany is starting to get a bit impatient about finding her mates. Is there any way we can introduce her to some of the men in your pack? Do you have... socials? Or something like that?"

I grinned at her. "She should just hang around Milly's for a few days. We *all* go there. If her mates are part of our pack, then she'll see them one day or the next."

Bella smiled. "That's not a bad idea. Thanks."

Elliot

"WHAT'S WRONG WITH YOU?" Tiffany asked me.

I stared at my mate and ignored the cute blonde. I sighed. "I need to go talk to Bella. Do you mind?"

She shrugged. "Not at all. Send Jonah to me so I have someone to talk to."

"Not a problem." I strolled over to where Jonah and Bella were chatting and smiling happily.

They turned toward me.

Bella's smile died, like a light inside of her was switched off.

Fuck. "Hey Jonah. Can I talk to Bella for a bit?"

Jonah stared at Bella.

She nodded as though giving him permission to leave her.

"Tiffany wanted you to go talk to her," I told him.

Jonah nodded and slunk away.

I wandered a bit further away from the group.

Bella followed me.

I knew that my wolf shifter brothers would likely be able to hear us, no matter how far I walked. "Hey," I began. "I just wanted to talk to you about yesterday."

Bella nodded, and kept her gaze on me, but didn't say anything.

I swallowed hard, pushing forward, despite how uncomfortable I was. "I can feel a... shift in how you feel about me. So, I just wanted to apologize again. Make sure you know that it won't happen again."

Her lips twisted in a strange smirk that made my gut sink. She didn't believe me. When she raised her gaze to mine, my heart dropped. "I don't think you can promise that" she said. "You're an Alpha. You're like... an Alpha's *Alpha*. You aren't meant to share a mate. You're meant to have your own."

I swallowed hard, forcing the lump in my throat down so I could speak. "I don't have another mate, Bella. You're it. Fate doesn't make these mistakes." That was what I'd come to realize. I'd been waiting for my Fated Mate, and I'd found her. So, what if she loved Jonah and Tommy as well? As long as she loved me, nothing else ultimately mattered.

She shook her head, glancing away. "Elliot, I think we should cut this... connection we have as soon as possible. It'll only get more painful, the longer we're together."

I froze, afraid to move. "Bella, what do you mean?"

She stared at the concrete and scuffed her shoes against the pavement. "I mean, we've only kissed once. You should be able to walk away from all of this relatively easily."

"Walk away?" I repeated. *Is she serious?*

She nodded. "I mean, you shouldn't have to share your mate, and it's obvious I'm not the right person for you. I'm quiet. I'm not nearly strong enough to handle someone with your strength—your possessive nature." She lifted her gaze long enough to look at me. Then as tears glimmered in her eyes, she looked away again.

"You don't mean that," I said. "You're, by definition, perfect for me, Bella." It hurt to admit that I *knew* she was perfect for me when I'd acted so poorly, almost as much as it hurt to hear her reject me.

She threw her head back and flicked her hair over her shoulder. "I can't do this, Elliot. You scare me. Your wolf. You. All of it. I can't handle you. I'm sorry."

A growl rose in my chest, and I pushed it down. "But you can handle Jonah and Tommy? Is that right? I'm too much for you, but they're *just* right? Like this is some kind of Goldilocks and the three bears porridge scenario?" Anger boiled inside me.

Bella sighed and shook her head, "See? You can't even acknowledge that the other two suit me better. It's obvious you can't change, so let's just stop pretending I'm right for you. You need someone so much better than me, Elliot. Stronger. Sexier..." She stopped midsentence, putting a hand to her head as though she had a sudden headache.

I reached for her, but she flinched, and I took my hand back. "Bella, please, I..." I wasn't sure what I was going to say next, but a strange sort of wind swept through the town. I inhaled sharply, a shiver of unease working its way down my throat. "Do you feel that?" I asked.

I glanced toward Tommy and Jonah just as the girls began to faint, falling toward the pavement.

All three of us dove simultaneously to save each of them from hurting themselves.

"What the hell...?" Bella drooped, and her knees seemed to give way because she was soon tumbling to the ground.

I reached out and grabbed her up into my arms, awkwardly pulling her limp body against me.

Tommy swung Ruby up into his arms carefully.

And Jonah pulled Tiffany's unconscious form into his embrace.

I leaned down toward Bella's face where her eyes were closed, and her mouth was open. Her breath fanned my cheek.

"She's still breathing," I said aloud with relief, even as panic pushed through me.

Tommy growled, deep in his chest. "We need to get them back to their moms. *Now*."

"Now?" I repeated, confused and terrified all at once which was an extremely unfamiliar feeling for me. Then I glanced up into the sky where a brewing darkness was beginning to gather. "Oh, fuck. That ain't natural."

"Let's go," Tommy yelled above the wind that had begun to howl like it had a mind and will of its own.

We ran for it, all three of us carrying a witch, through the main street where people ducked for cover, around the corner and down the street that would lead us back to Bella's house.

I was at the head of the group, carrying our precious cargo. When I glanced back, Tommy was right behind me with a pregnant Ruby and Jonah was a ways back. I'd have to help him with Tiffany.

Ahead, all three moms stood on the nature strip outside Bella's house, glancing from side to side, looking as terrified as I felt.

They ran toward us as we bolted to them.

"What happened?" Sherie cried, reaching out for Ruby.

"Let's get inside," I said raising my voice to be heard, pushing around the mothers. "Jonah needs help with Tiffany and the storm is about to hit."

The girls' moms went to help Jonah as lightning cracked in the sky above our heads, lighting up the whole town.

People screamed in fear and ran for their houses.

I pushed at the front door with my shoulder and went straight to the couches.

"I'm calling Jackson," Tommy said, placing Ruby carefully down on the couch nearest to him, then pulling out his cell. "He's going to want get here—and fast." Tommy walked away to call Ruby's triad.

I sat down with Bella in my lap and pulled her close.

Kathy dropped down in front of me and reached for her daughter's face. "Elliot, what happened?"

"We don't know. We were walking along the street. Bella and I were talking about, well, us. She put her hand to her head like she was experiencing a headache, then they all just passed out."

Kathy's eyes widened. "All of them? At the same time?"

I nodded. "Yeah, pretty much."

Kathy pushed to her feet and the mothers converged, whispering fiercely to each other.

"Hey!" I yelled, anger getting the better of me. "What's going on? What's happened to them?"

The mothers spun around to look at me.

Jonah was still holding Tiffany.

Her mom directed him to lay her down on the couch.

Kathy stepped forward; her brow furrowed. "We think it's the curse."

Thunder boomed over the house and the women jumped.

"What do you mean?" Jonah asked. "What's the curse doing now? Hasn't it taken enough from us?"

I nodded. *Yeah, especially our pack.*

Kathy's lips trembled as Sherie walked forward, dropping down in front of Ruby. "Ruby's pregnant with a girl."

"That's not possible, is it?" Tommy asked, back from speaking with Jackson. "They're on their way."

Kathy shivered. "The girls, Ruby included, are in essence.... the spell. The rules don't apply to them the same way they do everyone else. It's a magical loophole of sorts." She stopped and took a breath. "I believe that Ruby's baby will break the curse, if we can just keep her alive long enough to see her daughter born."

"So, what's wrong with them? Why are they all unconscious?" I asked, still not understanding what she was talking about.

"The curse is fighting back against the loophole," Rebecca said, checking on her daughter. "The spell doesn't want to be broken. All their lives are linked to it and it only exists because of *them*... So, if we can't find a way to unhook it, their lives will be forfeit."

CHAPTER 22
TOMMY

I walked over to where my best friend held our mate and put a hand to her head. "She's cold." Worry lanced through me.

Elliot growled. "Jonah, can you take her for me?" He stood up with Bella still in his arms.

Jonah sat down on the couch, accepting Bella's sleeping form into his care.

Then Elliot, the big idiot who Bella had been breaking up with when she fainted, began to strip off his shirt.

"What are you doing?" Kathy asked, staring at the huge form of Elliot's naked back.

Elliot twisted around to look at me, his eyes already shifting to his inner wolf. "I've got to do something. I can't stand around here and do nothing."

I didn't bother reiterating to him that Bella had technically already broken up with him.

Elliot wasn't going to let her go without a fight, and Bella didn't know Elliot well enough to understand just how stubborn he could be.

"Where are you going?" I asked, before he lost the ability to talk.

"I'm going to find the Manterri's..." Elliot said, as his teeth became pointed and garbled his speech. White fur sprouted through his skin, and he dropped to all fours to let the shift completely take him over.

"I'll get the door," I said, charging for the front door to let Elliot out, before one of the witches tried to stop him. The gale force winds hit me in the face when I opened the door.

But Elliot ran straight through the doorway and into the roiling storm.

Rain pelted down and, as I watched my friend disappear, my heart squeezed tightly in my chest. He may be a stubborn idiot, and I may owe him a beating, but *damn*, I couldn't imagine living my life without him around. I shut the door and turned back to the group.

All three moms stared at me like I'd lost my mind.

"Did he just say he was going looking for the Manterri's?" Kathy whispered.

I nodded. "Didn't Bella tell you?"

Kathy shook her head.

I sighed. "When Elliot went running the other night," *after losing his shit because he found us with Bella,* "he found the cousins. All three of them."

"They're alive?" Rebecca whispered, her hand straying to her heart and pressing against her breast.

I nodded. "We think so. Elliot said they wouldn't come back with him, but it looks like he's going to give it a second try."

The three older witches grabbed each other for support, staggering into nearby chairs.

Kathy lifted her hand and swung it around, clearing all the books off the floor and table.

"That's handy," I muttered. "Our house would always be clean, if we could do that."

Kathy ignored me. "We need to find a way to lift this spell."

The front door banged wide open and three wet, black wolves ran into the room.

I bolted for the front door and locked it shut this time as we weren't expecting anyone else that I was aware of. When I got back to the room, Jackson, Billy, and Darren were standing naked and wet in the lounge room.

"How is she?" they asked together.

"For goodness' sake," Sherie said, flicking her hand and magicking up three sets of jeans and black t-shirts for the guys.

"Thanks," Darren said, while Billy and Jackson went straight for their mate.

The storm brewed overhead, and the sparkling power of the lightning above lit up the sky.

Elliot

I RAN THROUGH THE TOWN, rain pelting my fur as thunder rolled through the sky. I was terrified—more so than I'd ever been in my entire life. My mate's life was in danger, and I was so afraid of losing her I couldn't even think straight.

Bella was my only mate. I'd never get another if she died. She was my only hope for happiness. Even if that hope was a tiny flame flickering hopelessly in the dark, especially after what I'd done so far to ruin her trust.

As I ran past the edges of the town, the storm cleared as though it had never been. The sky above my head became blue. The sun shone and the wind died down. I stopped running, my fur dripping wet, my eyes barely able to open from the sting of the wind. I shook myself, taking stock of my body. I had enough food in my gut, and a good sleep last night, I could run all day and reach the border by nightfall. It would hurt, but I could do it.

This time it wasn't anger driving me; it was pure panic. And a love that had grown with every minute since the moment I'd met my mate. Even if she wanted nothing to do with me after this, she couldn't die. I couldn't exist in a world where she wasn't.

I took the road around the next town, careful to dodge the city folk and took to running through the forests. I passed over the countryside, meeting cattle that leapt out of my path, and smaller, normal wolves who glared at me as I ran past. I didn't stop though my legs burned, desperate for rest. I kept my eyes peeled for danger and looked for any signs of the cousins I'd met just the other day.

I had no hope of helping Bella or her witchy cousins. I was no use to them where magic was involved. But I could find their fathers. I could bring them home. Maybe then the witches would have a chance of breaking the spell that held the Manterri's hostage in their own shifter bodies.

I ran long past the noon sun, watching it disappear on the horizon; stopping only briefly by a watering hole for some fresh water. Lapping it up with frantic gusto to soothe my parched throat. Then I kept moving. When night finally came, I was grateful for the dark, and the cold. My coat was drenched with sweat and the night air allowed me time to cool down.

There wasn't too far to go now. Last time I'd found the cousins, they'd been hanging around near the border. When I reached the state line, I slowed down to a trot and began to look for signs of wolf shifters. My heart pounded in my chest and my legs shook with sheer exhaustion, but I was nowhere near done with my quest. I wasn't going home without them.

The pack joked that I was an Alpha's *Alpha.* I'd never liked the responsibility of such a title and knew that when it came to our current pack dynamics, I'd never be called upon to do what a true Alpha would have done in the past. But I understood what it meant. I could command the respect of anyone in our pack. Those older than me. Those younger. The Alphas, the Betas, the Council and even the elders.

I'd never used my true power before, but one of the Manterri cousins had been Alpha-born, himself. And while the other two may follow me out of pure instinct, an Alpha wouldn't. Not unless I pushed the issue, which for the first time in my life, I might need to.

I lifted my nose and sniffed the air, catching the slightest scent of a wolf to the north. I took off running, jumping over logs and bolting around trees like my life depended on it.

When I finally found them, they were curled up around an old fire some human had stupidly forgotten to put out. The embers still glowed red and orange.

The largest of the three gray wolves got to his feet and growled at me.

I let go of my wolf, shifting back into human form. Staggering sideways under heavy fatigue, I finally collapsed to the ground beside the fire. The embers gave off only a small amount of heat. I put a hand to my aching stomach. "Fuck, I'm starving." *And cold.* I crawled over to the fire, rearranging the embers and sticking some dry wood onto the pile. The fire began to crackle and burn, lighting up once more.

I couldn't hear it, but I almost sensed the sigh in the other three wolves.

They moved closer, settling around me.

I leaned back against my hands and took a moment to catch my breath. I'd found them, and the relief was immense.

All three gray wolves were starved, their ribs protruding against their fur.

None of us really enjoyed eating in wolf form. It meant hunting down a live animal, killing it, and devouring it while still warm. We were taught as kids how to do it, as part of survival training. But it wasn't a preference and it wasn't fun. No wonder these guys were as thin as they were. They probably only ate the bare minimum amount of food necessary to stay alive. It looked like they were barely hanging on.

The fire began to crackle, and I reached forward to stir it up once more.

The wolves shuffled closer to me, tightening the circle around me, keeping me warm where the fire lacked.

I smiled at them. "Thanks."

They didn't respond, and I didn't expect them to.

Some wolves could communicate in a telepathic sense, but only members of a pack that ran together often. Brothers, sometimes, but not always.

I could imagine these three would read each other very well, especially after decades of being together—of being each other's only companions.

When I'd rested enough that my heart was no longer racing, the sweat had dried, and my legs no longer trembled, I pulled myself up so that I was seated to talk to them. They should be able to understand me. Unless they'd lost that sense too. "I'm Elliot Turnbridge. My father is elder Tony Turnbridge."

The largest of the gray wolves lifted his head and stared at me.

"My Fated Mate is Bella Swatch."

Another smaller gray wolf stuck his head up.

I turned to him. "You're Matthew Manterri?" He was Bella's dad, and half warlock. I looked at the largest of the three. "And you're Lucas?" Then at the final wolf. "Thomas."

The three of them stared at me, unmoving, barely breathing.

I could feel the tension within them. "I've come to ask you to come home. Back to the pack."

The wolves all stood up and began to turn away, their heads down, defeated.

I jumped to my feet. "Your daughters are all in grave danger."

They stopped.

"Yes, your daughters! You didn't know that Kathy and Rebecca and Sherie were pregnant, but they were. They gave birth to three daughters, all on Halloween."

The wolves turned to stare at me, unmoving. Focused. Listening.

My chest ached with pain at the thought of Bella at home, unconscious. "The girls are in real trouble. The curse that forced you three to remain wolf shifters forever is hurting them, and without you, I don't think their moms will be able to work out how to fix it."

There was a strange growl and a rumble, the men talking to each other in low-pitched wolf talk.

"I don't know if you can even go back to the pack. Or why you've stayed away this long. But if you can come back with me, you have to. You're the only lead we have."

The Alpha wolf began to turn away.

I let go of my humanity and shifted, letting my huge white wolf take over, allowing the anger to roll over my body and light me up from the inside. I growled loudly, standing over the Alpha and snarling. *You will come back. You will. For your daughters. And for yourselves.*

The two Betas bowed their heads, growling as they were forced to submit.

A small part of me hated having to do this, but a larger part reveled in being able to do something to help my mate. No matter the cost to myself or to my humanity. I'd gladly pay the price and have no regrets.

I growled harder, forcing the Alpha to do as I wanted—what my mate needed. Why they wouldn't come back, I didn't know. And quite frankly I didn't fucking care. Bella and her friends had grown up without their fathers and these men had lost half their lives. For whatever reasons they'd stayed away, I was sure we could fix it. Somehow. Someway. We had to.

The Alpha's head dropped in a show of aggression.

I snapped my jaws, feeling my heart pump and saliva pool in my gums. I didn't want to fight this wolf. He was weak. He was old. And he was one of my own. So, I dropped my head, made eye contact with the Alpha, and let the last thoughts go free. *Come back with me. Follow me now. If you don't, I will come back. And I will make you.*

I turned tail and started running home.

CHAPTER 23
TOMMY

The girls became red and started sweating around dinner time.

We took their temperature and all three were burning up at over one hundred and two degrees.

The moms panicked and called in other members of the Coven. They all hunched around the dining table, surrounded by books and herbs, spells, and crystals. There were witches and warlocks *everywhere*.

I sat quietly on the couch next to where Bella lay, watching over her.

"Do you think they're going to find the way out of this?" Jackson asked me from where he knelt on the floor, stroking Ruby's flushed face with a cool cloth.

The storm hadn't let up, and the rain was causing flooding in some of the houses around us. Only the magic of the Coven at the table in front of us kept this house safe.

"I wish we could just pick them up and take them home," I said in response, sighing with frustration. "Maybe they'd be safer with the pack?"

Jackson shook his head. "I don't understand any of this, so I'm just going to sit here and do as I'm told."

"You?" I huffed, almost laughing. "Since when? You're an Alpha, yourself."

Jackson was every bit as much of an Alpha as I was. Taking orders was not one of our fortes. But then neither was sitting back and just waiting for someone else to act. Jackson chuckled. "Since Ruby almost killed herself undoing the Halloween love spell. If it wasn't for us— hang on a second. Hey, Sherie!"

Ruby's mom looked up from the book she was studying. "Yeah?"

Jackson jumped to his feet, potentially onto something. "Could you use us to save the girls, like you did last time? They way you did on Halloween?"

Sherie pulled her glasses off her nose and stared at him in thought. "I suppose we could try. But Tiffany doesn't have any mates to draw strength from, Bella only has two here, and Ruby's pregnant. It's dangerous."

"Yeah, and so's sitting here waiting to see what happens," Jackson grumbled back.

"You could try Bella first," I said. "Jonah and I are up for *anything* that could bring Bella back." I glanced over at my brother who nodded.

Kathy looked at us. "But we need more than to just wake them up. We need to know what put them under in the first place. And who did it? I'm convinced someone who is still alive is pulling the strings on this spell. It's not simply the doing of the old High Warlock."

"Then who is it?" I asked.

"I bet you it's one of the High Council," Kathy said, grimacing as though angry.

"Like who?" Sherie asked. "Tabitha? I know she's a bitch, but do you really think she'd do this to our daughters?"

Kathy threw her hands in the air. "The High Council hate the wolf shifters, so why wouldn't they? Our daughters are making sure the pack line continues. The girls being Fated Mates with the pack boys is a nightmare for all those that want the shifter lines to fail."

I paced to the window and stared out; my brow bowed in confusion. "Why is it raining like this? Is it part of the spell? Or are they trying to stop us from leaving?" I turned back to the table of witches.

None of the strangers spoke.

Rebecca started to frantically flip through one of the books. "If the girls are being hexed, then perhaps we can protect them. There's a home enchantment spell that I saw earlier. It might not help Tiffany and Ruby but might bring Bella out of it. Here." She tapped a page and turned it toward Kathy.

Kathy swallowed. "I could try it, I suppose, but I'm not sure what good it will do to have Bella awake and not the others?"

It would help me.

Rebecca pushed the book over to where Kathy sat. "It will tell us if there's an external influence cursing the girls. If the protection charm wakes Bella, then we know it's coming from far away. If it doesn't, there's something internal going on here."

Kathy nodded and stood up, taking the book and going to stand in a strange spot near the kitchen.

"What's she doing?" I asked no-one in particular.

"Just finding the center of the house," Rebecca answered. "She'll create a shell of sorts that can cocoon everyone inside and hopefully stop whatever curse is hitting the girls."

"So, like a shield?" Darren queried.

"Exactly," Rebecca said.

Kathy began to read, to speak in a language I didn't understand.

The wind whirled around us, and the strangest, coldest sense of calm came over me. I sank to the couch, reaching out to hold Bella's hand.

Her skin felt warmer than it had been before.

"I think it's working," I said, breathless, not wanting to jinx it, but unable to keep the thought inside my head.

"Bella?" Jonah stroked her face. "Can you hear us?"

She rolled her head from side to side.

The woman behind us gasped.

I echoed the sound, happiness squeezing my chest. "Bella!"

Her eyelids flickered and slowly, too slowly, her eyes began to open. She saw me and frowned. "What happened?"

Thank you, God.

She tried to sit up.

Kathy rushed over to help us prop her up.

"Where's Tiffany and Ruby?" Bella asked. "Oh no, they're still there."

"Still where?" Jonah asked.

Bella turned around and stared at us. "The void. I left them in the void!"

Kathy reached out to touch her daughter. "What are you talking about, Bella?"

Bella put a hand to her head and turned so that she could slip her legs off the couch and put her feet on solid ground. "I can't explain it except that, there was nothing there. It was like a black room. We were all trapped there together. And we were just talking, waiting."

"A consciousness trap," Rebecca said with instant disgust and anger.

"A what?" I asked.

Bella sighed, rubbing her head. "It's a spell that collects your mind and traps it in a place your body can't reach. It's a complicated, very complex spell. Only a senior witch or warlock could perform it successfully."

Jackson slammed his fist into the opposite hand. "We need to find this bastard and put them out of their misery."

He was right. We needed to do something, and Jackson and I could rip apart a warlock. No problem. I turned to Kathy. "I assume you need to stay here to protect Bella, but where do we find the person who's doing this to them?"

Rebecca and Sherie stood up.

"They'll be at the church. There's nowhere else in town that has enough power to bolster a witch like this," Kathy said.

"And the rain?" I asked. "What's with the storm?"

Rebecca shook her head. "I don't know. I have to assume it's either a side effect of the dark magic, or it's an attempt to stop people trying to find her or him."

I grinned. "Luckily, wolves don't mind water."

Jackson cracked his knuckles. "I'm going with you."

"We are, too," Jonah and Billy said, jumping up. *My brothers.*

I turned to them and shook my head. "You need to stay here and look after everyone."

Jonah sulked.

Billy glared at me. "This is my mate's life too, Tommy."

"I know." I sighed and dropped my voice. "And if we don't make it back, it'll be your job to protect them, do you understand?"

Billy's eyes softened. "Fine."

"We're coming, too," Rebecca and Sherie said, stepping up as the Betas slunk away. "You're going to need the protection."

"Protection?" I asked, raising an eyebrow. "Jackson and I are both Alphas." We were the strongest of our pack. *Surely, we'd be capable of taking out a couple of distracted witches?*

Rebecca rolled her eyes. "I'm not talking about physical strength, boys. This witch is going to have a guard, and they will hurt you if they can. Kill you even if you get close enough. Sherie and I will keep a shield up so you can attack. We need to take them down before they kill our daughters."

Sherie shuddered. "Consciousness traps are dangerous. People go into them, and sometimes never come out."

"Never?" Jackson asked, glancing at Ruby with worry.

"Or if they do," Rebecca continued, "they're not sure which is the real world, and lose their minds anyway."

I clenched my teeth. "How long have they got?"

Rebecca exhaled sharply. "A few days at most."

"Then we haven't got a moment to lose. Let's go." I hurried to the front door and pulled off my shirt. "I hope you two have hurricane-ready umbrellas."

Rebecca and Sherie glanced at each other; determination written all over their tense faces. "Oh, we do."

Bella called out to me. "Tommy, please be careful!" She hadn't gotten up off the couch yet but was holding her hand out to me.

I couldn't stop myself from hurrying back to her, leaning down, and planting a kiss on her pouting lips. I cupped her cheek.

She looked pale and wan, but she was alive.

"You stay here, beautiful. I'll be back soon."

Bella's lip quivered. "What will I do if something happens to you?"

I chuckled. "Nothing will. Haven't you seen my reinforcements?" I pointed my thumb at Jackson and the two moms behind me.

Tears shimmered in Bella's eyes, but she nodded. "Please be careful. It's obvious these people will stop at nothing to tear us apart." Bella glanced around, alarmed. "Where's Elliot? He should go with you."

I grinned down at her. "Elliot left hours ago."

Bella frowned.

"He left?" She sighed and nodded so sadly it broke my heart. "Yeah. It makes sense. I told him that we shouldn't be together anymore. Of course, he left."

I shook my head. "That wasn't the reason, sweetheart. He's gone to find your dads and bring them home."

Her lips parted in a silent gasp, her eyes widening as though she couldn't believe what I'd just said. "I..."

I chuckled. "I've been friends with that knucklehead my whole life and I can tell you with certainty, he loves you. He's just having a hard time processing it all. I know you think it might be easier with just you and me and Jonah, but don't give up on him yet, yeah?"

Bella bit her lip, the unshed tears that had been swimming in her eyes spilling over and cascading down her cheeks. "Okay," she agreed.

"Good girl. Now..." I turned around and headed back to the front door, unbuckling my jeans and kicking off my shoes. "We're got an evil witch to take down."

"Or warlock," Sherie reminded me. "It could be anyone."

Jackson pulled off the black tank Sherie had magicked on him and rolled his shoulders and cracked his neck.

I nodded once. "Ready?"

He grunted in agreement.

I unlocked the front door, opening it a crack, then the wind banged it open in my face. I heard the exclamations of shock from the other witches in the room behind us but chose to ignore them and focus on what needed to be done. They could bolt the door again after we left. "Let's do it."

Together, Jackson and I shifted into our wolves and bounded out the front door and into the storm. Sherie and Rebecca were right behind us and, as I jumped down onto the road where the water was up to my shoulders, the need for the witches became suddenly apparent. I wasn't doggy paddling all the way to the church. If we couldn't run there, there was no point in being a wolf.

I was just about to shift back to human and start wading through what would be waist-deep water, when the river ahead of us running down the street, split like Moses and the Red Sea. I glanced back at the witches who were behind us.

Their arms were out, and their bodies were glowing like jewels of power.

I looked at Jackson, whose wolfy grin would have made me laugh if the circumstances weren't so dire. We had our way. *Time to go.* We took off, the witch moms at our backs and the road ahead of us clear. I didn't know what was going to happen, or if we were going to make it home again. But while we still had breath in our lungs, and our mates were at risk, I was going to fight for them.

I smiled as I ran through the streets, rain falling on us from above as thunder rolled across the sky. I'd never really given thought to the many reasons Bella had more than one mate, but for the first time, I was actually grateful for the fact.

Elliot was off conquering the cursed fathers.

I was here fighting the witches,

And Jonah was keeping our mate happy and safe at home.

Overall, I'd say we had all our bases covered. I just had to stay alive long enough to tell Bella I was happy about the fact she had all three of us.

CHAPTER 24
TOMMY

I ran through the empty streets, bolting through the rain, adrenaline pumping in my veins as Jackson and I made our way to the old church. How Sherie and Rebecca kept up with us, I didn't know. I had to assume they were traveling by magic.

When we finally reached the road that led up to the church, we slowed down and glanced back to find the witches right behind us. We'd finally cleared the areas where tsunami levels of rain were falling, and the moms were using their magic to create shield-like-umbrellas over us all for the drizzle that remained.

I shifted back, ignoring the fact that I was naked. It was more important that we spoke to the witches and organized a plan than wasted time worrying about their supposed modesty issues. "So, what's the plan? Where will they be?" I had to shout to be heard above the wind and the thunder that still assaulted the world around us.

Jackson shifted back too.

Sherie didn't bother covering us, as I was pretty sure she knew we'd be back in wolf mode pretty soon. "There will be at least two of them, witches or warlocks. One conducting the spell, the other protecting them. There may be more. An army of protectors even. We really have no idea how deep this runs until we're facing it head on."

"So, how do we take them out?" Jackson asked.

Rebecca looked at Sherie. "They hate wolf shifters. We could use that to our advantage somehow."

"So, we attack?" I asked. "Draw their attention away from you?"

Sherie frowned. "I don't like the sound of that. I'd never forgive myself if something happened to one of you."

I smiled to myself, enjoying the fact these witches had developed a natural affinity and bond with us now because of their daughters.

"So, one of you focus on protecting us, while the other one takes care of the bad witches?" I suggested.

Sherie glanced at Rebecca, who nodded. "We can do that. I'm better at protection spells, anyway," she said.

Rebecca grinned. "And I'm better at attacking spells. So, bring it on!" She stretched her arms and cracked her knuckles.

"All right then, let's do this." I turned to Jackson. "Divide and conquer? I'll come at them from the north."

Jackson nodded in agreement. "I'll cover the south."

We had a plan.

The witches rolled their hands, white sparkling magic pulsing around them.

Without wasting another moment, I shifted back to my wolf form.

Jackson followed suit.

We powered toward the church.

I bounded toward the north and was confronted by a male warlock.

He stood on the steps of the church, ready and waiting. His eyes looked crazy and unnatural, swirling with silver beneath the storm that played above him.

I put my head back and howled, drawing his attention.

Without a second's hesitation he fired magic directly at me.

Thanks to my fast reflexes I dodged out of the way unscathed. Not breaking my stride, I kept running, circling closer, growling and howling, the swirling white magic of protection around me like a shield. Jumping up I saw Sherie protecting Jackson. So, I dodged around a car, only to cop a purple ball of magic in the face. Pain burned my eyes and I dropped to the ground rolling onto my back and batting at my face futilely with my paws.

Then, Sherie was beside me like an angel, casting a spell over me.

The pain eased and my eyesight came back instantly. *Fuck. That was close.* I scrambled back to my feet and charged to the front door of the church for a second time.

The warlock was there, firing balls of blinding light at Jackson. I heard him yelp, and a thud as he hit the ground.

Oh no. My stomach lurched. I leaped over the steps, running straight for the warlock—intent on ending his days—when he suddenly disappeared. I skidded to a halt and peered around. He was gone, literally nowhere to be seen.

Sherie ran across the front of the church to help Jackson where he lay on his side, blood covering his pelt.

I couldn't help him now; he was in good hands. What I needed to do was stop whoever was casting this spell. Fear aside, I burst through the front door... but no one was inside. *Strange.* Racing through the rooms and hallways, water falling from my coat onto the hardwood floors, I made my way to the inner sanctum.

Tall candles were lit and surrounded the room, casting flickering shadows everywhere. Darkness consumed each corner, and flashes of light lit up the center of the room.

Rebecca stood at one end of the space, flames of magic dancing over her hands as she fought a blonde witch I'd never seen before, as well as the warlock who, moments ago, had been standing outside attacking us.

The warlock spun around, catching her off-guard.

Rebecca was hit in the side and fell to her knees.

I heard her pained gasp and saw red. With a growl, I charged forward with all my might. Before anyone could react, I jumped, teeth bared at the two people responsible for this spell that was hurting Bella, and all those she loved.

The blonde witch lifted her hand to throw a spell at me.

The warlock grabbed her arm. Then, they were gone.

I landed on the floor where they'd been standing, throwing my head left and right, but there was no sign of them. Only dust and black magic remained where they'd once been. *Damn it.* I rushed over to Rebecca.

She knelt, gasping for air and holding her belly.

I shifted back to human, needing my voice. But Sherie wouldn't hear me in here, though. So, I raced to the nearest window, pushed it open and screamed, "Sherie! Rebecca needs help!"

Sherie came bursting through the front doors of the church.

Jackson hobbled after her, holding his arm in a strange sort of way.

She went straight for Rebecca, summoning up her magic. She ran her hands over Rebecca, and magic arched from her fingers to the other woman, sparking and sizzling.

Rebecca let out a sigh, slumping on the spot.

I hurried over to Jackson. "You okay?"

Jackson nodded, dried blood caked over his chest and shoulder. "Yeah. That bastard got me good, but Sherie saved me. She's handy in a pinch, that's for sure."

I swallowed hard. Jackson could have died. We *all* could have. "Let's check on Rebecca," I said, turning back to the witches.

Sherie had Rebecca's arm around her, trying desperately to lift her up, but not quite managing it.

She looked at me with panic written all over her face. "I have to get her back to Kathy's house. *Now.*"

I nodded. She knew best when it came to magic. "How do we do that?"

"Can you do that transportational thing?" Jackson asked, grimacing in pain. "You know the thing you did to us?"

Rebecca inclined her head. "Yes, I can. It'll take most of my power, and you may feel a little sick, but hold on, okay?"

I nodded. "Whatever you want."

Jackson grabbed hold of my arm as I bent over and lifted Rebecca up and held her against my body.

"Let's go."

Sherie reached for us, and then we flew through time and space. We landed, smack bang, back into Kathy's flood water drenched front lawn. It was like being plopped straight into a cold swimming pool.

We went under, my breath trapped in my lungs. But I got my feet beneath me and stood, grabbing hold of Rebecca and lifting her up above the freezing cold water still running through the town.

She coughed and spluttered, ushing the hair out of her face.

"What happened?" I grated out.

Sherie groaned. "Sorry. I forgot about the protection spell Kathy's running. We need to get inside the old-fashioned way."

We waded through the water and staggered up the steps. The wind and rain were thankfully gone, but the town was still flooded.

Sherie reached out and rang the doorbell.

The door flung open a heartbeat later.

"You're alive!" Bella cried, flinging herself into my arms.

I let her grip me for one precious moment, loving the feel of her warmth against me. "Yeah, but we need to get inside, beautiful."

"Oh, yes. Sorry!" Bella dragged me inside and the others followed.

"Are Tiffany and Ruby waking up?" I asked, unnecessarily because as I stepped into the house the answer to my question was revealed.

Both girls were sitting up, eyes open, but looking pale and weak.

"You're both back." I grinned as relief overwhelmed me.

Kathy lowered her arms. "Is it safe to release the spell?" she asked.

I nodded. "I think so. They're gone. Disappeared into thin air."

"Thank God for that," Kathy said. "Oh dear, but what happened?" She rushed for Rebecca and Sherie.

I hobbled over to the couch, collapsed onto it, and threw back my head. "Fuck me, that was intense."

Bella rushed over and sat in my lap, wrapping her arms around me and sobbing. "I'm so glad you're all right."

I held her and smiled at Jonah who was looking more than a little relieved to have me back. "Everything go okay while I was gone?" I asked.

He shrugged. "You know, just the normal stuff. Witches doing spells. Magical comas. Storms, lightning, thunder."

I laughed. "Yeah, our life isn't exactly boring anymore, is it?" I glanced over at Billy who was holding Ruby close.

"She okay?" I asked, lifting my chin toward his pregnant mate.

Billy grinned. "Yep. Thanks to you four."

I glanced out the window and held my mate close. "Now, we've just got to wait and see what Elliot discovered."

There was silence in the room as everyone mulled over our words.

The witch and warlock who'd attacked our mates had disappeared, but they weren't dead, and I had the sneaking suspicion that they'd be back.

CHAPTER 25
BELLA

Mom and Sherie worked on Rebecca for ages, then put her into Mom's bed to rest. It was getting late, and dark, but no-one was going home. Not a chance. Our tiny house had never held so many people.

"Can we sleep here tonight?" Tommy asked. He glanced at my mom, then back at me. "That is if we're welcome?"

I nodded, then looked at Mom. "I'm exhausted. Can we set up some food for everyone, then head to bed?"

Mom nodded, then smiled. "That's a good idea, hon." She magicked up a large, long table in the middle of the room and began summoning food. The aroma of delicious hot meat pies, bowls of crispy, salted chips, steamed rice, and fragrant fried chicken soon filled the house.

I stood and stared, impressed with my mom's versatility. She didn't usually make so much at once—but then, she didn't normally need to feed a small army of witches and shifters.

When she was finally done, she said, "Dig in, everyone, please. Then we'll work out where everyone's going to sleep."

We ate as much as we were able and cleaned up.

Then Mom took over, organizing bedding for the rest of the clan.

"Good night, everyone," I called, dragging Jonah and Tommy to bed. Ironically, my room was big, but my bed was small. "Hang on a minute," I said, conjuring a small amount of magic to my fingers. Working a spell to make the bed larger, it grew until it was the size of a king, and easily took up half the bedroom now.

"Okay. I'm in the middle." I started to strip off, not caring about anything other than climbing into my bed and going to sleep. I got down to my tank and undies, stripped off my bra, then pulled back the covers.

Tommy and Jonah stared at me.

"Come on," I said, rolling my eyes. "I want both of you with me." I crawled over the bed, arranged the three pillows, and lay down with my head on the middle one.

Jonah and Tommy began to strip, though Tommy wore only the pants Mom had magicked on him when he'd arrived back here from their venture to the church.

I stared at them as their bodies were revealed to me. "You're both so beautiful."

They both blushed, simultaneously.

I giggled. *Who knew they'd be so coy?* "Come, please." I held my hands out to them, tired to the bone. I'd never felt so utterly exhausted before. I knew that if I closed my eyes for even a moment, I'd slide into a deep and blissful sleep instantly.

Jonah slid to my right and lay down.

Tommy lay down on my left.

I rolled onto my left side and laid a protective hand over Jonah. "Can you cuddle me from behind, Tommy? I have to lie on this side, sorry. Or I can't sleep."

"No problem," he said, spooning me from behind. He growled softly, his face buried in my neck.

I was too tired to react in any overt way, but feeling his hot body curl around mine was like sheer heaven. I could feel his masculinity pressing into me and sighed as I wiggled against them, glad I still had my knickers on.

He groaned and kissed my neck. "Keep doing that and you won't be wearing underwear for very long."

I sighed, smiled, and stopped wriggling. Now wasn't the time for that. "Thank you both for everything you did today." I adjusted my arm and placed my hand on Jonah's chest, my palm right over his heart.

He turned his head to look at me and smiled. "Tommy did most of it, Bella. I just stayed here."

"Exactly where I wanted you," I said, then yawned loudly. "I didn't realize how important having two mates would be until today. It was so good knowing that one of you could stay with me, while the other one went off to chase the bad guy. I would have been sick with worry if you'd left me all alone." I closed my eyes and felt sleep tugging at me through the darkness of my lashes.

"Elliot is your mate too. And he'll be back soon," Tommy whispered.

I sighed, not wanting to talk about that particular issue at the moment. Elliot was a complicated topic for me. I wanted him, but if he was the price that had to be paid to keep Jonah and Tommy by my side, then I would pay it. Even if it killed me. "Good night." I allowed sleep to claim me and dreamed of a wolf shifter running endlessly through the night, drinking from watering holes, and leaping large fences in single bounds.

THE NEXT MORNING I woke up with the covers pushed off the bed, and instead I was simply covered and wrapped in the hot arms of my mates. I blinked, trying not to move so I didn't wake them up. I couldn't believe that today was Sunday. *Has it really only been a few days since Thanksgiving?* The day before, I'd just met these men and realized they were meant to be in my life.

I had to go back to college tomorrow and the thought of normal life after what we'd gone through over the last few days just seemed wrong. And weird.

I was still lying on my left side with Tommy pressed up against my back, his arm slung possessively over my waist.

Jonah had rolled away and was flat on his belly, snoring peacefully away.

"Good morning," Tommy whispered into my ear.

I smiled as a shiver rippled through me, amazed that this all felt so normal. And *so* good. "Good morning," I said.

Tommy stroked my hips, then came up to cup my breasts beneath my tank.

Desire stirred in my belly, but I simply couldn't do more than sigh and lean into his touch. I still felt drained despite the solid sleep.

He must have felt my lack of desire because he pushed me over, so I lay on my back, and stared down at me with a worried look on his face. "Are you okay?"

I grimaced. "Yeah, I think so. But I'm so tired. I'm sorry."

He shook his head. "Never be sorry for wanting to wait, Bella. The time will be right when it's right. And I'll wait for you, forever." He leaned down and kissed me.

Jonah groaned loudly, rolling onto his back and stretching his arms above his head. "What are you guys talking about?"

I smiled at him. "Just saying how exhausted I am. And that I'm sorry all we did was sleep last night. I just... passed out."

Jonah smiled at me, then leaned over and kissed me too. "You're our mate, Bella. Your health is the most important thing to us. Everything else will happen in its own good time."

"Thanks." Despite their reassurance, I knew that I would always worry about whether I was enough for them. Perhaps that was just something I was going to have to work on personally; feeling more confident and comfortable within myself. My stomach suddenly grumbled, reminding me I hadn't eaten nearly enough last night in my exhausted state.

"Breakfast time?" Jonah said, sliding off the bed and grabbing for the clothes he'd left on the floor last night.

"Yeah," I said, not wanting to move.

Tommy bit my shoulder playfully. "Let's go, unless you want to see if we can make you come again?"

That got me moving. Not that I didn't want to experience that sort of pleasure with them again. I did, but with my body being utterly exhausted, and the worry about Elliot hanging over my head, I realized that this morning was probably not the time to try that again.

"Maybe tonight?" I asked as I pulled on some clean clothes and was rewarded with a grin. I had no idea what today held, but I was hoping I could start my life with my men soon. Guilt free. Worry free. Threat free. If that was at all possible.

We trundled down the stairs, the smell of fresh coffee in the air.

The hairs on the back of my neck stood on end. "What the..."

"What's wrong?" Tommy asked, coming up to grab my hand.

I turned around, looking for the source of the strange feeling.

"You guys ready for some breakfast?" my mom called from the kitchen, the smell of baked bread wafting toward us.

"Oh, hell yeah," Jonah said, heading off in search of food.

I looked around, uneasy. "Yeah, Mom. I just..." I had to find out where that feeling was coming from. Because I was pretty sure... *Oh, my God!* I rushed to the front door and flung it open wide.

There on the front lawn was a pile of wolves, all sleeping on the wet grass.

On the porch, was a naked, sleeping Elliot.

"Oh, my God," I breathed.

Elliot stirred, his huge body moving slowly as he woke, rolled over, and stretched out his back.

I couldn't stop staring. His body was absolutely exquisite. He was huge in every way, and his muscles looked so big and strong and thick. Then there was his dick, which I was embarrassed to admit was the largest of the three of my mates. And the most beautiful by far. It was long and thick, with a perfectly arrow-shaped head that made my insides pulse and pound with unexpected yearning. I looked away. *Damn it. Why is it that the one mate I've convinced myself I don't need, is the one whose body I want so bad?*

"Hey." Elliot pulled himself up to his feet.

I flicked my hand and conjured some black joggers on him, covering his delicious lower half. "Hey," I managed to return, trying to lift my gaze to his face, but not succeeding. *Damn, that chest...* I flicked my hand again, conjuring an ugly shapeless white t-shirt that somehow still managed to cling to his muscles in a way that made me want to run my hands all over him.

"Hey, man." Tommy went forward and embraced his friend. "How'd you go?"

Elliot hugged Tommy back for a mere second, then let him go, stepping back to point toward the front lawn. "I found them."

I fell back against the door frame and steadied myself by clinging to the wood. He'd found them. He'd found my father. *How were we ever going to repay him?*

"And you got them to come back," Tommy said. "How?"

Elliot shrugged. "Had to Dom them a bit."

"Dom them?" I repeated, staring at the three wolves still sleeping on the grass out the front of my mom's house. *Which one was my dad? The smallest one? Would he be the half warlock wolf?*

I saw some neighbors walk out their front door to grab a newspaper, then dart inside. Terrified.

Shit. We were going to have to get them inside soon or the neighbors were going to call animal rescue.

Elliot looked at me and answered my question. "I'm an Alpha, and so is Matthew. So, I had to, um, dominate him to force him to follow me."

I stared at him. "As in, you hurt him?" *He wouldn't have done that, would he?* That didn't fit with how I saw Elliot. Even with all his gruff strength, there was a good heart beneath it all, beating hard.

Elliot shook his head. "God, no. But wolves are pack animals and they respond to the strongest animal around. I just had to growl and threaten them a bit. They're all fine." He tilted his head. "Well, no. I mean they're weak, tired, And starving. But that wasn't me. That's twenty years of living in a body that's not your primary."

I didn't think I'd ever heard Elliot say so many words in a row, and I found myself captivated by his mouth. *Concentrate! Remember. You broke up with him. For his own good. For my own good. Stop looking at his lips! ...But then I promised Tommy I'd give Elliot another chance...*

I coughed to clear my throat, my mouth salivating at the smell of sweat and heat emanating off Elliot. *Focus.* "Do you think you could get them to come around the back? The neighbors are going to lose their minds if they see three wild animals hanging out in our front yard."

"Oh, yeah. Sure," Elliot said, and trotted down the steps.

I went around to the side of the house and opened the gate.

Elliot gently spoke to the wolves.

All three of them stood up and followed him around the side and past me.

One of the wolves stopped and sniffed me, staring at me like he knew me.

I stared back, my stomach aflutter.

"Um, hi," I said, my pulse pumping in my throat. Was this my... "Can he understand me?"

Elliot turned around and nodded, his face solemn. "Yeah, he can. And Bella? That's your dad, Matthew."

My mouth dropped open and I stared at the gray wolf that was almost as big as I was standing as a human.

"Oh. Well. Hi." *So eloquent.* "I'm Bella."

The wolf inclined his head as though bowing, then loped away.

I stared after him, noting the skinniness in his frame, the boniness of his back. The scars on his hide and tail made me flinch. How much trauma had he seen in his life? I locked the side gate and walked around the back to a flurry of activity. Someone must have seen us, or something, because everyone from inside the house had congregated in the back yard.

The noise was immense and the wolves seemed terrified, pressing against the back fence.

I ran forward, standing in front of them and putting my hands up. "They haven't been with people for like, twenty years. You need to back off."

Where I got the strength to stand in front of my best friends, all the moms, and the mates and yell at them, I had no idea.

Elliot came to stand beside me. "Bella's right. They need to rest, and eat. It's probably best if they come back to the pack and stay at our place, and you can all come visit in a few days."

There was an uproar from the witches, and I sighed.

"You take care of it," I said to Elliot, and left him to it. I turned around and walked over to the three cowering wolves and sat down on the ground with them.

They stared at me, then inched closer.

The arguing and sounds behind me grew quieter as I reached out and stroked the fur of my father's back. "I'm so sorry this happened to you."

He lay down and put his head in my lap. I stroked my hand through his fur, tears gathering and flowing down my cheeks unchecked.

Elliot knelt beside me. "Everyone's agreed to let them come back home with us and stay at Jackson's place because he has a better house and a bigger block."

I nodded. "That's great. Thank you." I wiped the tears from my face and turned to look up at my third mate—the one I'd rejected.

Elliot was frowning at me.

"Can we talk?" he asked quietly.

I coaxed my father's head off my lap and pushed myself to my feet. "Yes, I think we should."

Jackson shifted into his big black wolf to lead the gray wolves—our fathers—home, while the moms sobbed in pure relief and profound happiness.

Ruby went home with her men.

Tiffany stayed with my mom and hers.

I went home with Tommy, Jonah, and Elliot. It was high time we sorted out this mating triad thing, once and for all.

CHAPTER 26

BELLA

My stomach ached the whole drive back to the pack, knowing what I was going to have to say to Elliot.

I didn't need him. I couldn't possibly.

Someone like me didn't even need two men, but I would take the gift if Jonah and Tommy wanted me as well. They could share. They worked together well. They'd proven to me how much they cared about me with everything they did yesterday.

Elliot was jealous. And dominant. He could command an Alpha.

That was just too much for me.

We arrived back to the small home Elliot and Tommy lived in and I drifted inside, glancing around and wondering how this was going to work now.

Would we stay here and Elliot move out?

The idea filled me with a sadness I couldn't contain. A sob broke through and I covered my mouth to swallow hard.

No. Hold it together. This is for the best.

"Please let me go first," Elliot said, indicating the couch. "I know that you've made a decision about us, and I want you to hear me out before you try and break it off with me. Again."

I swallowed hard and nodded, hurrying over to the couch and sitting down.

Tommy and Jonah sat on the chairs around the dining room, quiet, but present. I could feel their love for me. Their support.

But they were giving Elliot time to talk, so I would allow it, too.

"You've decided to reject our mating, haven't you?" Elliot asked gently. "You've said as much, I know. But I need to be sure I understand what you meant."

I looked up, straining my neck to see him. "You're too tall up there."

Elliot sat down on the couch on the opposite side of the room.

He stared at me and waited.

I didn't want to say it all again, so I stared down at my hands clasped in my lap. "I don't think we're suited. I haven't from the start."

"Why would you think that?" Elliot asked.

I sighed and lifted my gaze to his. "Because I'm me. Haven't you noticed? I'm not strong, or confident, or like Ruby and Tiffany. I don't know what to do with three men. I'm not even sure I know what to do with one."

Elliot frowned. "I disagree."

"About which bit?" I'd made quite a few statements there.

"All of it. You are strong. You're brave, even. And I'm glad you're not like Ruby or Tiffany, because they're not meant to be my mate. You are. Which makes you perfect."

I pressed my lips together, thinking hard about what to say next. "Elliot, you're obviously not designed to live in a family like this one.

Which I can completely understand. Why would you want to share your mate with other men? I'm sure that there's another woman out there designed for you. Someone who doesn't make you share your life. Someone who can handle how sexy, and big you are. But it's not me."

I looked straight at him. I was doing a good job of being strong, being selfless.

"Is that what you want?" Elliot asked, pushing off the couch and onto his knees, then crawling over to me.

I took a deep breath, ignoring the tears that swelled in my eyes, then rolled down my cheeks. I forced my voice to stay even.

"What I want..." My voice broke, and I coughed to clear it. Then tried again. "I want...to do this right. To make the hard decisions now. The love spell I cast demands a payment for its use, and I know that losing you is what I must pay.... I..."

I shook myself and sniffed loudly, casting a quick spell across my face to dry my tears and runny nose. "You'll be happier without me, Elliot. Without Jonah and Tommy in your bed. I know you will."

"How could I be happy without my mate?" he asked quietly, looking straight at me and making everything in me cry and ache. "And I won't allow you to pay that sort of spell... fee. Losing you is something I can't live with."

It wasn't fair.

I forced myself to be strong. "You don't mean that, okay? Maybe Fate got it wrong?"

Elliot got up from the floor, sat down on the couch beside me, then grabbed me and pulled me into his lap.

"What are you doing?" I asked.

"Proving to you that we're meant to be together. As a wolf, there are several things that tell us who our mate is. Number one is the scent." He bent his head forward and inhaled deeply.

He groaned, a deep, sexy sound that made my belly clench with longing.

Then he lifted his head and stared at me with those dark blue eyes.

"Then there's the instant attraction, of course." He swallowed hard, his throat working. "When I saw you for the first time in Milly's, I thought I was going to shift right then and there. Lose control like some randy thirteen-year-old boy. I'm thirty-five, Bella. I've had my share of women. But no-one, and I mean no-one, has ever made me feel the way you do."

I didn't want to ask, but I desperately needed to know. "And how's that? How do I make you feel?"

My hands moved of their own accord, sliding over his chest and pressing against his heart that beat like a steam train.

He looked deep into my eyes and said, "Like my life will end if I can't be near you."

My mouth dropped open. "But you..."

"I know. I reacted badly when I saw you with Tommy and Jonah. I was jealous as sin. I wasn't mad at you. I was mad at them. At myself. At Fate. For giving me such an incredible mate, and me not being strong enough to deal with it. You're far more than I deserve, Bella, but if you'll let me love you... If you'll give me a second chance... I'll spend my whole life proving to you that we're meant to be together."

Tears filled my eyes and spilled over.

How was I going to fight against that?

I opened my mouth and flapped my lips like a fish, the words not coming out. "But the payment... the spell?"

"Fuck the spell," he said, gripping me tight. "Let it take payment in another way. We're meant to be together. It put us together. It can't possibly tear us apart."

When I didn't respond, Elliot's face fell and he said, "Unless you don't want me? And that's why you've avoided being with me?"

"Oh, God no," I said, pressing my hands closer. "I want you."

Too much. So much. It's scary.

"You do?" he asked. "Like I want you? Because when I kissed you that one time, you freaked out and didn't want me touching you. I figured you don't find me as attractive as you do Tommy and Jonah. I know I'm big, and you're small, but I won't hurt you, I promise."

The sweet words coming out of my huge Alpha made the tears flow even faster.

I desperately wiped at them, trying to get a handle on my emotions. On my body.

This was the punishment for the love spell. Feeling things I never thought I would. Loving someone I never thought I would.

Needing to love them, aching for them. It wasn't normal. And it scared me.

"You *are* afraid of me. I knew it. It's okay... I'll just..." Elliot slid me off his lap and made to stand up.

Panic flared so hard and fast I yelled, "No!"

I pushed him back against the couch cushion and threw my leg over his waist, straddling him so I could talk to him. So he couldn't leave.

"No?" Elliot repeated, his hands sliding over my thighs and around my hips.

I shivered, feeling need and lust coil deep inside me. "I want you... in a way I can't describe. It's scary how much I need you."

Elliot groaned as though someone had torn into his heart. The time for words had come and gone. Nothing was going to reassure either of us how right we were together, until we actually felt how good and right it was.

In the biblical sense.

I swooped down, gripping Elliot's face and kissing his lips in the most awkward, artless way possible. But I hoped I got points for enthusiasm.

He moaned and grabbed my ass tight, thrusting his tongue between my lips and making me gasp.

He grabbed hold of my hips, shifted to the edge of the couch, then stood up.

I squealed, but didn't fight him, wrapping my legs around his waist and holding onto him like a limpet to a rock.

"Hold on, beautiful."

He walked us into Tommy's bedroom, then let me slide down his body, to the floor.

The door closed behind us and I looked over to see Jonah and Tommy standing by the wall.

"I assume we're all invited?" Tommy asked.

I nodded, a squeal building in my throat. "Yes. Please. I want all my mates. Together. Please."

A week ago, the idea of making love to three men at all, let alone at once, had terrified me enough to make me avoid men altogether.

Now, staring at my three soul mates, all I felt was love—and excitement.

"How do we do this?" I asked, not even sure how we got naked, let alone how I was going to take them all into me.

Elliot chuckled. "Well, it would be great if you could get rid of all our clothes at once. You up for that, my gorgeous witch?"

He said the word with such affection, I found it impossible to deny him.

I nodded, and squealed as I whipped my hand around the room, magically removing the clothing from all four of us and sending it all into a large pile in the adjoining bathroom.

I gasped and covered my breasts with my hands, the stark reality of what I'd just done coming home to roost, with tingling tight nipples, and embarrassment flooding my face.

I stared at the men, their beautiful bodies now naked. Their cocks were hard and extended in front of them in anticipation of what was about to come.

"Oh, my God," I whispered.

Elliot laughed and rushed forward, scooping me up into his arms and walking toward the bed. "Time to make you ours, Bella."

I pressed my hands to his bare chest and relaxed into my Alpha. "And for me to make you mine."

Elliot put me down onto the bed and I shuffled up, laying on my back as he prowled over the top of me. As he stared down into my eyes

I saw his wolf. In the color of his eyes. In the sparkle of his teeth in his grin.

Now was not the time to be afraid.

Now was the time to embrace the wolf in me, and mate forever with the three men Fate had sent my way.

I reached up for Elliot's neck and dragged him down into a kiss.

CHAPTER 27
BELLA

I closed my eyes, overwhelmed by the feel of Elliot on top of me. He was pressed against me and I could feel... everything.

His cock against my thigh, pressing into me. His hard body against my soft one.

God, it felt good.

Overwhelmingly so.

I'm not sure I'm ever going to be the same after this.

Instead of being scared, I threw myself into the eye of the storm. I shifted my hips so that Elliot would lie between my thighs, and pressed my bare pussy against him.

He groaned and rolled to the side. "Damn, woman. For a virgin, you're a damn siren."

I stared at him. "Is that bad?"

He barked out a laugh. "God, no. What's bad is I'm going to struggle to control myself when you're this hot."

I didn't know what to say, so I tugged at his arm. "Come back."

"Not yet." He lifted his hand and called to the others. "Join us."

Jonah and Tommy came over and Tommy knelt at the bottom of the bed, grabbing my hips to pull me toward him.

"You're all good if I...?" Tommy asked Elliot.

I glanced at my Alpha, who grinned. "Oh, yeah. Get her as wet as possible."

Tommy dove between my thighs and I screamed as his mouth covered my pussy. "Oh, God!"

Elliot turned my head toward him and captured my lips with his.

I groaned and opened to him, letting his tongue sweep into my mouth as Tommy did magical things to my clit.

Jonah's hands were on my breasts, tweaking my nipples and rolling the sensitive flesh with his fingers.

The pleasure went on and on as they loved me from every angle.

I gasped after what felt like hours, breaking off from Elliot's kiss. It was too much. I was aching, deep inside.

"Can you put your fingers inside? Please?" I asked Tommy, wanting some relief from the pressure.

Tommy pulled away and Elliot said, "Oh, no. That's not the way you're coming this time."

He rolled on top of me and spread my thighs wide.

I lifted my legs, wanting to feel him where I was aching.

I stared up at him.

He held his weight on his arms. "You ready?"

I nodded. "Yes. Please."

I pulled at his arms and he grabbed his cock and positioned it at my entrance.

I gasped, my whole world zeroing in on that one spot between my thighs. I felt the thick head nudge my lips and I opened my thighs wider, wanting him inside me.

I knew it would hurt, but damn, the waiting was hurting more.

"Please, hurry!" I arched my back, urging him closer.

He surged forward in one long thrust.

I cried out, turning my head away to groan as he filled me completely. There was pain, but there was much more. A rightness. A deep pleasure. A bliss that no-one ever told me would exist when my mate finally made me his.

Oh, my God.

Tears tingled the edges of my eyes.

"Did I hurt you?" Elliot whispered from above.

I wanted to answer him, but I couldn't speak. I tossed my head from side to side to say no. I couldn't say the words. My throat was too tight with emotion.

I dug my nails into his arms, then reached down to grab his ass, finally opening my eyes to see him hovering above me, worried.

I swallowed hard. "Please. More."

The worry disappeared and he pulled away, only to drive home harder, and faster. I cried out, this time from pure pleasure.

Oh, God. I was going to cum so quickly. I could already feel the tightening in my belly.

Elliot's massive body rolled over mine and I lifted my legs to wrap them around his waist as he rode me faster and faster.

It was such an amazing feeling to be filled by him, to ache so much for that deep penetration and feel his body inside mine.

"Oh.. I..." I started to peak, so I grabbed onto his huge arms and threw my head back, gripping him as he thrust deep one more time.

My orgasm released, pulsing pleasure through me.

I screamed as Elliot groaned above me, biting into the side of my neck as he spilled himself inside me.

Hot pulses of his seed filled me and I cried out with the beauty of it all.

I pulled him down, wanting to feel the weight of him on top of me. He panted with exertion.

He rolled us onto the side and kissed me, before withdrawing and slowly moving away, a smile on his face.

"Wow," I said, wiping the sweat from my brow.

Then I looked to the side, where Tommy was waiting.

"You up for taking me, too?" he asked.

I nodded and held out my arms.

He grinned. "Jump on top."

He reached over and took me by the waist, flipping me over and pulling me up so I straddled him, then I looked down on his smiling face.

"How do I do this?" I said, glancing back at his thighs behind me, and wriggling over the thick cock that lay beneath me.

He chuckled. "Slide back a bit."

I did and he grabbed his cock in his hand and held it vertical. "Now go up and slide down on it."

I frowned, but pushed back, tilting my pelvis and feeling for the edge of him. As I moved back, he thrust up.

"Oh." When I felt him inside me, I slid down, his cock filling me up and my newly sensitized tissues relaxing around him. "Wow."

This was different.

Tommy grinned and cupped my breasts, stroking his thumbs over my nipples, then taking hold of my hips and moving me up and down.

"Ride me, beautiful."

I smiled down at him, enjoying taking some of the control as I moved up and down, but the more I moved, the tighter his grip on me became.

I gasped, not sure this was working for me. "I think I need more."

He grinned. "Hold on."

He flipped me over and once again I was on my back, Tommy driving into me.

Now this was what I wanted. I lifted my legs, taking him deeper and grabbing onto his shoulders, pulling him closer. Our lips met and I stroked my tongue along the seam, thrusting into his mouth and loving it when he sucked on my tongue.

The tingles were beginning to grow again, then Tommy's motions began to change, becoming jerky.

I pulled him into me, grabbing onto his tight ass, moaning as he filled me with his seed, mixing with Elliot's and making me ache for so much more.

Tommy kissed my lips and rolled onto his side, taking his weight off me.

I panted, exhausted in the best possible way. But the tingles in my belly called to me for more. Just one more.

Tommy kissed my nipple as he lay beside me, stroking his hand possessively over my hip.

I sat up on the bed. Jonah stood nearby, looking sheepish. Well, as sheepish as one can with an erection in hand.

"I'm assuming you want to wait until you're healed to take me?" Jonah asked. "I don't want to hurt you."

I glanced at Jonah's cock. He was smaller than Tommy and Elliot, which was a relief more than anything. *Perfect.*

"I want you, too," I said.

He walked forward, bent over, and kissed me gently.

"How about you roll over and get on all fours?" he whispered against my lips.

"Um, all right," I said, though the idea of sticking my butt in the air seemed a bit weird to me.

I turned over onto my hands and knees.

Jonah put his hands on me, stroking over my back and my ass.

"Open your legs for me, beautiful." He stroked the insides of my thighs until I opened for him.

"Good girl. Perfect."

He pushed on the small of my back, so I dropped down, then felt the tip of his cock at the entrance to my body.

That's what he wants.

I dropped my face closer to the blankets on the bed and pushed back.

He slid into me gently and I gasped out my pleasure at feeling the pressure of his cock from this angle.

Definitely different.

And awesome.

I sighed as he began moving in and out of me, stroking the fire Tommy had begun.

I grabbed for the bedding, my hands filling with nothing but blankets.

"Tommy. Elliot. Can you both come here?" I gasped. "Hold my hands. Please."

They climbed onto the bed, each of them lying down beside me.

Tommy gripped my left hand and Elliot gripped my right.

Elliot kissed the back of my neck, while Tommy reached under and cupped my breast with his hand.

"Oh, God!" I cried out, pleasure washing over me as my second orgasm crashed into me. I quivered and squeezed Jonah's cock.

Jonah groaned and began to move faster, harder. Fucking me the way I needed him to.

"More," I cried out. "More! Please."

There was one final orgasm moments away. I was sliding down a slippery slope. My skin was dotted with sweat. My pussy ached as he fucked me over and over.

Elliot slipped his hand beneath my belly, finding my clit and flicking the aching bud over and over again.

I began to scream into the mattress as the pleasure built and built, higher and higher.

"I'm gonna blow." Jonah gasped. "I can't hold on anymore."

I didn't want him to, but I couldn't say the words.

Jonah thrust his cock into me one more time, pushing me to the very precipice of the orgasmic cliff. There I hung. Time stood still.

Then Jonah began to cum, his orgasm pushing me through my own and I convulsed, safe in the arms of the three men I loved.

When Jonah finally pulled away, I was cocooned and dragged up to the pillows. I closed my eyes and grabbed for my men, wanting to feel all of them.

Tommy pressed a kiss to my forehead and I opened my eyes. "I love you," I managed to say, then twisted around. "I love all of you."

Elliot tugged my face to his for another kiss and I let my thoughts float away. I would never regret choosing my three mates.

The men Fate, and my Halloween magic, had sent to me.

WOLF MAGIC

PROLOGUE

TIFFANY

I'd been counting down the days to this night ever since we found Sherie's spell book all those years ago. Day one thousand and ninety-five had finally arrived! My twenty-first birthday and the night I'd looked forward to for *so* long.

Tonight, on Halloween, my friends and I would cast a spell that would save us from the devastation and loneliness which had followed our mothers around like a curse their whole lives.

"So, are we going to do this, or not?" Ruby asked, then stared at Bella and me individually. "Because there's no going back after this."

Her grin made me clap my hands together with glee and a ferocious sense of determination filled me. *I never want to go back after this. I want my soul mate more than anything!*

Growing up fatherless, the only children to three heartbroken witches, had been hard on us all. So, years ago, when Ruby found an ancient spell book her mother had buried under the stairs—carefully hidden beneath blankets and tucked away within a huge chest filled with clothes and other books—we'd read it.

Of course, we had. What teenage girls wouldn't have? Ruby had led the charge, and I'd been right behind her. I needed to know why a book had been so well hidden. Inside its pages we'd found an incantation that seemed to imply a guarantee that we could avoid the heartbreak of our mothers before us. I'd been the first one of us to voice my intention. "Hell yes! This is for us!" I said.

I hadn't wanted to wait. At eighteen, I was already working, had endured one terrible fail of a romantic night, and was ready for the man of my dreams to love me so that we could build a beautiful future together.

But Bella being typical bookworm Bella had done some research and realized that the spell was complicated and required a serious amount of power to successfully pull off, which was why all three of us would need to do it. *Together.* We decided that when we were old enough, and powerful enough, we'd make it happen come hell or high water.

The wind moved through the trees around us, rustling the leaves. A fall storm was coming. I shivered at the feeling of perfect premonition as it slid over me. This was it! *We are finally here!* About to do what we'd planned and talked about for so long.

The little house in the woods that Bella's family owned was the perfect location for secret nights and escapades like this one. No one would be able to see us, and as long as we all kept our mouths shut, nobody would know that on this Halloween night, our joint twenty-first birthday, we conducted a spell to call our true loves to us.

I nodded at Ruby fiercely. It was time to start the spell—it was now or never.

Fear flashed in Bella's eyes.

Ruby sighed. "Come on, Bella. You know we can't do this without you."

And she meant that quite literally, unfortunately. Bella was by far the strongest of us and the best at spell craft. She spent an inordinate amount of her time with her nose buried in books, which was probably why.

Damn it, Bella. Don't give up on us now.

Ruby pouted, narrowing her gaze on our friend. "Come on, Bella. *Please.*"

I bit my lower lip and tried not to worry. We'd been talking about this spell for years, planning every part of this night. And now that it was here, I couldn't bear to see our one chance to slip away. I opened my mouth to beg her not to chicken out, but she spoke first, and I breathed a sigh of relief.

"Okay, Ruby. I'm in. Let's do this."

I reached for Ruby's and Bella's free hands, forming a triangle of magic and perfect strength. These girls were my family, my best friends, and the closest I'd ever get to having real sisters.

I gripped their hands tighter and stared down at the ancient book that lay on the ground between us, the spell book Ruby had found all those years ago. Excitement skittered through me, but I pushed it down. It was time to focus on getting the spell right, not get overly excited about the outcome. *Horse before the cart!* I reminded myself. If we did this properly, we could enjoy all the excitement in the world—later.

Together, we began to chant in an ancient language that no-one used anymore, a magical dialect which had been long lost to time and memory.

I concentrated hard on my lines, reading from the book. Each verse of the spell called to the magic that rippled in our veins—to Fate—and most of all, to the unconditional love that we all so desperately desired and craved.

The spell began to hurt in a way I hadn't initially expected, and I frowned at the pain, focusing on the magic we were creating, and not the headache which pounded in my temples.

My legs began to shake. *No!* I locked my knees with grim determination, not willing to give in when we were so close. Maybe Bella was right, and this spell really was too big for us to handle... I clenched my hands into fists, willing myself to greater strength. The pain started to alleviate. I smiled with satisfaction and forged forward, reading faster, loving the swirl of magic which floated around us, bonding us together more tightly than we were before.

After tonight, we'd never end up like our mothers—abandoned and alone. And for that certainty I would pay any price.

The ancient book floated in the space between us, glowing and powerful. I watched the phenomenon with a growing sense of dread but grinned in spite of it. *We're doing it. This is actually freaking happening!*

Buoyed on, we began to chant louder, the words in our hearts building naturally as the spell came to a great crescendo. White light shone between our clenched fingers and power surged through us. I gripped Ruby's and Bella's hands harder. We were almost there.

We recited the final words of the spell and the white magic we'd conjured shot into the air above our heads with a cosmic *boom*, exploding in a spectacular eruption of color, like fireworks, sparkling against the dark night sky.

We were blown backward and apart by the power of the spell, our joined hands separating as we sailed through the air.

I landed hard on my ass on the dewy grass—the magic gone in an instant as it quickly dissipated. I shook my head, pushing my hands into the ground to hold myself up. *Whoa. That was so much more intense than I expected.*

"Is that it?" Ruby asked from about ten feet away.

The spell book that had been hovering in the air between us, landed in the dirt with a heavy thump, the cover closing of its own accord.

I jumped up, brushing the dirt from my pants as happiness flowed through me. We'd done it! Now, we just had to wait for our soul mates to find us. When they did, I'd have a husband. *And kids!* And a home filled with laughter and fun. I'd have everything I never did growing up. Tears gathered in my eyes, and I blinked them back. I couldn't believe it. We'd really finished the spell. My life-long wish was about to come true.

Ruby rose from her spot on the ground.

Bella got to her feet, too.

I closed my eyes and tilted back my head, breathing in the cool night air as the stars shimmered above. This was the start of the rest of my life. Now, I just had to exercise a little bit of patience, which was definitely going to be the hard part. I wanted my soul mate, now!

"So... back to the house for a celebratory drink?" Ruby asked, dusting off her hands.

Absolutely! "Sounds like a plan," I said, flicking my long blonde hair over my shoulder.

We turned and trekked back to the house. Once inside, we turned on the lights and Ruby used her magic to mix us up some cocktails the colors of the sunset—red, orange, and yellow, with a splash of dusky purple.

"Perfect," Ruby said as she picked up her glass that had been resting on the counter.

Bella and I plucked up our drinks as well and clinked them with Ruby's.

"Happy birthday, ladies," we chorused together, grinning as a group.

The best part of my birthday was getting to spend it with these two girls.

We all took a sip of our first legal drink and grimaced at the sheer amount of liquor Ruby had poured into our mix.

I gasped, my nose burning.

"Wow, that's strong," I said, blinking rapidly to clear my eyes, before I took another sip just for good measure.

Bella inhaled sharply and coughed, then waved her hand over the table in front of us, conjuring up a veritable feast of savory and sweet snacks. Chips, chocolate cake, cookies, and crackers with cheese littered the surface in front of us.

"Oh, perfect. Thanks, Belle!" Ruby said, grabbing a handful of chips and stuffing them in her mouth.

I took another sip of my drink. The alcohol warmed my belly and filled me with a nice, relaxed feeling.

"What's up, Bell-Bell?" Ruby asked.

I glanced between them. Was something wrong? What had I missed?

"Do you think it worked?" Bella asked quietly.

Ruby shrugged. "I don't know. I hope so. I mean, I guess we'll find out."

"I hope so too!" I said, my tone exasperated. "We've only been planning this since forever."

The other two sat down with me, around our tasty birthday spread on stools Ruby had conjured out of thin air. We chatted and ate, drank and laughed, celebrating the fact we had our whole lives ahead of us.

"What do you think your guy will look like?" I asked, directing my question to Ruby, being that Bella was sitting there looking like she was about to fall asleep.

Ruby laughed. "I really don't care, as long as he's nice."

"Nice? *Pah!*" I said, rolling my eyes. "I want my guy to be *hot*. With blue eyes, and massive muscles. A ripped six-pack..."

We talked all night and finally fell asleep sometime before dawn. I was the last to pass out because I was the most excited by far.

Ruby was still a little lost with what she wanted out of life.

Meanwhile, Bella was at college and had her sights set on a career. I'd already been working full time for three years and was *so* done with being single it wasn't funny. I wanted my man. I wanted a baby.

For me, the time until I found my soul mate couldn't pass quickly enough. Surely because of that, I'd be the first one to find my man...

CHAPTER 1

TIFFANY

I stepped into Ruby's new backyard and stroked my dad's fluffy head, running my fingers through the gray fur with a sigh. I was impressed with the health of his thickening pelt. He was healing so well since coming home and living at Jackson's house, no longer exiled to the wild and fending for himself.

"I brought you guys some chicken and vegetables," I announced as I walked over to the porch and laid out the supplies from my basket I'd brought. Mom had sent me with Tupperware tubs full of delicious, warm food. Something our fathers had no doubt missed—being condemned to their wolf forms—since our mothers fell pregnant with us.

I laid out three porcelain plates and served their food before stepping back to stare at their lunch. I hated the fact that our fathers had to be fed like, well, dogs. But until we found a way to break the spell, there was nothing for it but to deal.

I sat down on the porch step.

Two of the wolves stepped forward and began to eat their meals.

But my father stared at me, seeming almost embarrassed.

I didn't really know how he felt, but I could guess. I don't think he liked me watching him eat like a common mutt. "Can I feed you, Dad?" I offered.

The gray wolf shifter that was my father, a man I'd never actually met in the flesh, crouched down in front of me.

I picked up the plate I'd set out for him, took a piece of cooked chicken breast and held it out to him.

He took the meat carefully from my fingers and gulped it down.

The other two wolves were practically inhaling their lunch.

Poor things. So, I kept feeding my father, holding piece after piece out to him until the need to speak into the silence overwhelmed me. "You're going to think I'm so vain for saying this, but I literally have no-one else to talk to," I said. It was a strange admission for me. Once upon a time I'd considered myself the luckiest girl alive, to have two best friends who were closer to me than sisters. I'd always been able to tell them anything. But things were different now, and in that moment, I'd never felt so alone.

My dad tilted his large wolf head in a way that I took to mean, 'go for it'.

I smiled and went on. "I'm so... angry, Dad. Like... *all* the time. I don't know what to do about all these stupid feelings rolling around inside me. It feels like a storm! I shouldn't be mad, but I'm just so... lonely. And surprised to be honest. I thought I would be the first one to find my soul mate, and I still haven't found mine even though the other two have."

My dad tilted his head the other way.

I groaned. "Yeah, I know. I sound like a spoiled brat. But I don't mean to. It's just that…" I sighed. This was going to sound terrible, but I was going to say it anyway. "Everyone's always told me I'm the prettiest, the sexiest, of the three of us. You know? I'm certainly not the smartest or the kindest. But I thought that if anyone was going to find their man, or in this case, her men early, it would be me. I've been ready and waiting since my sweet sixteenth!"

That night I'd been set on losing my virginity, but the warlock I clumsily tried to seduce hadn't been 'up' to the task. For the one everyone called 'the blonde one', like I was some cheap Barbie doll, I certainly wasn't having much luck finding someone who'd have sex with me. Not that I was going to share *that* with my dad.

I was down to the mix of vegetables and the small remnants of chicken. "Here you go." I placed the plate down in front of him.

He ate the remaining food.

Then all three wolf shifters gathered near me, staring at me as though waiting for me to speak.

I sighed. "I know it sounds like I think I'm the prettiest or something, but I don't! Ruby's just beautiful. And Bella? She doesn't know it, but she's striking, no matter what she wears. It's just that… I guess I just thought someone would want me. At least as a wife. But I can't even find one mate." I took a deep breath and sighed. "Humans are scared of being with us and the warlocks have never liked us. I used to wonder why, but now that I know I'm half wolf shifter, I know why they don't find us attractive."

Humans and warlocks had one thing in common—a natural fear of wolf shifters, unless they were our mates.

"But I…" I knew I sounded like an impatient little bitch, so I stopped talking, frustrated even more now than when I'd begun. I needed to just get over myself, but I was sick of feeling like I wasn't special! I was, wasn't I? *To someone?* I stared at my father, a man who'd shifted into a wolf twenty-three years ago and had never been able to shift back.

We believed it was because of a curse the High Warlock had conjured before we were born, but we weren't totally sure about all the details. We only had our suspicions and what Tabitha had told us, but that bitch would say anything to hurt us. She would have lied about everything if it had suited her. But we would find out the truth. *Somehow.*

It saddened me to no end that my father had lost the chance to see me grow up. They'd all lost the chance to be married and have more children, or at least get to know the one daughter each of them had. And I was complaining because I was twenty-two, and still single? *At least I can eat with my hands!* I sobbed into those very hands. "I'm sorry. I'm being so childish and bitchy."

My dad put his head on my knee and growled a little.

I laughed at his expression, though there were tears in my eyes. "Who did this to you? To us?" I asked rhetorically. "I spent my whole life without a father... and I could have really used one."

Not that I was complaining about my mom. She was great. But there were times when a girl wanted a dad, though. A man to talk to. A male to give her a hug when things were rough. And for me... *now* was one of those times.

My dad moved so that he could lie on his side, then sighed heavily.

I chuckled to myself. He had such a great way of communicating, even without words.

"Hey, Tiff! I didn't realize you were here," Ruby called out from behind me, walking out the back door of her huge house.

I glanced up as she stood beside me. "Yeah. Sorry. I thought I'd deliver the food, then come in, but I got stuck talking."

Ruby grinned, her hand straying absently to her still-flat belly. "I come out here and talk to my dad all the time. We've told them to come and sleep in the lounge, but they don't seem to want to come inside, so yeah... Trying to make up for lost time, right?"

I shrugged and gestured to her belly. "How are you feeling?"

She smiled. "Just hit eight weeks and feeling violently ill most days." She laughed weakly, but I saw the truth on her face. She was pale and looked like she'd lost weight. "But I've been told it's a good sign. It means it's a strong pregnancy."

I forced myself to my feet. "Well, that's great to hear, Ruby."

My best friend was mated to three men and pregnant, and I still didn't have a boyfriend. Color me green with envy.

Ruby tilted her head at me. "What's up with you? You seem a little off."

I shook my head. "Oh, nothing." I indicated to the inside of the house. "You all ready for Christmas? Need any help with decorating or anything?"

Ruby's magic still hadn't returned, or if it had, she wasn't using it. We didn't know if it was due to the pregnancy—and her witch abilities would return after the baby was born—or if her magic was gone forever after what she'd endured last Halloween night. The night she'd fought on her own to remove the love spell we'd cast to find our soul mates in the first place.

"Come see," she said.

I waved goodbye to my dad as we walked up the stairs and into the huge house and stepped into the open plan living area. "Wow. You've gone all out," I breathed in awe. The once all-white house was now splattered with festive color. "What a tree!" I stared at the six-foot pine tree in the corner of the lounge room, lavished in gleaming gold and glittering silver baubles.

Ruby inhaled deeply. "Doesn't it smell great?"

I couldn't smell much, but assumed her heightened senses was a pregnancy thing. "Did the guys help you decorate?" I asked, glancing around at the tinsel lining the doorways, the twinkling lights, and strung-up mistletoe.

"Yeah, the old-fashioned way—with ladders, and sticky tape, and lots of cursing when everything fell down again!" She giggled. "I'm sure Mom will come by later and magic things up a bit."

Ruby's smile was infectious, and I grinned. "Most definitely." I sat down on one of the bar stools next to her large kitchen bench and sighed, my tummy growling loudly.

"Was that your stomach?" Ruby asked, pulling open the fridge door. "You want something to eat? Or drink?"

I nodded. "A drink would be great. Thanks."

Ruby poured me a soda.

I took a sip, the cold bubbles quenching some of my thirst, but not really doing much to bolster my mood.

Ruby grabbed a candy from a bowl nearby, before shoving it toward me, and popping one in her mouth. "These help with the nausea, so I need to suck them constantly."

I shrugged. "Go for it. Whatever makes you feel better." I traced an invisible pattern on the marble countertop, then stood up. "I probably should get going."

"Why? Are you working tonight?"

I was a hairdresser and had been working my ass off in the lead up to Christmas. "No, I've got the night off, thankfully. I've been doing overtime every day though, and I might need to work tomorrow." Tomorrow being Saturday, but since I'd worked all week, they'd given me Friday off. Christmas was on Monday, so at least I had a few days off after tomorrow.

"So, why are you rushing off then?"

I shrugged again, settling back down onto the stool. "You know. Just... Christmas stuff."

Ruby stared at me, her gaze searching. "What's going on with you, Tiff?"

"Nothing. What do you mean?"

Ruby rolled her eyes theatrically. "What do you mean, what do I mean? You're sad! It's so stinking obvious. Why won't you just talk openly about it? Bell and I are here for you, you know that right?"

I frowned and glared down at my hand, where my fingers still traced patterns on the marble countertop. I didn't want to admit to Ruby that she was right: I *was* sad—and lonely. I swallowed, not sure how to start that sentence.

I expected Ruby to take over the conversation like she normally did, being the life of our trio, and demand that I reveal all.

But she was pressing her hands into the counter and breathing hard like she was suddenly in pain.

I jumped to my feet, instantly alarmed. "Hey, Ruby. Are you okay?"

She was getting paler by the minute. She shook her head and stumbled sideways. "I... no..." Her eyes rolled back in her head, and she began to faint dead away to the floor.

"Ruby!" I wasn't close enough to catch her, but I threw out a spell on instinct and froze her, just inches before she hit the ground. I raced around the island and knelt, putting my arms beneath her before releasing the spell, so she fell into my waiting arms.

She was heavier than I anticipated, so I called on my magic and used a carrying spell to carefully transport her into the large bedroom on the ground floor. I pulled back the covers and used my magic to slide her into the bed, resting her head on the pillow. I dragged the covers over her and touched a hand to her cheek, then to my own face for comparison.

She was too cool, though I didn't know if that was a problem or not. Or was it only when you were too warm? I pressed my hands into my temples, a headache pounding inside my brain. "What do I do? What do I do?"

I didn't want to leave Ruby, but just sitting here and waiting for one of her mates to get home wasn't an option either. So, I pulled out my phone and checked the time. The guys wouldn't be home for hours and Bella was at college.

I stared at my cell screen and realized there was only one person I was comfortable calling. I hit the name on my favorites list and the phone began to ring. "Please pick up, please pick up," I chanted. She was at work, and I wasn't sure if she'd hear the ringtone or not. When her voice finally came through, I almost cried.

"Tiffany. What's happened?"

"Mom. You need to help me. Something's wrong with Ruby!"

CHAPTER 2
TIFFANY

Within moments of hanging up the phone, Mom used a transportation spell to get to me. After seeing the state of Ruby and deducing it came from a magical source, we didn't call the hospital. Instead, she called all the moms, and Bella. Within an hour, we had both generations together.

"Do you know what's wrong with her?" I asked Sherie, Ruby's mom, who was waving her hands over her daughter, analyzing the problem, white sparkling magic coursing over Ruby's body.

My mom stepped up next to me and squeezed my hand. "We don't know, honey. Sherie's doing a spell to stabilize Ruby, but from what we can tell the pregnancy is, um, more or less draining the life out of her."

I spun around and stared at her, aghast. "Are you telling me the baby's actually killing her?" That couldn't be true. Surely all pregnant moms felt like their life was being drained by their baby? Wasn't it said that the first trimester was always the worst?

Sherie dropped her hands and sighed, turning toward me with tears in her eyes. "Ruby's carrying a daughter, but the curse on the pack still means that no daughters are allowed to be born from this generation. Ruby's strong. She's managed so far, but I'm not sure how much longer the baby—or she—will last." Sherie bit her lip and stared at my mom, tears glistening in her scared eyes. "Do you think I should... if it would save her..."

I glanced between the two moms, trying to work out what they were referring to. When neither one spoke, and simply continued to stare at each other in long, knowing looks, I threw my hands up and said, "What are you talking about?"

Bella walked forward, a tear stain on one cheek. "They might be able to save Ruby—if they terminate the pregnancy."

"No!" I raced over to stand by Ruby who lay in the bed, helpless. She couldn't speak for herself, so I'd have to do it for her. I'd be her advocate. I knew in my heart she'd never want to end her baby's life. *Never!*

Not that I would physically be able to stop our moms if they really wanted to do it. They were much stronger than me. And ultimately, I was only half-witch, and had never really cared that much about perfecting my craft. I was a half-assed witch at the best of times. In this moment I regretted not focusing more on improving my magical skills.

But I could see how much pain was on both their faces and used that knowledge to my advantage. "You can't do it. You can't kill Ruby's baby!" I repeated. "She will never forgive you if you do."

The front door opened, and men's voices rang out throughout the house. "Ruby! You home, honey?"

"How are you feeling?" called another male voice. "Any better?"

Bella stared at the bedroom door, a look of worry on her face.

I clung to Ruby's headboard and called out, "We're in here!"

Two of Ruby's men stepped into the room, passing through one at a time.

Jackson had to turn his shoulders slightly to the side as he passed through since he was so damn big.

Darren didn't have a hope of sliding past him.

"What's going on?" Jackson asked, lingering near the doorway.

Darren hurried straight over to the bed, comfortable enough to come into the room with a full coven of witches hovering around his mate. But Darren was part-warlock, so he was always more comfortable around us than the other full-blooded wolves. Magic was a part of who he was, whether he could use it or not. "Is she okay?" Darren asked, reaching out for one of Ruby's hands and touching her fingers. "Shit, she's deathly cold."

Bella's mom, Kathy, stepped up. "We're pretty sure the pregnancy's killing her. So, we need to decide if we roll the dice and wait and see what's going to happen… or…" She let the unspoken words hang in the air.

Jackson took a step in the room. "Or, what?" he said, his voice rough with emotion. "We can't lose Ruby. I don't care what you have to do."

"We need to abort the pregnancy," Kathy said.

Darren gasped in shock and despair.

Jackson's face flashed with sharp pain, before he clenched his jaw and nodded once. "Do it."

I gasped at him. *No!* "Jackson, you don't mean that!" I turned to Darren.

He'd climbed onto the bed and was now lying down next to his mate, brushing her long red hair away from her face.

"Darren!"

He stared at me, his eyes shimmering with unshed tears. "We can't lose Ruby, Tiff. We can't. The three of us would die."

I wasn't sure if he meant it literally, but from the heavy feeling in the room, and the hardness in Jackson's face, they might. I stomped my foot, unwilling to give up. "No! Ruby will kill us if we do it! And that's assuming she even survives the process." I glared at the moms. "Can you guarantee that you can save her if you kill her baby?"

Mom glanced at Sherie. "We... can't. We don't know how tightly entwined Ruby and her daughter are with the spell. If we sever the connection, we could kill them both."

Jackson groaned and turned away, grabbing a hold of the door frame and squeezing so hard the wood cracked beneath his fingers.

I turned to Bella in desperation. Surely, she'd be on my side. "Come on, Bell! There has to be another way."

Bella chewed her lip before replying. "Well, I suppose we could do some sort of temporary stasis spell. We might be able to hold her like this for a few days. Maybe more. But any longer and you'll endanger the fetus anyway. It needs time to grow and change and keeping them like that too long will kill the baby."

"Why would you do that, then?" Darren asked from the bed.

"It would give us time to figure out what's going on," Bella said. "Maybe even find a way to break the curse once and for all."

"But you've been working on it for a month, and haven't gotten anywhere yet," Darren said, his tone thick with despair.

I wanted to shake him, shake them all. There was no way Ruby would give up this easily. If she wasn't in a coma right now, she'd slap them all silly! I glared at him. "It's the best hope we have, unless you can think of anything else that might save her?" I glanced from Darren to my mom, to Sherie, and then to Jackson.

They all shook their heads, or stared at the floor, unable or unwilling to look at me.

I took a deep breath, knowing that I was right in my determination to try and save them both. I knew that the fetus was young, and technically Ruby and her mates could try again for another baby if they saved Ruby. But she would never forgive us, or her mates, for killing her daughter. I knew my friend, and that was a certainty.

I closed my eyes and inside my mind I saw Ruby, cradling her infant daughter in her arms. She was a beautiful cherub with blonde hair and blue eyes, and my friend loved her more than anything in the world. I wasn't taking that away from her.

As I opened my eyes, tears spilled down my face as my heart ached with pain, realizing how far away from that vision we were. I brushed away the tears with haste. "We're saving them both. I don't care what we have to do. This curse was built from a place of ignorance and hatred. Surely the love you two have for your mates, and our moms have for our dads, is enough to break it!"

"It hasn't been enough so far," Bella said. "Unless the spell needs you to find your mates, too?" She smiled gently at me.

The soft joke made me sigh. "It might, but I think I've met every wolf in town now. *Twice.* My mates don't live here. Or they're not from this pack."

The room went deathly quiet, then the front door opened and closed again. "Hey, Ruby!"

Billy walked into the room wearing a leather jacket and I couldn't help the admiration that flowed through me. Of all Ruby's mates, Billy was my favorite: quiet, strong, sexy. The classic bad boy. His expression fell. "What happened?"

We filled him in, and by the time we'd finished, he was sitting on the blanket box, with his head in his hands, looking just as miserable as I felt.

"You have to save her," he said quietly, and when he looked up, his eyes flashed yellow with his wolf.

"Hey. Calm down. It's okay," Jackson said, squeezing Billy's shoulder.

Billy jumped up. "It's not okay. How are we meant to...?"

He stopped, swallowing audibly as he struggled to contain his emotions.

Bella, who in the past would have run from such a strong, emotional male, stepped closer. I watched her in admiration. Having two Alpha mates had really changed her.

"Billy. We're going to try and save both of them, but I've got a hunch that the only way we're going to break this spell is when all three of us have found our mates. Can you think of anyone that Tiffany hasn't met that she should? Or maybe she needs to meet some guys from other packs?"

"You really think us three finding our wolf shifter mates will break the curse?" I repeated. *Was Bella serious?* I crossed my arms over my chest, not liking the way they were talking about me. Like I was a problem or something. Or my singledom was part of the curse. Though if someone would point me in the right direction of my mates, I'd be grateful.

Bella nodded. "I think it's definitely a part of it. Think about what happened when I found my mates. Tabitha and David tried to kill us! The closer we get to finding love and happiness, the closer we get to destroying that spell."

I wasn't so sure about that. Tabitha had said the spell was grounded in us, but could love really break a spell that in the past we had assumed only our deaths could?

"You know I've tried everything, Bella," I grumbled. It wasn't like I hadn't tried to find my mates.

Billy jumped to his feet. "Hang on a second! I didn't even think..."

He turned to look at Jackson.

"What are you talking about?" Jackson asked.

"I was coming back to tell you I just saw Jase, Ollie, and Fin. They're home for Christmas!"

I frowned. I didn't recognize any of those names. "Who are they?"

"Do you think it's possible?" Jackson asked Billy, ignoring my question.

"Why not?" Billy said. "They're three wolf shifters. All Betas."

"They're all gray, too," Darren said from the bed.

I turned toward him. "What do you mean?" I was shaking now, and I wasn't sure why. I wasn't afraid, or cold. "What's that got to do with anything?"

"You're right!" Billy said, moving closer to the bed, excitement catching in his voice. He turned to me. "Do you remember at Thanksgiving? We were talking about the fact that all of Ruby's mates are white wolves..."

"Yeah, and all of Bella's are black." I shrugged. "And I joked that mine would be all brown..."

"Or gray!" Billy said, casting a worried look at Ruby.

I frowned. "Yeah, but you said that there weren't any gray wolves in your generation." Or he'd said they were unusual, or something like that.

Darren sat up. "They're super-rare. There are only three gray wolves in our whole pack our age, and they're three best friends, all Betas."

My heart pounded faster, a premonition-type wave flowing over me, making me shiver. "Then why haven't I met them?"

Darren glanced at Billy, who said, "Because last year they left the pack. They got frustrated at being single, and said they were going to go look for their mates, and they took off. They've been all over the country, I heard."

I bit my lip. *What if they've brought home a woman, or three?* "Do you really think they could be my mates?"

Jackson laughed. "Only one way to tell! Let's go introduce you."

I glanced at my mom, who nodded. "Go. We'll get to work on the stasis spell. See if we can hold Ruby and her baby long enough that we can break the curse that binds you all."

Bella hurried over to me. "I'll come with you. The moms can look after Ruby."

I grabbed Bella's hand. "Thanks." I needed the support, now more than ever.

The guys all stopped by the bed to kiss Ruby and whisper to her.

I tried not to listen out of respect for their privacy.

Once they were done, they charged out the door and Bella and I followed— hopefully to fulfil a date with destiny!

CHAPTER 3
OLIVER

I leaned back in the café booth, stretched my arms above my head and yawned. "Fuck, I'm tired. When are we going back to bed?" We'd been running all night for three days straight to get home in time for Christmas, and we'd made it with just a few days to spare. But I was fucking exhausted.

"You can go now if you want," Jase said, rolling his eyes at me. "But I'm getting some proper food in me first."

We'd stopped by our parents' places long enough to grab some clothes and say 'hi' to a few people, but we were all in desperate need of a relaxing warm shower and a hot meal.

Jase grabbed his knife and fork and held them as he waited for our food to arrive.

I groaned and went back to rolling my neck and shoulders, trying in vain to stretch out the muscles that were knotted as shit. "God, I'm sore. Being in shifter mode for too long messes with my back."

"Oh, my God," Fin said, glaring at me. "Would you stop your whining? We're home. We're starving. And Toni will be over with your burger soon. So just shut up. What more do you want?"

"Yeah, home and single. Still," I said, snorting in annoyance. I stared down at the table, going over the menu once again. Nothing had changed in the year we'd been gone. Nothing at all. "When are we leaving again?"

Fin stared at me like I'd grown a second head. "You want to leave again, already?"

I nodded. "Why not? Nothing's changed around here. We're still single and the pack still can't have daughters. I'm not going to sit around here and just wait for insanity." The loneliness of not having a mate got to me more than anything. Sometimes I thought I'd go crazy from a lack of touch—just some basic flesh to flesh affection.

Toni arrived with our food, cutting off my complaints.

"Looks great, thanks Toni," Jase said, grinning up at the girl we'd grown up with, but who'd ended up mating with one of the guys ten years older than us.

"Enjoy," she said with a grin. "It's good to have you guys back."

I didn't say anything, but grabbed my burger with both hands, watching the yellow egg yolk ooze over the greasy bacon and drip onto the fries beneath, absorbing the fatty goodness. I took a big bite, the juiciness of the meat patty, the cheese, and the freshness of the salad making me moan in bliss. *God*, we hadn't had enough good meals lately.

Jase laughed at me while he cut up his steak. "Hungry then?"

"Mmm... hm." I nodded and kept eating, sating a hunger I hadn't realized I'd been ignoring. Another problem with being in wolf form too long: None of us liked to hunt down animals and eat them raw the way normal wild wolves did. But if we didn't eat, by the time we were back in human form, we were absolutely ravenous. Shifting took a toll on our energy.

I ate my huge burger and all the fries, then stared at the pies on the counter. "I think I might go check out dessert."

"Go for it," Fin said, sitting back and rubbing his belly after downing his own burger. "Whatever you order, get me one too!"

I nodded with a grin and headed off to the front counter, inhaling deeply as the sweet smell of cherry pie filled my nostrils. *Mmm. Hell yes.* I grinned at Toni. "Can you bring over three slices of cherry pie with extra cream, please?"

Toni picked up her pad and pen and scrawled a note on it. "Sorry, Ollie. We have peach pie today. That okay?"

I sniffed again, my brow furrowing. "I'm sure I can smell cherries..." I drifted off as the scent grew stronger and stronger.

The bell above the door to the café rang.

I turned around to see who was walking in at the weird time between lunch and dinner and froze.

The three wolf shifters I knew well enough. I'd grown up with Jackson and Billy, and everyone knew the weird warlock-wolf Darren. But what had my heart beating in my throat was the sight of the woman standing with them. Not the brunette, though she was cute. It was the blonde.

Wow. I opened my mouth to call out to them but found myself growling low in my throat instead. *What the hell?* I put my hand up to signal to them.

Then Billy grabbed the blonde by the arm to get her attention and pointed at me.

I saw red. What the hell was he doing touching her? I charged for Billy, dancing around the tables and pushing chairs out of my way. They clattered to the floor in my wake. I heard someone yell out, but I didn't care. Billy had to take his hands off her. *Now.* Nothing was going to stop me getting hold of the guy touching my—

"Whoa, slow down, Ollie." Jackson surged forward, blocking my path. He grabbed me by both arms and pressed hard, stopping me in my tracks.

I growled at him.

He barked back. "Get a hold of yourself."

Jackson was an Alpha while Billy and I were both Betas. And though we didn't give much kudos to the original hierarchy of the pack, my genetics demanded that I listen to Jackson.

I shook myself and growled again, unable to speak though I wanted to. My teeth had shifted, and the sharp points of my fangs cut into my bottom lip. "I..."

"I know. You're struggling to control your wolf. You can't speak. And you want to kill Billy for touching Tiffany. I know. I can see it written all over your face."

I stared up at him. *How the hell does he know that?*

"Billy, just step away from Tiff for a bit, okay?" Jackson called over his shoulder, not taking his hands off my arms.

Billy took a decent sideways step.

My wolf calmed down instantly. My teeth retracted into my gums, and I could finally speak again. "Thanks."

"I'm not sure this was a good idea," Darren said, sidling up to the blonde that was making my wolf go berserk.

I growled at him.

Behind me, Fin and Jase hurried to join us.

"What's wrong? What's going on? What—" Fin's words were cut off as he too growled.

I glared at him. *What the fuck is wrong with us?*

"We better get outside. Quick," Darren said, tugging on the blonde and the brunette.

The girls followed him out the door without complaint.

I glanced back at my two best friends.

Their eyes were wild, and they looked as out of control as I was feeling. *There better be a good explanation for this.*

Jackson shook me a little. "Oliver. Look at me. Focus."

I stared up at him and clenched my jaw. He was an Alpha. I would listen to him and do as he said.

"You need to hold yourself together for two more minutes. Then you can shift and run until your heart's content, okay? I'll come with you. But do *not* let go of your wolf yet. Got it?"

I nodded as I gritted my teeth.

He glanced over at Fin and Jase. "You two as well. Agreed?"

They grunted their assent, and we stormed out into the open air together.

I inhaled deeply, finding it somehow easier to control the racing of my heart while we were outside, and I could no longer smell just how sweet the blonde was in the open air. Thankfully, I was standing upwind of her, and that gave me enough of a reprieve that I could get a handle on my wolf. "What's this?" I managed to get out between my teeth.

Jackson stood between us three guys and the two girls who were huddled together, staring at us.

Damn, she was beautiful. Long blonde hair, full lips, gorgeous blue eyes...

What I didn't like was the fact that Billy and Darren stood on either side of the girls as though they needed protecting. I could tell they were ready for a fight if it came down to it, and I found myself weighing up the pros and cons of taking them on.

Jackson was an Alpha, and we'd struggle to take him down, but the other two would be easier between the three of us.

A moment later two huge Alphas wandered up to the group. They grabbed the brunette up in their arms and both kissed her.

I glanced over at Fin and Jase. The tide had just turned. We wouldn't win this fight, no matter what we did now. Especially if we had to go up against that one... His name was Elliot. He was bigger than any Alpha I'd ever seen, and there were stories about his temper. They called him an Alpha's *Alpha.*

But as I watched him with the woman who had to be his mate, his care and affection showed a side to him I'd never expected to see. A softer side.

I took a step back, relaxing my stance. *Who are these girls?*

Jackson grinned at us. "Okay, you know what? I'm going to give you the crash course in everything you need to know. We've learned from experience what lies and secrets can do so I'm going give you the easy road. A path I wish I'd been able to take."

"Hurry," Fin said, trembling behind me. He was losing control of his wolf.

I reached out and pulled him back with me a bit. "It's easier if you're further away."

Fin didn't really like being in wolf form when he didn't have to be, so he would find this test harder than most.

Jackson nodded. "Okay. Well, basically, our mates are witches. They have three wolf mates each. Mine, Billy's, and Darren's mate isn't here. She's sick at home. Bella is mated to Elliot, Jonah, and Tommy. And Tiffany over there?" he said, gesturing to the gorgeous blonde. "Is yours."

My mouth dropped open. "No fucking way." I wasn't sharing my mate with anyone else! And there's no way Fate would send me a witch mate. That's not how things worked around here.

Jackson laughed. "*Yes,* way. Get over the fact they're witches, because they're half wolf shifter as well. They're the daughters of the Manterri cousins who went missing over twenty years ago."

"Seriously?" Jase asked.

"Tell them about the love spell," the blonde—Tiffany—called out.

I groaned at the effect her voice had on my inner wolf. I growled as my teeth began to shift once more. *Damn, she is sweet, and sexy, and hot.* More than anything I wanted to grab her, pull her beneath me, and sink my cock into her... I shook my head. *Focus!*

Jackson nodded. "The three girls cast a love spell on Halloween last year, calling for their soul mates. They didn't realize it would bring three wolf shifters for each of them."

Darren moved closer to Jackson. "But it isn't a spell that makes you love them, when you shouldn't. It just called out to us. Fate made us for them, and them for us."

"You. All. Share?" I managed to ask through gritted teeth with difficulty.

"Really?" Fin added.

Elliot laughed, the sound dark and deep. "You get over the jealousy crap." He shrugged. "They're worth it." He snuggled his tiny mate.

something shifted inside my chest.

I looked at Fin and Jase. "You guys feeling the same thing I am? Seriously?" These two guys were my best friends, my brothers-in-arms, but I'd never shared a woman with them, even on a casual night. I certainly never thought I'd have to share a Fated Mate for the rest of my lives with them.

They frowned at me,

So, I elaborated. "My mate's the blonde."

Fin nodded. "Yep."

"Me too," Jase added.

Tiffany squealed in this gorgeous way.

It made me want to go over and grab her. She sounded excited. Hell, she sounded hot. What sort of noises would she make when I got her into bed? Correction. When *we* got her into bed... I took a step toward her.

Jackson put out a hand and pressed it against my chest. "Ah. No. Trust me when I say you need a minute to process this. The girls will grab your clothes and we'll meet back at..." Jackson glanced at Tiffany.

Our mate whispered something to the brunette.

"Our place," said the brunette. "Let's leave Ruby to rest."

Jackson nodded then turned back to me, his jaw tight. "Okay. Let's go. To be honest, I could use a run too."

I groaned. "But we've been running for three days straight to get home in time for Christmas."

Jackson raised an eyebrow. "Which is probably the *only* reason you haven't wolfed out and lost control already. But seriously, let's go. You two as well." He pointed to Jase and Fin.

Jase tore off his shirt.

Tiffany's eyes bulged, and she licked her lips.

Oh, it was like that, was it? I ripped off my sweater and tossed it to the ground, staring at the woman I'd just been told was my mate. I'd traveled the whole fucking country, and she'd been right here all along? Just waiting for us to find her? A witch? A gorgeous half shifter? *Who I have to share with my two best friends.*

"Fucking hell," I said, then as I caught her eye, I saluted her and grinned the best I could manage. "See you soon." I let go of my humanity and shifted. I didn't like being in my wolf body as much as my human form, but it was an easy enough transition.

Jackson, Fin, and Jase shifted as well.

I took a moment to stare at my mate, or the woman Jackson had declared was mine at least. But it had to be true. *What other reason can there be for how I feel?* I wanted to kiss her, hold her, tuck her into my body, and keep her safe for all of time. And my wolf felt the same way. Every part of me acknowledged that she was the woman I'd been desperately searching for.

Jase nudged me with his head and with one last look at Tiffany's smiling, beautiful face, we took off, through the town, around several new buildings I'd never seen before, and dashed off into the forest.

Jackson took us the long way around the pack, running us through the woods and further than we'd normally go. We ran all the way to the witches' church and circled back home to the pack again.

Home. A place I'd thought was where dreams went to die. A place I'd initially refused to return to when Jase and Fin had wanted to, until my mom had called and begged for us to visit for Christmas.

But I could admit it now. This place, this pack, was where my heart truly lay. I'd just been so disappointed with how my life had turned out —so fucking lonely— that I'd run away from everything I'd ever known in an attempt to change it.

Now things were different. For the first time in forever, as we ran home, my wolf howled with happiness. After months, no, *years* of searching, our mate had found us. Finally.

Now we just had to sort out where we were going to live, and who she was going to sleep with. I'd bunked with Fin and Jase for way too many months, and I had no intention of sharing my mate with them. And I was damn sure they felt the exact same way about me.

TIFFANY

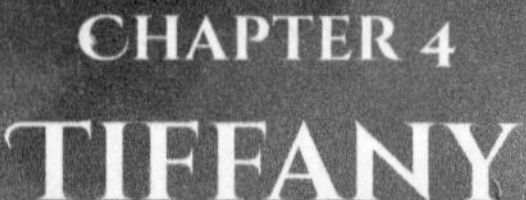

"Oh, my God, oh, my God, *oh, my God!*" I couldn't help the ridiculous words and nonsensical squealing that spilled out of me as the men shifted and ran away. *God, they were beautiful.* All three of them. And they were mine! I couldn't believe it. I slammed both hands over my mouth in an attempt to mute myself.

Bella laughed at me. "I knew they'd come for you. You just had to wait a little longer."

I deserved the 'I told you so' and I honestly didn't even care. I jumped at my best friend, sweeping her up into an epic hug and squeezing her tight. I never wanted to let go of these incredible feelings coursing through my veins. I literally shook with excitement, so happy I wanted to cry.

"They're good guys," Billy said from behind me. "Jackson and I grew up with them. They'll look after you, Tiff."

I drew back to stare at him, realizing I should probably ask him some questions—get some basic information on my three brand new mates. "Who are they? What are their names? What do they do?"

Before Billy could answer, Elliot interrupted. "And not that I mind, of course, but how come everyone's coming back to our place? We haven't built the extension yet. It's going to get super crowded real fast."

I hadn't thought about that. Bella's house was tiny, made for two bachelors who'd never planned on finding their mates. Now, there were four of them living there, and adding us into the equation was going to make things squeezy.

"You know, I've been thinking. Rather than extending, it might be easier to just buy that big place we were looking at last week," Tommy said. "Especially if Bella's going to have Tiff and Ruby around all the time. They each come in packs of four..."

I laughed, almost hysterically. *I* was included now, no longer left behind like an afterthought.

Then Bella answered Elliot's question, sobering us all. "Well, uh, Ruby's in some sort of sleep at the moment. Our moms are there looking after her, so I didn't really think it was a good idea to go back to Jackson's place and disturb everyone."

Elliot's smile dropped. "Shit. I had no idea, Bell. What's wrong with her? Do they know?"

"Is it the baby?" Tommy asked.

"Yeah, it is," Bella said quietly, almost reluctantly. "I'll explain as we walk. Grab some of the clothes with me Tiff, then let's go," Bella said, tugging on my arm.

I scooped up two pairs of jeans and a hoodie from the ground where the guys had left their clothes after they'd shifted. Bella grabbed the rest, and we walked away from Milly's and toward Bella's current accommodation.

The men and Bella discussed Ruby's condition.

I managed to wrangle Billy away from the group. "Hey, what can you tell me about my mates?" I asked.

Billy grinned at me. "The one who was doing most of the talking? That's Oliver, but everyone calls him Ollie. He's a grumpy bastard like me, but he's cool."

A guy like Billy? *Yeah*, I could totally cope with that.

"The other two are Fin and Jason. All three of them are Betas, so hopefully you won't need to deal with the overly jealous Alpha bullshit."

"Hey," Jackson called from behind us.

Billy just shrugged off his Alpha's playful protest before addressing me once more. "They were the only guys to leave the pack and look for their mate in other states. Even though everyone here is miserable, they actually did something about it. So, they've always been pretty determined to find you."

I bit my lip. That sounded like a dream. Men who wanted me... and only me. Men who'd traveled the whole country in their efforts to find me. "Thanks, Billy." *I needed that.*

We arrived at Bella's house which was a neat and tidy two-bedroom, two story house. It was much smaller than Ruby's place, but they obviously had plans to buy something bigger to accommodate them all as they were discussing. Especially, now that they were a family of four, and not two.

Billy began to back away. "I think I'll get going back to the house."

Darren went with him. "Me too. I want to check in on Ruby."

"Thanks guys," I said, rearranging the clothes I held to grip them tighter against my chest. Damn they smelled good. "Thanks for every-thing. I really appreciate you introducing us and everything. I'll message my mom later and see if the Coven needs our help trying to find a cure for all this."

We'd been doing research, and spells, trying to find the source of the curse so we could unhook it from ourselves. But with Ruby's sudden illness, and the fact she was carrying the only hope for future generations, finding a solution would become everyone's number one priority.

"You need to concentrate on your mates," Bella said, turning toward me and giving me a pointed stare. "If that's the key, us all needing to find love with the wolves; once you're mated, the curse might break."

I inhaled sharply at the thought of finally mating—of losing my virginity—and my chest tightened with anxiety. "It's definitely worth a shot," I admitted. I didn't really like the idea of ignoring Ruby's current plight to focus on my mates, but considering they were all I'd ever wanted, hopefully it would all come easily between us, and we'd soon have some kind of solution or answer. Just as Bella suggested. Which meant I'd be helping Ruby as well! *Not to mention our fathers.*

"We need to get back to work too," Elliot said, glancing at Tommy. "Or do you think one of us should stay here, you know, just in case."

Tommy nodded. "I'll stay, it's cool. Jackson will probably want to get back to Ruby when he returns. Someone should supervise the Betas."

He was probably right. If Jackson, Tommy, and Elliot were all gone, that only left Bella, me, and three men that I'd just met half an hour ago.

Elliot pecked Bella on the lips. "I'll only be a few hours, beautiful, but call if you need me to come home earlier."

Bella nodded and cupped her mate's face in a sweet caress that made my heart ache. "Thanks, Elliot."

He gave me a quick smile and bounded away.

"Come inside," Bella said, taking my hand and dragging me into the house.

When we stepped over the threshold, I glanced around. "Where do you guys all sleep? In one bedroom, like Ruby does?"

Bella's face turned a bright shade of crimson red.

I laughed. "Oh, come on, Bell. Don't be embarrassed." I put the guys' clothes down on the nearby couch.

Bella did the same with the articles she'd carried.

Tommy chuckled, grabbing sodas from the fridge, and tossed us each one. "Yeah. We all sleep in Elliot's room at the moment. It's on this floor, so easy access to the kitchen and he has the biggest bed. But if we get the new house that Elliot and I looked at last week, we'll be able to have two king beds in the one room and put them together. The master room is massive on that one."

"Which house is this?" Bella asked.

"The one near Jackson's," Tommy said casually. "One of the Elders built it for his son and grandkids, but they decided they couldn't afford the loan... And, anyway, not our business. But it's *big*. And it'll suit us in the future."

Tommy and Bella shared a pointed look.

I raised my eyebrows. "Don't tell me you're pregnant, already, too?"

"Oh, God no." Bella laughed, waving a hand as though dismissing my words. "But we do want kids. One day."

"Definitely," Tommy said with a broad grin. "As many as Bella will agree to."

Bella rolled her eyes. "I know, I know. Just let me finish college first," she added playfully.

I sighed and sank onto the couch, basking in their happiness. This morning I was so insanely jealous of what my friends had found that I would have curled into a ball and died if I'd had to listen to a sweet conversation like this again. But now that I knew my men had finally found me, I could relax and be at home around these people. *My people.* I truly, finally belonged and would be getting my happily ever after! "So, how many years have you got to go again, Bell? One?" I asked.

"Yeah, but that's not important at the moment. Tell me how you're feeling! Relieved that the love spell worked to bring your triad to you?"

I laughed. "A triad... Such a strange concept still."

Bella snorted. "Yeah, I know. When Ruby got three mates, my only thought was, *'God no, I could never do that'.*"

"What changed?" I probed curiously.

She shrugged. "Well, when you're in it, feeling it rather than just looking in from the outside, it feels right. Your perspective changes and you realize that it's natural, and normal, and perfect." She exchanged a glance with Tommy that made my insides twist and turn.

"I hope my triad will be as happy with me, as you guys obviously are, together," I said.

Tommy grinned and saluted me by lifting his can of soda. "They will be. That's the magic of Fated Mates. Even if there's crap at the start, jealousy and fights, you already know you're destined to be together and it makes you keep pushing forward, no matter what hurdles get in your way."

Bella sat on the couch and curled her legs up under her. "That's true. I struggled to believe it myself at the start. I thought that it would be better to let Elliot go, and just be with Jonah and Tommy. It seemed so much easier to be with them."

"Naw, thanks babe," Tommy said with a lop-sided grin.

I hadn't heard about this. "You were really going to let Elliot go?"

I stared at her; partly sure she'd gone crazy. Elliot was *hot*, with a capital H. Like crazy muscly, with a gorgeous face and a protective streak a mile wide. *What wasn't to like?*

Bella bit her lip and pulled a huge gray pillow onto her lap, hugging it tight to herself like a makeshift plush shield. "Yeah, well, at the time, I figured he was part of the punishment for using the love spell. The debt of pain I was meant to pay. I mean, I wanted him. I wanted him so much it hurt. But we're so different. I never thought we could make a relationship work."

I swallowed hard. *Shit!* "The payment... I'd totally forgotten about that part." Using the love spell had its consequences. Payment for services rendered. If the spell worked, it took something from you in return. I didn't want to lose my magic like Ruby had, or any of my mates like Bella almost had.

Bella shrugged. "We're here for you. No matter what. I'm sure everything's going to be okay."

I pulled my hair out of its high ponytail and ran my hands through the tangles. "Yeah, I suppose. *If* we can work out a way to break the curse."

Bella glanced out the door. "Speaking of which, I really should go visit my dad. It's been a few days since I last popped in."

I moved further along the couch and arranged myself in the corner of the chaise. "It's hard when they can't talk back, isn't it? But I still like hanging out with them."

She nodded, her eyes lighting up. "Yeah, me too."

"Do you think we'll ever get them back as, you know, humans?" I asked. Yesterday, it was my greatest wish, outside of finding my mates.

Bella inhaled slowly, then sighed. "I really hope so."

I slipped off my shoes and tucked my legs up under myself so I could cuddle into the couch the way Bella was. "Do you think they'll get back together, if we manage to get the dads back to their human forms?"

"Who?" Bella asked.

I grinned. "Our moms and dads, of course. All of them are still single. So, do you think they'll all just, you know, pick up where they left off twenty-three years ago?"

My mom had had so little time with my dad. One single night, after only a short time of dating. It seemed incredibly unfair.

Bella frowned, worry lines creasing her forehead. "I honestly don't know."

"If they're Fated Mates, they'll have no choice," Tommy said, his deep voice booming across the room. "They'll see each other again once the guys are in human form, and that'll be it. They'll have to be together. The fact that none of your moms remarried indicates they probably felt the bond."

"None of them have even tried dating," I said, feeling like that was a point that should be made. "I even encouraged my mom to date. When I was little, I'd point out the warlocks in the Coven who'd stare at her, or even humans in town I thought were nice. But she was never interested in any of them."

Bella shook her head. "My mom, either."

Tommy grunted. "Sounds like Fated Mates to me."

I opened my mouth to ask more questions about wolves and their mates, But the thud of loud footfalls landing on the porch sounded. I jumped to my feet, my heart thundering in my chest. They were here!

The front door burst open and four very naked men walked in. I didn't so much as glance at Jackson, but I couldn't help but stare at my three guys.

God, they are so beautiful. Lean. Muscled. Hard. Perfect.

"Do you guys mind if I head home? I want to go see Ruby." Jackson grabbed his jeans and pulled them on.

"Of course not. Go," I said.

"Thanks," he said before he scooped up his hoodie and headed for the door.

"I'll hang around," Tommy answered. "But let us know if Ruby wakes up."

Jackson saluted and headed out the door.

Once he was gone, I swallowed hard, unable to speak as I stared my men. My throat ached, and my belly was tight. *Oh, my God. So many men.* How was I ever going to handle all of... that?

The three guys stared at me with varying degrees of curiosity and sexual heat.

My face flamed with the blush of embarrassment and a hint of lust.

"Here you go, guys," Bella said, scooping up their clothes we'd carried home and dumping them in the middle of the room. "Throw some clothes on."

They nodded and began to re-dress.

I couldn't drag my eyes away from them and their incredible bodies, so strong and rippled with muscles. I didn't even bother trying to hide it. *They were mine, weren't they?* Three gray wolves, and me... their blonde witch.

CHAPTER 5
JASE

I clenched my jaw, my wolf flaring hard inside of me. I wanted to grab her and fuck her. I couldn't believe how strong the desire was. I normally prided myself on being pretty cool. Fun. Easy. But at this moment? Damn, I wanted my mate naked and under me.

I forced myself to pull on my jeans and sweater over my overheated body, my skin tingling and itchy with the need for a long shower. I tore my gaze from her gorgeous face and stared at Tommy. "Hey, man. I know it's early but..."

"You want a beer? Yeah. Of course." Tommy pulled a six pack from the fridge. "I know. I've needed a few of these myself since finding my mate." He handed me a bottle, then offered them to Ollie and Fin.

They took one each.

We weren't usually big drinkers, but today was a celebration day.

I think.

Fin glanced at me, and we both looked at Tiffany.

Where the hell do we go from here?

Fin walked over to the couch; his hand extended in greeting. "We weren't technically introduced earlier. I'm Fin."

Tiffany stood up off the couch, wobbling.

I rushed forward instinctively, grabbing onto her arms to support her. "Are you okay?" A shot of silver lightning pierced my nerves, pleasure shivering through my arm as we touched. "Holy shit..." I staggered sideways.

She grabbed for me, momentary panic in her eyes.

Another bolt of pleasure passed through me, and although I managed to stifle the moan—she didn't.

The groan that came from her throat sounded like she was aching for me just as much as I ached for her. It moved through me like a prayer, fulfilling every wish I'd ever had for myself.

I pulled her with me onto the couch.

"What was that?" Fin asked, frowning suspiciously at me.

I swallowed hard. I didn't really want to tell him, but if we were meant to be co-mates, I needed to man up and share. "Touch her, man. You'll feel it, I think."

Tiffany's eyes went wide.

I smiled reassuringly at her. "Go on. Try it."

"Okay." Tiffany put out her hand to Fin.

He gripped it and pulled her to her feet.

They both shivered as though someone had walked over their graves, as the saying went, though it was the complete opposite in this case. We'd just met our future. Our lives were only just beginning.

"Whoa," Fin said.

I turned around to call out to Mr. Grumpy Ass. "Hey, Ollie. Come over here."

Ollie strolled over with a grimace. "I'm Oliver."

She bowed her head sweetly. "I'm Tiffany."

She held out her delicate hand, her arm shaking. From apprehension, or nerves, I wasn't sure.

Ollie reached out and grabbed her hand, a moan escaping his lips as his eyes went wide.

Tiffany began to faint and all three of us jumped to grab her. We all connected, touching her at once, and the feeling was positively electric. Like touching a live wire, but in a good way.

I gasped.

We all panted as one but didn't move away, none of us willing to let her go.

She struggled to breathe as well, but turned to me, her blue eyes wide, her pupils huge and dilated with arousal. "And you're...?"

"Jase," I said. "Well, it's Jason, but I prefer Jase."

She wet her lips by sneaking out her tongue and licking them.

The move made me ache hard to kiss her. "So, what's next?" I asked, trying not to focus on how badly I wanted her. We had to take this slow. We couldn't rush and spook our Fated Mate.

Her beautiful lips lifted up into a grin. "Um, we move into a house and live happily ever after?"

And that was all it took. The beautiful atmosphere in the room broke as if Tiffany had dropped a crystal vase on the tiles beneath her feet.

All three of us stepped away.

Tiffany nearly collapsed.

The brunette rushed over to grab Tiffany's hand. "Are you okay? What was that all about?"

I frowned at the girl, who glared at us. "Um, and you're...?"

"I'm Bella," she said, straightening her spine but narrowing her eyes at me. "I'm mated to Elliot, Tommy, and Jonah."

"Jonah?" Fin asked. "Billy's little brother. He's a nice kid."

Bella pressed her lips together. "We're the same age. How old are you?"

From the kitchen, Tommy watched, shaking his head and grinning.

"Finding this amusing, huh?" I called out to him.

"Oh yeah," he said, joining us in the living room. "I was standing in your shoes a month ago, and I don't envy you at all. Speaking of which, I think I'm going to take my mate for a walk and show her the house we want to buy for her. Something nice and big." He grabbed Bella's hand.

"But…" she started to say.

"I think Tiff and the guys need a few minutes alone to talk. We won't be long. Twenty minutes tops." He glanced at Tiffany. "If that's okay with you?"

She nodded. "I'm pretty good at offensive spells. If any of them piss me off…" She raised her eyebrows and stared at each of us in turn. "They'll find out what a witch can do."

I took a step back and put up my hands. "We won't hurt you. I promise. Never." I'd never laid a finger on a woman, and as far as I knew, neither had Fin or Ollie.

"I think we should stay," Bella said, glancing at each of us as though she didn't approve of us. At all.

"Come on, sweetheart." Tommy dragged his reluctant mate from the room and closed the door behind them.

The room went quiet. Unnervingly so.

Tiffany slid onto the couch and indicated to the room. "Have a seat and explain to me what the hell just happened."

I grabbed a chair from the dining table, turned it around, and plonked myself down onto it.

Fin and Ollie found a spot on the large couch but didn't go anywhere near our new mate.

She'd really dumped a bucket of cold water on us with that comment about expecting a happily ever after. And a house. Did she want a baby by tomorrow, too? Although getting her pregnant sure would be fun, I wasn't sure I wanted kids so soon.

"Which part?" I asked, making sure I knew what she was talking about before I put my foot in it.

She rolled her eyes and sighed dramatically.

I blinked. Had she really just done that? I looked at the other guys, who were just as surprised as me.

"The part where we were all connected and hot, and I said something about a happily ever after and you all recoiled like typical human guys. What's wrong? Are you all afraid of commitment or something?"

My mouth gaped open. "Afraid of commitment? Us? We've just spent the last year traveling from state to state, looking for our mates."

Tiffany raised an eyebrow. "And how did you test these women to find out if they were your mates, exactly?"

"Oh, well..." I glanced at the floor, then over at the guys, hoping they'd take one for the team.

"So, you didn't just hold their hand, and test if there was a connection or not?" she pressed.

I met her gaze. She couldn't possibly think we'd gone all this time without a woman in our bed? What sort of men did she take us for? I forced out a laugh. "You don't need to lecture us. We all have a past. It's not like you're a virgin..."

"Yes, I am," she said, lifting her head and straightening her spine like she was affronted.

My mouth dropped open. "Are you serious?" I asked. "But you'd have to be, what, twenty-two, twenty-three?" That was, if my fast calculations about when the Manterri cousins went missing were right.

"I turned twenty-two on Halloween a few months ago. What's your point?" she asked, glaring at me.

"That you can't be a virgin," Ollie burst out "You're too fucking hot!"

Tiffany's cheeks went a bright shade of pink. "Well, while I appreciate the backhanded compliment, I have to inform you that no-one's wanted me before." She stood up and walked to the door. "And since you three seem to think I'm a liar, I think I'll join the rest of the guys and go hang out at Jackson's."

"No!" I said, jumping to my feet. "I'm sorry... I mean, we didn't mean to say you were lying. Of course, you wouldn't lie about something like that. But I've never had a..." I glanced at the other two guys.

They shook their heads.

"We've," I corrected myself, "never had a virgin."

Tiffany sniffed and wiped away the tears I hadn't even seen her cry. "Well, you still haven't, but I've been waiting for you. *Properly.* I haven't been fucking my way around the country, pretending I was looking for the right guy. So, excuse me while I check on my friend. At least her mates didn't run a mile when they found out she waited for them!" She flicked her gorgeous blonde hair over her shoulder, walked through the door, and slammed it shut on her way out.

I stared at the closed door, speechless. "Did that really just happen?" None of this made any sense. How had we gone from practically panting for her, to losing her in the next breath?

Ollie paced the room, cussing under his breath.

I sat down on the dining table chair and leaned back. "I don't get it." I shook my head. "Women."

"Well, it's her fault we freaked out, a bit," Ollie said, staring at me like I needed to agree with him. "We haven't even gotten to kiss her yet, and she's already talking about us buying her a house. What sort of chick does that?"

Fin huffed out a laugh. "*All* of them."

"Yeah, because they want the guy to pay for everything," I said.

We all chuckled, but beneath the laughter I could hear the thread of tension.

For guys of almost thirty, we didn't have anything to offer her. The other two guys knew it, and I knew it. When we'd been younger, we'd spent most of the money we made on food and booze and going out. There had been no reason to save for a rainy day—especially when there was no sign of a mate on the horizon.

Then last year when we'd decided to leave the pack, the little we'd saved had gone into travel expenses. We'd had to pick up some casual work along the way to pay our way as well, but we virtually had nothing left.

Fin sighed. "She's going to be disappointed when she realizes we can buy her sweet diddly-squat. I was planning on just crashing with my parents for a few days, before we headed off again."

"But if she's the one for us, we're staying, right?" I asked the others. "I mean, the whole point of traveling around was to look for our mates, and now that we've found her…"

"And we have to share her," Ollie said with a soft growl. "How do you guys feel about that?"

Silence descended over us. We were all Betas. None of us had a wide, arrogant Alpha streak. But none of us had prepared for this eventuality either.

"Well… I mean, it's not a preference," I said.

"God, no," Ollie said.

"I agree," Fin said. "But I don't care enough to walk away or anything. I mean, I'm not going to leave again to see if I can find another mate somewhere else. Do either of you want to try that after what we just felt?"

I crossed my arms over my chest and shook my head. "Not me. I've had enough of the loneliness."

A wolf shifter was a pack animal. A family man. Not having a mate, or the prospect of children, was what had driven us to leave our pack behind in the first place.

Tiffany was ours—mine—and despite this hiccup I wasn't leaving without her.

"Unless she wants to come with us? I mean, if you guys want to travel more, I'd be up for that. But she'd need to come along too."

Ollie scowled, still walking around the tidy little lounge room. "That's not likely. She'll have roots here. A family. Plus, you heard what she said. She wants a house. A big expensive one probably, like Tommy was talking about buying his mate."

Fin shrugged. "Looks like we've got to get jobs again then to support her."

"Yeah, and work out where we're going to sleep while we try to woo our mate back," I added, hating the idea that we'd pissed her off so royally already. "I'm not sure about you, but the shock has kind of worn off, now. And I'm starting to like the idea that she hasn't been with anyone else."

I more than liked it, truth be told. I fucking *loved* the idea that her pussy was waiting for me to be the one to taste it for the first time.

Ollie frowned.

But Fin laughed at me. "Yeah. It's hot."

"We've just got to convince her to give us another shot, I suppose." Worry settled in my chest, because the longer I sat here thinking about it, the more I realized we'd probably stuffed up a pretty critical time in the dating program. *Shit.*

I slapped myself in the head. *Oh, my God*. Jase could be so dense! We needed help. That was for God damn sure. I got to my feet and looked straight at Bella. "Um, we scared her off."

Bella frowned.

Tommy just laughed and headed for the kitchen.

He opened the fridge. "You guys hungry?"

I shook my head. "We ate at Milly's just before you arrived."

Tommy ignored my statement and started rummaging through his huge silver fridge.

Bella crossed her arms over her chest. "What did you do?"

Ollie threw his hands up in the air. "We didn't do... anything!"

She raised an eyebrow and gave me a reproachful look. "Fin?"

"Um, it's kind of hard to explain." I ran a hand through my hair that had grown to my shoulders. It needed a good cut, and I needed a long shower—two things that may have also contributed to our mate running for the damn hills.

"I'm not dumb, so about you try me?" Bella said.

There was an answering chuckle from the kitchen. The sound of the microwave could be heard a moment later, before the smell of fragrant lamb curry filled the room.

"What are you laughing at?" I asked Tommy, putting off the inevitable conversation with Bella a little longer.

He laughed louder. "You guys. If you knew how good it is to finally have a mate to love, you'd be chasing Tiffany down and begging forgiveness for whatever stupid thing you did."

My stomach tightened. A warning. We needed to listen to this guy.

I sighed and looked at Bella. "Tiffany said she was going to head over to Ruby's house. Could you show us the way?"

"Yeah, it's not far," Bella said, reaching for a purple sweater I hadn't noticed lying on the back of the sofa.

Outside it was getting darker and colder, not that we cared. As wolf shifters we never felt the cold, but as a witch, Bella wasn't so lucky. And from the way she shivered before wrapping the sweater around her shoulders and buttoning it up, she obviously felt it.

I made a mental note. *Tiffany's going to feel the cold in the future. So, no more sleeping outside or leaving all the windows open in winter.*

"You're not going to run after her, are you?" Ollie asked me, looking shocked.

I rounded on him. "Yeah, of course I am. Aren't you coming?"

Of the three of us, Ollie was the most cantankerous. A right pain in the ass most of the time. But he was as loyal and fierce as the day was long, so we put up with the other shit.

Ollie's jaw set.

I knew his answer. "Fine," I said, before I turned to Jase. "How about you? You coming?"

Jase looked between Ollie and me and frowned. "I'm not rapt about sharing a mate, but I'm damn sick of running all over the state looking for her. So, if Tiffany is the one for us, I'm in, no matter what I have to do." He stood up from his spot on the couch.

I assumed that meant he'd suck it up and get to work if we needed to buy a house for our new mate. He *did* say 'no matter what' after all. "Then let's go." I turned to Bella. "Lead the way."

Fin and I followed Bella out of the house and headed down the street. We didn't talk for a block or two, but soon Bella was at us again.

"Tiffany's one of the easiest people to get along with on the planet," Bella said. "She's super easygoing and doesn't take too much seriously, which is usually a plus. I don't get what you guys could have done to upset her enough that she would actually get up and leave."

I turned to Jase. "Um..."

Jase shrugged. "It's hard to explain, but we'll sort it out. We've probably spent too long on the road. We're a bit rusty on the talking to sensitive women front."

"Sensitive women?" Bella repeated, her voice rising higher as though she was mocking us.

"And the last thing we expected her to be, was a virgin. That was a bit of a shock too," he continued.

Bella stopped in her tracks.

Jase and I had to turn back around to look at her.

She held up both of her hands, her face twisting with anger. "Hang on a second. I'm sorry, but am I getting this right? She told you she was a virgin, and you guys... you possessive, protective, *stupid* wolf shifters... didn't want her to be? You thought it was, what, a bad thing that she saved herself for her soul mate?"

I glanced at Jase. "Well, when you put it like that..."

"You guys sound like fucking assholes!" Bella finished for me, crossing her arms over her chest.

I tilted my head and stared at her. "You know, I think I underestimated you."

She rolled her eyes, but the start of a smile played at the edges of her lips. "I may be a bookworm, and a bit of a wallflower, but I have three mates, two of whom are Alphas. So yeah, I'm not as quiet, or as weak as I look."

I nodded, grimacing in agreement. "I'm starting to get that." The very last thing we should do was underestimate our own mate, either.

"And Tiffany's not as tough as she looks," Bella said. "Everyone thinks because Tiff's the pretty one, that she's dumb, and slutty, and super confident or something. But she's got weaknesses and soft spots. And yes, she's still a virgin. We *all* swore to each other we'd wait for the right guy. Or in this case, *guys*. Why do you three have such a big problem with that?"

She swallowed and went a little red in the cheeks. "Elliot *loved* that about me—that I'd never been with anyone else, and never would be."

I smiled at her, loving the honesty and vulnerability in her eyes. She was sharing something special about herself so that we didn't screw this up.

"You're right. Of course, you're right. It was just... unexpected."

She cocked an eyebrow at me. "Would you have preferred her to have a list a mile long? Maybe she should try out a few of your pack mates? After all, there's a couple of dozen single guys just waiting for a woman to walk into their lives around here." She gestured to the rows of houses along the street.

A growl rolled through my chest, and

A similar noise came from Jase's throat.

I looked at Jase, surprised by his reaction. He'd always gone for the easy chick. He was too relaxed to work hard in any sort of relationship, especially a one-night stand. Yet he was looking as angry as I felt about Bella making such a suggestion.

When I glanced back at the little witch, she was grinning triumphantly. "*Exactly, you idiots!* You could barely stand it when Billy touched her arm. There's no way you could deal if she even entertained the idea of being with other men. So, next time the topic comes up, keep your bullshit opinions to yourselves." She turned and flicked her long dark hair over her shoulder and marched past us and down the street.

I couldn't help but chuckle as I stared after her. "Where have these sorts of women been all our lives?"

Growing up in a pack that hadn't birthed daughters in a whole generation meant that we'd never dated a lot. By the time we'd reached maturity, there hadn't been a girl born in ten years, and the scrabble for a mate became the obsession of most of the eligible males in our pack.

Jase, Ollie, and I hadn't been old enough to realize just how important it had been to grab whatever available girls there were. And by the time we did, all the good ones had been mated and snaffled up.

So, we'd had to indulge ourselves where we could, finding casual sex with random wolf shifter females from other packs. It had been the best way to deal with our growing sex drives. But we'd never met a girl like this. Strong. Defiant. Loyal to a fault. It was scintillating.

"It's probably because she's a witch," Jase mused. "Bet she's powerful too."

"Too right I am," Bella threw over her shoulder.

I laughed in surprise and amusement, then joined Jase in running to catch up with her.

We walked another couple of blocks together, then came across a massive two-story newly built house.

"Jackson lives here?" I asked, staring up at the monstrosity before us.

Jackson was only a year or two older than us. How did he have the money to afford something like this?

Bella nodded, heading for the side gate. "I'm going to go see my dad for a bit. You two go to the front door and ask Tiff to go for a walk or something. I won't be long. And don't screw this up!" Then Bella disappeared from sight.

I glanced at Jase. "Did she just say she was going into the back yard to talk to her dad? Isn't her dad one of the Manterri cousins?"

Jase shrugged. "I don't know and don't care at this point. Let's just go get Tiffany."

I smiled as we walked up the front steps of the massive house and knocked on the door.

We'd found my mate. *Our* mate. The one we'd been searching for all these years, and we'd finally found her. That was what I needed to focus on. What *we* needed to focus on. Nothing else mattered.

The door opened and an older woman with bright blue eyes opened the door. "Can I help you?" she asked.

"Yeah. We're looking for Tiffany. Is she here?" Jase asked.

I cringed. He sounded like a petulant teenager, not a thirty-year-old man.

The woman narrowed her eyes. "Yes, she is. Who can I say is calling?"

"Um..." Jase stammered under the weight of the woman's protective glare.

I cleared my throat. "I'm sorry. My name is Fin, and this is Jase. She'll know who we are, if you wouldn't mind asking her to come to the door? We'd really appreciate it."

The woman turned to look at me, her gaze flicking up and down my disheveled sweater and jeans. From the way her lip lifted in a slight sneer, it was obvious she found me lacking. She nodded once and closed the door in our faces.

"Do you think that could be Tiffany's mom?" Jase asked.

I tugged on my sweater, wishing I'd had the forethought to go home, have a shower, and get changed. "Yeah, she could be." The blue eyes had been the same.

"Great. Just great," Jase muttered.

"Yeah, we probably didn't make the best first impression."

"Do you think we should go get changed, or something? I mean..." Jase pulled at his hooded sweater. "I didn't think we'd meet our future mate at Milly's today, or I would have had a shave, or something." He ran his hand over his bristled chin and grimaced.

The front door opened, and our blonde mate stood in the doorway, her hair softly floating around her shoulders. Her eyes were red-rimmed.

"Hey, are you okay?" I asked, impulsively reaching out for her.

She shrugged off my hand. "I'm fine. What do you two want?"

"Ah..." I began. We hadn't really thought about what we were going to say when we got here. "We wanted to come over and apologize for our reactions earlier. I think we've been so used to traveling, and being in wolf form, we've lost half our good manners." I ran my hand through my hair and stared at the ground, realizing that it was actually true.

Jase cleared his throat. "Can we maybe take you out for dinner? Or do you want to do something tonight?"

She lifted her chin in a stubborn move that Ollie used all the time. "Where's Oliver?"

Jase chuckled. "You sound like his mom. No-one calls him Oliver except her."

Tiffany flicked her icy glare at Jase and he stopped laughing.

"Sorry," he muttered, put in his place.

Tiffany looked back at me. "I've seen my friends go through a lot of shit with their mates, so here's *my* deal, okay? I've been waiting for you guys for years... literally years... but I'm not going to be angry if one of you wants to jump ship. One woman sharing three guys isn't everyone's bag. I get that. So, I'll meet you at the burger place in town, at seven. It's called Sam's Burgers. Let Ollie know, okay?"

I stared at her, her conviction laden words at odds with her tear-streaked cheeks. "Um, tell Ollie what, exactly?"

"That you've all got one chance. I'm more than ready for my happily ever after. If you guys aren't, well, then, I suppose I'll be eating burgers by myself tonight." She went to close the door,

I put out a hand, pushing against the wood to stop her slamming the door in our faces. "You said Sam's Burgers?"

She nodded once, her mouth pulled tight, and her cheeks pinched. "That's right. In town." With that, she managed to push the door shut in our stupefied faces.

I turned to Jase. "Do you think Ollie can pull himself together in a few hours?"

Jase shook his head. "Nope. Never has before."

I inhaled deeply. This was going to get messy, fast. *Damn it.* If Tiffany and Ollie were as stubborn as each other, we would be in for a long fight. I patted Jase on the back and jogged down the stairs. "Come on. We've got the date of a lifetime to get ready for."

CHAPTER 7
TIFFANY

I moved aside the sheer white curtains on Ruby's front windows and stared at two of my three mates as they jogged off to God-knew-where. Hopefully home to get ready for burgers with me in three hours. But who knew? Life was full of surprises.

"Who were they?" My mom asked from behind me.

I jumped and turned to look at her, momentarily startled. "I think they're my Fated Mates."

Mom's eyes were worried and shadowed as she stared right back at me. "You *think*?"

"I mean, I know. Well..." I shook my head and laughed. I'd never been able to talk to my mom about boys at the best of times. You'd think it would be easier as you got older, but it still wasn't. I shook myself and looked Mom square in the eye. "Their names are Oliver, Jason, and Fin. And yes, they're all my soul mates, Mom. Just like Ruby, and Bella, I have three too."

"Where's the third one?" Mom asked, biting her lip.

I frowned. "He's my problem one."

There was a heavy beat of silence as Mom absorbed my words. Then her lips kicked up at the sides unexpectedly.

"I never told you this, but your dad didn't want to be with me when we first met."

I frowned. She'd never really told me anything about my father, but I hadn't expected that. "What do you mean?"

"I mean..." she turned and glanced toward the kitchen, where I assumed my father in wolf form would be lounging outside the back door on the porch. "He saw that I was a witch and wanted to run in the opposite direction."

"But you told me that you two were only together once," I reminded her.

Mom nodded. "We were. But by that point we'd known each other for almost a year, and it took him that long to get up the courage to follow his instincts and come to me."

"He fought the bond?" I asked, frowning. "Aren't you two Fated Mates?"

Mom sighed. "I'm not sure if we were or not, but I know I wanted him. More than anything. I hated the fact he didn't feel the same way."

"He probably did," I said, defending my dad on instinct. "But sometimes we let other shit get into our heads. Especially when it comes to the whole witches versus wolves thing."

My mom smiled at me. "That's true. So, my point being... don't be too harsh on your third, okay? You should appreciate that, more than anyone. Just because you want something to happen now, and be perfect, doesn't mean it will always work out like that. Unless you've forgotten about Miles?" Mom raised her eyebrows at me.

A flood of shame washed over me, and I looked away, horrified she'd brought up such a thing. I still couldn't believe I'd told her what had happened that night. "Mom. He has nothing to do with *now*."

"Of course, he does," Mom said, and walked over to take my chin in her hand.

I glared at her. "That's not fair."

"It is," Mom said, smiling fondly, despite the daggers I threw at her. "Miles made you feel unloved, unworthy, and undesirable. But you will be *all* of those things to your mates, and so much more. You just need to give them a little time to come up to standard. Guys aren't perfect you know, but then, neither are we." She turned and walked away.

I frowned after her. "What do you mean, 'to standard'?"

She raised an eyebrow at me. "You've had two months to wrap your head around the fact that your mates were probably going to be wolf shifters, and that there would probably be three of them— because you watched it happen with Ruby and Bella, right?"

I nodded, crossing my arms under my breasts. "Yeah, so?"

She chuckled. "These three guys came home for Christmas, according to Bella. They expected to have some food, see their parents, and head off into the wild blue yonder again. They had no idea they were coming home to their Fated Mate, who they now have to share, and who has been raised a full witch."

She stared at me long and hard and said the words she'd said to make me behave ever since I was a kid: "Come on, Tiffany. Be fair." She turned and left the room.

My mouth dropped open. "Be fair? Me! They're the ones that... that..." Don't want me as their mate. Who can't handle the fact they have to share me. And yet I wanted them! *All* of them! I staggered over to the nearby loveseat against the wall and fell onto it, staring around Ruby's gorgeous home. It wasn't fair. Ruby's mates jumped straight into bed with her, then moved her into a mansion!

Bella's mates almost died bringing her back from the abyss, and brought our dads home to us, too. Men we'd thought were dead or gone forever.

But my mates? I dashed the tears away as Bella walked into the room.

"Tiffany, hey, I... What's wrong?"

I got to my feet, shaking my head. "Oh, nothing... nothing. How's everything with you?"

Bella frowned. "Sit down. Talk to me."

I shook my head again, but let my friend pull me back onto the loveseat anyway. "I'm fine, Bella. Just being silly. We should go in and see Ruby." I made to get up again.

Bella grabbed my hands. "Don't make me cast a truth spell on you," she threatened with a smile. "You know I can do it."

I couldn't help but chuckle at that. "Yeah, I know you can do it." I sighed. "You're going to think I'm ridiculous as well. And I know I am! Ruby's in there, fighting for her life. Our dads are in the backyard, stuck in wolf form. We're linked to some twenty-three-year-old curse that's sucking the life out of the pack. And I'm..."

"Worried about your mates, and how the whole relationship is going to work?" She nodded. "I know. Been there, done that."

I sighed and hunched my shoulders, feeling deflated. "I just feel so selfish."

Bella wrapped her arm around my shoulders and squeezed tight. "You're not selfish at all, Tiff. You're just... impatient. You always have been. You want what you want, now. And there's nothing wrong with that. It drives you forward. I kind of admire that about you."

I sniffed and wiped my nose with my sleeve. "Thanks but telling me that I act like a toddler is not something to admire."

Bella laughed. "Tiff, you are strong, and capable, and loving, and loyal to a fault. Those three guys would be lucky to have you."

"They don't want me." I sniffed. "They want to keep fucking their way around the country, and I'm too... innocent for them."

I'd give them my virginity, the moment they asked for it. I wasn't attached to my sexless state the way Bella had been. I'd wanted it gone years ago. I threw my hands up in the air. "What do you even do with three guys in bed, Bella? I couldn't even handle one."

"You don't know that..."

I jumped to my feet. "Yes, I do." I sniffed and wiped my nose again with my hand, tears burning at the back of my throat. "I never told you guys, but I, well, I..."

Bella got to her feet. "What did you do?"

A hot wash of shame swept over me once more, but for the first time since it happened, I wanted to tell my friend. "I tried to seduce Miles when I was sixteen. You know, the warlock from school?"

Bella's eyes went big and wide. "Okay... what happened?"

"He couldn't... you know..." I indicated to my groin area. "He didn't want me. No matter what I did." As a naïve sixteen-year-old I'd done everything I could think of to get him to want me, but his dick had stayed as flaccid as a sausage from the butcher. *Softer even!*

Bella covered her mouth as though shocked, but there was a smile flirting with the edges of her mouth that made me want to smack her in the face.

"Bella! Don't you dare laugh at me."

"I'm not. I'm not, I promise," Bella said, shaking her head. "It's just that... Miles? Really? He's such a wimp. Totally not your sort of guy *at all.*"

I frowned at her. "He was cute enough. And I wanted a boyfriend. I wanted... someone to love me." Especially since my mom was always working to keep a roof over our heads and my dad had been nonexistent in my life. "I just..." I sighed.

Bella rushed forward and grabbed both my hands. "Tiffany Anderri, are you listening?"

"Yes."

"You are beautiful. You are fierce. And you have saved my life now, multiple times. I trust you with everything I hold dear, and I can tell you with no amount of bias, that you *are* loveable. You and your pack of men will get through whatever challenges you're about to face— together."

I finally forced myself to meet her gaze. "How do you know?"

"Because I have faith. In you. And in our love spell. Our magic would never have called upon three men who weren't perfect for you. Even if you can't see it just yet, I promise everything will work out. It will."

I snorted. "You can't possibly know that, Bell."

She grinned. "But I do. Want me to do a scrying session for you?"

I blinked. Bella had never offered to do one of those for me before, though I knew she was really good at them. "About what? My future?"

She nodded. "Just enough to give you some certainty in moving forward."

A wave of love for my best friend crashed into me. "Really, Bell? Are you sure?"

She nodded and went over to the coffee table, kneeling down in front of it and closing her eyes.

I glanced over toward the kitchen. "Here? Shouldn't we be in with the moms, checking on Ruby?"

She shook her head. "Mom and Rebecca are outside with ours dads. And I think that after the stress of today, we could both use some positive news, don't you?"

She was right there. I walked over and knelt down next to her on the soft carpet.

Bella had her hands out in front of her, wrapped around nothing. Then all of a sudden her scrying ball appeared out of nowhere, and now rested within the circle of her cupped hands.

"Where'd that come from?"

She shrugged. "Just transported it here, from home. It's not far."

I blinked. Bella's magic was *so* much more powerful than mine. "You seem super confident in this," I said to her, my heart pounding a little harder in my chest. Was Bella really going to tell me that everything was going to be fine? That I'd get my happily ever after with the three men Fate had made for me?

Bella closed her eyes and purple magic swirls began to manifest inside the ball. Around and around, it went. Bella focused on the scrying crystal, not speaking aloud.

My stomach dropped and twisted, making me feel sick. *Please let it be all good news.* I glanced toward the kitchen, where the family waited. *We could use some good news about now.*

Bella frowned, the lines between her eyes growing deeper. The smoke in the ball became black and she dropped her hands down, sighing.

"What is it? What did it say?" I asked.

Bella slumped backwards so she ended up sitting on her bum on the carpet.

I crossed my legs and faced her, sitting on the floor with her, my heart in my throat. "Tell me, Bella. What did it say?"

She shook her head. "I can't."

Fear lanced through me like a knife, cutting raw and deep. "Because it's really bad? Something happens to us? Or them? Please tell me something. *Anything.*" We'd gone into this scrying session with all the best intentions, or Bella had, but now I felt worse than I had before. *This is probably why she's never done this for me, or anyone I know.* The results were too varied. She had no control over what happened.

"I can't, because the future is too dark to see through it. There's like a black storm cloud headed our way, and my magic can't see past it."

"For me?" I asked, swallowing hard. *It's worse than I thought.*

Bella pinned me with an intense stare, her eyes still shimmering purple with her lingering magic. "For *all* of us."

When the guys told me that Tiffany had pretty much given us an ultimatum, be at a place of her choosing by seven tonight or piss off forever, my initial reaction was pretty bad, if I was honest. I'd said something along the lines of, "tell her to go to hell," and several other choice phrases...

But by the time seven o'clock rolled around, and the other two guys had taken off to meet Tiffany for dinner, I was beginning to have second thoughts. "Fuck. I should be there." I paced along the edge of the forest.

After the other guys had gone back to their parents' places to shower, and shave, I'd gone to the outskirts of town to shift. *To run away.*

Now that I was standing here alone, my temper had cooled, and all I could think about was the possible future I was losing. A wolf shifter only had a single Fated Mate—if we were lucky. If Tiffany was mine, then by turning my back on her, I was turning my back on the only chance of love I was ever going to get. I was basically flushing it down the toilet with a big old 'fuck you' salute.

My only chance of having a home and children. Did I really want to keep traveling? Have no roots. Never know what it was like to raise kids? An aching, tight pain of regret gnawed at my gut. This was my doing. My anger and stubbornness.

There was an intense magic in the air tonight. It couldn't be a coincidence. I could feel it. This was a major turning point in my life and despite my initial reaction of shock, I was beginning to think I'd made a seriously foolish mistake. *What the hell should I do now?*

Town was a fifteen-minute drive away, and I was already late! I started running I'm not sure why I didn't take off toward town in wolf form, but instead I just followed my feet and ran back to the first house we'd visited earlier today. I knocked on the door.

Bella answered with a confused frown on her face. "Ollie, what are you doing here?"

I got straight down to brass tacks. I didn't have time to waste. "I wasn't going to meet Tiffany at the café, but now I'm regretting it."

Elliot strode up behind his mate and slid a possessive hand around her waist. "Hey man. What's up?"

"I need to get into town. To some burger place," I said.

Bella nodded. "Sam's."

"Yeah! But Tiffany said seven, and it's already seven. I need to be there."

Bella grinned. "Worried you're going to miss out on having a powerful witch as your mate?"

"I... hadn't even thought much about the witch thing," I said, being honest. "I think I was more shocked that I had a mate, *at all.* I'd kind of gotten my head around the fact that it was never going to happen for me—for us." And part of me had been okay with that. *A very small part of me.* The part of me that had resigned itself to a life spent in the company of my two best friends... because that's all there was. Hoping for any more had been akin to emotional suicide. Daring to hope was a path that led to heartbreak and until now, I hadn't thought hope worth the risk. *Not really.*

Elliot chuckled. "Yeah, I thought that too until Bella came along." He wrapped both arms around his mate's waist and cuddled her openly. Such public displays of affection weren't super common around here. Especially for Alphas.

"I don't want to break this up, but can you call her? Or can I borrow a car?"

Bella's eyes lit up and she grinned. "I can do you one better."

A shiver of worry coursed down my back. "What can you do?"

"I can send you straight to her via magic, but I have to warn you that most wolves feel sick the first time they're transported."

I clenched my teeth. If feeling sick was the price to get back on track with my mate? I'd pay it a thousand times over. "Okay. Do it."

"Come in. Quickly," Bella said.

I followed them inside.

Elliot patted me on the back. "Take a teaspoon of cement and harden the fuck up, mate. These girls are worth the hassle," he said before He stepped away.

I faced the witch. "Go for it, Bella. And thank you."

She smiled. "Just try not to stuff it up once you get there, okay?" With a flick of her hand, white sparkles hit me...

And *zip!* I was suddenly standing next to a table, inside of a warm restaurant. I blinked, my stomach twisting and turning like I was about to vomit.

"Ollie!" Tiffany cried from her place, sitting in one of the café booths. "Where'd you come from?"

"I... um..." I tried to grab for the table nearest to me before I fell over, but my legs buckled beneath me. Instead of focusing on the pain in my shoulder as I hit the concrete floor, I simply focused on not throwing up. *Swallow. Just swallow.* I gulped. *Stay down.* I coached the contents of my stomach. "Whoa." I stayed where I fell, though hands from above grabbed for me to pull me up. I waved them off. "Give me a second. I just need to stay here for a sec."

"He'll be better in a minute," Tiffany said.

And I was. Within a few heartbeats, the nausea began to recede. Strength returned to my arms and legs, and I slowly pushed myself to my feet and brushed off whatever dust and grime I'd picked up from the floor.

Tiffany grinned at me. "So much for not making a scene."

I glanced around. Everyone in the small restaurant was whispering and staring. "Lucky it's not busy. May I join you?"

Tiff was sitting by herself on one side of the booth, with Fin and Jase sitting opposite her. Why they chose to sit so far away, I didn't know. She nodded.

I slid straight into the booth next to her, sliding my hand over her thigh.

She jumped at my touch, electricity sizzling between us.

And I reveled in her reaction. "I'm sorry I'm late," I said, though a possessive growl rose in my throat.

She swallowed visibly, but she didn't move my hand away. In fact, she seemed to slide a little closer. "It's okay. I kind of figured you weren't going to make it."

"Yeah, me too. But you know... Fate called." I grinned at her, and

her eyes shone at me as she stared at me, then she cleared her throat. "You traveled by magic to get here. So, I have to assume Bella helped you?"

I nodded.

She slid her hand over mine, where it rested on her thigh, but instead of pushing my hand away like I expected, she curled her fingers around mine, holding my hand in place. "That was very brave of you. I know transportation spells knock shifters around a bit."

I shrugged. "It was worth it. I would have kicked myself a thousand times over if I'd missed out on tonight."

Fin and Jase stared at me like I'd grown a second ass. "What?" they blurted in unison, before they shook their heads and grabbed the menus in front of them like they'd been snapped out of a trance.

I turned in my seat to stare at my mate. She was glowing. Her skin. Her gorgeous blonde hair. Her bright blue eyes. "You look beautiful."

She blushed, hot and red.

I chuckled. "Now you're even more beautiful."

She glanced down at the table as though embarrassed, then looked up at me through her thick, black eyelashes.

Desire flourished in my belly, deep and dark. I couldn't stop myself from reaching for her face and pulling her toward me. She was mine. I couldn't wait to taste her.

When our lips met, we both gasped at the sensation.

It was as tingly as fireworks exploding inside my skin, and as sweet as caramelized sugar all at once.

She melted into me.

I pulled her closer, pressing my lips hard against hers in a possessive kiss that I hoped showed her exactly what I wanted to do to her later. Virgin or not, she was ours. And I wasn't going to hold back. When I finally lifted my head, I stared down into her eyes and fell into them. She was heat, and light, and everything that was good in this world.

I swooped down for another kiss, this time tasting her with my tongue.

Someone nearby cleared their throat, and the noise finally broke through the cloud surrounding me.

I pulled back.

Tiffany giggled a little, pressing her fingers to her lips as though to stifle the noise—or imprint my kiss on her mouth forever.

"Who's hungry?" I asked, picking up the menu and forcing my gaze to the words I couldn't quite focus on just yet. My cock was throbbing, hard and persistent beneath the table. I wanted to grab my mate and strip us both naked so I could have my way with her. But I needed to keep a lid on it. At least for now.

While I stared at the menu, not caring one whit what I was about to eat, I had to think about where we were going to take Tiff tonight.

None of us had our own place. We'd planned on crashing at our parents' houses while we were here, but I wanted to take our mate somewhere we could seduce her. My old bedroom, with my king single bed and my parents in the next room, was *not* the way to do it.

"What made you change your mind?" Fin asked. "I didn't think you wanted to be part of this... family."

I glanced up at my friend, a guy I'd known my whole life, and for the first time noticed the hurt there. Had he thought I was rejecting *him*? That was weird. "I figured Fate doesn't fuck things up, but I was going to if I didn't get my ass over here."

"So, you believe we're Fated Mates now?" Tiffany asked. "That we will end up living together, and all that stuff?"

I tried to repress my immediate reaction to the whole, 'married with kids' thing. It was such a cliché. And as a family of four, surely we could break the rules a little? Make a future that we all wanted. *Something unique.*

"Yeah, I do believe it," I admitted, and swallowed against the thickness in my throat. "I think the problem was... I never expected to find a mate at all, period. I'd talked myself into believing I'd be single forever. So, when you showed up, and I had that intense, 'I need to fuck you right now', reaction... What's wrong?"

Tiffany had practically choked on her water, coughing and spluttering into her napkin.

Fin groaned. "She's a virgin, Ollie. You can't say things like that."

She shook her head, coughing to clear her throat. "No. You can. I just... I'm not used to it, that's all. I'm not made of glass."

"Yeah, what happened there?" Fin asked, perplexed. "The guys around here blind or something?"

She smiled at the compliment and tilted her head. "Well, Ruby, Bella, and I made a pact a few years ago after we found the spell book.

The one that showed us how to call our soul mates to us. None of us wanted to play around. We just wanted one guy—the right guy. So, we all swore that we'd wait until after the spell was cast, so then we wouldn't get hurt."

"Get hurt?" I asked, frowning in confusion. *Is sex really that painful for a girl?*

"We all grew up with mothers who'd been abandoned by our fathers, or so they thought at the time. None of our moms ever dated again after we were born. And they obviously didn't remarry or have other kids. It was sad, seeing our moms so lonely and depressed. It put us off dating. We just wanted the right one."

"That's understandable," I said, glancing over at Fin and Jase.

We couldn't relate to that sort of upbringing, ourselves. Our parents had all mated young, and stayed together, forever. Break ups within wolf pairings were as rare as hens' teeth. But I could imagine that having her sort of childhood would have changed how she saw life. And marriage. And men.

"Plus," Tiffany went on. "None of the guys around us were interested in dating us anyway. We thought it had something to do with our moms being single, but now we know it was probably our wolf shifter blood. The warlocks our age didn't want us, and the humans practically ran in the opposite direction..." She shrugged, but pain crossed her face.

I slid my hand onto her thigh again, as close to her pussy as I dared and squeezed gently.

She jumped a little, casting a furtive glance my way.

"Their loss," I said. "I'm sorry for being a fuckwit before. About the whole virginity thing. That was stupid."

She bit her lip. "Yeah, well, I thought it was a bit weird. But as long as you guys are okay about it now?"

"As long as you're not attached to it, because I'm hoping to part you with it as soon as possible."

"Oh, um... yeah." She glanced across the table. "All three of you want to do that, right?"

"Hell yes," Jase said.

Fin grinned. "Of course. As soon as you're ready to mate with us, I'm in. I can't speak for the other guys, but I've been waiting for you for a decade, Tiff."

Tiffany smiled at him, flashing her brilliant white teeth. "That's a long time."

I slid my little finger even closer to the juncture of her thighs, watching heat flush her beautiful cheeks. "Yes, it is."

She grabbed my hand, holding it a couple of inches away from its destination. "Well, it's all yours. But should we eat dinner first?"

I laughed aloud at that one. This girl was so much more innocent than she appeared. I had to remember that. She was sweet in a way I'd never appreciated in a woman before. "Yes, gorgeous. We can wait until after dinner."

No point losing her virginity on an empty stomach, after all.

I couldn't wait to claim her, but how we were going to do this, all three of us sharing a single woman, God only knew!

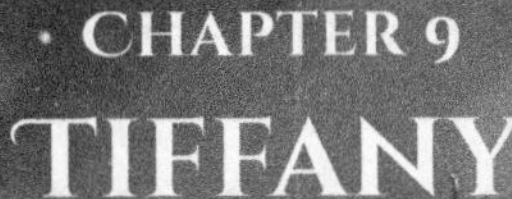

CHAPTER 9
TIFFANY

I spent the entirety of dinner wriggling in my seat, trying to keep my head above the waves of arousal that hit me every time I caught the lust in my mates' gazes. And when I wasn't trying to distract myself from how uncomfortable and *hot* under the collar, they were making me, I was laughing at their antics.

They were all gorgeous—but in totally different ways.

Ollie was assertive, sarcastic, and had a dirty way of talking that both embarrassed me and turned me on at the same time. He had short dark hair and incredibly dark eyes that made me want to stare into their depths to try and discover his secrets.

Fin on the other hand was relaxed, and sweet, and almost too beautiful to look at. He had tanned skin, bright blue eyes, and dirty blond hair that fell all the way down to his shoulders. He was better looking than me!

And Jase? Well, he made me shift in my seat the most. He was funny, and lovely, and had an edgy hardness to his looks that made me think he'd be great in bed.

That was one of the things I loved about having mates older than me. Although I hated the idea of them having had so many women before me—in fact, the jealousy made me sick if I dwelled too much upon it—I loved that they'd know what they were doing. Our first time, *my* first time, wouldn't be two ridiculous teenagers fumbling in the dark, with no discernable idea about what either one should be doing.

And thank God they knew what they were doing, because I certainly didn't. If anything, I was intensely afraid I was going to disappoint them. The only guy I'd ever tried to seduce had found me to be the biggest turnoff. Those memories had haunted me for years, and I was pretty sure that if my mates ended up having the same reaction to my touch, I would absolutely die of shame.

We finished our meals and paid. Then it was time to get up and leave the warmth of the familiar restaurant. I didn't have to be home by any specific time tonight. I didn't have a curfew at my age and my mom knew where I was, but I had no idea what the guys wanted to do.

"Do you three want to see my house?" I asked, aiming for as casual a tone of voice as possible. "Or are we calling it a night now?"

The three men exchanged glances.

Then Fin turned to me, his face as serious as a seizure. "We don't have a house like Ruby's and Bella's mates. We'd planned on just staying at our parents' houses over Christmas, then heading off again."

"Um... okay." I frowned at them. What did that have to do with our plans for the night? "That didn't answer my question."

The guys exchanged glances again.

"What we mean is, we don't have the money to offer you the

immediate home and future the other guys did for their mates." Jase finally said, his lips twisted as though he was annoyed.

I opened my mouth to answer, but he rushed to interrupt me.

"But we will. We'll all get jobs and rent a place to start with. Then we'll save up for a home for you. We'll be the mates you deserve, Tiffany. We promise."

Ah, so that's what the problem is! I smiled at them. I didn't care about those things. All I wanted was a man, or in this case, three men, who actually wanted me. The rest would take care of itself in the long term, like it did for all partnerships. "Well, I might have a solution to that in the short term. Are you guys up for a bit of a walk?"

Ollie's eyebrows drew down into a frown, but he ended up nodding. "Okay. Yeah, sure."

I led them along the main street and through the town, chatting the whole time about family and life. Nothing too serious.

We laughed the whole way.

Ruby and Bella knew about this secret of mine, but as someone who didn't like to talk about money, it wasn't something I casually told many people. When we finally reached a little town house with a white picket fence, I stood proudly in front of it, beaming at them.

"What's this?" Jase asked, glancing up at the house.

"Is this where you and your mom live?" Fin asked.

I shook my head with a grin. "Nope! This is *my* place."

"What do you mean?" Ollie said, sounding confused. "I thought you lived with your mom?"

"I do," I said with a sigh. "Long story short. I wasn't very good at school, so got out as soon as possible and went straight to work as a hairdresser. I lived with my mom and didn't have a lot of expenses, so when I had the down payment, I bought this place." I indicated the property I'd bought at just nineteen years old.

"It's been leased out since I bought it, and it's only got two bedrooms, so it's not huge or anything. But if you guys would help me pay the mortgage off, because I can't afford to do it on my own, then we could live here together. Then maybe, after a while, we could get something bigger? Maybe something closer to the pack if you want?"

I had no idea if they'd want to live in town with me. Wolf shifters and humans didn't mix very well, but it was the best option I could see. My tenants had been making noise about moving out soon anyway, and instead of re-leasing it I could move us in, and we'd have an instant home for our new little family.

Now that I thought about it, with the way the bedrooms were arranged next to each other, we could even knock out the dividing wall between the two and make it one big bedroom. If that was what they wanted...

I didn't want to tell them my plans out loud. They seemed a little gun-shy when it came to talking about the future. Or had, up until just now. They seemed to be coming around to the idea of us being together. Slowly, but surely.

"Are you serious?" Ollie said, his mouth dropping open.

I frowned at him. "Ah, yeah. Why?"

He chuckled loudly. "Because it's fucking awesome! How... how did you do this?"

I shrugged. "I work hard."

They all grinned at me.

"Looks like we're the ones that are going to have to lift our game, huh boys?" Ollie said.

The other two shook their heads and laughed in agreement.

Ollie grabbed me and swung me up into his arms. "Looks like you have the future sorted, gorgeous. But we need somewhere to take you tonight. Is there a motel nearby?"

A shiver of premonition moved through me. *Yes. This was the right path for me.* "Ah, yes," I said, running my fingers up his arms and loving the feeling of his strong muscles beneath my palms. "There's two, I think. The nicer one is a block or so from here."

I knew most people in town, and we'd probably start an absolute firestorm of gossip if anyone saw me going into a motel with three hunky guys, but I couldn't stop the shiver of excitement that passed through me at the thought.

Ollie's dark eyes lit up. "Lead the way."

He took my hand and I managed to walk calmly, without screaming, all the way to the motel.

Mercifully, the guy behind the desk was a stranger, an amazing thing in a town as small as ours, and we got the biggest room they had. The clerk looked at us weirdly but didn't question Fin when he handed over some cash and took the key card. In fact, the guy looked a touch scared if anything.

Humans had issues with shifters, and it was obvious as the guy paled that my three wolves had him feeling beyond his normal levels of inadequacy.

We went up to the room and shut the door.

My stomach was all knotted up and there was an aching pulse deep in my belly that I couldn't ignore. I was fifty percent nerves and anxiety, and fifty percent excitement and horniness. It was a heady and dizzying combination.

Ollie reached for me first.

I put a hand up to his chest, pressing against it, hard enough to stop him. I needed to get something off my chest first. "Thank you for coming to the restaurant tonight. I know I was pushy with what I said about you having to be there and everything. I shouldn't have been like that."

Mom had made me see clearly just how petty I'd been. Just because I'd been waiting for them, and technically they'd been looking for me, hadn't meant they were as prepared for the 'till death do us part' bit as I was. Especially since they had to share me.

Ollie slid his hands around my waist, then grabbed my ass and hauled me into his body.

I gasped, heat bursting to life in my core like a flower unfurling.

The hardness beneath his jeans pressed against me.

I almost moaned at the feel, relief sweeping through me. I wasn't going to be disappointed tonight. *This time will be different.*

"I shouldn't have been so resistant to what Fate had planned for me," Ollie said, then ducked his head and kissed the side of my neck.

I melted into him.

He nipped and sucked his way up the column of my throat. "You're meant for us, and we're meant for you. And it's time we made you ours."

His whispered words were everything I'd ever wanted to hear, and I closed my eyes against the wave of arousal that swept over me.

He slid his hands up underneath the back of my top.

I cupped his face, drawing his mouth to mine. A moan escaped my lips as a tingle of awareness passed over me. It wasn't as strong or as strange as the first time we'd touched, but it was still there, letting me know that I'd made the right choice. That this man, this shifter, was one of the incredible men made just for me.

Ollie swept his tongue into my mouth, surprising me with the growl that rolled through him.

I pulled back, feeling the eyes of the other two guys upon me. With a coy grimace, I grabbed hold of Ollie's hand, so I didn't get disconnected from him, and looked at Fin and Jase. "I need to have a quick bathroom break; then can we have a chat about how this is going to happen? I'm a little bit nervous about the whole, three guys on one girl... thing."

Ollie chuckled. "We've never done this before either, so I think we're going to need to feel our way through things."

"Let's check out the bathroom," Jase said, walking through the large room and opening the ensuite door. He turned back to me with a grin. "If you want some privacy for a minute, go for it, but after you're done, I could really use a shower. The other guys too. So, do you want to watch us for a bit first? Get comfortable with us before we take you to bed?"

My mouth dropped open. "All three of you are going to shower, together?" I was going to get to look at them naked, together, like... now? I wasn't really prepared for that. But then, was I prepared for any of this craziness Fate had dealt me?

Jase nodded, then pretended to sniff his friend. "Ollie needs a shower more than me."

"Hey!" Ollie swatted at him, then shrugged sheepishly. "It is true."

Jase tilted his head toward the bathroom. "The shower is massive. So, you go do whatever you've got to do and when you're ready, we'll all come have a quick shower and wash the day off."

"More like the past *week,*" Fin said with a grin. "We've been running for days to come home to you."

I shivered, loving their expressions and the fact they were giving me this time to get more comfortable—and to ramp up the heat and tension before getting into bed together. *Best foreplay ever!* I gave them a grin, then ducked into the bathroom and shut the door behind me.

Oh my god! *Bloody, wow.* This was really happening.

CHAPTER 10
TIFFANY

I pressed my forehead against the closed door and shut my eyes. This was really happening. After practically ten years of wondering what my first time would be like, who it would be with, and how it would go... I now had the answer. My first time was going to be with three men who were destined to be mine, and who I was going to see completely naked, in this bathroom, in about five minutes.

I could barely breathe with the excitement saturating every part of me.

"You okay in there?" someone called out.

I think it was Fin. "Yeah. Yeah. All good," I called back, pushing myself up and turning around to check out this supposedly massive bathroom.

Jase was right. The ensuite was more like a wet room, with floor-to-ceiling tiles, one large glass panel separating the shower from the room, and two large shower heads so at least two people could shower at once. *Probably more.*

I bit my lip and shivered as a sense of true longing rippled through me. I'd never be alone again. I wondered if I'd ever truly wrap my head around that concept. *I have my mates!* I could almost scream.

I hurried to finish my bathroom necessities, then stripped off to take a quick shower myself. If they were going to be kissing, and licking, and smelling me in all of those places... I wanted to be as fresh as possible. I needed every bit of body confidence I could get in front of these three gorgeous, more experienced guys!

When I was warm, clean, and dry, I glanced around the bathroom. I didn't really want to put on the clothes I'd been wearing to dinner. It felt wrong after washing myself so thoroughly. So, I grabbed the fluffy white robe that was hanging on the back of the door and slipped it on.

It wasn't exactly fancy lingerie, but it would give the guys easy access at least. After I tied the belt around the robe, I opened the door and met Fin's eyes. "All done," I said cheerfully.

He grinned back at me. "Great." Then he began to pull off his clothes.

I glanced away, getting more and more embarrassed with each article of clothing that disappeared. I tried to find somewhere to look that wouldn't make the heat climb further up my face, but everywhere my gaze landed, there was a naked man. *Holy shit!*

Ollie, Jase, and Fin had all completely stripped, and they sauntered forward to come into the bathroom,

I hurried back, dragging the door open with me.

Fin swaggered in, all big shoulders and awesome six-pack. "Hey," he said with a grin as he walked into the shower and flicked on the water.

Jase was next. He was huge in every way; shoulders, arms, even his cock was so long it made me look away, mortified to be staring.

Ollie slid an arm around my waist and tugged me into him.

I squealed when my hands came up to press against his huge, hot pecs. "Whoa."

He chuckled and kissed me quickly on the mouth, then strode over to the shower and stood at the opening, waiting his turn.

I bit my lip and glanced at the floor, the white tiles beneath my feet. My stomach tightened with both excitement and arousal, and there was the most incredible pull to look at my men. I knew I was allowed to, and they wanted me to, but I'd literally never seen a naked man in real life before. My teenage experience with the warlock had been in the dark, and I'd been the one to turn off the lights. I hadn't wanted to see all his dirty, ugly private bits.

Curiosity eventually got the better of me and I lifted my head to peep at the men washing themselves in the shower. My mouth dropped open, and my heart started to pound with a whole new level of arousal. *Oh. My. God.* They were fucking beautiful! Their bodies were all sculpted and made of pure muscle. They looked strong, and lithe and hot, all at once—like a team of Olympian gods.

Ollie grinned at me as he scrubbed his body with suds, then stepped beneath the water and washed the soap away. "We won't be long, gorgeous girl. Unless you want to join us in here?"

I opened my mouth to respond, then just shook my head, more embarrassed now. I would have loved to say I had the confidence to throw off the robe and strut into the shower like a boss to join them. Maybe even make love to them in there, with my back pressed against the cold tiles and my head beneath the warm water.

I shivered, my pussy throbbing in dire need. "I'm, ah..." I couldn't finish the sentence, and I couldn't stop staring at them. I was trapped by their beauty, as if drawn in by their gravity.

They flicked off the water and began to grab towels, the water droplets running down their exquisite bodies, their wet hair hanging over their eyes in a deliciously feral and rogue way.

I licked my lips, my mouth suddenly dry. *How is this real?*

They moved toward me...

And I bolted into the bedroom. Out of the frying pan and into the fire. "Um..." I didn't know what to say or what to do. How did you even start a session like the one we were about to have?

Ollie reached for my hand and tugged me toward him. "Don't think, gorgeous. Just feel how right this all is." He cupped my face and pulled me into him for a kiss.

I closed my eyes, slid my hands up his chest to wrap my arms around his neck, and gave myself over to the storm of passion sweeping me up. This was my future, my fate. And hopefully the path to break the curse and give us back the lives we were always meant to have.

Jase grabbed for the robe at my shoulders.

Ollie undid the knot in the belt around my waist.

I broke the kiss and leaned back.

Jase peeled the robe down my arms.

And Ollie pulled back to stare down at my naked body, a dark hunger evident in his eyes. "Fuck, you're more beautiful than I even imagined you would be."

Every part of me screamed that I needed to cover up, to raise my arms and hide my body from Ollie's view. But I didn't. That would have undermined everything we were trying to build. They desired me. They wanted to look. So, I lifted my chin and let him stare at me, trying to bury the anxiety and embarrassment that threatened to consume me.

That's when Jase grabbed my hand and spun me around so he could look his fill as well.

I struggled not to reach for the robe that had dropped to the floor, once again feeling vulnerable under my mate's stare. But as my gaze caught on his heavy, thick erection, I swallowed down my squeal of embarrassment and instead focused on their need for me.

Then Jase dragged me into his arms for my first kiss with him.

I moaned as my pelvis cradled his narrow hips, and my breasts pressed against his chest.

Jase grabbed me by the waist and lifted me.

I clung to his shoulders and wrapped my legs around his hips as he walked me to the bed.

He rolled onto the soft surface and landed on top of me.

I couldn't stop all of my focus going straight to the way his cock poked into my belly. I looked over his shoulder at the other two, obscenely staring at the way their cocks jutted out from their bodies also. The relief I felt was palpable. I grinned and went back to kissing Jase, but he stopped and stared at me strangely. "What were you looking at just then?"

"Um..."

He nipped my jaw with his teeth. "You can tell us the truth. Always, gorgeous."

I shook my head. "I was just looking at the other guys. That's all."

He chuckled. "There was something in your face I couldn't quite decipher. What was it? Is it fear? Are you scared about tonight?"

"No, it's not that." I sighed. I didn't want to get into it, but they may as well know the real truth about me and the reasons I had the hang-ups I did. "There was one guy I dated for a little while in high school, when I was sixteen. And when we were fooling around, he couldn't, you know, get it up. He said it was my fault. That I was repulsive and ugly." I swallowed the lump in my throat as I practically spat the words out, wanting to be rid of them once for all.

Jase's eyebrows climbed his forehead, then he began to pull back and get off me.

I grabbed for him, horrified that he would leave me after I'd revealed such a private and painful thing to him. "No, please. Don't go!" I panicked. "I didn't mean to upset you."

Jase laughed. "I'm not leaving, sweetheart. Not in a million years. I just wanted to show you that we don't have *that* issue." He stood next to Ollie and grinned at me. "Look your fill, sweetheart."

I sat up on the bed and looked from face to face. They were deadly serious. They were happy for me to just stare at them to my heart's content. "Really?"

Ollie grunted. "Fuck yeah. Go for it."

I slid to the edge of the bed and studied them, from their intense eyes to their long, hard cocks, all lined up and ready for me.

Ollie grinned then charged toward me. "I hope that's enough for now, because it's our turn to love on you." He pushed me back onto the bed and kneeled on the floor between my legs, spreading my thighs open.

"What are you doing?" I cried out in shock.

The other two slid onto the bed with me.

Ollie stared up at my face. "I'm making sure you're so hot and wet for me, by the time I slide into you, you'll be begging me for it."

Oh, my God. I covered my face with my hands and lay back on the bed, mortified. I couldn't handle him talking like that, saying those sorts of words to me. But at the same time, they circled around and around in my head, easing the pain of the past and cementing the path to the future.

Fin slid his hands over my breasts and nipples.

I dropped my hands to stare up at him. I couldn't hide from this—from them.

Jase turned my face toward him and started kissing me.

I cried out against his lips as I felt Ollie's tongue slide down my pussy. His groans of pleasure broke me. And I cried out again as his tongue thrust inside me. "Oh, fuck!" I moaned, arching my back and loving every second of what they were doing to me.

I was being kissed, touched, licked, and sucked from every conceivable angle. Three mouths were on me. Three sets of loving, knowledgeable hands. There was nothing to do but moan with ecstasy and let them have their way with me. This is what I'd waited for, for so long...

By the time Ollie climbed up between my thighs to lay on top of me, I was a shivering pile of pulsing, triggered nerve endings, unable to do anything but focus on how good everything felt. And how much better it was going to be when Ollie finally appeased the ache throbbing deep in my belly.

"You ready for me?" he whispered into my ear as he pressed his weight down upon me.

I wrapped my thighs around his waist and bucked up at him, needing something to ease the ache inside me. I nodded, biting my bottom lip hard. *I'm ready.*

Ollie pushed himself up on his hands.

I grabbed for his back, trying to drag him back down again. "Please."

"Please what?" he asked, his gaze intense.

I tilted my hips as invitingly as I could. I wanted—needed—to cum so bad.

Ollie tilted his head and I saw the same stubbornness that others saw in me. He wanted me to say it. He was going to make me spell it out. He was going to make me beg, just as he said.

I swallowed down my stupid embarrassed pride. "*Please* fuck me."

A growl sounded from around me, above me, within me, and the wolf shifter on top of me, my mate, bent his head to consume me with a kiss.

CHAPTER 11
OLIVER

When my mate said those three magic words, I almost blew all over her belly like some teenage kid who couldn't hold his load. My wolf howled inside my head, and I had to stop, clench my jaw, and force him back into the recesses of my mind.

I would not do anything to hurt Tiffany, and that meant keeping my wolf locked up tight. She wasn't ready for that. Not yet. It was her first time... So, I grabbed my cock and rubbed my flesh along her slit, then up to tap the head against her clit.

She cried out, arching her back and digging her nails into my arms.

"Please..." she begged; her voice tinged with a sweet note of desperation. "*Ollie...*"

I was only human after all. I set my cock at her entrance and nudged the head inside. Hot, wet heat engulfed me, and I groaned, thrusting forward as slowly as I could, considering my lust was riding me hard as the damn Devil, like an inferno at my back.

I paused, waiting a moment for her to adjust to me. She was barely breathing as I slid into her and the last thing I wanted to do was hurt her. But from what I'd heard, there would be a little pain, no matter how gentle I was. So, I kissed her neck and rocked my hips forward slowly, sinking deeper and deeper. Then I surged forward with one final push.

A soft cry of pain whispered from her lips and her eyes closed.

I was fully seated inside her, my flesh to hers. I rested my body carefully on hers so that I could whisper in her ear. "Are you okay, gorgeous?"

She nodded against my face and gripped me tight, both with her hands, and inside where my cock was hard and ready for more. She opened her eyes and met my gaze. "Yes. Please don't stop. I need you."

Growling as I began to move, I slid in and out of her as she gasped with every hilt-deep thrust of my cock into her luscious pussy. I fucked harder and faster, riding her until she was screaming for me. I held on so tight to the reins of control, I had to clench my fists against the sheets and bite my own knuckle to stop from coming before her.

When I heard her breath hitch, felt her back arch, then her pussy clamp down on me, I cried out with relief as I pumped into her.

She came all over my cock.

And I reveled in the magical feeling, finally able to let myself go as my own orgasm crashed over me with a breath-taking brutality I've never experienced before. I dropped my head and instinctively bit into the soft flesh of her shoulder as I pulsed my seed into her, claiming her. *My mate.*

"Oh, my God. That was amazing," Tiffany whispered.

I finally lifted my head and kissed her softly on the lips. She could say that again. My head was still spinning. I grinned. "You had enough? Or...?" I glanced to the side of her, where my two best friends waited for their chance to be with our mate.

"We can wait if you're sore," Fin said, always the gentleman.

I withdrew from her and slid off the bed to stand up. My legs wobbled and I ended up sitting on the end of the bed.

Tiffany looked from one of them to the other, her expression one of worry.

I wasn't sure why. "Are you sore?" I asked gently. "Or are you afraid of rejecting them? It's okay. You can be honest with us. We're not going to force you."

She sat up, shaking her head. "No. It's not that. Not at all. I... would love... more. If that's okay? I just didn't know how they felt about, you know... I mean, they just watched me make love to you."

I grinned and glanced at my friends. "Tell her." I wasn't blind. I could see how aroused they still were. Our mating hadn't done anything to dim their desire.

"Come here," Jase said, drawing Tiff closer to him, before taking her and rolling her over so he was positioned on top of her.

I sat and watched as, one after the other, Jase and Fin made love to Tiff. I'd assumed it would cause a panic within me, an unshakeable anger and jealousy. But my wolf was sated and pleased. Watching Tiffany receive more love, and more pleasure, was shockingly satisfying to me and my inner wolf. She would always be loved and cared for now. Even if we weren't around—she'd always have one or more of us. And I knew my best friends like the back of my hand. They'd look after her if it ever came down to it.

When finally everyone had mated, the room went quiet and still.

I tilted my head at Tiff.

She was lying provocatively on her back, her chest rising and falling rapidly as she struggled to catch her breath.

"How are you feeling, gorgeous girl?"

She groaned, pulling herself up to a seated position. "Guilty as all hell," she said with a grin. "Here I am enjoying myself with you three, and Ruby's at home fighting for her bloody life."

I frowned. "You're going to have to explain that to us. I don't think we ever got the entire story."

She ran a hand through her disheveled hair. "Well, basically, we found out a month or so ago that the old High Warlock of our Coven had used our mothers to put a curse on your pack, so that no-one would ever be able to sire a daughter, and as as a result the pack's line would die out."

My jaw dropped open. "Fucking... what? Where's that old bastard now?"

She cringed. "He's dead, actually. He died last year, which takes me to the even more horrible part. Around Thanksgiving, someone put a curse on the three of us—Ruby, Bella, and me. We all ended up in a magical coma, and well, long story short, we found out it was some of the current members of the witch council who was conducting the curse."

"I hope they got theirs." Fin growled, his eyes flashing.

Tiffany sighed. "Not really, unfortunately. The other boys did their best, but they escaped. We all came out of it in the end, but the worst part is that one of the witches told us that the old High Warlock had grounded the original spell in us—Ruby, Bella, and me."

"Grounded?" Jase asked. "What's that mean exactly?"

I was glad he asked, because I sure as hell didn't know.

"It means that we can't break the spell unless all three of us die. It's connected to our very lives."

My mouth dropped open.

"No fucking way!" Jase said.

My thoughts exactly.

Tiffany laughed. "Yeah, I know. It's insane. So, Bella is hoping that we can break the curse another way—by me mating with you three. Now that we're mated, it means all three of us witches are connected to the pack, and hopefully the curse can be done away with."

"What's with Ruby then?" I asked, still confused about how everything fitted together.

Tiffany's lips trembled. "Ruby's pregnancy is slowly killing her, according to our moms, but ultimately, it's all linked to the spell. Ruby's managed to conceive a girl, which she wasn't meant to be able to. But as she's part of the spell, it seems that she and her daughter are trying to break it on their own... but it's not working. The spell is far too strong, so they've put Ruby into a magical coma to try and buy us a few more days to see if we can break the damn thing once and for all."

"And if you can't find another way around it...?" Jase asked.

"Then they'll have to try and get rid of the baby," Tiff said, her eyes shimmering with unshed tears. "Which will destroy Ruby when she wakes up. She'd never forgive us, any of us, if we let our moms go through with it. But..."

I wrapped my arm around her shoulders and pulled her into my body.

She cuddled in closer, sighing against my chest, clearly needing comfort.

Now, I understood the pressure she felt to make sure everything went smoothly with us. Tiffany had her best friend's mortality on her mind. "That's a shit choice," I said, not able to make it sound pretty. Choosing between a best friend and her child wasn't a decision I'd want to give to my worst enemy. It was cruelty incarnate.

She nodded against my shoulder. "Yeah, it is, but we can't lose Ruby. We can't."

I kissed the top of her head. "You won't."

Jase reached over and squeezed her arm. "Yeah, let's hope that we've just broken the spell. You're mated, so are Ruby and Bella. And all to wolves of the pack that were cursed in the first place, so you never know. Don't give up hope, yet Tiff."

Tiffany sat up. "You're right! We should go back home and see how everyone is." She got to her feet, looking excited.

I shook my head, reaching for her hand with a wry smile. "It's past eleven now, gorgeous. How about we all have showers and get a decent night's sleep? Then first thing in the morning we can head back to the pack grounds and see how your friend is faring."

She stared at me, as though weighing my words. "You're probably right. I'll just message my mom and ask her how Ruby is and let her know I'm not coming home." She headed off to find her cell phone.

I watched her gorgeous ass move as she walked away. *Damn, I could just bite that...*

"How are we doing the bed?" Jase asked.

I frowned at him. "What do you mean?"

He gestured to the two large king beds separated by a small table.

"I'm not sleeping without Tiffany," I said.

"Neither am we," said the other two guys.

Tiffany walked back over, still naked and glorious. Her cheeks were pink, her nipples tight and perky. Every part of her was just crying out to be loved all over again. "Can't we just move that table out of the way and push the beds together?" she asked. "That's what Ruby's mates do, I think. They have two king beds connected. Then we can all sleep together."

I pulled our clever mate into my side, her soft skin against me making me ache for her once more. "Sounds like a plan."

We got straight to work.

Jase lifted the small bedside table out.

Then Fin pushed the two beds together.

Tiffany giggled as she crawled across one giant bed and climbed beneath the sheets.

I jumped onto the same bed that she had and slid beneath the covers, pulling her close.

The other two guys got in too.

Fin huffed over the fact he was the furthest away. "I can't even touch her."

"Fine. Try this," Jase said, pulling Tiffany over to him, then rolling her up so that she was lying on his chest facing up.

I shuffled nearer, reaching for her belly.

Fin rolled closer as well.

Tiffany looked from me to Fin, then back again. Then she laughed, a purely happy, sweet sound that a part of me wanted to memorize and remember always. "You know I'm not going to be able to sleep like this, right?" she said, grinning at me, but not moving to get off Jase, nor stopping anyone from touching her.

"Yeah. That's fine," I said.

"Just give us a few minutes," Jase pleaded from beneath her.

"Fine by me," Tiffany said, nestling in. "I've been waiting for you guys for forever. I can wait for sleep. I've had a lifetime of that."

I frowned. There she was talking about waiting for us, like she was old and on the shelf, which she was nowhere near being. "I'm not trying to be rude or anything, gorgeous, but aren't you, like, only twenty-two?"

Tiffany jutted her chin out. "Yeah, so?"

"So," Fin began gently, "we're all thirty-ish. We've been waiting for you for a *lot* longer that you've been waiting for us. So why does it sound like you think twenty-two is old to find your mates?"

She frowned, her brow furrowing in the middle in the cutest way.

I wanted to reach over and use my thumb to massage the stress away.

"You're right. I suppose it's not long compared to a woman in her thirties, or whatever. I've just wanted a husband since I was young. Too young, you guys would think, and I just..." She sighed, shifting as though she was uncomfortable. "I feel like my life can finally begin now. That probably doesn't make sense to you three."

I chuckled and rolled onto my back, tucking a hand beneath my head and staring up at the ceiling. "You have to remember how we grew up, gorgeous. By the time we were eighteen, it was obvious there was something wrong with the pack. There hadn't been a female born in over a decade, and although we'd grown up with a lot of girls, they all got married off to their mates and we were left standing, so to speak."

"We'd kind of gotten our heads around the fact that we'd never find a mate," Jase said quietly.

"Especially after a year of searching the country," Fin added.

Tiffany looked from me to Jase and back again. "So, you're saying..."

I turned onto my side again to face her. "I suppose we're saying forgive us if we're a bit slow on the uptake. You are a *huge* surprise to us, Tiffany. Actually, scratch that. You are literally a miracle to us."

Tiffany's eyes lit up and she smiled brightly at me, before her smile faded. "What will be a miracle is if we can save Ruby and her baby and bring our dads back from their cursed wolf forms."

"Come here, gorgeous." I pulled her from Jase's chest, and rolled her perfect naked body away from me so I could spoon in behind and her other mates could reach for her too.

I leaned forward, whispering into her ear. "I know there's a lot of other stressors in your life, but for tonight, let's just enjoy how amazing this is. We found you, and you found us. There's a miracle in that. We'll tackle the rest as it comes."

She nodded and pulled my arm tighter around her. "It is, but will it be enough?"

I couldn't say anything more after that. What was there to say, except for... *I fucking hope so.* All of our intertwined futures depended on it.

Waking up with my arm wrapped firmly around Tiffany's warm, naked body, was bliss. Her head rested on my chest and her hair tickled my nose. I opened my eyes and turned my head slowly, not wanting to wake her up. Judging from the loud snores around me, Fin and Ollie weren't awake yet either.

I stared at Tiffany for a long moment, drinking in the miracle of our mate. A few days ago, I'd been totally bummed about having to come home for Christmas and to our slowly dying pack.

I'd wanted to stay up in Ontario, happily ignoring the fact that we didn't have much of a future but choosing to accept that our present had been good enough.

We'd had a cheap place to stay, a little work, girls, and beer. It had been simple, and it certainly didn't make me jump for joy or anything, but it had been better than the depression I knew would be waiting for me when I got home. To my parents with no grandchildren. To the pack with no women.

Instead, this obligatory family trip had turned into the best thing that had ever happened to me. I'd found my mate, a person I was sure hadn't existed.

The boys and I had tried almost twenty packs, over ten states, and not one had a woman who held a candle to how I felt when I was near Tiffany. She made me feel like a man again. I was finally beginning to feel whole once more. Like my life had a purpose now.

And the fact she already owned a property despite being so young? That had blown me away. She was driven and fearless. We could all learn a lot from her, and in that way, I felt unworthy of her. But we would make it up to her. I was certain. I'd spend the rest of my life making sure that she was loved and taken care of. This was only the beginning of our lifetime together, after all.

"Mm, good morning," Tiffany said softly.

"Good morning," I said, trying to match how quiet she was being.

She still hadn't opened her eyes, but her dark eyelashes fanned out against her cheeks in a beautiful way.

"Damn, you're perfect," I said, tucking her long blonde hair behind her ear and letting my eyes trail down her neck to the swell of her perky breasts. If I'd been a photographer, there would be no way I'd be able to stay in bed and just stare at her. I would have wanted to jump up and grab my camera so I could capture the exquisiteness of my mate for all of time.

She opened her eyes and stared up at me, looking a little wary. "What do you mean?" she asked, pulling the sheet higher so her pink nipples disappeared from my view.

I tried not to be too disappointed that she was covering herself up.

It wasn't like she was a super confident woman of the world. Not yet anyway. I grinned at her. "Well, let's start with your perfect face, your cute nose, and your stubborn chin." I kissed the tip of her nose, then her plump lips, just because I could; not because my cock was beginning to stir beneath the sheets now that she was awake.

"Yeah…"

"You're determined, courageous, and obviously stubborn," I said, then kissed her forehead and both cheeks this time.

She drew back to frown at me. "You know all this already, do you?"

"Absolutely."

"Anything else?" she asked, and the men on either side of us began to stir.

I reached under the covers, flipped her onto her back, and climbed on top of her possessively. "Yeah," I growled. "You're so hot I can't wait for you to have our babies."

Her eyes widened as her legs opened for me.

I didn't try to slide inside her just yet; I didn't trust her body not to be sore still from last night.

"You want to have kids soon, too?" she whispered.

I grinned. "Sweetheart, with you? Even today isn't too soon."

She turned her head toward Ollie. "Do you all feel that way?"

Ollie slid forward and kissed her lips, getting too close to me in that move. "Yeah. Of course."

I bumped forward, pressing my hard cock against Tiffany's pussy.

She flinched.

I withdrew straight away. "Tender?"

She nodded, sitting up, her pink-tipped breasts just calling out to be kissed. "Can we have a shower then head back to the pack? I'm really excited to see if our mating has changed anything back home."

"Yeah, of course," I said, sliding off the bed and standing, willing my cock to behave and go down. Even after being rejected so nicely, I was still more than enthusiastic for her.

Tiffany got up, eyeing my wayward appendage. "I suppose, if you like…" Worry filled her eyes.

There was no way I was going near her if she was feeling like that.

The other two guys were already tugging on their clothes already, anyway—we all silently agreed.

I reached out for her and pulled her close. "No. We'll wait until you want us again."

"Oh, it's not that I don't want you," she said, running her hands up my arms, while pressing her naked body into mine.

I shivered and forced myself to focus. "No. You're sore, and there's a lot going on today. Let's get dressed and head over to the pack." That was the absolute last thing I wanted to do, though.

She went up on her tiptoes and kissed me, the sweetness of her lips making me moan with a renewed hunger. "Thanks, Jase." She bounded over to her clothes and dressed.

Damn it. I wasn't prepared for how desperately I'd want my mate. I ran a hand down my face, then lumbered over to my own pile of clothes and pulled on my jeans and shirt from last night. "You looked pretty wiped out when you zipped in last night, Ollie," I said. "What happened there?"

Ollie shrugged. "Not sure. Bella said it's normal to feel shit when you first transport. Or get transported. Don't know what it's called."

Tiffany giggled from the corner. "It's called a transportational spell. And yeah, it affects shifters the most. Though I'm not sure why exactly. But I've been told its kind of like a bad travel sickness."

Ollie pulled on his work boots and grinned. "It was worth it to get to you last night. And I'd do it again."

I rolled my eyes. "You just wanted to make a dramatic entrance."

The guys laughed and together we made our way out of the motel and onto the street.

I filled my lungs with fresh air, breathing deep. The sun was warm on my face, the air crisp. It wasn't just a new day, but a new start to our life. I took Tiffany's hand and began walking toward our car. "Do you want to grab some breakfast, or..."

"I really want to just get to Ruby's. We can probably get some food at Milly's or something if you guys are hungry," she offered.

I opened the car door.

Tiffany jumped inside. She really was desperate to get home.

I slid into the driver's seat, a little disappointed that we couldn't spoil our girl with sex and breakfast in bed this morning.

Ollie and Fin climbed into the back of the car, ready to go.

I turned the key in the ignition. I needed to focus. Today wasn't about us. There was a lot more going on with Tiffany, and her family, and the pack.

"Do you go to Milly's a lot?" I asked, as we started the drive back to the pack.

Tiffany burst out laughing. "You could say I've practically *lived* there the past month or so."

"Why would you do that?" I asked. "The burgers are good and all. But..."

She bit her lip and glanced out the window. "You're going to think I'm crazy."

"Not likely," Fin said. "Tell us."

Tiffany sighed loud enough to be heard throughout the car. "I was the last one of my friends to find my soul mate, and since we all assumed that my mates would be from your pack as well, Jackson and Billy recommended I hang around Milly's since the pack *all* go in there. But sitting there by myself, day after day, just made me feel lonelier. And since I'm a witch, not many of the guys even wanted to chat with me, let alone look at me as being their possible mate, so..." She crossed her arms over her chest.

I reached across the car to grip her knee. "Of course, they didn't come over. They weren't your mates, gorgeous. And I'm sorry you had to wait so long for us to come home."

She turned to me and pouted prettily. "Yeah. You guys should have been here waiting for me. I would have found you so much earlier."

I smiled at her, then looked back at the road, turning into the pack's territory. "We're almost at Ruby's place, so hopefully you'll get some good news soon."

Tiffany slid to the edge of her seat. "Can you imagine if the spell has broken? We would be total heroes." She laughed to herself.

I glanced at the rearview mirror and at the two other guys. I didn't know anything, *literally* anything about curses, but I couldn't imagine them being broken easily. "Let's go see," I said as I pulled the car into a park on the opposite side of the street to where Jackson lived. "Looks like there's a few people here."

"Yeah," she said, pointing to a small blue mini. "That's my mom's car. And there's Ruby's mom. Looks like everyone's here." Tiff got out of the car, crossed the road, and rushed up to the front door.

We got out of the car more slowly.

A cold premonition rolled over me. There was no cheering coming from inside the house, and there was no happiness abounding in the streets. I would have assumed that if we'd broken the spell that had held our pack hostage for over twenty-two years, there would have been some sign of a celebration. "What do you think?" I asked Ollie and Fin. "Do you think anything will be different?"

Both guys looked at me, dread in their eyes.

"Nope," Ollie said, glancing down at the sidewalk and thrusting both hands into his pockets. "I think our mate is going to be sorely disappointed soon and we're going to have to deal with the fall out."

Tiffany glanced over her shoulder as she opened the front door, a huge grin on her face. She called out. "Come on, guys!" And ran into the house.

I groaned. "I know we're not warlocks or anything, but I've got a feeling this is going to be bad."

Fin shuddered. "Me too. And I don't want Tiffany to be upset, but she's going to be."

A soft cry came from inside the house.

My ears pricked up. "You guys hear that?"

Ollie groaned. "Yep. Shifter hearing sucks sometimes. Let's go."

I thrust my hands into my jeans pockets too and led the charge across the road and up to the front door. Someone was crying inside, and every part of me hurt to think it was our new mate.

Tears flowed down my face as I stared at my best friend lying on her death bed. Ruby was as pale as Snow White from the fairytale, but her lips weren't a ruby red, and her hair wasn't a raven black. Instead, my friend's normally lustrous red hair was limp, and carrot colored. Even her lips were pale.

"What's happened to her?" I sobbed, stumbling over to the bed. I slid onto the bed with her and reached for her hand. "I thought the stasis spell was going to help her stay in a stable condition!"

My mom put an arm around my shoulders. "It's meant to, honey.

But unfortunately, as you can see, she's just getting worse, and a stasis spell is only ever temporary."

My throat burned with tears, and I swallowed hard to force the lump down so I could speak again. I'd been hoping, so much, that I would arrive at Ruby's to find her awake and healthy, and our father's human again. *Stupid, Tiffany. Stupid.* As if I was going to be central to breaking the spell.

Bella was sitting on the other side of the bed.

Ruby's mom hovered around the room.

"Our moms have done everything they can, Tiff," Bella said. "But it's possible we're going to have to..."

"No," I said, shaking my head. "*No.* You can't. We need more time."

Bella cleared her throat.

I turned around to face her.

"Have you mated with your triad?"

I nodded, another tear slipping unwanted down my cheek. *Traitor. I'm trying to be strong here.* "Yeah, I did. I was hoping it would help."

Bella smiled softly. "Yeah, so did I. Obviously our happiness isn't linked to breaking this curse, after all."

I wiped away the next tear that fell. "Only our deaths."

"Don't talk like that," Mom said. "We're not going to let anything happen to you. And we're going to save Ruby. There has to be a way."

"What about her baby?" I asked.

Jackson, who I hadn't noticed hanging around the back corner of the room, stood up and walked out. That answered my question.

My guys' voices came from the front of the house, and a wave of happiness spread through me. There *was* some good to focus on, but not here. Not today. Rather than railing against the inevitable, I chose to focus on what could be done. "So, what are our options?"

"Abort the pregnancy is probably the best one at this stage," my mom said. and

Ruby's mom sobbed. She covered her mouth and closed her eyes.

My heart went out to Sherie. I loved Ruby like a sister, but her mom must be in so much anguish over this decision. Not that we really had much of a choice it seemed. Lose one or lose them both.

"Okay," I said, nodding, taking it all in. "But what else?"

My mom sniffed, her eyes filled with sadness. "There isn't anything else."

"How long can you give us before you do anything?" I asked. *Forgive me, Ruby.*

Mom glanced over at Sherie. "About twenty-four hours. No more. After that, I don't think we'll be able to bring Ruby back at all."

That was another day. One more day. We had time. Then I realized we were missing someone. Bella's mom wasn't present. "Where's Kathy?"

"She's at the church, talking to some of the Coven members," Bella said. "We got a lead on where Tabitha had disappeared to, and Mom was just following up."

"What lead?"

"Her mom," Sherie said. "She still lives in town."

"Her mom?" I asked. "Why would that be important?"

"Oh! We didn't tell you," Bella said. "We found out that Tabitha was actually the daughter of the old High Warlock. He never married her mom, and it was all hush-hush when she was born... but that's why she's on the council. Or was. And why she's such a strong witch."

"You mean *bitch*," I corrected, flicking my hair over my shoulder, fire brewing inside me.

Bella chuckled.

Even Sherie gave me a half smile against her tears.

Mom tapped me on the shoulder.

I turned to give her my attention.

"But it also explains why she cursed you three last month and attacked Bella's mates."

I nodded. It was starting to make sense. They were right. "And why she hates wolf shifters so much."

"What do you mean?" Mom asked, tilting her head.

"She was *really* nasty to Ruby when we went to the church to ask them questions," I said. "She told her that she was a traitor. If her father hated wolf shifters so much that he cursed the whole pack, then he probably passed that prejudice onto her." Bigotry and hatred ran in families. Not the way blue eyes did, of course. It was taught. Handed down. It wasn't a coincidence.

"Do you really think the answer lies with the High Warlock and his daughter?" Bella asked.

I shrugged. "It looks like it might. The High Warlock told the pack Elders that he cursed them using our moms. Then Tabitha told us the spell was grounded with us. Which sucks by the way. Now we learn she's actually his daughter, so of course she knew about all that from the very beginning." The pieces of the puzzle were all clicking into place.

"But how the hell do we break the spell without dying?" I asked, more to myself.

According to Tabitha, us dying was the only way we were going to lift the spell. *But then she would say that, wouldn't she? She probably just wants us dead along with the wolves.*

"We could look into the past and see what they did. How they did it. See if the answer is there," Bella whispered fiercely, like we were holding a conspiracy meeting.

"Bella, *no.* You can't," my mom said flatly, like it was absolutely not an option.

"She can't, what?" I didn't understand. "And why would Bella do it?"

Bella stared at me. "Because the moms need to stay here and keep Ruby stable. They can't leave. But I can."

"It's dangerous to look into the past, Bella. You know you're not meant to," my mom said.

Sherie chewed on her bottom lip. She looked worried, but not enough to intervene, apparently—not when her own daughter's life was on the line.

Ollie stuck his head in and met my gaze "Are you okay, gorgeous?"

I waved my hand at him. It was obvious he didn't want to step into the room with all the witches and their emotions charging the space.

"Yeah, I'm okay. You guys catch up with Jackson and I'll be out in a bit."

He winked at me and smiled at Bella. "Thanks again for last night, Bella."

She lifted her chin and nodded like a teacher admonishing him. "I'm just glad you got your ass into gear and asked for help."

"Never too old to learn, I guess," he said. With that, he popped back out.

I glanced at Bella. "Thank you for helping him get to me last night."

Bella ran a hand through her hair. "It was nice to be asked, actually."

I didn't muse on the fact that Bella had bonded with one of my mates. I could feel the tiny barb of jealousy and tried hard to push it away. In the past, Bella wouldn't have even looked at a man. Now that she was bonded to three of them, she seemed more confident about, well, *everything*.

I shook myself. "Back to the past thing. I don't really understand what you want to do, and why it's so dangerous."

Bella watched Ruby before replying. "Scrying into the future or the past is frowned upon, but I've always been good at it."

"So, you can look into the past and see what they did to us? Really? Even back before we were born?"

Bella glanced at Sherie, then back at me. "Yeah, I can."

"It's dangerous, Bella!" Sherie said, clearly realizing how serious Bella was about endangering herself. "You don't understand! Your mind could get lost in the past, forever."

"We don't have any other choice," Bella said stiffly with determination. "What other solutions have you come up with?" Bella put both hands on her hips and held Sherie's eye.

Sherie finally collapsed on the bed and faced her daughter, caressing Ruby's cheek. "She wouldn't want you to put your life on the line, Bella. I know that much."

"I can do this," Bella said. "In fact, I think we should do it right now."

Sherie jumped to her feet. "We should wait for your mom, at least, please."

"There's no time," Bella said. "We need to work out what he did so we can undo it. That might take us the full day, maybe longer. We have to start as soon as possible." Bella grabbed my hand and tugged me toward the door to the bedroom. "Can you ask your mates to wait outside? I'll get set up in the dining room." She pulled me into the lounge.

My three gorgeous mates were all milling around the island in the kitchen.

Jackson was frying up eggs and bacon by the smell of it and toast was piling up.

"Maybe we can do it in the front room?" I asked.

The small lounge at the front of the house was more like a formal sitting room.

"Everything okay, gorgeous?" Ollie asked, turning around to look at me as he bit down on some buttery toast.

I nodded. "Bella's going try a spell that might help us find out where this curse came from in the first place."

His eyebrows climbed high on his forehead. "Cool. Need us for anything?"

I grinned at him. I loved that he offered, but what was a wolf shifter going to do to help with a scrying spell?

"Do you want some breakfast?" Ollie asked me, grabbing for a plate.

I shook my head. I was too nervous to eat. "I'll join you guys later."

"Come on," Bella said, and dragged me into the front room.

My mom appeared through the door as we settled on the ground.

Bella pulled her scrying crystal from her bag. "Got it with me this time," she said with a smile.

"You know, a séance would probably be more effective for this,"

Mom said as she kneeled down on the carpet on the other side of the coffee table. "Since the High Warlock passed away last year."

Bella arranged the crystal ball on the table and knelt in front of it, her attention zeroing in on the object. "I don't want to speak to the dead. I just want to know what happened that day." Bella closed her eyes as the purple magic began to swirl inside the orb.

"You didn't explain why this was so dangerous," I whispered to my mom.

"We don't know exactly why," Mom said, her gaze flicking from me to Bella, and back again. "We just know that looking into the past can be dangerous. Like Sherie said, we know a witch's consciousness can get lost…"

Bella gasped and took her hands off the orb. Her eyes flew open, and she stared at me, her expression wracked with shock. "Oh, my God. It wasn't him."

I frowned. "What do you mean? Who's he? And what didn't he do?"

"It wasn't the High Warlock," she said. "The spell he cast on us when our moms were pregnant was literally just to stop us from shifting. He didn't do anything else. He didn't harm us in any way beyond that."

I frowned at her. "That's impossible. You said that the wolf Elders admitted that the High Warlock told them that he, himself had cursed them."

Bella pressed her lips together. "Well, he was lying. Or someone else did the curse instead and he took the credit for it. Either way, it wasn't him."

I slumped. "But we need to find out who did it and how. Can you follow the curse back in time? Or follow Tabitha maybe? What's another way to find the solution?"

Bella straightened up, pulled a hair elastic from her wrist, and tied her long dark hair up in a messy bun on top of her head. She was getting her serious on. "I can try."

"Bella," my mom said, "I know you two are ignoring me, but I'll warn you again, this is *dangerous.*"

Bella shrugged. "I don't care. We're running out of time, and I know Ruby would do the same for me."

This time when Bella focused on the crystal ball, I felt the energy in the room shift. Something cold, and evil, was here. "Um, Bella... I'm not sure about this..."

Too late. She was already in. The smoke was swirling inside the scrying crystal, but this time the magic wasn't purple. It had turned a strange, sickly, and murky green. Sweat dotted Bella's brow and then she began to shake.

CHAPTER 14
TIFFANY

Worry punched me in the stomach, making me sick, and I reached out for Bella.

"*No!* Don't touch her," Mom warned, her command like the crack of a whip.

My arm froze mid-air.

The front door slammed open a moment later.

"What is she doing?" Kathy cried as she ran in and kneeled beside her daughter.

Bella's forehead creased as she frowned, concentrating hard on the crystal ball in front of her. "The key isn't Tabitha..." she panted, grimacing as she searched deeper, further into the past for our answer. "It's... her *mom*."

I gasped. "Could her mom have cursed the wolves? Maybe the High Warlock told her about us, and she linked the spell to us as babies?"

Bella shook her head trying not to break her focus. "No, it's not that. There's more—" Bella threw her head back suddenly and gasped for air, her eyes wide.

"Bella, come back," I pleaded, resisting the urge to grab her hand. "You've done enough."

She shook her head, her eyelids fluttering uncontrollably as her mouth fell open.

I looked between Kathy and my mom, panic swelling in my chest. "What's wrong with her? Why isn't she breaking the connection?"

Kathy leaned forward, studying her daughter intently. "She's looking for an answer, perhaps one she shouldn't know. The reason we ban looking into the past is because we don't know what's there; or how it will affect the future, or the person doing the scrying. Bella is forcing herself well past her limits for Ruby and the baby."

"What can we do?" I asked, scrambling to my feet in frustration. My heart thundered in my chest, and I couldn't stop tugging on my hair. I wanted to save Ruby and the baby too, but none of us wanted Bella to sacrifice herself! "What can you see, Bella?" I asked in desperation.

"They want us... to die..." Bella gasped. Then she whimpered in a way that had me kneeling quickly next to her again, desperate to help.

I looked across the table at my mom. "What do I do?"

She shook her head. "We can't do anything, Tiffany. I told you it was too dangerous. Bella knew the risks. This was her choice."

I slammed my hand down on the coffee table in outrage. "At least Bella is trying to do something to help! You three have done nothing but want to end Ruby's pregnancy!" That wasn't entirely fair, I realized. And yelling at my mom wasn't going to help.

Bella began to scream, her eyes wild.

Tears ran down my face. I felt completely helpless.

Then Bella fell deathly silent and slumped toward me.

I caught her in my arms, fully expecting to be shocked with the power of her magic, but there was nothing. I glanced at the crystal ball. The murky green smoke had dissipated, but there was a crack in the glass. "What happened to her?" I asked, hoisting my friend up as best I could.

Kathy reached over and checked Bella's pulse.

I stared at Bella's mom, my mouth open as I awaited an answer. *No. It's not possible.* "Tell me she's not…"

"She's alive," Kathy said. "Barely. Let's get her up."

I shook my head, determined to be of some use in this God-awful situation. "I've got this." I uttered the same levitation spell that I'd used on Ruby and slowly lifted Bella up in the air. I walked her carefully toward the bed where my other friend slept.

"What the fuck?" Ollie said, jumping to his feet from where he sat on a kitchen stool.

"What happened to her?" Jackson demanded, racing around the island to come up next to where Bella floated through the air as though she was asleep like some fairy tale princess.

I didn't bother wiping the tears from my face. I needed both hands to hold onto the spell that was carrying my friend to the bedroom. "Bella tried to look into the past, to see who cursed us, but she went too far—we think. She's passed out." I looked up at Jackson pointedly, trying to silently communicate that this really wasn't good.

He paled and nodded, understanding flickering in his gaze. "I'll go find Elliot." He raced off without another word.

I continued to maintain the levitation spell to get Bella into Ruby's bedroom. "Can you pull back the blankets, please?" I asked Sherie, who was still there, sitting a silent vigil by her daughter's bedside.

Sherie jumped up to help and tugged back the covers. "What happened?"

I lowered Bella gently, resting her on the mattress, her head on the pillow. Then I let go of the spell and pulled the blankets up over her with care. "We don't know," I said without looking at her. "She went searching for answers, and she hasn't come back again."

Sherie hurried over to the other moms, their frantic whispers filling the air around me.

But I couldn't drag my gaze from my two best friends. The sisters of my heart. My blood cousins.

Ruby was my fierce friend. She was the outspoken one. Eternally stubborn and great at magic. Bella, meanwhile, was my smart friend. She was good at everything, except speaking in large crowds. She was the most powerful of us all and she made me so grateful to be her friend.

Another tear ran down my face and this time I grabbed a tissue from the bedside table and wiped it away. "What are we going to do?" I asked the moms as I turned around to look at them.

They turned to face me.

All three of them seemed as lost as I felt. And despite the twenty-five years of life experience they had on me, I felt like I was the one who was older and wiser and more in control. "We have to do something," I said, "but what?"

My mum bit her lip. "All I can think is that we've already lost two of you and we can't lose you as well, Tiffany."

"Why would you lose me as well?" I asked. Then it came to me like a bright flash of lightning—an idea. "What if you put me into some sort of deathlike state?" I asked.

"What do you mean?" Mom countered, swallowing hard.

"I mean that the curse is linked to all three of us and our lives, and according to you, both Bella and Ruby are already as close to death as you can get. If you guys use magic to put me under as well, maybe we could trick the curse long enough for it to break!"

"That's crazy," Mom said, shaking her head.

"It may be," I replied with a smile, "but if it works then we might be able to save everyone and we won't have to die to do it."

The moms looked at each other, and there was finally a flare of hope glimmering through their fear.

I used that to my advantage. "Don't you all want our fathers back in human form? Don't you want to spend the rest of your lives loving the men that you should've had by your sides for the last twenty-three years? Don't you want to take back the lives that were stolen from you?"

Sherie looked at my mom, then at Kathy.

They were thinking about it.

"Could it really work?" Sherie asked.

Kathy tapped her lips as though she were reasoning out the logistics of it all. "I suppose... if it's true that the girls' lives are linked to the curse... But to do it, we'd actually need to stop their hearts. All at the same time. It'd be the only sure way to really fool the spell into accepting they were all gone."

I swallowed hard, the lump in my throat threatening to constrict my speech. "Could you do it?" I pressed. "Without really killing us, preferably?"

"If we did it as one, we could hold them that way for... what's safe?" Mom asked.

"Sixty seconds at the very most," Kathy said firmly.

Sherie nodded. "Sixty seconds should be safe enough, for Ruby's baby as well. If we tilt them all upside down the blood will rush closer to their hearts and brains."

My heart began to pound with fear. They were really going to do it. They were going to stop our hearts so that technically, we would all be 'dead'. "Okay, how do we do this then?" I asked, my voice breaking with stress.

My mom turned toward me. "We don't know if it will work, Tiff. Not for certain. Perhaps it's not worth the risk."

"Of course, it is!" I blazed. "You're three talented and powerful witches. Surely you can do something. What would you need?"

Mom turned to Kathy. "What do you think, Kath?"

Kathy walked to the head of the bed and put her hand out to feel Bella's cheek. "I think we need to do *something*. And it might be our best bet. This is only getting worse and worse. We almost lost them all to Tabitha's spell last month and now... this?" She sighed. "We need anchors."

"Anchors?" I repeated.

"Yes," Kathy said, spinning toward me. "The three of us can conduct the spell, but it would be safer if you three had another person to hold onto you during the minute you're gone. Someone to pull you back—someone you love."

"Our mates!" I cried. "Just one? Or would all three be better?"

Our moms exchanged glances.

"Traditionally, one lover would be enough. But since the three of you have three men each, I don't see why more would be a bad thing," Sherie said.

"It may even be enough to bring Bella back to us," Kathy said. "I can tweak the spell to pull Bella back up to consciousness as they rise."

"I can do the same for Ruby," Sherie said, "if we decide we want them all awake." A tear slid down her face.

It was in that moment I realized that our moms had planned on aborting Ruby's baby while she was still in a magical coma.

"Bring us all back," I demanded in a tone that challenged any opposition. *Ruby has the right to be a part of the decision.* Even if I knew deep down what she would likely choose. "If you can," I added.

"If we can," Mom repeated.

I tapped my fingers on the end of the bed, noticing for the first time just how big the damn thing was. There was about ten feet between Ruby and Bella. *I've got to get one of these when all this mess is sorted out.* Last night worked well pretty with the two king beds pushed together, but this would be better. I shook myself to clear my mind. "So, what's the next step? Gather all our mates?"

"Yes," Sherie said. "Meanwhile, we need to go home and collect some specific herbs for the incantation."

Kathy nodded, frowning in thought. "I need to get a book from my house too. And my wand."

My eyebrows climbed up my forehead. We didn't use wands much, almost at all, really. We were taught from a young age to do magic without them. But from what Bella had told me in the past, it would magnify a witch's power when necessity called for it.

"So, what?" I asked. "Meet back here in... an hour?"

It would take our moms half an hour to drive to town and back.

Sherie shook her head. "No. Make it fifteen minutes. We'll travel the quick way. We don't have the time to waste."

The three moms stood together, shared a look, clicked their fingers, and they were gone.

I swayed on my feet, a wave of exhaustion making me close my eyes and reach for the foot board.

We'd been running for too long. Since before we were born our fathers had been cursed, and with that spell, it had cursed our whole lives; us girls to be fatherless and our mothers to be husbandless. It was time for it all to end. No matter what price we had to pay. No matter what I had to do. There had to be an end in sight.

I walked out the door the old-fashioned way and went about explaining to my mates what I was about to do.

Elliot the Alpha tore into the house looking for Bella like a bull in a China shop. Jackson had obviously successfully conveyed the seriousness of our situation.

I sighed. It was time to tell nine of the most possessive, strong, paranormal men that their mates were about to die... And that they had to hold us while our hearts stopped.

Lucky me.

CHAPTER 15

OLIVER

"Sorry, what?" There was *no way* I just heard my mate correctly. "Ah, no. You're not fucking doing that!"

"I have to. We all have to," Tiff said, impassioned.

I shook my head and growled in frustration, crossing my arms over my chest to stop myself from reaching for her. Why wasn't anyone else telling her she was crazy? Surely the other guys felt the same way I did?

"You want to... die?" Fin asked, his tone showing he was as clearly as baffled as I was.

"Hell no!" She glared at him in indignation. "How can you even think that?"

All three of us, her mates, relaxed into the couch a little easier upon hearing that.

"But that doesn't mean I don't have to do it," she added quietly.

I groaned and sat up straighter. *Great*, all that tension was back. "I... don't get it," I said, then glanced around the room at the other guys.

Tiffany had sent Jackson and Elliot out to find the others, and within ten minutes, all nine of us witch mates were crammed into the lounge together. Three Alphas. Five Betas. And a warlock-wolf just for something different. We made for a pretty impressive unit, and in a way, I felt lucky to be included in such an elite group.

"Explain it to me again," Elliot said, his voice rough with emotion. "What happened to Bella?"

Tiffany swallowed hard.

I reached for her hand, gripping it to offer my support.

Elliot was by far the most intimidating of us all, and although I could tell he was trying hard to control his anger, it was still currently directed at Tiffany—*my* mate.

"Um..."

There was a glimmer of light, then suddenly three older ladies materialized into the kitchen, chattering away like birds.

"Oh," one of them said.

Then all three turned to look at us.

The one on the left, who had dark hair, grinned. "That is *a lot* of men." Tiffany's mom put a hand over her mouth, I think to stop the laugh from exploding through. Now really wasn't the time to laugh.

To be fair, though, from her perspective, *yeah*, there were a lot of guys in this room and a shit load of testosterone.

Elliot stood up.

I stared up at him. *Damn*, he was tall.

"Kathy. What happened to Bella?" he asked, unsatisfied with Tiff's slow start.

Bella's mom stepped forward, putting a trembling hand on the marble kitchen counter that stood between the women and us. "I don't know for sure," she answered. "But she was doing a spell that allowed her to look into the past. And when she did, she seems to have gotten lost somehow. The magic that it required was too much for her to take. We rarely delve into the past for exactly this reason."

Bella's other mates stood up.

"What can we do?" they asked in unison.

I stood up as well. "We don't want Tiffany risking herself."

Tiff glared at me.

"But we'll do anything to help you fix this," I added quickly.

"Good," Tiffany's mom said, stepping forward. "We're going to need all nine of you to make sure we get our daughters back."

"Explain that to me." Fin said, coming to stand next to me.

"Basically," Kathy began, "we need all nine of you to hold your mates in your arms, so that when we re-start their hearts and bring them back to us, they have an anchor to hold onto. Something worth returning for. The journey back isn't always easy."

"We'd do it," Tiffany's mom interrupted, glancing at her witch friends, "but the spell itself is going to need all of our combined magic and power, so we need to be able to focus on that."

"If you need a timekeeper," Jase said, "I'm freakishly good at measuring time. I can tell you exactly when sixty seconds is up."

Tiffany's mom smiled gently at him. "We'll use someone's phone and alarm just to be sure, but... there is a possibility... if something goes wrong with us, or the spell, or the electronics in the room, then yes. Keep count of the sixty seconds they're going under for, just to be safe. Please."

Jase was weirdly good at telling the time. He never wore a watch, and yet he still always knew what the time was, right down to the minute. Or how long had lapsed from one event to another.

Jackson clapped his hands together. "All right, how are we doing this?"

"Let's go into the bedroom," Kathy advised, and she began arranging people.

Ruby's mates all got on the massive bed to take her in their arms.

"Make sure her feet are raised above her head. The blood needs to stay in their brains and hearts as long as possible, so hopefully they won't even realize their hearts stopped beating for a whole minute," said Kathy.

I held Tiffany's hand in mine and dragged her closer to me. "We only just found you. You are not allowed to die on us. Do you hear me?" I whispered in her ear. I understood that this spell was purely a ploy, a trick, of sorts to break the curse. But Tiffany's heart *really* was going to stop beating and it was obvious from the fear I could scent in the room, that there was a real danger here of things going terribly wrong.

Tiffany turned her head.

Our gazes connected, clashing with the heat and passion of two stubborn people in love.

I swallowed hard as the realization hit me. I loved this woman already. *Now I really can't lose her.*

Tiffany pressed her lips to mine, kissing me like a woman drowning, searching for the air within me.

I kissed her with every pent-up emotion inside of me. I held nothing back as my tongue swept inside her mouth and my hands squeezed her body tight to me.

Then, too soon, she pulled away from me, smiling up at me with tears in her eyes. "I'm not going anywhere. But what you three need to understand, is that these two girls are the closest things I've ever had to sisters. They're my cousins by blood, but they've been my whole entire world since we were kids. Nothing can stop me from helping them."

"Then we're here for you, whatever you need," Jase said, stepping up and tugging Tiff into him.

I glanced at the bed, where Bella's mates had picked her up and now held her in their arms.

Ruby's mates had done the same.

"It's your turn, Tiff," Tiffany's mom said as she touched her daughter gently on the arm.

Tiff inhaled sharply, then nodded. "Let's do this." She climbed onto the end of the massive bed.

I took a moment to assess the size of it. "Whoa, is this like... custom made?"

Jackson glanced over at me, where he sat at the other end holding Ruby's head. "Yeah."

He didn't expand further, so I made a mental note to ask about it later—when all this was over.

Jase and Fin sat down.

Tiffany lay over them.

I climbed on too.

She stretched her legs over me. "You'll need to hold my legs up once the spell is going," Tiffany said to me, her eyes wide with barely restrained fright.

I nodded. *She's so brave.* "Not a problem, babe. I've got you."

"We're ready to start," Bella's mom said.

The moms walked around the room and stood at each end of the bed.

One on the left, one on the right, one at the end near us.

A triangle of power.

Three daughters. Three mothers. Three mates for Ruby, Bella, and Tiffany.

Strange pattern, really.

"It's important than none of you freak out, run out, or attempt to touch us, okay?" Bella's mom said as she tossed some sort of smelly powder in the air. She spoke some strange words, then using her magic, she made the powder hover over the three girls and sprinkle down over them.

Tiffany lay back and didn't say anything. She closed her eyes and began to breathe deeply.

"Why would we do that?" Fin asked.

Kathy's lips trembled into a weary smile. "Because it's about to get intense in here. We're trying to break a twenty-three-year-old curse and none of us have done this spell before. Instructions still hold. No matter what, do not let go of your mates. You are their literal anchor in this world, gentlemen, and without you, we might all lose them forever."

My heart squeezed tight at the thought of losing Tiffany for even a minute, let alone forever.

Kathy narrowed her eyes and glared at me. "And *do not* leave that bed."

I nodded once. *I got it.*

The three protective moms moved into their final positions.

Kathy pulled out a wand from one of the pockets hidden within the long folds of her skirts.

My mouth dropped open. "Whoa." *A fucking wand!*

"Concentrate!" Fin snarled, whacking me in the chest.

I growled at him and gripped Tiffany's legs tighter. "I am, but this is some freaky shit!"

All three moms began to speak in a language I didn't understand. Smoke soon filled the room, beginning at carpet level then rising up, like we were in some sort of band with special effects on stage or something.

"Who turned on the smoke machine?" I mumbled under my breath.

There was a loud growl from the other side of the bed.

I took that as a sign that I needed to shut the fuck up. It sounded like Elliot, or one of the other Alphas.

Tiffany began to gasp and struggle against us.

"Hold her," Jase said.

All three of us clung tighter to our mate as she kicked and moaned in pain.

The mom's voices grew higher, and louder.

Tiffany screamed.

I swore under my breath and held tight to my mate. The sound unnerved my very soul. Every instinct in me raged to protect her, but there was nothing I could do but follow the witches' instructions. *This is getting seriously intense.*

Tiffany stopped, sagging over us. Then she stopped breathing.

"Lift her legs!" someone yelled from across the smoke-filled bedroom.

I jumped, then grabbed hold of Tiffany's ankles and lifted them high in the air.

She was still. And cold. And pale.

I shook from the stress of it all and time seemed to cease holding any meaning.

"Oh, my God. Oh, my God," Jase was saying beside me. "That's thirty seconds."

My wolf howled inside my mind and I began to shiver. *No. No!* I would not shift. I would not abandon my mate or ruin this spell. There was too much at stake!

The moms' continued chanting.

"That's fifty seconds!" Jase yelled out, a bit louder this time.

White light suddenly erupted from the center of the bed and exploded through the room. The aftershock swept through all of us, humming with magical electricity. Wind kicked up around the room, and the curtains flapped so hard that the curtain rod twisted free.

My vision was obscured by the strength of the wind in my face. I lifted Tiffany's legs higher, until her butt was up in the air as well out of sheer panic.

"That's sixty seconds!" Jase yelled at the top of his lungs over the roar of wind that filled the room. "Stop!"

The moms ceased chanting. Then, as one, they collapsed to the ground.

The wind died, the smoke evaporated as though it had never been, and an unsettling stillness descended.

Next to me, Tiffany's mom lay in a heap on the floor. Her eyes were closed and her mouth was open as though she were panting for breath and utterly exhausted.

"Is she alive?" I asked to no one in particular. "Quick, check her breathing!"

Fin reached out and pressed his fingers against Tiffany's neck.

"Fuck, what have we done?" he said.

My heart pounded even harder than it already had been.

Jackson called out to his Beta. "Look, I can see her breathing, check her pulse. Quick Billy."

There was a frantic rush to check all three mates for their breathing, their heartbeat, any signs of life.

All the moms were still passed out and hadn't moved. Considering the sort of spell they'd just conducted, literally draining the life and taking the heartbeat from their daughters, I could only imagine how much effort and strength all three of the older witches had to exert to maintain control.

"Hang on, wait, look!" Jase said.

I stared at Tiffany's face. Her color began to return. The paleness that had haunted her cheeks disappeared and the pinkness came back. Then her perky, gorgeous breasts began to rise and fall with each breath she took.

She opened her eyes and looked up at us.

The tangible sense of relief that washed over me made me weak.

"Did it work?" she whispered, her voice hoarse.

CHAPTER 16
TIFFANY

I feel like I've been hit by a truck. My skin was clammy, my heart was pounding, and there was an overall fatigue throughout my whole body that was stifling. I felt completely drained of energy. And when I opened my eyes, I was still lying on my back with my legs in the air, fully clothed and surrounded by all three of my mates.

"Well?" I asked them, looking between each of their intense sets of eyes. "Did it work?"

Jase ran a hand over my forehead and down my cheek. "How do we know if it worked or not?" he lovingly asked.

I sighed. "Help me up, please." I reached for Jase and Fin.

They grabbed an arm each and slowly pulled me back up again.

Meanwhile, Ollie gently let my legs go.

Soon I was sitting upright on Ruby's bed, my head spinning. I turned around and glanced at my two best friends who were still being held by their mates. "How are they?" I asked. "Is Ruby okay? Is Bella all right?" I scoured their forms for signs of life. My heart was in my throat and my stomach was twisting with anxiety, but I counted my heartbeats... one, two, three. I held my breath.

Just as I was about to resign myself to the fact that my friends weren't going to wake, Bella's eyes fluttered open.

She sat up between her mates and put a hand to her head. "What happened?"

"Your scrying spell knocked you out," I said. "You put in too much power or something."

Bella shook her head at me. "No, it wasn't that. It was something in the past. Something in that group of witches and warlocks. I couldn't get out of there without the right information."

"What did you learn?" I asked. "Can you remember anything now?"

"Don't worry about any of that now," Tommy said evenly.

"You're alive," Elliot said. "That's all that matters."

Bella smiled at them but then she looked at me and said, "I have a few things to tell both of you."

I gazed over at Jackson who was still holding Ruby. "Is she awake?"

"I don't know," Jackson answered. "I think she's alive. Her heart is beating but she isn't waking up."

"Hang on, wait a second," Darren said. "Her eyelids are moving! I think she's waking up."

Excitement flashed through me, and I couldn't contain my smile as Ruby opened her eyes for the first time in days.

She looked from one person to another. "What's happened? What's everyone doing here?" Then she giggled. "And why is everyone in our bedroom?"

I scrambled across the bed as I laughed and dragged her into my arms, hugging her close while pushing her big mates out of the way. "I can't believe you're alive," I said, then pulled back and gazed at her. "How are you feeling?"

Ruby stared at me as though she didn't understand the question. "I'm okay, I suppose. How are you?"

I laughed out loud at her casual response. I couldn't help myself. It seemed simply amazing to me that she was sitting there looking at me and talking to me as though nothing was wrong—when half an hour ago we were concerned she wouldn't even make it through the day.

A sudden thought hit me and I jumped, sliding off the bed with excitement. "We need to go check and see if our dads are still in wolf form." I glanced down at Sherie, who was still lying on the floor. I kneeled beside her and put my fingers to her neck, checking for a pulse, to see if her heart was still beating. She seemed all right, so I told Ruby to see if she could do anything to get the moms to wake up.

I bolted out the door and into the backyard and stopped dead on the patio.

The three gray wolves, still in animal form, lounged on the grass.

I stumbled forward with so many mixed emotions pulsing through me that I couldn't stand. I pushed my hands against the wood of the railing as I stared at the wolves. It didn't work. There's no way it worked, if our dads were still in wolf form.

There was the sound of steps behind me and a hand slid across my shoulder. "Does this mean the spell tonight didn't work?" It was Ollie.

I looked up at him. "I don't think so. But it was worth a try."

I certainly had no regrets. We'd gotten Ruby back at least. But if the pack and our dads were part of the same spell, then the three of us being dead for one minute hadn't broken the curse.

Ollie kissed me gently and then led me back inside to the kitchen area for a glass of water. Within a few minutes, the room was full of people and this time Bella and Ruby were on their feet. The moms were up and about too, milling around and checking on everyone.

Someone's phone rang and Elliot reached for his cell. "Hey Dad, I'm just a little busy with something, can I call you—" he stopped, and then said, "No way! Seriously? I can't believe it." He turned to stare at me, his eyes wide. Something had happened. "Yeah, yeah, I'll tell them," Elliot said, then hung up the phone.

"What was it?" Tommy asked.

"You won't believe it," Elliott said, "but Cynthia gave birth today."

"Cynthia, as in Nathaniel's mate?" Tommy said.

"Yeah." Elliot grinned. "They thought they were having a boy… like we always do. But… she just had a little girl!"

"Bullshit," Tommy said.

Elliot laughed, his deep chuckle rolling through the room. "Yeah, that's kind of what I was thinking, but my dad would never bullshit about something like that."

Ruby's face lit up, her hand moving to her belly. "Does that mean we *did* break the spell? Could we have broken the curse on the pack?"

"But the dads are still wolves," I said. "We didn't break the curse."

Bella turned to me. "Unless the spell on our dads and the curse on the pack was done by two people, not one. They would have had to link each spell to two different things. If the pack's curse is linked to us, then by dying metaphorically and physically for a single minute, we've broken that curse. But if our dads' inability to return to human form was done by another witch or a warlock, then we need to find out the link to that."

I stared at her "You said you had to talk to Ruby and me about something you saw when you were scrying," I prompted.

Bella nodded slowly. "Yeah, I do, and it's starting to make more sense now that I know that the dads and the pack were affected by two different spells."

Our mates and the pack members started to chat happily over their cells, talking about the prospect of the curse finally being broken. It meant daughters for the pack. It meant mates for the sons of their friends.

I went over to Ruby and held her hand. "Do you think we can go and talk now?"

Although I was relieved that the pack's curse was finally broken, assuming the birth of the first daughter in twenty-three years proved that it had been, I was worried about the fact that our fathers were still in wolf form.

The moms stayed in the kitchen to prepare food. They were looking pale, but relieved.

Bella glanced that way and said, "Yeah, Ruby, is there anywhere we can go and have a quick chat about what I saw?"

Ruby nodded. "Let's go upstairs to one of the spare bedrooms, and let these guys celebrate the fact that the pack now has a future." Her hand slipped down to cover her stomach once more. "And hopefully, so do I..." A smile rippled on her lips, and I knew deep down that some part of her knew that she almost lost her life and that of her baby.

Ruby walked toward the stairs and called out to Jackson that she was just heading upstairs with us for ten minutes and would be back soon.

The three of us went up the stairs and into a bedroom with a nice queen-sized bed.

Ruby shut the door behind us. "Sit on the bed if you like," she said.

Ruby and I ended up sitting on the bed and faced Bella.

She paced up and down the bedroom.

"What did you see, Bella? Can you remember?" I asked.

"Yes. I remember everything. But before we move on, I need to say thank you. I know that you put yourself in harm's way for us."

Ruby glanced from Bella to me, and back again. "What did I miss?"

I laughed. "Only the fact that the curse on the pack almost killed you and your baby. The only way to save you was to try and get rid of the pregnancy, and even then the moms weren't sure that you would survive the process."

Ruby gasped, blatant surprise and pain on her face. Then she slid her hand down to hold her pregnant stomach. "They wouldn't..."

Bella smiled gently at her. "They would have, and almost did. Your mates and the moms would have done anything to save you, Ruby. I must admit that I was willing to do anything to save you, too." Tears slipped down her cheeks. "I'm so sorry."

Ruby nodded slowly. "I understand. I suppose if the roles were reversed, I would've done the same thing for either of you."

Bella smiled sadly again. "Well, Tiffany wouldn't have. She fought to save you and the baby. Elliot told me that it was her idea to get them to kill her, as well as us temporarily, to try and break the curse."

Ruby turned to me and smiled, tears in her eyes and glistening on her eyelashes. "Really? You fought for me and my baby?"

"Of course, I did," I said. "You're like a sister to me. Even more so."

"Thank you, Tiffany. I don't know how to thank you for saving me and my daughter. I think I would've been completely heartbroken if I'd woken up and she was gone."

I reached out and held Ruby's hands where they were lying in her lap. "I couldn't let them do what they wanted to do, even though I knew that their intentions were all good and they just wanted to save you."

"You did the right thing, obviously," Ruby said. "We broke the curse."

"We have one more thing to do," Bella said. "We need to break the curse on our dads, so we can finally have our families back together again."

"Who is it linked to?" Ruby asked.

"What do you mean, *who* is it linked to?" I asked.

Bella turned to me. "A spell this strong needs to be grounded in *someone*. It wasn't the High Warlock who did it though. He didn't do this side spell. It was someone who hates the wolves just as much as he did."

"Who was it, Bella?" Ruby asked, clutching her belly protectively.

I wanted to know the answer to the same question.

CHAPTER 17

TIFFANY

"Come on, Bella, please tell us." The need to know who we had to find and sort out was eating away at me. If it was one of the witches from the Coven, then we could handle that. If it was Tabitha? We might have more of a problem. No-one had seen her since she cursed us a month ago...

Bella crossed her arms over her chest and bit her lip, her expression one of anxiety.

Ruby jumped to her feet. "Come on! Tell us, Bella. *Please*."

Bella huffed out a big sigh. "I'm not sure what we're going to do about it. It was Tabitha's mother. She's the one who hates the wolves just as much as the old High Warlock did."

My mouth dropped open. *Is she serious?* The bad guy that we were chasing was some... what? Seventy-year-old witch?

"Seriously?" Ruby said, voicing my thoughts aloud. "What does she have against the pack?"

Bella shook her head sadly. "From what I could see while I was looking back into the past, there was a reason the High Warlock never married. He was in love with a woman who was the Fated Mate to one of the wolves in the pack, which meant that rather than marrying the High Warlock which she was destined to do according to our laws, she ran off and married the wolf shifter instead." She smiled suddenly, which surprised me.

What was funny about the situation?

Then she continued. "I'm pretty sure she was my grandmother, and Darren's as well."

Ruby chuckled at that too. "Darren will be *rapt* to hear that. He loves stories about our family."

I got to my feet since Ruby and Bella were now standing in the middle of the bedroom; I felt silly being the only one still sitting on the bed. "I'm sorry, I don't quite get why this is a big deal?" I couldn't work out the connection between Tabitha and our dads. *Sure, they were wolf shifters, but still...?*

Bella turned to me. "The High Warlock never married anyone. He went to his grave as an unmarried man still mourning the loss of the one woman he loved."

That didn't make sense. "But he had a daughter. Tabitha." I interjected. Had I missed something?

Bella smiled but it failed to reach her eyes. She still looked sad. "Yes, he did. That's the problem. He never married anyone because he could never love anyone but my grandmother. The woman who left him. But he sired a child with another woman, and I believe that Tabitha's mother loved him very much. She expected him to marry her and have more children and a life with her. But he never did."

"Why would he do that, though?" Ruby asked. "Because he couldn't get over your grandmother leaving him?"

"Probably," Bella said. "From what I saw, Tabitha's mother grew insanely jealous of my grandmother because of how the High Warlock loved her. So, she was left as a single mother raising a daughter, still living in the same town, within the same Coven, as a man that she loved, but who wouldn't marry her. And with that envy grew a hatred for the pack that only soured and continued to get worse over time."

"So, who did the curse that linked us to the pack?" I asked. "Was it Tabitha or the High Warlock?" I was getting confused about who'd done what. *God, hate convolutes so much!*

"I believe that Tabitha's mother did both spells," Bella said finally. "The spell that was grounded in us and was linked to the pack's 'infertility'. But she also did another spell to punish our fathers for daring to impregnate our mothers, powerful witches, when they had no right to —according to her. And I believe she grounded that spell in her own daughter, to ensure our mothers and fathers suffered as long as she did."

Ruby and I gasped in union.

I put a hand over my mouth. *No way.*

"She wouldn't do such a thing, surely?" Ruby said.

"I think she did," Bella answered. "It would make sense if she wanted our fathers punished as long as possible. Her daughter is about ten years older than us and will live a lot longer than her mother will. And as we already know, when the individual that the spell is grounded in dies, then the spell breaks."

I couldn't believe that a mother would use her own daughter to ground a spell born of such hatred. *Surely that could cause long term effects?* "So, does that mean we need to find Tabitha and..." I didn't want to have to voice aloud that we needed to kill her, which it seemed we obviously did. So, I decided on a slightly more tactful route. "Does that mean we need to find a way of unlinking the grounding, then? Because I'm not leaving our dads in wolf form forever. I want my dad back."

Bella and Ruby stared at me, neither speaking.

I'd stunned them. *Great.* I bit my lip, forcing the tears I felt burning in my eyes to retreat. "I've never said that out loud before, but I do. I can't believe that for so many years I thought they'd abandoned us and our moms. Imagine what it would've been like for them! To have to leave their pack and everything they'd ever known. *To leave us.* To miss out on everything they could've had in their life, all because some stupid witch decided that they'd overstepped some ridiculous personal mortality line." I wiped away the hot tears that fell on my cheeks and swallowed hard. It was all so unfair.

Bella nodded. "You're right. It sucks on such a major level and yes, to answer your question. We need to find Tabitha and we need to work out if there's any way of unlinking the grounding—other than death."

We all knew the answer to that. We'd spent a month researching the topic and hadn't found one single good answer.

"We can always ask our moms to do the heart stopping spell on Tabitha as well, maybe?" I said. "We did it. We survived. And it worked." I was willing to do anything to have my dad in my life.

"So, what are we going to do?" Ruby asked.

"We need to find Tabitha," Bella said, "but I think the key is going to be to find her mother."

That sounded ominous. Were we going to use her mom as bait? Or could we put some sort of spell on her mother that would attract Tabitha to come back to town? Assuming she'd left.

"Do you think we need to ask our mates for help?" I asked. I was pretty sure the wolves were going to want to help us out, but I was also a little worried that they wouldn't stop at a heart-stopping spell once they got their hands on the woman who had tried to kill us a month ago.

"I think Elliot would probably kill her if he found her," Bella said.

She looked truly worried at the prospect. Elliot was an Alpha's alpha, one of the strongest and largest men of the pack. He was also known for being uncontrollable and for having an almighty temper on him.

Bella seemed to be able to control him extremely well but if he came across the woman who had tried to kill his mate, and had almost succeeded, would he be able to control his wolf long enough to leave Tabitha unharmed?

Though that would unhook our dads from the spell.

"Well, we need to do something," Ruby said. "I don't know what it is, but I feel like we're running out of time."

"At least we've severed the link to the curse on the pack," Bella said. "That's huge."

Bella was right. What we had achieved today was nothing short of incredible. We'd saved the pack from literal extinction, and we'd saved Ruby and her daughter as well.

Was it selfish to feel like we were losing the battle when my father was still lying in the sun outside in the backyard in his animal form?

He should be inside chatting with my mom about what we were going to do, enjoying a coffee or a homemade cookie. I didn't know what dads did, and I didn't really care, as long as I finally got to have one.

There was a knock on the spare bedroom door.

"Can we come in?" my mom called out hesitantly.

I walked over and opened the door with a smile. "Yeah, of course."

My mom rushed in and hugged me tightly.

I didn't question her sudden need for affection. I just hugged her tightly back. Over Mom's shoulder, I watched Kathy and Sherie do the same with their daughters, each holding Ruby and Bella in a firm embrace.

Ruby hugged her mom, before pulling back and glaring at her. "I can't believe you were going to abort my baby!"

A stab of guilt hit me. *I probably shouldn't have told her that.*

Sherie sighed and nodded. "To my shame, yes, to save you I would have."

Ruby's eyes welled up with tears, but just when I thought she might scream, or lash out at her mom in anger, she nodded in understanding and wiped the tears away that fell on her cheeks. "I guess I'm lucky that I had Tiffany there fighting for me and my little one."

All five women turned to me and stared.

I shook my head as heat flushed up my cheeks. "You would have done the same for me."

Ruby smiled.

I felt a swell of love in the room stronger than anything I'd ever felt before.

"Maybe, maybe not," Ruby said, shaking her head. "We'll never know. But you're amazing, Tiff. I know you don't see it sometimes, but you're *so* strong. And I really admire you."

I had to look away. My nose was tingling, and my throat was thick with emotion. I'd always felt inferior to my friend. Less nice. Less smart. Less beautiful. "I suppose being the most stubborn has its benefits," I offered.

Ruby crossed the room and hugged me. "It does when it comes with a heart of gold. Thank you again, Tiff."

I nodded and closed my eyes, so I didn't embarrass myself again.

"So, you three saved the day?" Sherie said, coughing to clear her throat. "The pack is finally free."

I pulled away from Ruby. "Well, it was you three who performed the spell," I said to our moms. "Your power and talent saved the pack. But we saved Ruby, too, and that's the best part for me."

Kathy turned to her daughter, her face suddenly somber. "Is there something you need to share with us?"

Bella nodded with a grimace. "I saw more than I was meant to while I was scrying into the past."

"And what did you find out?" my mom asked, her brows downturned heavily.

Bella sighed. "Basically, that the High Warlock didn't conduct any of the spells. It was his girlfriend, or lover, or whatever you want to call her."

"Eloisa?" Mom said, sounding surprised.

"Is that Tabitha's mom?" I asked. "Because she's apparently the key to it all."

Mom turned to me, her eyes wide and strangely frightened. "Yes. Eloisa is Tabitha's mother... and the old High Warlock's half-sister."

CHAPTER 18

TIFFANY

"What? No way!" My mouth dropped open. "Surely, that can't be right?"

Bella stepped forward. "You don't really mean that the High Warlock had a child with his *own* half-sister? I must have misheard you."

If Bella had misheard it, so had I, because that was exactly what it sounded like Mom said.

Sherie pressed her fingers into her temples as though she had a migraine building, then she nodded. "You heard correctly, all right. It's the greatest secret, and shame, of our Coven."

531

My mouth gaped wide like a fish.

Ruby put both hands up as though she was saying 'hold on'. "Are you telling me that Tabitha is the product of a half-brother-and-sister coupling?"

Our moms nodded.

I snorted. "No wonder she's so fucked up."

"Tiffany!" My mom admonished me.

"What? It's true!" I glared back at her.

Mom's mouth twisted as though she was trying not to laugh.

How screwed up must that poor woman be? Both genetically and mentally? I wondered.

"How did something like that even happen?" Bella spluttered.

Sherie ran a hand through her hair. "Well, we're not a hundred percent sure."

"Some people say she was the one to cast a love spell on him," Kathy whispered.

"And some say he didn't realize she was his half-sister until it was too late," my mom added.

I stared at the moms, aghast. "Seriously? How did he not know?" That must have been one hell of a love spell to ensure that someone as powerful as the High Warlock was not able to see the person he was having sex with or feel their connection.

"Well, they didn't grow up together," my mom explained. "Eloisa herself was the product of an affair, so she didn't spend her childhood here in town. Her mother took her far away and no one really knew who she or who her biological father were. But when Eloisa returned to join our Coven twenty-something years later, she seduced the High Warlock. At the time no one cared, until she was suddenly pregnant—and her blood lines revealed."

Bella shook her head, understanding dawning upon her. "That's *why* he couldn't marry her."

"Exactly," Sherie said. "He probably would have, even though he didn't love her, for the sake of Tabitha. But it was literally impossible given the revelations."

"And she still kept the baby?" I asked, shocked at the stupidity of the woman. "Something could have been *really* wrong with the fetus. Like... genetically."

Mom blew out her breath. "Don't we know it! From what I was told, Eloisa disappeared after her parentage was revealed and returned six months later, babe in arms."

"What did the High Warlock have to say?" Bella asked.

I glanced around the room. The tension was high. Nothing like incest, gossip, and intrigue to keep a group of women engrossed in a conversation.

Sherie shrugged. "What could he say? The child was already born. So, everything was just hushed up. Eloisa was told to keep quiet about her biological father and everyone just went on with their lives. Or so we thought."

I shook my head. "Eloisa must have been obsessed with the High Warlock to do such a sick thing. To seduce her own brother, then cast spells to destroy the wolf pack from the next town."

"All because she was jealous of her brother's love for another woman," Ruby said, filling in the blanks. "Yuck."

The door opened and Fin popped his head in. "Everything okay in here, ladies?"

I nodded, strolling over to my gorgeous mate. "Yeah, we're all good." *Though our moms just revealed a pretty disturbing piece of information.*

Fin grabbed my hand, entwining our fingers and pulling me into his side. "The guys want to go celebrate. And we want you to come meet our parents. Can you do that? Or do you have to stay here...?" He glanced at my mom and the other women behind me.

I turned to them and raised an eyebrow. "I think we deserve the night off to celebrate the win, don't you? We have Ruby back, her baby is safe, and the pack is saved. Surely, we can attack the dad problem tomorrow?"

Truthfully, part of me wanted to work it all out *now*. After all, our fathers deserved just as much focus and sacrifice as we'd dedicated to saving the pack and Ruby today. But given the insanity of what had just come to light, I needed time out. Just a short one.

Ruby brushed back her hair. "Definitely. Don't know about you guys, but I'm exhausted and hungry, and want to crawl into bed with my mates and thank Fate and everyone else," she said, sending a smile my way, "who saved me and my baby today."

My stomach grumbled. "I definitely should have some breakfast soon."

"It's past lunch time now," Fin said, "but Milly's has an all-day breakfast menu. And my mom's house isn't far from there."

I grinned at him. Milly's was in the center of town. No one's place was far from there. "Sounds great."

We all dispersed.

The moms stayed to cook in Ruby's kitchen and chat with our dads about everything that had happened.

Meanwhile, Bella's mates whisked her off, saying something about wanting to see their new house, but I was pretty sure they were just dragging her home to bed.

How Bella got lucky enough to score three mates that constantly wanted to have sex with her, was beyond me. She was the last one I would have thought to have horny Alphas all over her, but maybe that was just my jealousy talking. On the flip side, my mates were dragging me to meet their moms. *That's pretty special, I guess.*

I groaned to myself as I was led out the door to Milly's for a massive late lunch that consisted of way too many pancakes and delicious, frothy milkshakes.

Meeting three mothers-in-law in one afternoon was not something I'd ever expected to have to do in my lifetime, but it wasn't as bad as I thought it would be. The pack as a whole were all in a state of elation, and my future mothers-in-law were just grateful their sons had finally found a mate. The fact that I was a witch didn't seem to worry any of them at all.

By the time dinner rolled around, I was exhausted in a bone-deep way that only a long night's sleep was going to fix. "I think I'm going to head home," I told the guys as we stood outside Milly's once more. "I need my own bed, and preferably one of my mom's amazing home-cooked meals."

When I said home cooked, I meant magicked up, but still. My mom made the best ribs, chicken, and soups, and stews. I wanted something hot and soothing before I succumbed to a deep, desperately needed sleep.

"Can we come with you?" Jase asked casually.

My mouth dropped open. "Really? You want to come to Mom's house with me?"

"Yeah, of course." Fin stepped closer and threw an arm over my shoulders.

"How big is your bed?" Ollie chimed in, the light of excitement flaring in his eyes. "Can we sleep over?" He waggled his eyebrows suggestively.

I got the distinct feeling he wasn't thinking about sleeping. I laughed as heat bloomed in my belly. Despite my exhaustion, I could definitely go for another session with my mates. As long as it didn't last *all* night. Not tonight, anyway. "Let me just check with my mom. I'd love you guys to all be able to come back and sleep at my place." I pulled out my cell phone from my pocket and texted Mom. My bed was only queen sized, but a little magic would fix that up no problem.

Mom replied that she would be home late, if not early in the morning. She had plans with Kathy and Sherie to brew up some potions that might help our dads with their shifting abilities.

I quickly told her I was bringing the guys home to sleep, and that I'd see her in the morning. I waited with bated breath to see her reply,

But it seems I didn't need to worry at all. She just sent through a smiling emoji with hearts for eyes, which made my anxiety swim away. She was fine with me bringing my three soul mates back to our house.

Which means I might get more than a good night's kiss from them all!

"It's all good. We can go," I said, grinning as I slid my cell into the back pocket of my jeans.

"Great. I'll drive," Jase said, grabbing onto my hand and pulling me down the street.

I wasn't as good as my mom was with food and recipes, but I could magic up a few pizzas, I was sure. Enough for dinner tonight anyway.

The drive home was relatively quiet, and I shut my eyes for most of the trip. It really had been the most massive day. And Christmas was only a couple of days away. Though, this one wouldn't be quite the same as all the others. I now already had the only thing I had ever wanted. I wondered what Santa might bring me to top this.

"You're going to have to direct me, sweetheart. Sorry," Jase said quietly. "I don't know how to get to your mom's house."

I opened my eyes and shook myself awake. "Yes! Of course. Sorry." I directed Jase to the small house I loved. The one I'd spent my whole life growing up in. Mom had worked her ass to the bone to pay it off, and I admired her so much for her courage in being a single parent. It wasn't something I thought I had the guts to do, and hopefully I never would have to face parenting alone when the time came.

"This is it?" Ollie asked from the back seat. "You sure it's going to fit us all?"

I blew a raspberry at Ollie. "I know it looks tiny, but you'll be fine."

From the outside the house looked a little like a dollhouse, with intricate lacing around the porch and only a single window to the right of the front door. But my mom had extended the back, and my bedroom was huge.

I led the guys inside and we all sat around the small kitchen table. "Pizza?" I asked, lifting my hands up and wriggling my fingers. "And what sort?"

The guys excitedly called out a collection of requests and extra toppings.

In two seconds flat, I magicked up dinner for us all.

"Whoa."

"That's awesome."

They all laughed as large pizzas materialized out of thin air.

I grimaced at the end product. "I'm sorry if they're a bit over-cooked. My mom's the chef in the family. Not me. I'm more of a survival cook when it comes to food."

"No. It's perfect," they all chorused and hoed into the food.

Ten minutes later, the pizzas were gone. And I was finally full. I staggered up the stairs to show the guys my bedroom. I pushed open the door, already lifting my hand to magic up the biggest bed I could fit in this room. "Give me one sec, and I'll fix our sleeping arrangements." I wriggled my fingers and sent an expansion spell at my bed.

The mattress widened and the pillows elongated. I pushed it all the way to the edge of both sides of my room, then stopped. It wasn't quite the size of two king beds pushed together, but it would do for tonight. "What do you think?" I asked, waving my arms at the end result like a game show host.

Ollie chuckled and swept me up in his arms.

I squealed as my feet left the ground and grabbed hold of his neck, scared he'd drop me.

He walked over to the bed that still held my woven purple blanket Bella's mom had made for me last Christmas and dumped me down onto the mattress. "You want to go to sleep straight away?" Ollie asked, then reached over his shoulder and tugged his shirt over his head.

That's not fair. My mouth ran dry at the sight of his bare chest. The beauty of him. He had a light sprinkling of hair over thick, perfect muscles. "Well, not straight away," I teased. "Why?"

Ollie chuckled, then pushed his jeans down his thighs. "Because I can't wait to fuck you again." He grinned at me.

All my insides burned with instant heat and I chewed on my lower lip.

Then he stopped, and his smile fell. "Unless you can't...? Then of course I'll wait. I didn't mean—"

Damn, the man was way too hot to be that thoughtful as well. Instead of expressing my thoughts with words, I walked forward, dropped down on my knees, and did something I'd wanted to do since I first saw Ollie naked.

I sucked his cock.

CHAPTER 19
TIFFANY

Taking Ollie's cock in my hand, I leaned forward to wrap my mouth around the head. It was about the bravest thing I'd ever done. My heart pounded like it had the power of a steam engine behind it and my anxiety over being rejected had my stomach tying itself into twisty knots.

A single long groan from Ollie as he slipped his fingers through my hair and gripped me tight to him had my worries melting away. "*Fuck...* Tiff. That. Is. So. Perfect."

I moved up and down his shaft, loving the heat and softness of his skin beneath my tongue—the feel of him in my mouth—and the musky scent of him in my nose.

The other two guys moved around us.

And when I lifted my head to see what they were doing, I found that they were standing next to Ollie, naked too. And waiting their turn. Glancing up, I met Jase's gaze. Lust burned in his eyes. I kissed the end of Ollie's cock and turned toward Jase, ready to taste my second cock.

He stepped closer, thrusting his hips out so I could easily grab hold of his shaft.

I tugged his flesh into my mouth. Jase tasted different to Ollie, somehow. Sweeter, smoother. The difference intrigued and titillated me, and I felt myself growing even wetter between my thighs in response. I sucked and teased, treating him with the same attention I had Ollie.

Then Fin stepped closer, hungry for his turn.

I smiled as I took my final mate's cock into my warm mouth. Fin was the hardest by far. Waiting his turn hadn't done anything to dampen his desire.

I had only managed a few sensuous licks of his long, delicious cock before he interrupted me.

He lifted me up and carried me to bed. "You need to be naked, too," he growled.

I couldn't agree more. I was so ready for this. I started to lift my hips and pull at my jeans, when I realized I had magic at my fingertips. *Jeepers, Tiffany!* I chastised myself. Without a second thought I clicked my fingers and made all my clothes disappear, sending them all to the wash basket in the laundry; a neat trick I'd learned as a teenager. But back then it had been for practicality, not sexuality...

"That's more like it," Ollie said, lying down beside me. He went straight for my breasts, cupping them and setting his lips to my nipples.

I gasped at the strange, new, and pleasurable feeling and grabbed for his head, holding him closer, tighter, wanting more.

He didn't disappoint. Suckling deeply, he forced me to arch my back to get even closer.

Fin lay down on the other side of me and slid his hand between my legs while he kissed me.

I turned my head to give him better access to my mouth, opening for him in every way he wanted. I shivered with need and anticipation. *It's finally happening... after the years of hurt and rejection I'd lived with, it was really happening; and it felt wonderful!*

His fingers slipped deftly over my clit and between my folds,

I gasped against his mouth as my desire for them grew even higher and more intense. It was literally unlike anything I'd ever experienced.

Fin's fingers masterfully manipulated me like he had it down to an artform. around and around his hand moved, making me climb the peak of my ecstasy higher still.

Ollie's mouth continued to love on my breasts with an ardent passion.

I moaned aloud, unashamed, grabbing for my men, wanting them closer.

"Come here," Ollie said, rolling back and away from me. "Climb on top."

I kissed Fin once more before climbing over to Ollie and instinctively throwing my leg over his waist.

He grabbed my hips and lifted me up and back.

I quickly got the idea and tilted my hips for him, reveling in the feel of him as his cock slid beneath me.

"Damn, I need you," he ground out, a note of feral lust in his voice.

I stared down at him as I tilted back, engulfing his cock slowly, one inch at a time, before sliding down until I was completely stretched beyond belief. I gasped out, throwing my head back. I could scarcely believe it. Ollie was inside me. *I'm not a virgin anymore!*

"Hey beautiful. Want to come all together, tonight?" Jase asked with a gleam in his eye.

I glanced left and right, finding Jase and Fin positioned on either side of me, standing on the bed, their cocks seductively at my eye level.

"How...?" I began to ask.

"Use your hands," Fin said, thrusting his hips forward so that I understood.

I nodded and reached for them, wrapping my fingers around each of their cocks; grateful they were being open and understanding about just how new this all was to me.

Fin and Jase groaned in unison.

Ollie seized me around the waist and thrust up into me.

I moaned with pleasure, feeling the heat of the room begin to overwhelm me. The smell of sex was everywhere. The men above and below me moaned with pleasure as I rode and stroked their cocks with fervor.

"Fuck! I'm going to blow soon. You're *too* fucking hot... my mate," Ollie groaned beneath me,

I felt the tightening of my own orgasm building within my belly and I bore down harder, desperate to take as much of him as I could.

Ollie cried out as he flooded me with his seed.

The warm pulses of his orgasm filled me, and I gasped at the unparallelled pleasure that tore through my body. Glancing down at my mate, a rush of love overwhelmed me at seeing the tortured expression of pleasure on his face.

He squeezed his eyes shut tightly as he fell into his post-orgasm bliss. Then he opened his eyes and they were glazed with lust and emotion.

I grinned at him. "I love making you come." And I meant it. It might be my first time with a man, but it felt special to share something so raw and deep; and not just with any guy, but with someone who just so happened to be one of my three Fates Mates.

He chuckled. "You're far too beautiful for me."

I glanced up at my other two mates, their cocks were thick and swollen with my frantic attempts at mid-coitus stroking. "What should we do now?"

Jase and Fin stared at each other for a minute, then looked down at me. "Do you think you could take us both at the same time?" they said together.

"Um... you mean—" I was pretty sure they meant by putting one of them in my ass, and although that sounded almost *impossible* to imagine, I'd quizzed Ruby on the concept, and she'd told me the spell she'd used to make it easy and pain-free.

I chewed on my lip, a thrill of anxiety racing through me as I nodded. "I can do that."

Fin's eyes widened, then he jumped down and off the bed. "Where's the lube?"

I laughed and shook my head. "We don't need it. I can use a spell instead." I carefully eased off Ollie's sated cock.

With a lazy, satisfied smile, the most dominant of my three Betas rolled out of the way.

Jase flopped down onto the bed, on his back. "Jump on, beautiful. Let's see if we can make you cum."

I wanted that too. I ached deep inside my belly with emptiness and need. Ollie had brought me close, but not all the way and I craved that same release. I climbed on top of Jase, my thighs trembling.

He grabbed his own cock, slid me backwards, and pulled me down onto his shaft without pretense.

I gasped at the pressure and pain that came with taking him so quickly.

"I won't last long," he promised, groaning as he grabbed tight to my hips. "Your pussy is fucking divine, Tiffany."

I would have blushed if I could have, but in that moment all my blood seemed to be centered deep in my pussy, throbbing with a heartbeat of its own around Jase's thick cock.

Fin put his hand on my lower back, then slid his fingers down to open my ass cheeks. "You sure about this, sweetheart?" he pressed.

His concern was sweet, but I nodded and said the short spell Ruby had taught me. It would lube me up and take away the pain—or so she said.

"Yes. Please. I want to feel you."

Fin pressed the head of his cock to my asshole and pushed forward.

I gasped, waiting for the pain I was sure would inevitably follow, but instead there was only the delicious slide of his cock inside me, opening me up, and filling me. I closed my eyes at the warring sensations and leaned forward, loving the feel of Jase's kisses on my neck and face.

"Please," I whispered to him. "You need to move." I was as full as I could get, with the perfect pressure on all my pleasure spots, but without them doing more, I was never going to reach climax.

Both men obeyed my request, pulling out, before thrusting back into me with perfect timing.

I cried out at the feeling of being so horribly empty, then so deliciously full a moment later. It was a beautiful, yet agonizing torture.

They began to move faster, picking up pace as they fucked me together.

I moaned, over and over again, until I was a blithering mess of incoherent sounds and gasps. Then my first orgasm crashed over me with an unexpected brutality, and I screamed, shuddering between my two mates.

Jase began to thrust up into me harder and faster, punishing my clit over and over. Seconds later he cried out and thrust up with wild abandon, coming inside me.

His orgasm set off a second round of orgasms within my belly, making my pussy convulse and clench with a chaotic and breathtaking rhythm. I bit my lip as I convulsed in raptures.

Fin groaned, a primitive *growly* sound, as he sunk deep into my ass and came, too.

He was so deep I felt his balls slap against me as they spasmed and shot his seed deep inside me. Scarcely a heartbeat had passed when I felt a hand in my hair and knew it was Ollie, moving closer to be a part of this amazing moment. Collapsing down onto Jase's chest, I opened my eyes.

Ollie gazed down at me, love written all over his face. He bent and dropped a kiss on my swollen lips. "That was incredibly hot," he whispered to me.

I couldn't help but laugh. It *had* been hot. Hotter than I had ever imagined sex could be.

Fin slipped from my body, as starry eyed as Ollie.

Jase carried me to the ensuite shower.

We all washed quickly, then staggered back to my bed and fell into a pile of well satisfied, orgasm and hot shower relaxed bodies.

I was asleep before the covers were pulled up. I'd never been so happy.

WHEN I WOKE up the next morning, something had changed—and it wasn't for the better. I reached out for Jase, who was closest to me, and shook his arm. "Hey, we've got to get up. Something's wrong." My stomach twisted when Jase didn't respond. I sat up, looking to my right where Ollie lay stretched out over the bottom half of the bed. "Hey!" I called out to my triad of men. "Are you guys, okay?"

They groaned as a whole, all three of them opening their eyes and slowly pulling themselves up into a seated position.

Oh, thank God for that. They were just sound asleep.

"It's early," Ollie moaned, stretching his arms over his head.

"What's wrong, beautiful?" Jase asked, sliding closer. He pressed a tender kiss to my bare shoulder.

I took a moment to enjoy this incredible feeling, this experience I'd been gifted by Fate, one I'd been dreaming of for *so* long. Of waking up surrounded by heat and flesh and muscles. Three men in my bed who would love me, in time. *Hopefully.*

"I don't know," I said, answering Jase's question. "But something's wrong. I can just feel it. I might go check on my mom. See if she's okay." I didn't know what made me think of my mom, first, but I didn't question my intuition. It was a witch's best friend, according to, well, everyone.

I slid out of the bed and grabbed my robe from the back of the door.

My stomach rolled like I was going to be sick, and my skin crawled with a worrying sense of premonition. I glanced back at my bed.

Fin was laying on his belly staring at me with big sad puppy dog eyes.

I had to assume because I'd left without cuddles or kisses.

Jase pushed his long hair out of his eyes, looking sexier than any man had the right to.

Ollie was leaning back on his arms, displaying his gorgeous body to me.

I groaned in frustration but turned away with determination. "I'll be right back!" What sort of sane woman got out of her bed when it contained three men who were naked and probably hoping for good-morning-sex?

I slapped myself in the forehead as I hurried down the stairs. I was crazy to be doing this. But I would just check on my mom, where she would be sleeping safely in her bed on the first floor, then I would run back upstairs to my mates. *I might need to use that lubricating and pain killer spell again,* I mused. I was a little sore in my nether regions if I was being perfectly honest. Three scorching hot wolf shifters was a lot to handle!

I pushed open her door, adjusting my robe as I went. I was still naked beneath, which made this that much more inappropriate. "Mom?" I whispered. If she was sound asleep, I didn't want to wake her. I also didn't want to shock the hell out of her by creeping into her bedroom at what felt like the middle of the night.

Frightening a witch never ended well.

I stepped into her darkened bedroom and glanced at the clock beside her bed. It was seven in the morning. *Not too early. Good.* Then my gaze fell on her bed. It hadn't been slept in. The seventeen hundred pillows she slept with were undisturbed and still piled perfectly in the middle of the mattress.

As I turned to go back upstairs another shiver of premonition shivered through me.

Mom hadn't come home last night. That wasn't the indication that something was wrong. After all, she'd been with her two best friends last night, and my father was in wolf form nearby. They could have fallen asleep on the couches, or they could still be up drinking and chatting. *Who knew with those three?*

But as I ran upstairs to get my cell phone, I had to swallow down the bile that rose. Terrible thoughts surfaced in my mind, unbidden. No matter what happened, I couldn't lose my mom. She'd been my only parent, my rock, my entire life. I hit the green button to call her. The phone went immediately to voice mail... She never turned off her phone.

I hit my mental panic button and started yelling for the guys. "Get dressed. We need to go!" Something was very wrong. It was Christmas Eve, and everything inside my witchy body told me I had to find my mom—and now.

CHAPTER 20
JASE

"It's okay. Sweetheart, just breathe." I concentrated on the road, and not the sound of my mate hyperventilating in the passenger seat next to me. I was already driving as fast as I safely could at twice the speed limit. I couldn't go any faster without killing us all, so I tried to keep Tiffany calm.

Back at the house, she'd run upstairs to tell us that something was wrong with her mom, and that we had to go back to the pack right away. We'd all thrown on our clothes and dashed to the car at her command. She was the queen of our world and if she said move—we did.

When we asked her what was wrong with her mom, she'd started to tremble and couldn't tell us. I wasn't sure if she even knew what was going on. Tiffany was pale and sweating and shaking like a leaf in the breeze. That couldn't be a good sign, surely? But what did I know about witches, anyway? Except that they were powerful and beautiful and loving.

I hoped that when we arrived at Ruby's house, all the moms would just be sitting around with their phones off, chatting away, simply engrossed in conversation and good company and nothing more. Those women looked like firm friends that could talk an entire day away if they set their minds to it. And in this instance, perhaps it was the whole night?

"Have you heard from anyone else this morning?" Ollie asked tentatively. "Has Ruby or any of the others contacted you?"

Tiff pulled out her cell phone in a flurry from her purse and started typing madly. "You're right. They were at Ruby's house. She should know if something's wrong with my mom!" She smiled at me, though she still trembled, before her concentration returned to tapping away at her phone.

"We're almost there, Tiff," I said, slowing down to pull into the main road that led right up to the town at the heart of pack's territory.

"You're right. I know you're right," she said reassuring herself. "We'll arrive at Ruby's and Mom will be fine. She'll be asleep. Her phone battery probably died overnight. I'm worrying about *nothing*." She combed her hair up into a ponytail with her fingers, then pulled it down again seconds later.

My heart pounded a little bit harder as we stopped outside Ruby's house.

Tiff launched herself out of the car and ran for the front door like an Olympian.

I glanced at the clock on the dashboard. It was barely seven-thirty in the morning. I looked over my shoulder at the guys in the backseat. "I hope they're all awake."

Ollie chuckled. "They will be soon enough if they're not already."

Fin sighed. "Come on. We better get in there."

We all got out of the car and began walking up to the front steps.

I sniffed the air, inhaling deeply, my wolf senses kicking into overdrive. "Tiff's right," I said. "Something's wrong. Can you guys' smell that, too?"

There was a scent on the breeze, like acid.

Ollie sniffed the air, then concern washed over his features. He charged for the front door and swung it open with an almighty slam as he darted inside.

Sharing a fleeting, worried glance, Fin and I followed shortly after.

Inside, nothing seemed out of place, but something seemed off about the house. "Where are they all?" I asked.

The house was clean and eerily quiet.

A bedroom door opened and Jackson walked out completely naked.

Not that I particularly cared. As shifters, we were used to seeing each other naked all the time. It was an entirely natural part of life when you constantly shifted between one form and another.

Tiffany shrieked and covered her eyes.

I realized she felt quite differently about the matter.

"What's going on?" Jackson mumbled sleepily. "Not that it's a problem, but what are you guys doing in my house this early?"

Tiffany turned away with a strange, strangled sound. She said, while facing the kitchen, "I'm sorry we barged in like this, but I have this *really* bad feeling something's wrong with my mom."

Ruby appeared from behind Jackson seconds after, wearing a long black t-shirt that obviously belonged to one of her mates. Thankfully, it was long enough to cover her modesty. It fell all the way to her knees.

"What's going on, Tiff?" she asked, then she turned to her mate with a wry grin. "Go put some clothes on, Jackson. Tiffany doesn't want to see all of that."

Jackson shrugged and headed back into the bedroom as asked.

Ruby walked around Jackson and up to her best friend. "Tiff, what's going on?"

Tiffany turned around, her eyes brimming with unshed tears. "Something's wrong with my mom. I just know it. I'm probably being silly. Please tell me I'm being silly. Where are they?" she begged, the words practically tumbling out of her.

Ruby frowned and ran a hand through her tangled long red hair. "What do you mean, where are they?"

Uh-oh.

"I thought they were with you guys," Ruby said. "As in, I thought Rebecca had gone home. We went to bed around midnight and the three moms were still at it, talking and mixing spells. Didn't she come home sometime during the early hours?"

Tiffany shook her head, tears falling down her cheeks now. "No, she didn't. Her bed hasn't been slept in and I woke up with the worst feeling of dread."

Ruby tilted her head to the side. "You know the moms sometimes have sleepovers. Could your mom have maybe gone back to Kathy's place since you texted to say that you were going home with your guys? Perhaps she just didn't want to... intrude, you know?"

Tiffany brightened instantly, a smile stretching across her lips. "Oh my God. You're probably right! Of course, Mom wouldn't want to come back to our house if she knew I was there with my mates." She smacked her forehead as she flushed a rosy shade of pink. "I'll message Kathy right now and see what they're doing."

I sniffed the air again. Something still wasn't right, though. "Ruby, do you mind if I check out the back?"

Ruby's eyebrows flicked up, but she didn't deny my request. "Yeah, of course I don't mind. Do you want to go see the dads?"

I nodded, because what else was I going to say? That I, too, had a feeling of premonition that something was seriously wrong? "Thanks." I went in the direction she pointed, through the kitchen and the laundry. The back door put me straight onto the porch.

I stopped and stared at the carnage before me.

All three moms were laying on the grass beside each of their wolves, in various positions of defensiveness. There was some smoke and fire damage to the grass, and from what I could tell there had been one hell of a fight.

I ran a hand through my hair. "Fucking hell!"

Tiffany's mom was lying on her side with her wolf mate half covering her protectively. He had blood caked into his fur all the way along his ribs.

I turned back to the house and called out. "Tiff! Ruby! You guys need to come out here. *Now.*"

The back door swung open. Tiffany walked out, her brow furrowed in confusion.

I reached for her just as she saw what lay on the back grass.

She let loose a sob that broke my heart as her knees gave way and she crumpled.

I grabbed for her and held her against me, stopping her from falling to the ground.

Ruby came up behind us. "What's going on? Holy shit!" She ran down the stairs and fell to her knees beside her parents reaching for her mom to check for a pulse.

I held Tiffany's sobbing form to me tightly and called out to the guys inside. "Ollie! Get Jackson and the other guys. Quick." I turned back to Ruby, who seemed a lot calmer than Tiffany.

She crawled from one witch to another, gently petting each wolf as she went.

"Are they alive?" I asked, terrified on Tiff's behalf, for the answer. How was Tiffany going to survive losing her mom *and* her dad, especially before she'd even gotten a chance to know him?

Ruby nodded, pressing the back of her hand to her nose, I assumed to stop herself from crying. "They're alive. Just."

Jackson and Billy burst through the door. They scooped up Ruby and carried her back to the porch and away from the macabre display before us.

We all stood together, staring at the bodies laid out on the lawn.

"Should we get some help?" I asked. "Or blankets? An ambulance? What do we do here?"

Wolf shifters were rarely sick as a rule, until they died. We didn't have many doctors, nor did we use the local hospital for anything other than the women birthing babies. Or if someone had experienced a minor injuring or cut off a finger.

Tiffany wiped at her face and gulped. "This is the work of a warlock. Or a witch. We can't do anything, except kill the one responsible."

I lifted her face to mine by raising up her chin. "What do you mean? *Who* did this?"

She bit her trembling lip and shook her head. "We don't know. I don't know... I don't know..."

I pulled her in close, hoping the warmth of my body would comfort her in some small way. "What should we do, Ruby?" I asked.

She shuddered in Jackson's arms.

Fin and Ollie rushed outside, reaching for Tiffany.

I handed her over to them. "Go on. Take her inside. She's freezing." I turned back to Ruby.

She looked pale and exhausted.

"What can we do?"

Her keen gaze rose and met mine. "It looks like there was a fight of some sort and an explosion. Someone set off a spell. Maybe it was intended to kill them, I can't be sure. Either way, they didn't succeed, and have instead put them all into an unconscious state." She shook her head as though trying to clear her thoughts. "We need to get Bella." Her eyes were unfocused now. "She'll know what to do. She's the brains." Ruby turned to go inside.

Bella would probably be at her place with her three mates. Hopefully, she was well enough to diagnose the problem and work out the solution. She'd already almost died looking for answers.

I flicked my gaze back to the yard and the occupants still lying on the grass as though they were asleep. *What the hell have we gotten ourselves into?*

CHAPTER 21
TIFFANY

I shook all over, with fear more than anything else. Who had done this to our parents?

Fin and Ollie held me in their laps on the couch, trying to warm me,

But I still couldn't stop shivering—and it wasn't just the cold.

Ruby walked into the kitchen and grabbed her cell phone.

I pushed out of Ollie's arms and staggered to my feet. "Who are you calling?"

Ruby put the phone to her ear. "Bella. Surely, she can work out what's happened... Hey Bella. Sorry to wake you. Yeah, can you feel it?"

I stared at her. Did the other two feel the same creeping premonition that I had this morning?

"Ah-huh. You need to get over here ASAP, Bell. No, I won't tell you on the phone, just get your butt over here and—"

Before Ruby could finish the sentence, Bella materialized in the lounge room.

She put her hands on her hips. "What are you doing here so early, Tiff? Shouldn't you be celebrating with your new mates somewhere?"

I swallowed hard so I didn't cry. "I woke up and I knew something was wrong. I checked Mom's bedroom and she hadn't slept in it all night. So, I called her, and you know my mom always has her phone on because she's on call for work all the time."

Bella dropped her arms at her side. "Well, where is she then?"

I sniffed to stop the tears from leaking out of my eyes. "She's in the back yard. They all are."

"What do you mean, they all are?" Bella's eyes grew wide, then she bolted for the back door like a bird on the wing.

We all followed but didn't get to her in time to warn her.

Her yell of anguish sounded through the air as she threw herself toward her mom and dad.

I pushed open the back door.

Bella ran her hands all over her mom, from her ankles to her waist, to her neck, then her hands.

What she was looking for, I didn't know. I'd skipped so many parts of magic class when I was at school, I was lucky I knew what I did. "What's she doing?" I finally asked Ruby, then turned as the back door opened again.

"Coffee?" Darren asked, holding a mug out to each of us.

Ruby took hers with a grateful smile.

I grabbed for mine. "Thank you so much." Boy, did I need it this morning. I added some sugar with a wiggle of my magical fingers, then turned back to the surreal and bloody scene that had rocked us to our cores.

Bella was crawling from one mother to another, checking each of them for signs of... something.

"I think she's trying to diagnose what's wrong with them," Ruby suggested, then took a sip of her coffee.

Steam rose off the top of my mug, and I blew on it once, before wrapping one arm around my middle. I still felt sick to my stomach and couldn't shake it.

"What do you think it is?" I asked. "Poison? Or just the aftershocks of a powerful blast?"

Ruby shook her head. "Truthfully? No idea, though it looks like someone waged one hell of a battle out here."

The more I looked, the more evidence I saw that proved Ruby's suspicions. There were black scorch marks on the grass and even on some of the fur on the wolves. Mine and Bella's fathers had blood in their fur, and yet everyone still appeared to be breathing—*at least for now.*

"What do you think it was, Bell?" Ruby called out. "Do you want a coffee or anything?"

Bella got to her feet, dusted the grass off her hands and the tears off her cheeks. "No. I'm okay." She walked over to the porch and shivered from the cold. "Let's go inside."

We followed her in, where all the mates were sitting, including Bella's three.

Jackson and Darren were in the kitchen, frying up bacon from the smell of the room.

Meanwhile, the three of us girls huddled on a single couch, holding hands like we used to when we were little.

I trembled with an invasive shot of fear that passed through me. These girls were all I had left if my mom died.

"Stop thinking the worst," Bella said, squeezing my hand.

I smiled at her meekly. "Stop reading my mind."

"What do you think it is, Bella?" Ruby asked again. "What can we do?"

Bella sighed. "I think they were in an epic battle last night. How you didn't hear anything, Ruby? I have no freaking idea."

Ruby nodded, guilt written all over her face. "I don't know how we didn't hear anything, either. When we went to bed and all three of our moms were just chatting, cooking, and making a potion. Bella's mom was reading a spell book..." Ruby stopped, then jumped to her feet.

"What is it, Ruby?" I asked.

"The book! It was full of location spells. I bet they tried to find Tabitha, or Eloisa, or both." She ran for the kitchen and started pulling out drawers, then rushed to the corner pantry. "Where would they have put it?" she fussed. "Oh. Here! Got it!" She pulled a massive tome of a book off one of the high shelves, then staggered with it.

Jackson grabbed it from her and helped her carry it over to the coffee table. He dropped it down on the table and it made a loud thumping noise.

I jumped, even though I'd been expecting it. I was really jangled.

"That is one hell of a heavy book!" Jackson remarked.

"Thanks, hon," Ruby said to her massive mountain of a man.

He grinned in return and headed back to the kitchen to keep feeding the troops.

I gazed over to my own mates anxiously.

In between bites of hot food and sips of steaming coffee, kept shooting me looks of mutual concern.

Ruby kneeled on the carpet and flicked through the pages of the book. "Here it is." She tapped on a spell in front of her. "Just before I went to bed, I saw this over my mom's shoulder. It was this symbol that caught my eye." She pointed at the picture at the top of the page. "This is what they must have been doing last night."

Bella lowered herself to her knees and pulled the book toward her, reading the page rapidly. She gasped, her hand flying to her mouth in shock. "They *wouldn't*."

"What is it?" I pressed as my stomach twisted itself in knots.

"It's a location spell, but one that is only intended for those that you can't find any other way. It literally tears that person out of their life and whatever they're doing and sets them right in front of you. If Tabitha had that happen to her, I would have to say she'd be the kind of witch to shoot first and ask questions later."

"You think she tried to kill our parents?" I asked, aghast. *What a psychotic monster!*

Bella nodded and shook her head in dismay. "It's not a stretch to imagine, Tiff."

Ruby frowned. "But then why are they all still alive?"

Bella ran a hand through her hair. "Because our moms are powerful witches who would have put up preemptive barriers. That would account for why you couldn't hear them, Ruby. I bet they put up a protective bubble, or something, and they were essentially sound-proofed."

Ruby leaned back against the couch. "Oh, thank God for that. I thought there was something seriously wrong with me; that I could have done something to..."

Bella shook her head and reached out a hand to our best friend. "It's not your fault, Ruby. But this does beg one question."

"What's that?" I asked, trying desperately to find my courage for the sake of our mothers.

"How fucking powerful is this witch?" she finished.

I burst out laughing. I couldn't help it. Bella never swore, not like that anyway.

"What?" Bella said, her lips twitching at the sides. Though she knew exactly what I found funny.

"Nothing. Sorry. You're right. How fucking powerful is she? And is the 'she' Tabitha? Are you sure it isn't *her* mom?"

Ruby pushed herself up so she could sit back on the couch. "Do you really think Tabitha's mom is capable of what happened outside? Isn't she ancient by now?"

I shrugged. "I have no idea. How old would she be anyway? Seventy? But we know one thing—she's capable of some pretty fucked up things. You know what she did with the High Warlock and every-thing. And if she's the product of an affair as well, then no one really knows her parentage either. She could have all sorts of weird stuff in her genes."

Bella and Ruby looked between each other, then nodded.

"You're right," Ruby said. "It could be either of them, so we need to be really careful about how we approach this."

"I don't care about Tabitha *or* Eloisa," I said stiffly. "They can go jump off a cliff for all I care. I just want my mom back and I want my dad too."

"Eloisa and Tabitha are the key to the curse that's holding our dads in wolf form," Bella said. "Unfortunately, I think we're going to have to find them and work out a way to break the link."

I raised an eyebrow. "Break the link? You *know* we don't have any idea how to break that link except through death."

"So, we kill them," Ruby said with a fierce grin. "I'm sure we can manage to do the spell to them that the moms did to us. Their hearts only have to stop for sixty seconds or maybe a little bit longer to break the spell."

I took a minute to think about it. Then I turned to my friends. "Do you think we need to ask the Coven for some help? How are we even going to find them?"

Bella shook her head. "I don't think we should involve anybody else. I believe we can do it ourselves. It's too dangerous to risk involving others. Anyway, this is our battle."

I wasn't so sure we could do it on our own. Our moms were more powerful than us, and yet they were all outside, in comas having been hit with a single spell. Or so we assumed. "Should we ask our mates to help us then?"

"What do you mean?" Ruby asked. "How can they help?"

"I'm just thinking out loud here, but Tabitha and her mom hate the wolves, so that has to give us some sort of advantage, surely? And our moms have used spells before that have had our mates ground us and amplify our magic. Maybe we could try the same spell but be better equipped than our moms went into it?"

I let my idea ruminate for a moment before continuing. "Or we could just leave Tabitha and her mom alone," I suggested, though I was pretty sure this was one of those times where hoping the issue would resolve itself, wouldn't work.

Bella shook her head. "We can't. We need to get them here and break the spells they cast on our moms and dads. Without them, we'll never get our dads back, and we may never be able to wake our moms up again, either," she said matter-of-factly with a chilling edge.

I groaned. *I knew it.* This was all going to come down to a single fight. Them versus us.

"So what are you thinking of for a spell, in regard to us and our mates?" Bella asked me, ever the pragmatic one.

"I didn't have any other ideas on how to actually achieve the practical side of what I was suggesting." I laughed humorlessly. "I was hoping you would know a spell that could do that. You *are* the resident bookworm, after all."

Bella tapped her fingers against her lips in thought. Then she held out her hands in front of her over the coffee table and transported several books from somewhere.

I had to assume they came from her mom's house or her new home with her mates.

"What have you got there?" Ruby asked curiously.

"Books, obviously," Bella said with a grin. "I'm pretty sure I know which spell your mom used, Ruby, to save you on Halloween. She pulled magic from the earth and channeled it through your mates. Because they're shifters and therefore super-strong paranormals, they survived the process. She was able to harness ancient magic through them and pull you back into the realm of the living. Tiffany is right in that we can probably use our mates to bolster our magic and our power so that we don't get wiped off the face of the planet if we try to locate and transport Tabitha to us."

"You seriously think we should do it?" Ruby asked, her mouth open as though she was surprised that we might actually follow through.

Bella opened the books in front of her and flicked through the pages. "Yes, I do. I don't think we have any other choice. We need to wake them up and we need to break this curse once and for all. It all comes down to one single witch and I *know* in my gut that it's Tabitha. It has to be. Eloisa used to be a key player but she's not anymore. She didn't ground any of the spells in herself because she knew she'd die first. It's all based around Tabitha. It just makes the most sense."

"So, Eloisa isn't in the picture?" I asked.

Bella laughed. "We should never discount her mother. You know that moms can be over-protective, especially when they only have a single daughter and no husband to rely on."

I couldn't help but laugh at that one. "That's funny. I've never thought about how much Tabitha and us are alike. You know, except for the fact that she is the product of incest and totally fucked in the head. But I get the fact that she was raised by a single mom who considered her the center of the universe."

I glanced toward the door that led outside into Ruby's backyard where our moms still lay helpless. "Do you think they're okay?" I asked, sobering, then bit my lip at the idea of my mom being in pain. "Or are they, like, torturing them inside their own minds and bodies? Trapped?"

Bella shook her head in denial. "I hope they're in some sort of dream-like sleep."

I hoped so too. I couldn't stand the idea of my mom being trapped and going insane or being in some kind of excruciating pain. "Okay then, so what's the plan?" I asked. "Do the same spell as our moms did last night? We find Tabitha, make her heart stop for one minute—break the spell—and free our parents forever?"

Ruby and Bella glanced at each other, then at me.

Our favorite red-head grinned. "Yeah. Easy, right?"

I rolled my eyes. "Yeah, totally easy." *For a full coven with advanced powers, maybe.*

"We have our mates to ground us and to draw power from, if they'll allow us to," Bella said, tapping a page. "I have the spell right here."

"Okay, so, supercharge our powers using our wolf mates, then do everything I just said," I repeated, my heart pounding in a mixture of fear and excitement.

"And we've got to try not to die," Ruby said, without smiling. "I have a baby onboard, remember."

I groaned. *Shit.* We were dealing with a real lunatic witch after all. That was a possibility. *We might not survive this...* I realized bleakly. "Okay." I sighed. "So, supercharge, do the spells, and don't die—in that order."

"Yeah, that's pretty much it," Bella said with a grimace.

I covered my face with my hands. *Damn it.* We were never getting out of this in one piece! Just when I'd almost attained everything I'd ever wanted. And it was Christmas, tomorrow, too. *What fucking bad timing is this?*

OLLIE

"You want us to do... *what*?" I blinked at my mate, not sure I understood what she was asking exactly.

We were all sitting around in a 'witch mate' circle. All nine of us crammed into Jackson's lounge room, our three beautiful, unique, and powerful witch mates in the middle of the circle, standing as they explained some crazy plan about taking down a wicked witch.

Tiffany glanced at Ruby.

Ruby sighed. "It's basically..."

Jackson groaned from where he lounged back on the couch. "It's basically crap," he said with an echoing sigh, as he shifted his legs. He was restless and didn't seem able to find a comfortable spot to settle. "It hurts like a bitch, I'll be honest. But if Ruby needs my strength to survive whatever they've got to do to save their parents, then she can have all of it."

I had no idea what to say. It was obvious that Jackson and some of the other guys had been through this before. I didn't want to look like a wimp or an idiot but having a witch drain my power or strength kind of scared the shit out of me. I glanced at the other guys who were looking just as worried as I was. At least I wasn't alone in my misgivings, which made me feel a little better. This was some seriously heavy shit.

Tiffany sat down on the couch next to me. Then she reached over and took my hand. "Witches get more powerful with time and age," she explained. "Genetics helps too. Ruby and I are only half witches, and we aren't very old. Bella is more powerful than us, but even so, if our three moms ended up like that outside, going up against this one witch? Then there's no way the three of us can take her on and win, without you."

I clenched my jaw and told myself to harden the fuck up. We'd said that we would do whatever Tiffany needed of us. This was what came with being in a mated couple or, in our case, a full family: sacrifice. It was time to put our money where our mouths were. "And it's going to hurt like a bastard, like you said, Jack?"

Jackson laughed, though there wasn't much humor in the sound. "Oh, yeah. Billy and Darren passed out from it last time."

Billy growled at him.

"I think it was only my strength as an Alpha that kept me going, to be fair," Jackson added to calm his Beta.

I had to laugh. "Seriously?"

Billy glared at me. "You won't understand until it's actually done to you."

I tried not to grimace, but I knew that I probably hadn't succeeded when Tiffany stared at my face for too long.

She withdrew her hand and stood up. "It's okay if you can't. It will leave me more vulnerable of course, but if Ruby and Bella have the strength to do the spell, we can probably get through it without your help." Her tone was one of disappointment and understanding all at once and it cracked something inside me.

I grabbed for her hand and pulled her back so that she was sitting on my lap. There was no way I was losing my mate over this. *Not a chance in hell!* We'd gotten into a lot of trouble and had countless injuries throughout our lives already, and ultimately, I wasn't afraid of a little bit of pain. It would be a small price to pay for the love of my mate.

It was just the unknown that terrified me. And the magical element. I knew next to nothing about witches. All of this was new territory. A whole new world.

Fin and Jase reached over and took Tiff's hands in theirs. "We'll do it," they said.

I nodded and tried to ignore the quiver of panic that rose at the idea of what they were talking about. Weren't they anxious too? Or were they simply braver than me? I sighed at the thought. I needed to hold my own. "All right. What else do we need to know?" I asked, turning to the other two witches in the room.

Bella opened the book she'd been holding and pointed to a page with elaborate and intricate pictures and lots of strange, cursive writing.

I couldn't even read it. I assumed it was in some sort of ancient magical language that they could decipher, and we couldn't.

"This spell will help bolster our power through you guys." She flipped a couple of pages, put that book down, then picked up another one. "And this is the spell our moms used the other day to stop our hearts and break the curse on the pack."

"And you intend to do both of those?" I asked, following as closely as I could.

Tiffany nodded. "On different people obviously. We'll have to do 'boosting power' on each other, and then the 'heart stopping' spell will be cast on Tabitha when she arrives."

"What do you mean, *when she arrives?*" Jase asked, one brow furrowed.

Bella gasped. "Oh yeah. Of course, sorry! There's a third spell we need to do as well." She rummaged through the pile of books and finally pulled up a massive Bible-looking thing, with heavy leather binding and old gold lettering. "There's a spell to locate Tabitha—the witch we're looking for. This spell will locate her and physically bring her to us."

Elliot stood. "Is that what your mothers did last night?"

I stared at him. Either he had really in tune instincts or he knew these witches better than I did. I would never have put those two things together.

Bella nodded, her eyes big and round as she stared at Elliot with a measure of pride. "Yes, hon. I think that's what they did, but we weren't here so I'm only guessing."

Elliot grumbled, a deep growl rolling through the room. "So, it's dangerous, Bella?"

She hesitated. "Technically, it is, as you can see from what happened outside. If it's true that this spell is what our moms did, then Tabitha is far more powerful than our moms ever realized."

"Or she just got the drop on them," Tommy offered. "We came up against her at the church over Thanksgiving, and she didn't win that fight. She ran away like a coward."

I didn't know what they were talking about, and I wasn't sure I wanted to know. These witches had been through hell and back over the last few months it seemed. Between finding their mates and trying to save their fathers, not to mention helping our whole pack by breaking the curse, it had been an eventful year to say the least.

"Do you think they can do it?" I asked Elliot, holding his gaze with some trouble. I forced myself to straighten and swallow down any foolish Beta-bowing tendencies my genetics still craved.

Elliot nodded. "Yeah. These girls are made of courage and fire. It's just... Bella's *my* mate..."

Once again, I was struck by how much power these girls had over their mates. We would literally walk over glass for them if we needed to, and it was obvious the other mates already had done so, proving their mettle. They were our greatest gifts and also our undoing. They were our strength and our weaknesses. And losing them would mean our deaths.

My chest ached with the thought. What would I do if Tiffany was hurt or killed? Just get back on the road and try to find another mate? I swallowed the hot, sour bile that rose in my throat. *No fucking way.* She was my one and *only* mate. There would be no other. Ever. I would never love anyone else, and because of that, I would offer up whatever strength my Beta blood gave me. "I can't lose you," I whispered to Tiffany, pressing my nose into her hair and inhaling her cherry sweet scent.

She pulled back and stared at me. "You won't. But we have to do this."

Some of the other guys surged to their feet.

"Well, let's do this then," Tommy said.

Tiffany slipped off my lap and stood with the others.

I glanced at Jase and Fin.

They nodded and clenched their jaws.

"What's the plan?" Tiffany asked Bella.

"We need to find a safe space to channel the energy of our mates, and make sure Tabitha doesn't hurt anyone else."

"I bet that's what our moms did wrong," Ruby said. "They probably put up the protection bubble so they wouldn't affect the pack or wake us up."

Tiffany nodded. "Total waste of a spell and power considering they got blasted after that, anyway."

Bella inhaled sharply, running both hands through her dark hair. "Where to go... where to go? Ah-ha! The church. It has to be. It's the only place I know that's big enough, safe enough, and..."

"The sacred grounds amplify your magic naturally," Darren finished for her.

Everyone turned to look at him.

He flushed a hot red and shrugged. "What? I learned a thing or two the night Ruby almost died on us."

I shuddered and shared a look with Jase. It sounded like all the guys had almost lost their Fated Mate at one time or another. There was obviously a happy ending, because they all stood here happy and well. But I wasn't sure I wanted to go through the same trial by fire all the other mates had needed to. I felt conflicted. Anxious, brave, ready, and afraid all at once and it was maddening! I wasn't used to acknowledging my feelings like the others...

I reached for Tiffany, grabbing her hand for attention. I needed to do *something*. I was feeling impatient and impotent. My wolf clawed at my mind to get out. "What can we do?"

Tiffany bit her lip. "It's probably best if you guys get to the church grounds manually. It'll drain you to be transported."

I nodded. I didn't want to say it out loud, but I definitely didn't want to go through that shit way of traveling again.

"You're right, Tiff," Ruby said. "We need to go together, and transportation would be the quickest. Grab the books and whatever else we need. The guys can shift and run if they want. Or drive, if they want to be boring." She winked at them.

"So, we should go, like, now?" I asked, already beginning to tug at my clothes. My skin was itching for the shift.

Tiffany nodded. "Go. We'll meet you there."

Elliot and Tommy sauntered up, all huge and bold. "We'll go with you."

Darren stepped closer. "I don't need to shift. I'll go with the girls."

I nodded and began to let go of my humanity.

"I'm going to call Maddi and Paula, my mom's friends from the Coven and see if they'll watch over our moms," Ruby said, grabbing for her cell phone and dialing.

I let the shift fully take me. I fell to the floor, my arms turning to legs as gray fur sprouted through my skin.

A huge black wolf appeared in front of me, then a white one.

Whoa. They were fucking big.

They tilted their heads at me.

I followed them out the front door of Ruby's house and into the fresh air, taking a deep breath as Jase and Fin joined me.

Together, we stood shoulder to shoulder.

A part of me still couldn't believe that I was sharing a mate with my two best friends, but at the same time, it was as natural as breathing. We were a family. A team. Our own pack. And today, we were going to help our girl kick ass, and hopefully get her home—still in one piece.

CHAPTER 23

TIFFANY

My two best friends, and Darren, collected everything we needed for the spells: protection charms to wear, crystals for boosting our power, and of course the books that Bella needed to recite the incantations from.

All eight of the other mates shifted into their wolf forms and took off toward the church.

We were left in a lounge room that looked like a fire alarm had gone off. There were shirts, and hoodies, and tanks, and jeans strewn everywhere.

Ruby huffed with a hand on her hip. "Just look at this place."

"Do we need to take any of this with us?" I asked.

Ruby began to giggle.

"What's funny?" I asked.

"Sorry, I was just picturing it. The three of us trying to conduct this super-powerful spell, with a ring of huge, naked men all around us." She stopped to laugh again. "It'll look like some sort of weird, pagan ritual."

I shuddered. I'd only had sex twice now. I wasn't sure I'd be able to focus on the magic I needed to perform if *all* of our well-built mates were standing around us, butt naked. Just seeing Jackson nude for a second this morning had made me feel more embarrassed than I'd ever been in my life. He was Ruby's, not mine. I didn't want to look at all that... stuff. I had my very own to worry about—and was very satisfied. "Okay, so, we'll grab their jeans," I said.

Bella reached for my arm before I went to scoop them all up. "Allow me." She flicked her fingers in the air and all eight pairs of jeans floated up, then she neatly folded them on the couch in a pile.

"Are we almost ready to go, then?" I asked, glancing around at the things we had to take with us. "We look like we might need a car."

Ruby nodded. "Probably a good idea, though we need to wait for Paula to arrive." The doorbell peeled and Ruby grinned. "Never mind, I think she's here. Hopefully, she can cast some sort of stabilizing spell for our moms or think of something to do to help them that we didn't." Ruby set off to open the front door.

I turned to Bella. "Are you okay?"

She nodded. "Of course. Why?"

I grabbed her hand and squeezed it. As she was the most introverted and quiet of the three of us, it was easy to assume Bella was fine, when in actuality she probably wasn't. It was always best to check in with her, just in case. "A lot of the stress of this plan has come to rest on your shoulders. I know it's not fair, and I'm sorry I can't do more, Bella."

She turned to me so she could look me in the eye. "I'm fine, honestly. I have you and Ruby, and all our mates there. We're going to do this. We're going to get our lives back to how they should have *always* been. We were robbed in the past. I'll be damned if I lose anything more in the future."

I sniffed as the heat of tears as they tingled in the back of my nose and eyes. "You're right," I said, and hugged her tight. "I believe in you —in us. We can do this."

Ruby walked back into the room.

Behind her followed a pale-looking Paula, a woman I'd seen from past Coven meetings on occasion. She had curly red hair and a dress sense similar to Kathy's. She wore an orange quilted skirt and a bright green flowing blouse. And I intuitively knew we could trust her.

"Paula. You know my friends, Bella and Tiffany," said Ruby.

The older woman ran a frazzled hand through her curly hair. "I do, but I don't think I've spoken to you girls before. It's nice to officially meet you."

"Nice to meet you too," I automatically replied. "Thank you for coming to stay with them. We didn't want to leave our mothers alone."

Paula's eyebrows lowered in a frown. "I can't believe they took on Tabitha and she did this." Paula wrapped her arms around her chest. "I'll do what I can, though I doubt I'll be able to do much more than sit with them."

"That's all we need, today." Bella said quietly. "Thank you for coming on such short notice, Paula."

"We really need to get going, so let me show you where they are. They're just right out here," Ruby said, directing Paula through the lounge room.

I didn't follow. I didn't want to go outside and see my mom like that again. The next time I saw her, I wanted her to be awake, and I wanted to see my dad in human form for the first time. I wanted us to be a family. That was the dream anyway.

"Should we pack the car while we wait for Ruby?" Darren asked, grabbing some water bottles from the fridge. "Or do you guys want to transport there?"

I didn't know which I preferred, but I had a thought on the idea. "Do you think it would maybe be better to save our energy and magic for the big show down?"

Bella picked up one of the books and held it to her chest. "Yeah, I do. Transportation takes quite a bit of magic, and we're going to need every drop we have in reserve."

I nodded at Bella before turning to the half-warlock. "Let's go pack the car then," I said, picking up the pile of eight pairs of jeans. "Who's got the biggest truck?"

Darren chuckled. "Jackson, I think. His keys are in the bedroom. Let me go grab them and we can pack."

After we finished packing up the vehicle, we jumped into Jackson's truck and headed for the church grounds. It took fifteen minutes by car, but the wolves could run straight through the forest, so they'd probably already beaten us there.

"The boys are going to have to wait for us," I said.

"Doesn't matter," Ruby mused, staring out the window. "They can't do anything before we get there, anyway."

I turned to Ruby, a thought occurring to me. "How are you going to do this, Ruby? I mean, how's your magic at the moment?"

Since Halloween a few months ago, Ruby had said her magic was literally gone. She couldn't use it.

I hadn't been sure if that was entirely true, or if her pregnancy simply made her too fearful to even try.

Ruby sighed and wriggled her fingers. "There's magic there. It's been coming back a little every day. But I've been too afraid to try anything. The pregnancy takes *so* much out of me, and I don't know how this is going to go. But I'll give it everything I've got."

Even if that means losing the baby? I wondered to myself.

"We'll be there for you," Darren said from the driver's seat. "All the way. No matter what. You can take all my power, plus more."

Ruby smiled, though I could see the pain and weight of the world in her eyes. "Thanks, honey."

We were quiet for the rest of the drive. When we arrived, a pack of eight wolves prowled around the church car park.

"The zoo's in town," Darren joked, as he drove slowly through the pack.

The wolves dispersed and I watched them in awe. Black, white, and gray. We had all three beautiful colors between us.

As we climbed out of the car, they began to shift back to human form.

I grabbed the pile of jeans from the trunk and threw them toward the men. "We brought your pants!" I looked quickly away. There were so many dicks I just couldn't cope until they were all covered.

"Let's go set up," Ruby said, calling to me from the truck.

I ran to her and grabbed some of the books and crystals, glad to be away from the dick-fest. "Where do you want to put all this?"

"Under the tree where they took me," Ruby said, shivering.

"Where's that?"

"This way." Ruby trudged off behind the church, her arms full of crystals and a blanket.

Bella grabbed the rest of the spell books.

Meanwhile, Darren grabbed everything we hadn't,

Then we all walked over the frost covered grass to stand near the graveyard, where a large tree stood in the middle of nowhere.

"Here?" I asked.

Darren shuddered and put everything down. "Damn, this place has some bad memories attached to it."

Ruby stood, staring at the tree, her hand protectively resting on her stomach.

"Bella," I called out.

She was placing the spell books down and arranging them for the best vantage point.

"Yeah?"

I sighed heavily. *How am I going to say this without offending anyone?* "Do you think we should, I don't know, protect Ruby somehow?"

"What do you mean?" Bella asked, glancing up.

"I'll be fine!" Ruby said with a frown.

I ignored her and focused on Bella. "Ruby hasn't used any magic since Halloween. What if something happens—to her, or the baby? I know you and I can't do it ourselves, but... I'm worried."

Ruby groaned and rolled her eyes. "Ugh. Tiff! Seriously?"

Bella put a hand to her mouth. "Oh, my God. I'd completely forgotten that your magic had taken a leave of absence since you became pregnant."

Ruby threw her hands up in the air in frustration. "I *have* magic! I'm still a bloody witch. I've just been... worried about using it."

I stared at Bella. "So, what do we do?"

Bella bit her lip. "With the magic in the hallowed ground here, and her mates to bolster her, Ruby should be okay to channel all of that into herself. She wouldn't even need to use a lot of her own magic."

Ruby groaned again. "Guys! I can do it."

I turned to her and glared. "Ruby, we didn't save you and your daughter to lose you now. I know you want to do everything you can to save our parents, but we don't want you accidently sacrificing anything in the process. Got it?" I said with conviction. If there was one thing I was good at, it was being independent and standing on my ground when life required it.

Darren stepped closer. "I can help," he said. I've been working on my warlock abilities, and if you can work out a way to channel what magic I have into Ruby, I'll gladly give it up to protect her."

Ruby turned to her warlock-wolf and threw herself into his arms.

I looked at Bella. This was going to come down to *us*. Bella had more raw power, that much was true, but I had the will, and it was made of tempered steel. I wanted my parents back, whole and alive, and human. I didn't care what I had to do, and I could be as stubborn as a mule, if my mom was anyone to go by.

The guys headed toward us, walking around the church like a

photoshoot for some sexy magazine. All I could see were huge pecs, tight abs, and great arms strolling in slow motion.

Bella began to arrange everyone into formation—a triangle—the strongest shape; a literal pyramid of power. She grabbed me and moved me over a few feet, then called out to my guys. "Can you three stand behind her, please? One hand on her shoulder."

They all reached out and touched me as instructed.

I shivered at the feeling of their strength against me. I closed my eyes, and a wash of premonition crashed over me. *She's coming,* I realized. She was searching for us. My eyes popped open again. "We need to hurry," I urged Bella. "She's coming. I can feel her."

Bella stared at me for a moment, shock written all over her expression, then picked up her pace. "Ruby, here. Quick. And you guys, hands on her shoulders. My guys, come here. Okay!" She snatched up one of the books when we were all finally in order. "Hold onto your lunches, boys. This is going to get *rough.*"

"Do we have to hold on to our mate the whole time?" Ollie called out.

I was glad he asked, because I wanted to know that, too. Would breaking the physical connection jeopardize the success of the plan?

"You don't have to if the pain gets too much," Bella said. "Your nearby presence is enough; but it would help, so hold on as long as you can! Even if you're on the ground and it's just to her ankle. Okay, I'm going to do the translocation spell." Then she pointed to the book in front of me. "I want you to hit her with the heart stopping spell as soon as you've got eyes on her, okay?"

I nodded, fueling my resolve. "I will." I would cast that spell not matter what. I had the earth of my ancestors beneath my feet and the touch and support of my mates around me. My whole fairy tale future with my parents was on the line. I could manage the spell.

"What about me?" Ruby asked.

Bella broke away from her mates to place a book in front of Ruby. "The land here will boost our natural powers anyway, but if you can do this spell, it's the one that will drag our mates' strength from them and into us, that would be amazing."

Ruby flexed her fingers with determination. "I can do it."

"And I can help," Darren said, standing beside her. "Use me for anything you need, Ruby. Drain the fuck out me. Whatever it takes."

I glanced at the sacred triangles we made. Three small triangles that came together to form a greater triangle of power. In witchcraft, the triangle was used for so many incantations that it was truly mind boggling. And here we were... three witches with three mates a piece, and with three spells that needed casting. I smiled at my friends. "Looks like this was meant to be. Three spells for the three of us."

Ruby smiled at me, her eyes shimmering with tears. "I always said we were perfect together."

"Mom always told us we were meant to be," Bella said, though her throat choked up on the words.

I clenched my jaw, struggling against the flood of emotion and the tingles of premonition tickling at my neck. "I love you both. Let's do this." I looked down at the spell book that was my task and summoned my magic to the forefront of my mind. My fingers pulsed with living power as I lifted the spell book into the air in front of me and stared at the timeless transcription with intense focus.

I read it over and over again, ready to cast the spell the moment I saw the bitch of a witch who'd cursed my parents—our parents.

Ruby began to reciting in the ancient language of the warlocks, calling out to the witch powers within all of us to entwine with our supernatural mates, and to draw their strength into our own bodies.

I began to ache and burn in the strangest way.

Behind me, my mates groaned and gasped. One of their hands dug deeper into my shoulder.

I didn't dare look back to see what was happening with them, I had to stay focused. Everything rode on this.

Bella began to glow with the white light of magic and power.

Her men stared at the ground with stony and determined expressions.

Tommy's arm shook as he gripped Bella.

I could only imagine the type of power an Alpha had—*and Bella has two of them!* The whisper of something akin to hope fluttered in my heart. We were really doing this! We'd succeed where our mothers had failed.

Then Bella began to speak, and evil was headed our way.

The chanting around me grew louder and louder beneath the cool winter sky.

Ruby recited the spell that dragged my mates' natural power from them.

I could feel their combined strength coursing through my veins like fire. Wriggling my fingers, I prepared myself to cast the spell that would stop Tabitha's heart the moment she materialized within the confines of our sacred triangle.

The air began to change, shimmering and rippling with white light and sparking with magical electricity. A person began to form in front of us, about our height, thin, and with dark hair. I could see through her as though she were a ghost. She was not quite material yet, but she was coming.

Bella began to speak faster, and louder as the spells wove around us.

One of my mates fell to the ground behind me; I wasn't sure which. But I felt the dip in my magical power immediately. Whoever it was, he groaned, valiantly grabbing my ankle a moment later. The power surged within me once more, like I'd been plugged back into an electrical socket.

The witch, Tabitha, became more defined.

I stared at the spell I would soon have to cast. The words stood out, highlighted against the page as if enhanced by a luminescent enchantment. I absolutely had to get the timing just right. I had to pinpoint the exact moment the spell would work on her, and I assumed it would be most effective and successful when she was almost fully here and present with us.

But she was fighting the spell, that was obvious.

Ruby was sweating, and her voice rose until she was yelling.

Tabitha faded in and out, like an old TV getting reception, then losing it again. She raised her hand and began to speak.

That was my cue. I had to act. *Now*. Before she flattened us all. With conviction I spoke the words of my spell.

She turned on me, glaring with evil, glowing eyes.

I could feel her spell trying to reach me—to touch me—but I held firm. I reached deep into the well of power my mates were sacrificing for me. Seizing hold of a power I'd never known could exist. I chanted louder and with renewed force.

Pain ripped through my belly and nails scratched at my face.

I put a hand to my cheek and glanced at my fingers. My hand came away covered in red blood. *That bitch.* Narrowing my gaze at her, I chanted harder, pushing every bit of energy I had at my disposal into the spell.

Ruby hit the deck opposite me. She was on her knees, barely speaking.

I could feel the well of power waning.

The groans and moans of pain from our mates had almost stopped.

Ruby's spell was scarcely holding up.

I needed to take Tabitha out. Now.

Tabitha was almost completely visible and wasn't anywhere close to being legally dead.

I glanced at Bella.

She swayed on her feet. She wasn't going to last much longer either.

I couldn't do it myself. I wasn't designed to do it myself. This was a team effort. We were all in or nothing. Without stopping the spell, I reached out each hand and called Ruby and Bella to me using magic.

They slid toward me on the grass, drawn as if with an invisible rope.

Their mates crawled or staggered after them, determined as all hell to stand by their women, their queens.

This was going to work! I reached forward just as my second mate fell to the grass behind me.

Bella reached desperately for my hand,

Then Ruby connected with me by grasping onto my fingers like her life depended on it.

I brought the book toward me. "My spell. Together. *Now.*"

Tabitha fired toward me.

Bella flung out her hand and managed a shield of sorts that blasted us all backwards and out of the damage zone of Tabitha's spell.

I ended up on my ass, my mates sprawled haphazardly around me. "We can't lose! We're getting our parents back!" I cried out, surging to my feet. I grabbed my friends' hands and began to cast the strongest spell I'd ever cast in my life. With every word, I forced my power forward like a wave.

Bella's voice joined mine. It was weak but I could hear her.

Then Ruby joined in, whispering the words of the spell with everything she had left.

Tabitha fought me, pushing back against my magic with brutal force. She raised her hand to fire another blast of destruction our way.

I braced for the impact, but it hit me with bone-breaking strength, nonetheless, cutting my face and snapping my ribs. I cried out as pain ricocheted through me, hot tears of agony streaming down my face. *No. No! You will not win*, I screamed in my mind.

Tabitha's eyelids began to flutter and she moaned.

She's exerting too much of her own power, I realized. *She's weakening! That... or our spell is working!* I squeezed Bella's hand and tugged on Ruby's fingers. The pain in my chest flared so brutally I wheezed. I closed my eyes as I tugged harder on my mates' power.

Tabitha began to scream and clutched at her chest.

I pushed more power into the spell, practically tearing it from everyone around me.

Then the sound stopped.

I opened my eyes.

She lay flat on her back on the grass.

Ruby climbed to her feet, quietly repeating the spell we all knew by heart now.

"Thirty seconds," Jase said from somewhere behind us, so quiet I could barely hear him.

I fell to my knees next to Ruby. The pain was so intense I struggled to stay awake. Black spots formed at the edges of my vision, threatening to blur my grip on consciousness.

Finally, after what felt like an eternity, Jase said, "Forty-five seconds."

I swayed where I knelt, uttering the spell one more time. Slowly and with purpose. Dragging crisp air into my lungs with each painful breath. It felt like there were a thousand needles splintering outward from my ribs, but I had to keep going.

"Sixty...." Jase whispered, then cleared his throat loudly. "Stop!"

And just like that I let go of the spell that I had recited a hundred times and gratefully allowed the darkness to take me.

I SWALLOWED HARD. I needed water. "Mom... I..."

"I'm here sweetheart. Here's a glass of water. Drink."

I struggled to open my eyes. "Mom? What happened? Mom..." I sat bolt upright, my head spinning, and stared at the woman in front of me. My rock. My family. My mother. "You're okay! What happened? Where am I?" I rambled in shock, confusion, and excitement.

Mom chuckled as she petted my shoulder. "We're home, sweetheart. Relax. This is your room and your bed. Though, I don't remember it being quite this big."

I grimaced. I'd forgotten to put my bed back to normal size after my night with my mates. "Oh yeah. Sorry about that. I—" Cutting myself off, I put a hand to my head, pain pounding behind my temples with a vengeance.

"Lie back on the pillows." Mom pulled a multitude of pillows around me and stacked them up so I could recline comfortably, remain mostly sitting up. "How are your ribs?" she asked. "And your head? I fixed up what I could, but there could be residual pain. Drink this." Mom handed me a mug.

I didn't ask what was in it. I didn't need to. This woman had looked after me since the day I was born and I trusted her with my life. "Thanks." I took a few sips and frowned. *Definitely a healing potion.* They always tasted like crap. I swallowed as much as I could, then handed it back, since my bedside tables had disappeared to accommodate my now ridiculously large bed. The potion was mercifully fast working, and a soothing effect soon stole over my whole body, making me sigh as the last of the pain in my head floated away.

"What happened, Mom?" I asked. "Is everyone okay? Where are my mates? Are the other moms okay?"

Mom sat down on the bed with me. "Yes. Everyone's okay, Tiffany.

Your mates are all downstairs eating me out of house and home." She giggled, a sound I hadn't heard in years. "Lucky I'm a witch, or I'd go broke trying to feed those guys." Her gaze softened. "Thanks to you, sweetheart, everyone is alive and well. I am so, *so* proud of you."

I laughed. "For the weakest witch in the group, I did okay, yeah?" I leaned back against the pillows before experiencing a light bulb moment. "Hang on a second. Did you say 'everyone' is okay? As in..." I didn't want to say it out loud in case we hadn't done it. In case we hadn't succeeded in saving *everyone*.

"As in...?" Mom prompted, smiling softly.

There was a light in her eyes I didn't think I'd ever seen before, and I had to swallow hard to stop myself bursting into tears. "As in did we break the curse? As in... is Dad...?"

Mom stood up with a big smile and took a few steps back. Then she turned toward my half-open bedroom door. "You can come in now."

A man stepped into my room so quietly I didn't hear his footfalls, but I could see him. Right there. In front of me.

"It's you." I swung my legs off the bed and stood up.

"Hi Tiffany," he said, his throat scratchy and husky, like he hadn't used it in twenty years. Which in actuality, he hadn't. He had light brown hair, shot through with silver. He had a wide jaw, my blue eyes, and was way too thin to be healthy. Mom was going to have to get some food into him, stat.

He stepped toward me, almost shyly. Then he met my gaze and smiled. "You saved us. You saved us *all.*"

Tears burned my nose and my eyes. "Dad." I staggered forward.

He forward in a heartbeat, wrapping his arms around me.

I sobbed against his chest. "I've missed you so much," I whispered. as

He held me tight. "Shh... Everything's okay now. I'm never leaving you ever again. Come here, Rebecca." He reached out his arm and brought my mom in for our first family cuddle.

She stroked my hair, a familiar and comforting gesture that settled my nerves and my fast-beating heart.

I closed my eyes and drank in the moment I'd waited my whole life for. I had my family together. Every pain and sacrifice, every tear and ounce of loneliness had been worth it. Our courage and unwavering faith in reuniting our families had finally paid off. And nothing was going to break us apart ever again.

EPILOGUE

TIFFANY

One day later.
Christmas Day.

There had been a bit of a fight over where Christmas was going to be held this year. In the end, Bella won the right to host our first ever family day. The new house they'd bought was even bigger than Ruby's place and could actually fit *all* of us together in the living room.

Bella had created a positively massive table. At one end sat our three moms and our dads, all cuddled together like hopeless, love-struck teenagers; holding onto each other like they were never going to let go.

Although I wanted to tease them for it, I almost cried every time I looked at my mom's happy face.

"Hey beautiful," Jase said, sliding into the seat beside me. "Does Bella know there's no food on the table?" He glanced forlornly at the pristine white tablecloth topped with festive decorations and new plates.

I laughed. "You need to wait and watch. This is a witches Christmas, after all. There has to be some magic!"

He huffed playfully and didn't ask any further questions.

I reached over the table to grab Ollie's and Fin's attention from where they sat on the other side of me. "Hey, I got word from my tenant yesterday, by the way. I didn't check my phone until late, but they're wanting to leave my house early in the New Year, so if you guys want to, we can get in and start painting, or knocking down walls or whatever, around the fifteenth."

Ollie grinned. "Hell yes! I can't wait to get a space where we don't have to be quiet."

I blushed and glanced down at the table. Since when were we quiet?

Bella stood up at the head of the table, Elliot and Tommy on either side of her. "Thank you all so much for coming to our first ever full family Christmas!"

Cheers erupted around the table as we all clapped and laughed with unparalleled joy. It'd certainly been a long time coming.

"I am thankful for so many things this year," Bella went on, glancing from one mate to the other. Then she slid a hand onto Jonah's shoulder, where he sat on her right. "My mates, my friends, my mom. But most of all I am grateful to finally have my dad back. Words really aren't enough to describe how much we've missed your presence in our lives, but know that we have *always* wanted you home with us and we are so grateful you came back."

I glanced at my dad, who had an arm slung over my mom's shoulders.

Our gazes met and he smiled at me.

My throat tightened and my heart swelled. I finally had *everything* I'd ever wanted. My mates. My father. And with time, hopefully I'd be blessed with a family of my own. A big one. With at least three kids— hopefully more!

Bella lifted her hands. "Ladies? Shall we feed our men?"

I nodded and rose to my feet, happiness filling me up like never before as I lifted my arms.

Ruby stood up just down the table from me.

And at the end, all three mothers joined us.

We began to weave our magic, creating our favorite traditional Christmas dishes.

Bella took care of the meats; summoning up enormous festive hams, pork with perfect crackling, tender beef, and succulent seasoned chicken.

I created a hearty deluge of piping hot rosemary and garlic roasted potatoes, with pumpkin and yams to compliment Bella's contribution.

Kathy and Sherie handled the side dishes, offering up loads of steamed seasonal greens, as well as a variety of gravies and condiments.

My mom made an array of sweet baked pies and heart-achingly beautiful desserts that deserved their own cookbook cover.

And last, but certainly not least, Ruby took care of beverages. and candy.

By the time we were done, the table was the prettiest thing I'd ever seen, and I could hear our mates' stomachs rumble around us like rolling thunder.

I sat down with a laugh at Jase. "How's that? Christmassy enough, now?"

He stared with hungry eyes at the table, practically salivating, then lifted an eyebrow at me. "Can you do fresh, hot bread rolls and butter?"

I laughed at his simple, wholesome request. "Of course!" I wriggled my fingers and created a huge breadbasket right in front of him piled high with rolls decorated by scored patterns and floral designs. *Perfect.*

"Just brilliant," he sighed.

Jackson stood and raised his glass of whiskey on the rocks. "One toast before we all get started on this magnificent feast." He lay a hand down on Ruby's shoulder.

She smiled and reached up to entwine their fingers.

"To our beautiful and strong Halloween witches. May they always love us, spoil us, and do amazing things to enrich our lives. From the bottom of our hearts, we love you."

I glanced at Bella and Ruby with a smile on my face that could rival the sun, unable to stop the tears as they flowed freely down my cheeks.

The men around the table all stood. "To our Halloween witches!" they cheered.

We lifted our drinks and then, together, drank as one.

I committed the moment to memory as joy swelled my heart. Our story would be passed down through generations of wolves, witches, and warlocks. Generations that would now be born and flourish because three best friends had the courage to rewrite their Fates.

THE END.

Thank you *so* much for reading the last of the
Whychoose Witches trilogy.

If you enjoyed this Fated Mates, Reverse Harem Paranormal Romance,
you'll LOVE my series: ***The Woodland Wolf Packs***! It's a trilogy of three
standalone romances, all intertwined within the same world.

You can download Book 1 for FREE:
https://books2read.com/the-packs-mate!
Or *read on* for an exclusive Sneak Peek into Book 1, **The Pack's Mate...**

CHAPTER 1

DEXTER

My pack's community grounds looked nothing like they did when I was a child. The once soft grass was gone, worn down to dirt. The area, central to our town, was littered with beer bottles and cigarette butts; the playground equipment long since hauled off into the woods by jack-ass youths.

The sun was only just rising, but we were all up, ready to start a long day's work. The heavy scent of testosterone filled the air. My all-male pack—consisted of Taylor and Jay, men with whom I'd bonded since we grew up together—

A sigh ripped through my throat as I glanced at the rock-strewn dirt at my feet. The pack before me was a powerful and depressing sight I'd grown tired of. For a whole generation now, the Woodlands pack had not born a single female. *Not one.* For almost sixty years the elders of my pack had questioned what happened to our breed. And what might happen to our genetic lines if there were no female mates to carry our children for future generations.

My mother and her sisters were some of the last pack-born women and each had produced at least three sons. What went wrong? To this day, no one knows. What we do know is that there will be no more children born to our purebred wolf-shifting women. It's impossible now. The last of our fertile females matured past breeding age almost twenty years ago; so, there's no longer any hope of a savior being born for our pack.

Something must be done. If we don't find women to breed with soon, our pack will become extinct. Great family lines that have existed beyond memory will die out and the world will be poorer for it. There was obviously only one option that remained... to bring human women into the pack.

We needed to venture into the cities and acquire human females for breeding. No one knows if the plan will actually work, as it's never been attempted before.

We have a unique pairing system called Fated Mates in our world. Wolf shifters in my pack only breed with their true mate, the one chosen for them by Fate itself.

I've always been told that I would recognize my mate by her scent. There would be an instant attraction, an undeniable bond from the moment we touched. I won't actually *know*, as I've never experienced it before. No one my age has. We must rely on the stories our parents tell us, which seem to change with time, just like myths and fairy tales.

So, what should we believe? It's tough to discern between the fact and fiction that has grown over the years. And if there were to be no more wolf-born women, would that bond still exist outside of the community? *Probably not.* We were in entirely uncharted territory and no one in the pack knew, not even the elders. And everyone was afraid of what would become of us if the bond failed.

"Dex! Come quickly. It's your dad." Taylor, my Beta, came running atoward me at break-neck speed and grabbed my arm.

My dad? "Where is he? What's happened?"

"Come on!" Taylor turned on his heel and ran toward my parents' home.

I followed behind, not thinking twice.

My father had been feeling unwell for months, and as one of the elders in our pack, that was a bad omen for everyone. They're meant to be the strongest of us. He can't die. *Not yet.* Not until we've secured the continuation of our bloodline. *I'll be lost without him.*

Taylor led me straight into the lounge where my father was laying on the couch and my mother was on the floor, kneeling over him protectively. His face was deathly pale, and his breath wheezed in and out of his chest like it took all of his energy just to stay alive to see the next moment.

"What happened?" I asked as I crouched down next to my mother.

Mom turned and squeezed my hand. "Please, Dexter, please. Take him to the hospital in Little Creek."

Little Creek was the nearest human town. "Mom, no. You know that's not our way. They'd notice he's not human. They wouldn't be able to make sense of our differences. It could endanger what's left of the pack."

We had a healer in our pack but he was rarely required for anything other than alleviating and mending fighting injuries. Our paranormal genetics meant that we healed extremely fast and rarely fell ill, unless it was something extremely serious or inexplicable.

My mom grabbed my shoulders with surprising force. "Dexter, you listen to me. I am not ready to lose him. Not yet. He can't die. Do you understand? Take him to a doctor. Now. *Please.*"

I looked toward my father.

He met my gaze with his own.

He didn't nod, but he didn't shake his head no, either.

And for the first time ever, I saw fear in my father's eyes. He didn't want to die. And just like that the decision was made for me. I had to take him in. "Taylor, grab Jay and the truck. Bring it 'round the front. I'll carry Dad out."

Taylor looked at me for a moment, as though questioning the soundness of my logic. But in the end, he followed my instructions as any good Beta would.

"Thank you, Dexter! Thank you," my mother said as she stood up and moved out of the way quickly, relief flooding her features.

I leaned down and lifted my father up over my shoulder, grunting with the effort. He couldn't assist in any way himself, so he was dead weight and he weighed more than me. And up until yesterday, he was still as strong as ever. Or so I'd thought.

With due care I arranged his arm over my shoulder and wrapped my arms around his waist so that I could carry him out to the truck. "Let's go, Dad." I didn't know if a human hospital could save him, but if there was any chance, then I had to try. Losing an elder would be risking the pack anyway, no matter how you looked at it. Mom was right.

I limped outside under the weight of my father's bulk. His ragged breathing echoed in my ear and his skin was clammy beneath my palms. "Are you sure this is what you want, Dad?" I asked a second time as the vehicle pulled up.

If my father didn't want the humans to help him, then I wouldn't force him. And I wouldn't do anything without his consent.

My father nodded against me, but just barely. He was growing weaker by the minute.

Okay. I was doing the right thing. It's what both my parents wanted. There was no arguing about that. "Let's go then, old man."

That earned me the briefest of smiles from my dad as I hefted him to the back seat of the full-sized truck.

Taylor helped me get him situated comfortably.

Then I climbed into the driver's seat. I adjusted the rear vision mirror so I could see my father's ashen face. "Little River is an hour away, so don't you dare die on us before we get you there, Dad." I bolstered my words with a threatening growl.

There was a weak laugh in the back seat from my dad.

Jay slid onto the floor behind my seat, at my father's feet, the perfect Omega. Lucky, we had trucks or he would never have fit.

My pack was in and my father wasn't getting any better just sitting here.

"Let's go." I planted my foot on the accelerator, and we took off toward the nearest town. I drove the roads as safely as possible, my heart thundering in my chest the closer we drew to Little River.

"Let's hope the human stories have been exaggerated, huh?" Taylor joked, trying to ease some of the tension in the truck.

The silence had become overwhelming.

I managed to smile. "Yeah, I think as long as none of us go shifting in the middle of the city, we'll be fine."

All of us of mating age ventured into the cities for clandestine sexual encounters with random strangers occasionally, but we never went anywhere near the heart of the city. Nor did we ever go to their hospitals or doctors when we were injured, for fear of the possibility of having our blood tested which resulted in them discovering a difference that they could not medically or scientifically explain.

We'd been told ever since we were kids how much the humans hated us. That they feared anything different, and that we'd be locked up in a zoo, or dissected on a scientist's table if they discovered who and what we were.

Taylor grinned. "Yeah, I hope so."

We drove the rest of the hour in silence, broken only by the chilling and unsettling rasp of my father's labored breathing.

Taylor pulled out his cell phone and directed me to the hospital using the maps feature. "Turn left here. It should be on our right."

The hair on my arms stood on end as we passed through the human city. *So much light, so many people.* There were a thousand shops and cars, and noise everywhere. It felt overwhelming. There was simply too much of *everything*. It was a level of chaos and cacophony we weren't accustomed to.

I pulled up outside the Emergency Department next to a hospital that stood a hundred feet tall. "I'll take Dad in. Taylor, park the truck and meet me inside. Jay, help me if you can."

Jay nodded and slid out the door easily, his agile, lithe body making everything easier for him.

I jumped out, opened the rear door and reached into the back seat for my father's heavy, but failing form. His wheezing was getting progressively worse. He was really struggling to breathe now, and his lips were a ghostly shade of blue. I pulled my dad along the seat, hard.

Adrenaline pumped through my bloodstream, making my muscles bulge and tingle with strength. My inner wolf instincts were telling me that time was running out.

Jay got under my father's other arm, attempting to alleviate some of his weight.

Then together we carried him toward the sliding doors.

They *whooshed* open and two men rushed out to meet us. "Do you need help?" they asked.

The foreign human scent rolling off their bodies made my hackles rise. I grabbed for my father's huge bulk, a growl ripping through my throat as they attempted to take him from me.

Taylor pushed at me. "Dexter, they want to help. Let him go."

Fighting back the red shifting haze was harder than I thought. *What am I doing?* I had to calm down, and fast. *Focus on Dad. Why you're here.* I gulped at the air and forced my arms to unhook their death-like grip. "It's my father. He can't breathe... I think it's his heart."

"We need a gurney out here!" One of the men yelled.

Another man in uniform came running up with a white bed on wheels.

The man who'd called for the gurney touched my arm. "It's okay. We're going to take care of him."

I helped them put my dad on the bed, my heart pounding with the fear and ferocity of my wolf as I struggled to keep him in check.

They wasted no time and wheeled him away quickly.

My father's skin was gray and sweaty, his eyes were closed, and he didn't seem to be moving at all.

"What the hell are they going to do to him?" I asked Jay.

He squeezed my arm hard. "Let's follow them and find out."

I walked into a human hospital for the first time ever and it was surreal. I'd spent my life in the woods, fighting bear shifters, and protecting my pack from outsiders, yet this truly was the strangest scene I'd ever witnessed. The fluorescent lights burned my eyes, and the stark, white walls stretched up before me and all around me like an enormous clinical maze.

I skidded to a halt before an indoor cage. The sign said *Reception Desk*, but it was a cage of sorts, nonetheless. *How do humans live and work in places like this?*

A woman approached us.

I searched my instincts. Despite the fact I hadn't seen a human woman in months, she did nothing for me.

Her face was too coarse and pinched. Her aura felt wrong and unattractive. "Can I get you to fill in some forms for the man they just brought in?" She handed me a black clipboard and a pen.

I nodded numbly and managed to relax enough to sit on an uncomfortable plastic chair with Jay at my side.

Taylor came running in the door, spotted us and took the vacant seat on my right.

It was the three of us against the world, as it's always been. We were pack mates; an Alpha, Beta, and Omega. Brothers, not by blood, but by a bond stronger than any other I'd shared.

"Whoa, I'd forgotten how hot these women could be." Taylor whistled as more nurses moved about and other patients staggered into the Emergency Room.

I shrugged my shoulders and focused on the human's paperwork. "You're welcome to them, Taylor."

The pack took turns travelling to town, hitting up the bars. Finding women to bed for the night. I'd always struggled with fucking women I wasn't connected to. Slaking my lust while still keeping my passions under control so I wouldn't hurt a fragile humans is not how I was designed. The Alpha wolf inside me craved the constant contact of my true mate. A woman to love and protect. Someone to complete me and bear my children.

"What's wrong with you, Dex? It's been months since we came to town. You must be horny as all hell."

I was. But I'd been running miles a day to keep the demons at bay. "I am," I admitted. "But I don't want any of these." I gestured to the room as a whole and glanced up again.

A young blonde woman stumbled over her own feet as she stared at us.

I rolled my eyes and kept my focus on the paperwork. "When my mate shows up, let me know."

Jay sighed. "We may not have mates, Dex. A real mate is a wolf shifter and pack-born. You know that's not our path. We're out of luck."

I looked over at my Omega, battling to keep my anger at bay, my gut burning at his words. "What is, then? To die without a mate? To simply grow old and be childless?"

Jay's mouth set in the familiar grim line he always adopted when upset. "We're still a family, Dexter."

"I know that." But still, I looked away.

A lot of the men in our pack were happy with their situation, but I wasn't. We'd grown up as one, huge pack, and at adulthood—at twenty-one years of age—we were ranked and chose who would share our own pack.

I was ranked an Alpha, of course. All three of my brothers were Alphas, the same as my father. As an Alpha, I was given the authority to choose a Beta and an Omega to complete my immediate family, my pack. I was lucky. It had been an easy choice. Jay and Taylor had been my best friends from childhood, and it felt perfectly natural when we built a house and moved in together.

But we were missing our mates, and despite how much I loved the guys, we weren't complete. There was a massive hole in my heart, and my life, and even if the other men didn't feel it as much as I did, it was still there. It was like a special, sacred piece was missing.

The receptionist returned to claim the clipboard full of information. Then we were left to our own devices for what felt like hours.

"What's taking so long?" Taylor asked, as he restlessly shifted on his chair, before he stood up, and began pacing once again.

We took turns wearing out the floor in the waiting area. There was nothing else to do.

I leaned forward on the chair and watched the white swinging doors that my father had disappeared behind. Over and over they opened and closed. And nothing happened. But eventually the doors opened, and a woman walked through. One I hadn't seen before.

I sat up straighter, my shifter rising to the surface. Who was she? And why did I suddenly want to take her in my arms and kiss the life out of her?

She was obviously a physician. I could tell that much by her uniform. She wore blue scrubs and running shoes that were well worn. She spoke briefly to the nurse and headed toward us.

I jumped to my feet, my heart pounding like I'd just run a marathon. and my skin itched and vibrated like my wolf was about to spring forth.

"Dexter Monaghan?" she asked, meeting my gaze for the first time, her sapphire blue eyes clashed with mine.

A growl rolled through my chest.

"Are you all right?" she asked, narrowing her eyes at my unexpected reaction.

Jay audibly gasped.

And Taylor went rigid beside me.

I could feel them reacting to her in the same way that my shifter was, which should have been impossible. We were meant to have our own mates. And she was *mine*. I couldn't explain it. I didn't need to. I just knew it. Maybe there was still some truth to those passed down stories after all. I turned to my pack mates. "Go, wait in the car. I'll be out as soon as I can."

Jay nodded mutely and began to back begrudgingly away.

But Taylor set his jaw. "No. I..."

I dropped my gaze away from my mate and stared at Jay, willing him to do my bidding. As the Alpha, my will was law, but I rarely exercised it. I never wanted blind obedience. I'd always firmly believed that bred insolence and contempt. I wanted loyalty and love. And that was earned over time. Then I focused on my Beta. "Taylor. *Go.*"

Together they fled as casually as their instincts allowed.

With that sorted, I turned my attention back to the woman before me. "Doctor...?"

"I'm Doctor Claire Masterson. I'm the physician treating your father."

"Claire..." I managed to say her name, even though all I wanted to do was put her over my shoulder and throw her into the back of our truck.

She looked at me strangely again.

I obviously wasn't behaving normally, and I didn't want to scare her off. *But how to do that?* "I'm sorry, Doctor. Please continue."

She straightened up, her throat working up and down as she swallowed hard. The woman looked almost as uncomfortable as I was.

Perhaps she feels this strange electric connection too?

"Your father had a massive heart attack. A cardiologist has been paged, and I believe they will operate tonight, inserting stents into his abdominal aorta. I'm here to give you an update and to let you know that there is a very good chance he'll survive and recover. You got him here just in time."

Thank you, God. Relief winged its way through my heart with such intensity that it robbed me of breath for a moment. I'd talked myself into thinking there was no way my father could die today, but from the look of this woman's face, it could have almost been a very real possibility.

My mother had said she couldn't live without my father, and hopefully she wouldn't have to. Not for another three decades or so at least.

"How long until he can come home?" I pressed.

She cocked her head to the side as if it were a silly question to be asking this early on. "Let's just take this one day at a time."

I ignored her human pragmaticism. She didn't understand what my father was, nor what his healing capacities were. "We live an hour away. I need to get my mother in to see him. If you could give me a rough estimate, I can let her know."

Claire hugged the clip board to her chest with a small grimace.

"Best case scenario, he may be home within two weeks. But he'll need to be managed by a local doctor moving forwards."

She didn't know that my dad's shifter genes would heal him as long as the doctors could repair the damage to his heart.

"Thank you, Doctor." I extended my hand to shake hers, my arm trembling with anticipation of her touch. According to the old stories passed down by my parents and pack elders, I would know my mate the moment I touched her. Now was the moment of truth.

Claire reached over and took my hand. Her gasp was as loud as mine.

Electricity pulsed between us like a thunderstorm besieged by lightning on a dark night. It would have taken out my knees if I wasn't so determined to stand.

Claire wasn't so lucky. Her eyes rolled back into her head, and she began to crumble to the ground like a falling house of cards.

I stepped forward and swept her up into my arms before she could hit the floor.

Her eyes fluttered as she struggled in vain to stay awake. She stared up at me with a confused expression, her eyelids dropping to half-mast. "What happened?"

"The mating call."

Her eyes closed upon hearing my answer and her body went limp in my arms.

I looked around. Not a single soul had noticed what had just happened. The waiting room was a hive of activity, and the medical professionals all seemed to be concentrating on their various tasks at hand and not the room at large. I turned slowly and began walking toward the hospital's exit doors.

"Excuse me!" I heard a woman call out behind me.

I kept walking, forcing my legs to keep moving, even though the scent of Claire made me want to kneel on the ground and thank the Fates for sending her to me. I couldn't stop or they'd take her away from me. I couldn't have that.

Once I got out into the fresh air it was easier to breathe and I sucked in a huge lungful. My head cleared a little and I began to wonder what the hell I was doing.

"Dexter!" Taylor called out from about ten feet away, having pulled the truck up near the entrance.

I didn't pause to think about it again. There was no time for reason or logic right now. I was running on instinct alone. I went straight for the truck with Claire still firmly nestled in my arms.

"Hey!" There were noises indicating a commotion behind me and I was pretty sure Claire's absence from the hospital had finally been noticed.

Taylor opened the back door without asking any questions and

I put her into the back seat. "Step on it!" I commanded before I jumped into the back with her and held her tightly against me.

Taylor slammed the door, leaped into the driver seat, turned on the engine and fish-tailed it out of the parking lot like a real rally car driver.

I looked down on the unconscious doctor in my arms. She was a human and without doubt... my Fated Mate. *What the hell have I just done?*

～

Download '**The Pack's Mate**' now:
https://books2read.com/the-packs-mate